The
BEACH
TRAP

The
BEACH
TRAP

Ali Brady

BERKLEY
New York

BERKLEY
An imprint of Penguin Random House LLC
penguinrandomhouse.com

Library of Congress Cataloging-in-Publication Data

Names: Brady, Ali, author.
Title: The beach trap / Ali Brady.
Description: First edition. | New York: Berkley, 2022.
Identifiers: LCCN 2021047261 (print) | LCCN 2021047262 (ebook) |
ISBN 9780593440155 (trade paperback) | ISBN 9780593440162 (ebook)
Subjects: LCGFT: Domestic fiction. | Novels.
Classification: LCC PS3602.R342875 B43 2022 (print) |
LCC PS3602.R342875 (ebook) | DDC 813/.6—dc23/eng/20211004
LC record available at https://lccn.loc.gov/2021047261
LC ebook record available at https://lccn.loc.gov/2021047262

First Edition: June 2022

Printed in the United States of America
1   3   5   7   9   10   8   6   4   2

Book design by Ashley Tucker

For our parents,
Kathy and Randy, Merrie and Jim

The

BEACH
TRAP

PROLOGUE

2007

THERE'S SOMETHING UNIQUE ABOUT FRIENDSHIPS FORGED
between girls at summer camp. Maybe it's being away from home,
separated from other friends or family, and the need for some
kind of connection to ward off homesickness. It could be the
setting, all that fresh air, the tall trees and sparkling lake water,
or the fact that each day feels never-ending, like the camp itself
is a miniature universe. Whatever it is, these friendships are special: tinged with the scent of campfire; solidified in whispered
conversations in the dark cabin; strengthened by secrets shared
and pranks pulled. Magical.

If Kat Steiner and Blake O'Neill hadn't met at such a camp,
they never would have become friends; their lives were as different as the lives of two twelve-year-old girls could be. Kat lived in
Atlanta with her mom and dad in a big, fancy house in a wealthy
neighborhood. She had thick, wavy brown hair, and her mother
took her to an expensive salon every six weeks for a deep conditioning treatment. She attended an exclusive Jewish private
school, where she was one of the most popular girls in her class.

She took piano and tennis lessons, spent her weekends at the mall with her friends, and always wore the right brand of jeans.

Blake lived outside Minneapolis in a cozy house with her grandparents. She had wispy, pin-straight blond hair, and her grandmother trimmed the split ends with nail scissors every few months. She went to a public junior high school where she kept her head down and tried not to attract attention. She spent her weekends reading books and helping her grandparents with chores around the house. She'd never had many close friends, and she didn't even know what the right brand of jeans was.

But on that first day of Camp Chickawah, on the shore of a small lake in northeast Minnesota, as the throng of girls was sorted into their cabin groups, something between Kat and Blake clicked. Maybe it was because Kat was out of her element, absent her trusty group of followers, and she was looking for someone willing to fill that role. Blake never would've been brave enough to approach Kat on her own, and in fact, when their counselor told the girls in Cabin 10 to find someone to share bunks with, she spiraled into a panic. She was seriously contemplating running down the bumpy dirt road that led away from camp, catching up to her grandpa in his old pickup truck, and begging him to take her back home.

Then Kat turned to Blake, her brown eyes shining, and said, "Wanna be bunkmates?"

Blake couldn't believe her luck. "Okay," she said, breathless.

And so it began.

After that, they were inseparable, a unit of two that had become one, Kat-and-Blake giggling in their bunks at night, Kat-and-Blake paddling a canoe on the lake, Kat-and-Blake making matching friendship bracelets during craft time. And in the second-to-last week of camp, they teamed up for the Camp Chickawah talent show together. They'd chosen to lip-sync to the song "Build

Me Up Buttercup" by The Foundations, because they'd both grown up listening to it in the car with their parents. Plus, it had an echo that lent itself conveniently to two different parts.

Kat took the lead, of course, and Blake was happy to let her. They were in the dining hall rehearsing, Blake standing directly behind Kat. Kat started with the first line of the chorus, and Blake popped her head out for the echoing "Build me up!"

Kat was feeling pretty pleased about how it was going when the door to the dining hall opened and someone walked in.

It was their counselor, Rainbow, which wasn't her real name— all the camp counselors took special names for the summer. The nickname usually fit her, but not today. Right then she looked like a storm cloud, the kind that gets heavy and swollen before the rain starts to fall.

Both girls stopped and looked up. Blake stepped out from behind Kat.

"Kat," Rainbow said, "I need to talk to you."

Kat's first thought was that Rainbow had figured out that last night she'd snuck out of the cabin to take a late-night canoe ride on the lake. Blake had been there, too, of course, but Kat had been the instigator.

"Okay," Kat said, steeling herself.

Rainbow glanced at Blake. "Alone," she said.

With those words, Blake knew instinctively that Rainbow was bringing bad news to Kat. She recognized the expression on the counselor's face; her school secretary had looked just like this on the day Blake's mother had died in the car accident. White face, tight mouth, sort of flustered and fluttery.

"Blake can stay," Kat said. "She's my best friend."

Blake's chest swelled with warmth; she hadn't been anyone's best friend in years. Not since moving to Minnesota to live with her grandparents.

She stepped closer to Kat and the two girls linked hands.

"Okay," Rainbow said. "I'm so sorry, Kat, but your grandfather has passed away. Your father is coming to pick you up—he's on the first flight out tomorrow."

Kat blinked. Her first thought was dismay that she wouldn't be able to do the lip sync—they'd practiced so hard, and there was no way Blake could do it on her own, and they were supposed to have hot fudge sundaes after the talent show.

But then it hit her: Sabba was dead. He was the only grandfather she'd ever known, because her mother's father had died when Kat was just a baby. Her eyes filled with tears as a thousand memories rushed into her mind: the time he'd tricked her into jumping into the ocean water even though it was freezing, how he'd hide one of her shoes so she couldn't leave when it was time to go, and that he gave the very best hugs in the world.

Meanwhile, Blake's heart ached for her friend. She knew what it was like to lose someone—she'd been through it more than once. She squeezed Kat's hand tighter, sending a silent message: *I'm here for you.*

Kat squeezed back. *Thank you.*

"You should head up to the cabin and start packing," Rainbow said. "We have dinner soon and then campfire, and your dad will be here pretty early tomorrow."

"Can Blake help me pack?" Kat asked, her voice shaky. The last thing she wanted right now was to be alone.

Rainbow's face softened. "Of course."

IN THE DARK, musty cabin, Kat pulled her giant suitcase out from under the bunk and laid it open on Blake's bottom-bunk mattress. Blake sat at the foot of the bed and helped Kat fold her clothes and place them into her suitcase. She didn't know what to say—Kat was usually the one to fill the silence with her chatter, her jokes and ideas. Now she seemed like a candle that had been snuffed out.

After Blake's mother had died, she'd wanted so badly to talk about her mom, but it seemed to make other people uncomfortable. She'd been desperate for someone to share stories and memories with, and she wondered if Kat might feel the same way.

So Blake took a deep breath and said, "Were you and your grandpa close?"

Kat blinked away a few stray tears. "Yeah."

"What was he like?"

Kat's chest felt like it was being squeezed by a giant fist, like her ribs might splinter. She swallowed down a sob and said the first thing that came to mind: "He—he always had butterscotch candies in his pockets for me."

"My granddad always has Jolly Ranchers in his pockets," Blake said. "He likes the peach ones the best. They're, like, super hard to find, so whenever we stop at a gas station or grocery store, we always look for them. For Christmas last year I filled his stocking with them, right up to the brim. He laughed so hard he almost fell off the couch."

Kat sniffed. She liked the image of Blake's grandpa laughing on Christmas morning. The tight fist around her chest eased, just a bit. "Every summer, we go to my grandpa's beach house in Destin—that's in Florida. There's white sand and it's right on the ocean, and we'd spend all day on the boat, swimming and looking for dolphins."

Blake couldn't help feeling a small twinge of envy. She'd already known that Kat came from a different world, a wealthier world—the brand names on her clothes and shoes made that clear. But her grandpa had a whole beach house and a boat to go out in the *ocean*? Blake's granddad had a beat-up old fishing boat that they'd take out on the lake sometimes.

"I don't know what I'd do if my granddad died," Blake blurted, then instantly regretted it. Kat's face had gone white. "Sorry—that's not what I meant. It's just that my grandparents are like my parents now. I've lived with them since my mom died."

Kat gave her a curious look. She realized that despite all the time they'd spent together, she didn't know much about her best friend's life outside camp. "What about your dad?"

Blake pulled her bony knees into her chest and hugged them. "I—I don't know where he is. After my mom died, I didn't see him anymore."

The words felt like ash in her mouth. All those long, lonely nights after her mom's accident, longing for her daddy, wishing he would come.

"What happened to him?" Kat said, knowing it was maybe not very nice to pry, but her curiosity about Blake's past was a nice distraction from the pain in her chest.

Blake hesitated; she hated talking about this. For a full year after her mom died, Blake had held on to the hope that her dad would come get her, bring her to live with him. He always called her his very best girl—so where was he? He hadn't even come to the funeral. The only explanation, in Blake's mind, was that he didn't know what had happened.

But then one day her grandparents had sat her down and explained things to her.

"He—" Blake took a deep breath. This was the first time she'd said this out loud, and her cheeks burned with shame. "My parents weren't married. My dad had another family."

Kat saw the flush spreading across Blake's face and reached

out to squeeze her hand. "And he just abandoned you after your mom died?"

Blake nodded, unable to speak.

This seemed unbelievable to Kat. Her father wasn't perfect, but she couldn't imagine a world in which he'd just disappear from her life. "But you knew him before your mom died?"

Blake's face lit up in a big smile. "Oh yeah. He would stay with us all the time. A couple weekends a month, sometimes a whole week. We'd play catch in the front yard; we'd pick up donuts from our favorite place in the morning for breakfast; we'd have movie marathons and stay up until midnight." Then her smile faltered. "Anyway. You're lucky your dad is around all the time. Lucky that he's coming to get you."

Kat bit her lip. "Well, I love my dad, but he works a ton, and yeah, I see him every day, but he's always super busy. He golfs a lot, and most nights, he's not even home in time for dinner."

Blake had a hard time imagining that—her dad had given Blake all his attention when he visited. All his love. Which was exactly why it had been so difficult to understand why he'd just disappeared after her mom died. Even if he had another family, hadn't he missed *her*?

This was why she had begged her grandparents to send her to Camp Chickawah—her father had gone to the boys' side of the camp as a kid. She'd thought it might help her feel closer to him, doing things he loved in a place he used to go. Now the whole idea felt silly and babyish, and she was glad she hadn't mentioned anything about it to Kat.

The door to the cabin opened, interrupting their conversation, and in marched the rest of their cabinmates. Immediately the other girls rushed over to Kat, hugging her, surrounding her with support and love, saying that they were so sorry she had to leave early.

. . .

THE NEXT MORNING, Blake stayed back from sailing so she could help Kat take her things to the main lodge. Blake knew it was selfish, but she felt like her own heart was breaking; without Kat, what would she do here? How would she get through these final weeks of camp?

Kat felt like she was in a daze; none of this seemed real. She'd spent most of the night crying into her pillow. But she kept reminding herself that soon her dad would be there, and he'd make everything okay.

When they reached the lodge, Kat stopped and pulled something out of her backpack. It was an old, tattered teddy bear with one eye. "I'm giving you Beary," Kat said.

"Wait, why?" Blake said. "Don't you need him?"

She had seen Kat sleep with the stuffed animal every night, then hastily hide it inside her pillowcase in the morning before the other girls woke up.

Kat swallowed, then shook her head. "Keep him until you can give him back to me in person. That way we *have* to see each other again."

Blake took the bear and tucked him under her arm, aware that this was a rare honor.

"You have to promise to stay in touch," Kat said. "I'll send you a letter as soon as I get home, okay?"

"Of course," Blake said. "Best friends forever, right?"

They had braided each other's hair that morning in two French braids—Blake's straight blond hair usually looked nothing like Kat's thick chestnut waves, but there was a sense of solidarity in the hairstyle. Like they were connected.

Kat threw her arms around Blake and hugged her.

Out of the corner of her eye, Kat saw a car pull up outside

the lodge. The car wasn't familiar, but when she recognized the man in the driver's seat, her broken heart leapt.

"That's my dad," she said. She rushed toward him, wanting nothing more than to have his arms around her. And there he was, stepping out of the car, her handsome father with his wavy brown hair, his shiny shoes and crisp button-down shirt.

"Hey, Kitty Kat," he said, pulling her in for a hug.

Kat took a deep breath of his familiar smell, the Hugo Boss cologne he'd always worn. When she pulled away, his face looked sad and tired, and all of a sudden it hit her: his father had died, and she realized that someday *he* would die, too, and she buried her face in his chest and let loose a flurry of sobs.

Behind her, Blake watched the scene, frozen with shock. Her entire body felt like it had turned to ice. She couldn't breathe. She couldn't speak. It couldn't be him, she told herself. It couldn't be him here, now, with his arms around her best friend.

But it was. He was dressed more formally than Blake remembered, and he was a few years older, but it was definitely him.

"Dad?" The word fell out of her mouth and hung in the air.

He looked up, and their eyes locked. "Blake?"

Kat pulled away from her dad, glancing back and forth between Blake's face and his. Her mind swirled with confusion. Why had Blake said that? How did her father know Blake? It made no sense.

Her dad looked just as dazed as Kat felt, but there was something else in his eyes: recognition. And something underneath that, something Kat had never seen before in her smart, confident, handsome father.

Shame.

"Get in the car, Kitty Kat," he said abruptly.

"But—" Kat protested.

He opened the car door nearest her and gave her a look that

meant business. Obediently, she slid into the back seat of the rental car, and he shut the door behind her, sealing her in the silent, leather-scented interior.

Outside, Blake stood stock-still.

Her father was here.

Kat's father was here.

Her father was Kat's father.

He turned to face her. Her dad, the man she'd cried for every night for months. The man who'd disappeared when she needed him most.

Blake wanted to ask him a million questions, she wanted to run up to him and beat her fists on his chest and demand answers, but she still couldn't move. Couldn't speak.

His dark eyes met hers. For one split second, Blake thought he was going to open his arms and pull her into an embrace. But then he blinked. He turned around. Got in the car. And shut the door.

Kat, sitting in the back seat with her heart pounding, stared at him. "Daddy? What's going on? How do you know Blake?"

"Not now," he said, and started the car.

"But, Daddy—"

"I said *not now*, Kitty."

Kat shut her mouth. She knew better than to argue. But as the car pulled away, she turned around in her seat to look at her best friend through the rear window. She was still standing outside the lodge in her green Camp Chickawah T-shirt, her mouth hanging open.

The car drove away, bouncing gently on the dirt road, and Kat watched as Blake's pale face grew smaller and smaller in the distance.

FIFTEEN YEARS
LATER

CHAPTER ONE

KAT

THE LAUGHTER OF TEENAGE GIRLS WITHOUT A WORRY IN the world might be my very favorite sound. Of course, these girls aren't nearly as carefree as I'd been at their age.

When I was fifteen, my biggest problems were the fact that my BFF Jill and I both had a crush on the same boy, and that my parents wouldn't let me buy clothes from Hollister because they weren't ladylike.

These girls have adult-size problems: Luna's mom is in prison again; LaTasha's living with her sister, who works three jobs just to make ends meet; and Chelsea told me her mom couldn't afford groceries last week.

While their stories break my heart, their laughter puts it back together again. As a volunteer at the Peachtree Boys' and Girls' Center, I know I'm here to be the helper, but honestly, they help me, too.

Outside these four walls, my world is focused on designer labels and fashion trends—but inside, I'm reminded that safety, stability, and unconditional love have so much more value.

"What do you think, Miss Kat?" Chelsea asks, holding her tissue-paper-flower headband up for me to see.

Since they're too young for margaritas, we're celebrating Cinco de Mayo with an arts and crafts project I saw on TikTok, making Frida Kahlo–inspired floral crowns.

"Very festive." I try to match Chelsea's smile with one of my own, and hope she can't see through it. The girls are so in tune to troubles that I make a conscious effort to leave mine at the door. But you can't always control when grief decides to rear its ugly head.

"How about me?" Jackie asks, striking a pose with her tissue flowers.

"Gorgeous," I tell her, as I fold sheets of pink and orange tissue together to make a flower of my own. While the girls tolerate these crafty activities, I genuinely love them. They remind me of simpler times back at summer camp when we told time by the morning reveille and the dinner bell, when a swim in the lake counted as bathing and the only thing on my agenda was soaking up every minute.

"You can take my picture if you want," Jackie offers, batting her eyelashes.

My smile falters. Ever since the girls found me on Instagram, they've been not-so-subtly hinting they'd like to be featured in my feed.

"It's against the rules," I remind her. "It's for your privacy that I'm not allowed to post your pictures."

"I won't tell," Jackie says with a sly smile.

"Me either," Chelsea chimes in.

"But one of her seventy-five million followers might," La-Tasha adds.

"Seventy-five thousand," I say, correcting her, although both numbers are so beyond the girls' comprehension the difference doesn't mean much.

"Y'all are crazy," Luna says, ripping a sheet of tissue paper she's supposed to be folding into a flower. "She don't care about no rules. She just doesn't want to ruin her fancy image by hanging out with the likes of us."

"That's not true," I tell Luna, lowering my voice so it doesn't sound defensive. "I'm sure my followers would love to know I spend time volunteering—but I don't hang out with you guys for the likes."

"Then why do you?" LaTasha asks.

"Because I like you," I tell her. "I like all of you."

The girls light up, all except for Luna, who scowls. I wish I could tell her that I understand, that I know how hard it can be to let new people into your heart once you've been hurt. But they have trained counselors to help with the heavy things like that—I'm just here to be a positive role model and supportive friend.

My phone buzzes with an alarm, reminding me there's somewhere else I have to be. As much as I'd like to skip the meeting and stay here, I know my mom would kill me. And one death in the family this year is more than enough.

I FIND A parking spot outside Tin Lizzy's in Midtown, where sounds of drunk, happy people drift out the open windows. I wish I could join them and drown my sorrows in a giant margarita and an order of buffalo shrimp.

The restaurant is Mexicanish, which makes it a perfect place for white yuppies to celebrate a holiday that doesn't belong to them. Not that I'm any better than they are—an imposter in my own right, on my way to play the role of a supportive daughter, comforting her grieving mother.

It's been just over a month since my dad passed away. He had a heart attack sitting at his desk, where his secretary found him after she realized he hadn't left for his lunch meeting.

My father lived for his work as a commercial real estate developer, so it seemed appropriate that that's where he died. I can't stop thinking about the moment it happened, wondering what his last thoughts were—if he looked at the framed family photo he kept on his desk and thought about me and Mom, or at the stack of papers he'd never be able to finish.

Probably the latter.

While I loved my dad—idolized him, really—he always seemed more interested in the news or whatever game was on TV than the desperate girl clamoring for his affection.

Even back then, I knew I wasn't the kind of daughter he wanted. I collected Barbies instead of baseball cards, built scrapbooks instead of model cars, and the ultimate sin: I grew up to have a career he couldn't easily explain, much less understand.

One of our last conversations ended with him asking when I'd finally grow up and get a "real" job—even though I've monetized my Instagram account with enough sponsorships that the income alone has been paying my bills for almost a year.

But no matter how much success I had, David's daughter the social media influencer would never measure up to Paul's daughter the tax attorney, Stephen's son the lawyer, or Brian's daughter the financial planner. I hate that he died disappointed in me.

The blast of cold air-conditioning makes me shiver as I walk into the lobby of Callahan and Callahan, the firm handling my father's affairs. There's something familiar about the room, and I have the glimmer of a memory of being here once before. I was nine or ten, tagging along with my dad on an errand to sign some Very Important Papers. I remember the hunter-green walls and the rich mahogany furniture feeling like a library, and I knew I was supposed to be a Good Girl.

While dad and the senior Callahan spoke in hushed tones about a small trust for a child in Michigan or Minnesota, I sat so still and quiet it was like I wasn't even there. Which was what my dad wanted. For me to be invisible.

And it must have worked, because when they finished talking, my dad turned and walked out of the room, leaving me alone with the stern-faced lawyer. My dad came back a few minutes later, growling at me to "come on," as if it were my fault he'd left me.

Back in the same room all these years later, the pressure of being the perfect daughter is as strong as it ever was.

I find my mother sitting in the private waiting lounge, impeccably dressed as always. She makes being a widow look good in her all-black Eileen Fisher ensemble—wide-leg slacks, a cashmere sweater, and a black-and-white silk scarf with just a pop of gold. Her hair, the same chestnut shade as mine, is smooth and straight thanks to the keratin treatments we both get every twelve weeks.

Looking down at my own outfit—black jeans with a Topshop floral blouse—I realize my mom is representing my brand philosophy that "life is a fashion show" even more than I am. Although, in my defense, I did have the challenge of dressing for two very different audiences.

"Hey, Mom," I say, giving her a kiss on the cheek.

"Hi, sweetheart," she says, crossing and uncrossing her legs.

I take a seat beside my mom and glance down at her hands resting in her lap. If it weren't for the small tic of spinning her wedding ring around her finger, I wouldn't know she was nervous.

From everything I've heard, the reading of a will is just a formality, but for my mom, this is a whole new frontier. My dad took care of this sort of thing for their entire thirty-year marriage, so I imagine it's overwhelming for her to suddenly be the one in charge.

I place my hand on my mom's back in what I hope is a comforting gesture. We've never been a touchy-feely family, but when she turns and offers me a small smile, I give one back to her.

After what feels like long enough but not too long, I bring my hand back and rest it in my lap. Like mother, like daughter, I start to twirl my own ring—a Yurman classic in topaz I got for my twenty-fifth birthday. Although unlike my mother, I actually have a reason to be nervous. There's a very good chance the secret I've been keeping for my dad for the last fifteen years is about to be revealed.

Suddenly, I'm twelve years old again, sitting in the back seat of my dad's rental car, wondering how many times a heart can break. *My dad and my best friend. My best friend and my dad.*

"Not now," he'd said when I asked him about it as we drove away, down the bumpy dirt road. Of course, I knew he really meant "not ever." Our family didn't believe in talking about unpleasant things when they could just as easily be ignored. It was practically our family motto to put on a happy face, even if you were shattered on the inside.

After I got through the shock of my grandfather's funeral, I'd tried to believe Blake hadn't known we shared a father. Sure, she had told me that her father had another family, and she knew my last name was Steiner, but I desperately wanted to give her the benefit of the doubt. I wanted to believe it was all a big misunderstanding, that she was just as much a victim as I was.

But then I got her letter.

In the months after camp, Blake sent several letters, but I barely read them and never wrote back. I had nothing to say to her after I read that she'd gone to Camp Chickawah in an attempt to get closer to her father. To *my* father.

The feeling of betrayal was as sharp as a knife in my back:

Blake had never wanted to be my friend. She'd been using me to get to my dad, and who knows what would have happened if my grandfather hadn't died, if she'd come to visit me in Atlanta like we'd talked about.

After reading that first letter, I shut Blake O'Neill out of my life and out of my mind. The memory of her eventually settled like a stone in the pit of my stomach—something that flared up every once in a while when I saw a young girl with blond wispy hair, or when I heard "Build Me Up Buttercup" on the radio.

Still, I kept the secret. I wasn't sure if I was protecting my dad from being found out, or protecting my mom from being hurt. I just knew it was my responsibility to keep my family together.

Now my dad is gone, but the secret is still here, wedged between my mom and me, like a crack in the foundation our family was built on.

A door opens into the lobby and Scott, the junior Callahan, walks out. He looks about my mom's age, tall and sturdy, like he played football in college before following in his father's footsteps. He flashes us the same sympathetic smile I recognize from when he introduced himself during shiva.

"Eleanor." He greets my mother before turning to me. "Katherine."

"Kat," I say, correcting him. I'm not sure why I bother, except that I already feel so out of sorts in this situation that I at least want the comfort of my name.

Mr. Callahan nods and leads Mom and me back to his office. He takes a seat behind his massive desk and invites us to sit in the plush chairs facing him.

"Ladies," he says, clearing his throat. "I'm afraid I have some difficult news."

My breath hitches and I brace myself for the impact of a crash that's been fifteen years in the making. I clench my fists, afraid not of the news, but of how my mom will take it: if she'll fall apart, if she'll be mad at my dad, or at me since I'm the only one left to blame.

"At the time of his passing, David was on the verge of bankruptcy," the lawyer says.

I exhale and lean back into my chair at the same time my mom leans forward in hers. That was not the bombshell of truth I'd been expecting.

"That can't be right," my mom says, her voice slightly wavering.

For the first time, I realize the weight of what the lawyer actually revealed. It wasn't *the* secret, but it was one that could have an even greater impact on my mom's life.

I keep my eyes focused on the lawyer, not brave enough to glance at my mom beside me as we both wait for the man to say he's made a mistake. But Scott Callahan's face is set in an all-business expression, any signs of warmth or familiarity left out in the lobby.

"David unfortunately made a few bad investments," he says, "including one in a friend's business that, well, for lack of better words, tanked. David was the main investor."

My mom shakes her head. "But—"

"He leveraged most of your investment portfolio, and there's not much left in savings—although the house is fully paid for, and it's yours." He says those last words as if my mother should take comfort that while she's lost her husband, all her money, and any sense of safety or security, at least she isn't homeless.

But I'm with my mom—there must be a mistake. If my dad had been hemorrhaging money, there's no way he would've gotten a brand-new Porsche just a few months ago. And the month before that, he bought me the checkered Louis bag I'd been eyeing.

Those were not the actions of a man who'd lost all his money. But they were, I realize, the actions of a man who carried on like normal, living a charade until the very end, even as his world crumbled around him. And now that he's gone, we're left to clean up his mess without so much as a broom.

"I suggest you take some time to process this news," the lawyer says. "But when you're ready, I think it would be smart to sell the house and move to a smaller place. I imagine you'll be able to live quite comfortably."

Quite comfortably? My mom's lips narrow into a thin line at Callahan's dismissive words. The Buckhead house isn't just a house. It's a symbol of my mom's status, a place to entertain and show off her exquisite taste in art and design. I could no sooner see her moving into a condo than I could picture her getting a tattoo.

"For Katherine, er, Kat," he says, correcting himself, "your father left a small sum of money, ten thousand dollars. And as far as the beach house in Destin . . ."

My heart lifts at the thought of my grandparents' Florida beach house. Some of my best memories took place at that house, on the rare lazy summer days my dad would leave his work at the office and join me in the ocean, catching waves while Mom watched from the white-sand shore. I didn't realize my dad knew how much those days and the house meant to me. My eyes well with tears at this final, thoughtful gift.

"Your father left half of the house to you, and the other half"—he pauses—"to your half sister."

My stomach twists in a giant knot at his words. Blake may be my father's daughter, but she's not my sister—half or otherwise. But now is hardly the time to correct him.

I've had fifteen years to process this news, but my mom hasn't had the same luxury. I take a deep breath and turn toward her, bracing myself for the worst. But she looks as stoic and serene as ever. Her head is held high and her eyes are trained on the stack of papers on Callahan's desk. I watch, waiting for her stone face to crack as the truth inevitably hits her the same way the news about the money had.

But she doesn't so much as flinch, and I get the sinking feeling that this isn't news to her. Suddenly, I'm the one who's shocked that the secret I helped my father keep for the last fifteen years wasn't a secret at all.

All the years of guilt and shame at being an accomplice to his deceit are gone in an instant, replaced by a flash of anger.

I remember the one time I'd been brave enough to bring Blake up again. It was approaching summer the year after we'd met, a few months after her letters had stopped coming. I was mad at my dad for missing the father-daughter dance at the Jewish Community Center, and I wanted to hurt him as much as he'd hurt me. So I asked if he'd talked to Blake recently.

A shadow crossed his face at the mention of her name, and he snapped like a tight rubber band, yelling in a hushed voice that my mother was in the next room. I realized then that it would be impossible to hurt him without taking my innocent mother down, too.

As much as I want to ask my mom when and how she found out, I know this isn't the time or place. I imagine she's already mortified that this lawyer knows the ugly truth behind the picture-perfect family image she's taken so much pride in portraying for the last three decades. And all she's got left to show for it is a house she might lose, too.

Scott Callahan looks at me, clearly waiting for an emotional response, possibly tears. But he won't get any of that from me. I am my father's daughter, after all.

Instead, I take a deep breath and smile, all while cursing the day Blake O'Neill was born.

CHAPTER TWO

BLAKE

"BLAKE!" A LITTLE VOICE CALLS. "I NEED YOU!"

I straighten up from where I'm zipping a suitcase. "Yes, Charlotte?"

"I . . . I need help with my button." My four-year-old charge is in her bathroom, a gorgeous space with a soaking tub and a walk-in shower. Her "princess suite" is larger than the apartment my mom and I lived in when I was her age.

"I'll be right there," I say, smiling because I adore the little nugget, even though her parents represent everything that's wrong in the world. "Make sure you flush the toilet, okay?"

"Blake!" another voice calls. This one's older, more distinguished. Slightly impatient. Charlotte's mother, my boss, will have to come first.

"Yes, Mrs. Vanderhaaven?" I poke my head out Charlotte's bedroom door. She rushes past me and down the stairs, a blur of blond hair and expensive perfume.

"Do you know where the children's passports are?" she says over her shoulder. "I *asked* you to keep track of them for me because, as you *know*, they're incredibly important, Blake. Literally the *most* important thing when one is planning a trip to a different *country*. I don't know if you're aware of this, but we're catching a flight to Paris in two hours."

I take a cleansing breath. "The kids' passports are in your handbag, by the front door," I call down to her, then lower my voice to a whisper. "Just like I told you."

My phone rings in the back pocket of my jeans, and I silence it. No time for that now—my mission is to help the family avoid a *Home Alone*–style dash through the airport, because while Mrs. Vanderhaaven wears overpriced athleisure ninety percent of the time, I've never actually seen her break a sweat.

"Blake! I can't find my shoes!" Zachary hollers from his bedroom across the hall. He has one volume setting: eardrum bursting. "They're nowhere! They disappeared into thin air!"

I stick my head in the doorway of his room, where he's sitting in the middle of the floor with both hands fisting in his curly blond hair.

"Your red Jordans?" I say, pointing. "Buddy, they're on the chair where I set your clothes out for today."

"Fanks!" he shouts.

Just like I told you, I think to myself but do not say. He's only six years old; he gets a pass.

"Blake!" That's the fourth person calling my name in as many minutes. Mr. Vanderhaaven's deep voice echoes from the master bedroom down the hall. "Did you pick up the dry cleaning? My pants—I was going to wear those pants, you know the ones with the little thing on the pocket . . ."

I step into the hallway. "They're hanging in your closet, behind the door."

"Ah yes. I could've sworn they weren't here a moment ago."

I stifle a laugh. The man would lose his nose if it wasn't attached to his face, as my grandma used to say. My phone rings again, and again I silence it.

"I need help tying my shoes!" Zachary shouts from his room.

"I will never, ever be able to do my button!" Charlotte wails from her bathroom.

"Blake! Are the children ready?" Mrs. Vanderhaaven calls from downstairs. "The car service is here."

"They'll be right down," I say.

Closing my eyes, I rub my temples to tame the building headache. If I can make it through the next fifteen minutes, I won't have to see any of these people for the next three months. Though I will miss Charlotte and Zachary—they've become my buddies over the past two years—and I will definitely miss going to France. And I already miss the two hundred dollars I paid to get my first-ever passport.

I was supposed to be on their flight, nannying for the entire summer while they stay in a villa in the French countryside. But last week, just *seven days* ago, Mrs. Vanderhaaven informed me that they'd decided to hire a French nanny. I'd be staying home to watch the dog, she added, as if it wasn't even a question.

I'd imagined spending my summer exploring the countryside with my two little charges, not hanging out with a hyperactive designer-breed dog. It was a massive disappointment. Not to mention a huge drop in pay. But being a dog nanny is better than being unemployed, and since I'm a live-in employee with no home of my own, I don't have another option.

As if on cue, the dog bounds up the stairs, nearly knocking me over as he rushes into Zachary's room. He's a forty-pound ginger-colored labradoodle purchased from an elite breeder in New Zealand for the tidy sum of five thousand dollars, which is ridiculous for what is essentially an expensive mutt. You'd think he drank straight espresso from his water bowl for all the energy he has. He drives me insane.

"Max!" Zachary shouts, delighted as they start to wrestle. Usually, I'd break it up because Mrs. Vanderhaaven hates when Zachary gets his clothes all wrinkly, but Charlotte is now weeping quietly in the bathroom.

I rush in to find her flat on her back on the tile floor, tears sliding down her face.

"I tried and tried but it was just so hard for my fingers," she says, sniffing.

"No big deal!" I keep my voice sunny; Charlotte is known for dissolving into tears, and Mrs. Vanderhaaven doesn't like that, either. I lift her onto her feet. "Up you go. Let's do that button . . . there. You look lovely."

Even though we don't have much time, I can't help smiling. She really is a beautiful little girl, with soft golden curls and big blue eyes.

"I will miss you, Blakey," she says, throwing her arms around my neck.

I squeeze her little body and inhale; she smells like syrup from the whole wheat waffles I made for breakfast. "I'll miss you too, baby cakes. Now let's go—your mother is waiting."

I take her hand in one of mine and heft her suitcase with the other, and we head across the hall. I tie Zachary's shoelaces—he thanks me with a sloppy kiss on the cheek—then send them both down the stairs. The dog lumbers after them, blissfully unaware that the children he adores are leaving and he'll be stuck with me all summer.

Mr. Vanderhaaven rushes down the hall from his room, redfaced and bumbling, and grabs the kids' suitcases, one in each hand.

"Thanks, Blake," he calls over his shoulder. "You're a wonder."

I pick up the children's carry-on bags—two-hundred-dollar backpacks made by some designer Swedish brand—and follow him downstairs.

Outside, a driver is loading suitcases into a sleek black SUV. The next few minutes are a flurry of commotion: the children shouting their goodbyes to me and the dog ("Miss you, Blake! Miss you, Max!"); Mrs. Vanderhaaven checking her handbag for the passports ("Blake, where are the—oh"); Mr. Vanderhaaven reminding me that the lawn care service will come tomorrow ("Make sure they weed the flower beds this time"). And then they all load up, the doors shut, and they're off.

I stand on the sidewalk in front of their house, holding the dog's collar so he doesn't follow them. When the SUV rolls out of sight, I release the dog's collar. He looks up at me, like, *Now what?*

I have no idea, dog.

As we head back into the kitchen, my phone rings again, and I pull it out of my pocket. *Shaky Oaks Assisted Living.* My heart skips a beat; have they been calling all this time?

"Hello?" I say, answering.

"Hi, Blake, it's Martina. Your grandfather is missing."

"IT'S GOING TO be okay," Martina reassures me through the phone. "I'm on my way to get him. The manager at Dee's called me—you remember Shawn? He's making him a milkshake right now."

I'm pacing in the Vanderhaavens' massive living room, next to a gleaming grand piano that no one plays. My heart gives a guilty squeeze at the thought of Granddad walking to the diner where he used to take me for a burger and fries after a long day working on the house. I wonder if he's lonely, if he misses me.

Thank goodness my oldest friend is a nurse at his facility—Martina Rojas has known me since middle school and remembers Granddad from before he started to change. Even more important, he remembers her. Usually.

"Thank you so much," I say. "But how did he get all the way there? It's what, like, two miles away?"

"I don't know—it happened before I came on shift." Martina's voice is serious, as is the situation. "He's going to be fine, okay? I'm almost there. Once I get him home, I'll check on him as much as I can today."

Granddad has been at Shaky Oaks for two years, and despite the fact that the name of the facility seems to be a direct insult to its inhabitants, he seems happy there. However, his memory continues to worsen. His side of the facility isn't set up for taking care of someone who needs a high level of supervision—which is exactly what Vincent, the director of the place, told me a month ago.

"I don't worry about him when you're there," I tell Martina, "but the days you're not . . . and if Vincent found out . . ."

"He won't find out," she promises. "I'll make sure of that. But, Blake, if things get worse, he'll need to move to the memory care unit."

My stomach twists in a tight knot. We can afford Granddad's current place with his social security payments plus the better part of my nanny salary, but the memory care building is four times more expensive. There's no way I can afford that.

"Maybe he won't get worse," I say, even though that's wishful thinking. Alzheimer's always gets worse.

"I'm pulling into the parking lot," Martina says. "I can see him through the window. I'll call you in a bit, okay?"

Relief rushes through me. "Thank you," I say again.

After hanging up, I sit on the stiff white couch and put my

head in my hands. The dog leaps up next to me, and I wave him off—not because I care about Mrs. Vanderhaaven's rules about the furniture, but because he smells like stale Doritos and he's always sticking his wet nose in my hand. He sits by my feet and stares up at me with a mournful expression in his liquid brown eyes. I know how he feels. Like the whole world has turned upside down and he can't figure out how he got here.

Two years ago, my crafty grandfather sold his house and moved himself into Shaky Oaks without even telling me until it was done. I would've moved back home in a heartbeat as soon as I found out he was struggling, but he said he didn't want me to waste the best years of my life taking care of him. I would've happily done it, though.

Besides, I loved that house. He'd built it himself, and I'd spent much of my childhood puttering around, fixing things with Granddad, baking in the kitchen with Grandma. It was the one place on earth that felt like home.

Not that the house was worth much; they'd taken out a second mortgage to pay for my college tuition. Which was a complete waste, because I dropped out my senior year to come home during Grandma's chemotherapy treatments. After she passed away, I couldn't muster up the strength to return to school. I still feel guilty for using my grandparents' money and not even finishing my degree.

I got the nanny job with the Vanderhaavens because their home in Liston Heights, a fancy suburb of Minneapolis, is only a forty-five-minute drive and I can visit Granddad every weekend. It would've been difficult to be away from him all summer if I'd gone to France, but the Vanderhaavens had promised a huge salary bump because I'd be essentially solo with the kids while they did whatever rich people do when they don't have to actually parent their children. That bonus would have paid for a few months in the memory care unit, giving me some time to figure out what to do next.

But now? I'm at a loss. I need a better-paying job, but I don't have any real skills unless you count reading bedtime stories in funny voices and convincing small children to take baths. Without that college degree, a lot of positions are out of my reach. But I have to figure something out. Fast.

My phone rings again, and I answer it quickly. "Martina? How is he?"

There's a pause. "Is this Blake O'Neill?"

It's an unfamiliar voice, a man's. My chest tightens; has something happened to Granddad?

"That's me," I say.

"My name is Scott Callahan. I'm the estate attorney for David Steiner."

My mouth falls open. In a flash I'm back at Camp Chickawah, standing in front of the lodge, watching my father turn his back on me.

"Estate attorney?" I whisper.

"Yes. Mr. Steiner died several weeks ago. I'm calling to let you know that he's left you something. It's a beach house, Ms. O'Neill. In Florida."

"YOUR NO-GOOD, ASSHOLE, cheating, lying bum of a father left you a house?" Martina squeals. "That's crazy. But crazy good, right?"

It's been two hours since my call from Scott Callahan, and I'm heading down the hall of Granddad's assisted living center to his apartment. Martina, in purple scrubs with her dark hair up in a curly bun, is next to me, a huge smile on her face.

"Half a beach house," I say, correcting her. I'm still stunned.

I spent the entire drive, the dog in the back seat with his head hanging out the window, repeating Callahan's words over and over in my mind:

It's a joint inheritance with your half sister, Katherine. The house belongs equally to the two of you, and neither of you can sell it without the other's permission.

I don't want this house. Just the thought of a place where my father spent happy moments hanging out with his real daughter, the daughter he chose over me, makes me want to vomit. I'm not sure what I'm supposed to do next. Call Kat and discuss it? Nope. Not going to happen. Luckily, Callahan said he would act as a go-between.

An image floats through my mind of Kat at twelve, hair in two brown braids, practically bouncing on her toes in anticipation of seeing her dad. My heart gives a reluctant squeeze of empathy. She adored him. I know what it's like to lose a parent, and I wouldn't wish that on anyone.

Then my heart gives a mean kick: *my* father is dead, too, and he pretended like I didn't exist for the past fifteen years.

"Oh my god!" Martina says. She's holding her phone out to show a real estate listing with a seven-figure asking price. "Did you see what houses on the beach in Destin are worth?"

I did. It was one of the first things I checked. Another reason I'm still stunned—I was raised by people who scrimped and saved, who worked hard for every dollar they earned. This feels too good to be true.

We've reached Granddad's door and I knock.

"Come in! Come in!" My eyes prick with tears at hearing his familiar voice, round and plummy. As a kid, I legit thought he voiced Winnie-the-Pooh in the old cartoons.

When I walk in, Granddad is sitting on the sofa in his studio apartment, watching a John Wayne movie on the television. His eyes light up as he comes over to envelop me in a big, soft hug.

"Isn't this the best surprise!" he says. "My favorite grand-daughter is here."

I give him a kiss on his scruffy cheek. "I'm your only grand-daughter."

"I got rid of the others so you wouldn't have any competition."

It's easy, in moments like this, to pretend he's exactly the same. That there isn't an invisible thief in his brain, stealing away his memories, his personality. His symptoms come and go, but right now, I can tell he's my granddad. One hundred percent.

Martina waves. "Have a good visit, you two. Ellis, I'll be back soon with your afternoon meds."

"Meds? We don't need no stinking meds," he says with a wink, paraphrasing one of his other favorite westerns.

Martina walks away, laughing to herself, and I sit next to Granddad.

"How are you?" I ask.

"Oh, tolerable. Can't complain."

That's my granddad. He never complains.

"I heard you went on a walk today to Dee's."

His eyes cloud over, and I'm nervous that he doesn't remember, even though it happened a few hours ago. Then he smiles. "You know the food here is terrible, Blakers. I needed a big, juicy burger."

I take his hand and squeeze. "You can't go wandering off. It scared me to death, Granddad."

"Well, I'm sorry about that. The last thing I want to do is upset my girl."

I'm not sure what to tell him about the beach house inheritance. He always gets angry when the subject of my father comes up, and I don't want to upset him. But I would like to discuss this with him. Granddad didn't have fancy college degrees or a lot of money, but he's always been pragmatic and smart, and I value his opinion.

"Random question," I say, walking over to the kitchenette. He's been losing weight, so I keep one cupboard stocked full of candy and cookies. "If you owned a house in another state and you needed to sell it, how would you go about doing that?"

I grab a container of chocolate-covered almonds and bring it back to the couch.

"Why would you have a house you don't live in? Give me a couple of those, Blakers."

I shake some nuts into his open hand. Onscreen, John Wayne is rounding up a group of inexperienced boys for a cattle drive. It's one of Granddad's favorites, *The Cowboys*. The first time I watched it with him, I was dumbfounded when John Wayne's character died. *He's dead?* I remember thinking. *Just . . . gone?* The Duke wasn't supposed to die.

My father's face flashes through my mind: standing in my mom's little kitchen in Nashville, singing "Sweet Caroline" as he flipped a pancake.

He's dead.

Blinking the memory away, I look over at Granddad. "Hypothetically. How would you go about selling a house in a different state? Get a good real estate agent?"

I'm certain Kat will buy me out, but I want her to pay a fair price. She grew up the daughter of a wealthy businessman, so I'm sure she's inherited his savvy.

"Wouldn't trust anyone else to do it for me, that's for damn sure. If you want something done right, you have to do it yourself," he says, which I must've heard a thousand times growing up.

That's been Granddad's philosophy his entire life. As a general contractor, he checked on every site every single day, making sure the work was going as expected.

Can I just pack up and head down to Destin? I've never been to Florida, and the gas money alone will probably be more than what I usually spend in a month. But he's right—if I want to make sure I don't get screwed out of this "inheritance," I need to be there.

Gunshots echo from the television, and Granddad nods at the screen. "Now, that's a man who knew how to take care of things himself."

I'm about ready to ask him another question, but his eyes have lost their focus. I know from experience that he's drifted somewhere into the past. So, I sit back against the sofa and pop a few chocolate-covered almonds in my mouth.

I hardly taste them, because my mind is running through options. I could take the dog with me—I assume the Vanderhaavens won't care. It'll be a long drive, but if I get a real estate agent and an appraiser to meet me there, hopefully I can wrap this up within a couple of days.

I'm not sure how to feel right now—I feel like I've stuck my hand on an electric fence, my body all buzzy and twitching—but it's nothing like the overwhelming despair I experienced back when my mom died. I grieved my father a long time ago, after he skipped merrily out of my life, and I guess I'm done with all that, which is good. I have enough on my plate without adding any messy emotional crap for a man who left me twice by choice. Once when I was nine, and again when I was twelve.

Glancing at Granddad, I nod to myself. He's absolutely right. I'm going to take this unexpected windfall and do something useful with it—make sure my grandfather is taken care of. After everything he's done for me, it's the least I can do. There's no need to revisit the past, to get all sentimental about my departed father, and definitely no need to reconnect with Kat. She never responded to a single letter I sent her after camp. Not even the one that was stained with tears.

I'll drive to Destin, figure out a fair price for the house, and sell it. Just get in, get out, and get on my way.

CHAPTER THREE

KAT

IT'S MOTHER'S DAY, WHICH MEANS BRUNCH AT THE CLUB. For as long as I can remember, my mom and I have had a just-the-two-of-us buffet breakfast to start her special day. Even though my dad never—not once—participated in this annual event, his absence is felt around our table.

Probably because it's his fault this tradition is likely coming to an end. I feel a pang of guilt at thinking less-than-kind thoughts about my dad—I know you're supposed to only remember good things about the dead, but my relationship with my father was complicated.

And so, apparently, is grief. One minute, I'm totally fine, and the next, an ad for male pattern baldness will have me in tears.

In my defense, it's fact, not opinion, that my dad's risky financial decisions are the reason my mother has to rethink every expense in her life. And I imagine the country club membership will be one of the first things to go once she comes to terms with her new reality. A reality where the only club she'll be able to afford is the free-sub-of-the-month club at Subway.

Luxury comes at a price, and nothing at the club says

"affordable," although I wonder if there's a way I could negotiate a deal for my mom in exchange for showcasing the country club in my feed to bring in a younger audience.

Everywhere I look, I see potential posts. They clearly put care into every detail—including the centerpiece at our table. There's not a carnation in sight; the bouquet looks crafted, with purple hydrangeas, white orchids, and pink tulips.

I snap a picture to add to my Instagram story. The one I posted earlier—a selfie in a gilded mirror from the ladies' lounge with a poll asking my followers to rate my dress—is already getting high engagement. So far, ninety-five percent of them have answered LOVE IT, which means I'm obsessing about the five percent who answered MEH.

But you can't make everyone happy, I remind myself as I add the floral photo to my stories. I add one more picture, a shot I snapped of my mom smiling when we first sat down a few minutes ago. She's wearing a fitted white blazer over a blue floral print dress from Chico's—an outfit that complements my white slim-fit dress with a blue blazer.

I was five when I suggested we dress to complement each other instead of matching like most other mother-daughter duos. She was delighted, and ever since, our love of fashion has united us.

When I look back up from my phone, my mother's smile is gone.

"I know you love what you do," she says, "but given our situation, it might be time to find a real job."

"What I do is very real," I counter, glancing down at my phone, where the screen is already filled with hearts and comments from my followers: people who see me, who love me, and who look to me for advice, buying the products and services I recommend. The products and services I get *paid* to recommend.

Just last week, I was invited to pitch a year-long contract with one of the hottest brands in fashion.

"I'm making more than double what Dr. Rosen's office paid me," I tell her.

My dad had called in a favor to get me a job as an office manager at the family practice of one of his golf buddies after I graduated college with an English degree and no serious job leads.

It paid well and the work was easy, which made the days drag. But the worst part was the scrubs I was forced to wear every single day.

Not only was the shade of pink putrid, but the fit was so unflattering that they were unfollow-worthy—which is why I had to keep any glimpse of them off IG. It was worth the extra effort to get dressed at home in my own clothes each morning, changing once I got to the office in the same bathrooms where people peed in cups for urine samples.

"It was a good job," my mom says, dropping her voice to a whisper in case any of her "friends" are in earshot.

"It was suffocating," I say, defiantly keeping my voice at a normal level. I didn't know how miserable I'd been until the day after I quit, when I woke up and threw those damn scrubs in the trash.

Being my own boss on my own time, wearing my own clothes with no one to answer to but myself, was more freeing than having dad's credit card at Phipps Plaza. Worth so much more than any stupid 401(k).

Sure, quitting had been a gamble, but I was betting on myself. And if there's one thing I know, it's that I'm the only one I can count on. My dad taught me that.

"You want to know what's suffocating?" my mom says, leaning across the table toward me, her voice a low rumble. "Being sixty-two and finding out the money's gone, your husband is gone, and you don't have a way to make a living."

Her voice shakes and my heart breaks. I shouldn't be surprised my mom has just been putting on a good face—she's the one who taught me how: *Smile through the pain, darling; never let them see you cry.* But I'd hoped she'd be real with me. Our family of three is down to two. If it gets any smaller, it will be just me.

Rebellious tears fill my eyes, and I blink them away. It's my turn to be the strong one. If I let her know I'm here for her, that I understand what she's going through, maybe then she'll open up and we can finally have a conversation about the secret I thought I'd been hiding for all those years.

I reach across the table and take her hand in mine. Her bottom lip quivers ever so slightly before she turns it into a bright, phony smile. Someone must be watching.

Sure enough, my mother lifts her hand and does a princess-style wave to Janet Rosenbaum and her daughter, making their way back from the buffet. Mrs. Rosenbaum smiles and nods, but instead of coming to say hello like she might have done two months ago, she hurries her daughter toward their table.

I watch my mom's face for a sign of hurt, but if she noticed the snub, she doesn't let it show. Her porcelain mask is back on, but I had a glimpse of her real, vulnerable self, and I take this opportunity to ask one of the questions that's been on my mind for the last week. I start with the easier of the two questions, approaching the conversation like the icy lake at camp, dipping a toe in to test the water.

"Did you know?" I ask. "About the money?"

She shakes her head so subtly I might have missed it if I wasn't looking for it.

"Have you found out about any of the investments?" I ask. "Who these 'friends' of his were?"

She shakes her head again.

The knotted ball of grief I've been carrying around since the day he died twists, morphing into anger and frustration. "How could he have been so stupid?"

I expect my mom to agree with me—after all, she's the one left holding the empty purse—but her face hardens as if I'd just insulted her.

"Kina hora," she says, a throwback to her great-great-grandmother and the Yiddish phrase that's the Jewish equivalent of knocking on wood to ward off evil. "I will not have you speaking ill of your father."

I lean back in my chair and stare at the woman across from me. She's obviously grieving the loss of her husband, but I imagine her feelings are as complicated as mine are. Maybe even more so.

It seems the theoretical water is still too cold, and I retreat from the conversation. If she's not willing to talk about the money problems, there's no chance in hell she'll be willing to discuss the whole illegitimate-child-by-another-woman situation.

Before I can think of a safe topic to change the subject to, the waitress approaches, her smile matching my mother's.

"Are y'all doing the buffet?" she asks.

"Yes," my mother says, pushing her chair back and standing up, officially ending our conversation. "Come now, Kat. You know what they say, calories don't count on Mother's Day!"

The waitress and my mother both laugh and turn to look at me. But I can't bring myself to pretend there's anything funny about this day. Or my life.

MONDAY MORNING, THINGS are looking up as I settle into my desk with an oat-milk latte at half past ten—a benefit of being my own boss.

I open Instagram and check my insights for the previous week. Engagement is up—but not as much as it had been the week before. I frown and flip back to my feed, wondering what it was that improved my visibility in the algorithm two weeks ago.

This is the unglamorous side of my job that my parents don't see or appreciate. I do more than post pretty pictures with witty captions. There's a science to the art: strategy and research, testing with trial and error.

My grid is bright and airy by design. Every fourth picture is of me, since I am my brand. Two posts a week are videos where I'm doing my signature #KatWalk, turning ordinary places into a fashion runway. The fish market last week—a sponsored post with Frye boots, Alice + Olivia short-shorts, and a plain white tank from H&M—got crazy engagement; people love seeing beauty in unexpected places.

The rest of my grid is full of artful shots of products or beautiful things I eat, drink, and discover throughout my day. Avocado toast is always a guaranteed spike in numbers, and so are before-and-after cosmetic product demos—my top post of all time is a Sephora-sponsored series that compared Too Faced Better Than Sex mascara to Charlotte Tilbury's Pillow Talk Push Up Lashes.

When my head starts spinning from all the insights and data, I close Instagram and bring up the email I haven't stopped thinking about since I got it last Friday.

The email is from the head of marketing and publicity for Rachel Worthington, former child star turned national treasure. Once she conquered the big screen, she went behind the camera and started producing, then created her own book club before expanding her brand to a modern/Southern fashion line and, rumor has it, a soon-to-be-announced home décor line.

A few months ago, I did a sponsored post for her clothing line about gingham making a long-overdue comeback. The deal hadn't been for much money, but I took it with the hope it could turn into something more.

Another gamble that looks like it's paid off. The company is looking for three influencers to do a year-long partnership with events, social media posts, giveaways, and more—and I have been personally invited to apply.

I know it's still a long shot; everyone who is anyone is throwing their virtual hat in the ring. Not only is it for Rachel Worthington, *the* trendsetter herself, but it's a six-figure deal that would be sure to take a modest account like mine and skyrocket it to fame.

Even though I have the short email memorized, I read it again:

Kat darling,

Wanted to make sure this was on your radar. Loved your take on gingham, and hope you'll consider applying.

xx
Brenda

Brenda Jenkins
Senior Vice President, Marketing and Publicity
Rachel Worthington, Inc.

I wonder how it feels when a person gets to a point where they have to incorporate themselves. And if that would ever be possible for someone like me.

Before I can go too far down that dreamscape, my phone dings with a five-minute warning for the phone call I've been dreading. A rude intrusion of reality into the fantasy my life appears to be.

TEN MINUTES LATER, I'm rolling my eyes, grateful this isn't a video conference. I don't think I could keep a straight face listening to the junior Callahan wax poetic about my late father. It would be one thing if his words were sincere, but they're not.

"Even the brightest men make mistakes," Scott Callahan says. "But at the end of the day, our lives are a tapestry of our wrongs and our rights."

I mumble in agreement and wonder if he's reading from a badly written manual on how to talk to grieving families after you've detonated a last will and testament bomb on their lives.

"As they say, time heals all wounds—and what doesn't kill us makes us stronger." My father's lawyer stops short, as if just realizing he would have been better off with a cliché that didn't invoke death. He tries to cover his tracks, adding, "Your father loved you very much."

Even though there's no warmth to the man's voice, my heart constricts at the words I always craved from my father. My dad usually said "love you, too" when I said it first, but he wasn't one to initiate words or gestures of love. Maybe because he knew how desperate I was to hear it. Or maybe because that part of him was broken.

I feel the prickle of tears and blink them away. My father would be the first to remind me that if I want people to take me seriously, I have to act serious.

"Have you talked to *her* about the house?" I ask, interrupting Callahan before he goes any further into his uninspired script.

"Your half sister?" he asks, as if there could be anyone else.

"Please don't call her that," I tell him—trying to keep the

emotion out of my voice. The word "sister" implies love and a shared history. She is none of those things. She represents secrets and lies and betrayal, nothing I need or want in my life.

Scott Callahan clears his throat, then says, "We spoke late last week."

"And?" I say, annoyed he's making me ask.

"And I can't share details of our conversation, but your—er, Blake—mentioned getting an appraisal on the house to see what it was worth."

My stomach clenches with the realization that Blake O'Neill isn't going to make this easy for me. It's hard to imagine her playing hardball—in my head, she's still twelve years old, awkward, and shy, a girl who didn't know the difference between a debit and a credit card.

"Can she do that?" I ask, afraid to hear the answer.

"She can't sell it without you, but it's her right to get an appraisal."

"I . . . I . . ." I stammer, trying to put my anguish into words. The beach house isn't something you can put a price tag on. It's more than a place; it's a living memory. My grandparents bought the three-bedroom house in Destin a million years ago, when my dad was just a kid, and I grew up spending spring breaks and summer vacations there.

Most of the good memories I have with my dad are at that house: holding hands as we chased waves, the two of us against the ocean; making the world's best s'mores, letting our marshmallows catch fire for one brief moment; rainy days curled up on the couch watching classic movies. Destin was the one place where he left work behind and focused on my mom and me.

The sudden onset of memories makes my throat tighten, and once again, stubborn tears threaten to fall. I just lost my dad. I can't lose our beach house, too.

"She can't sell it," I say.

"That's correct," the lawyer says. "She can't sell it without your signature. Don't worry about that."

I exhale, but I'm still worried. I'm terrified Blake is going to storm into my life and take what little I have left of my dad, the way she tried to when we were young. But it didn't work then, and it won't work now.

"Your father was a smart man," Scott Callahan says.

I nod, forgetting he can't see me. My father was one of the smartest men I know, which is why he was so successful. At least he had been. And it's probably why he was able to pull the wool over all our eyes.

"He wouldn't have left the house to you both if he didn't have a plan—maybe he wanted to bring you two together? Coordinate a little reunion."

I scoff at the thought. This man clearly didn't know my father— not the real David Steiner. He would never, ever, not in a million years want his dirty little secret to be exposed.

We know people in Destin. People know us. They knew my grandparents. If any of those people found out about this, they would talk. And if there's one thing my dad hated, it was people talking about his personal business.

I might not have known everything about my dad, but I know that.

Before Callahan can hit me with another tired cliché, I end the call. Blake can get that appraisal, but it won't change anything. That house belongs to me.

CHAPTER FOUR

BLAKE

MY LIFE IS ABOUT TO CHANGE FOREVER.

That phrase has been rattling around my head during my journey to Destin. I divided the twenty-hour drive into two days, which felt even longer because I had to stop and let the Vanderhaavens' dog out to pee every three hours. Now my butt is sore and my eyes are gritty with fatigue, but I'm almost there. And the closer I get, the louder those words echo: *My life is about to change forever. Forever.*

The dog is in the back seat, sticking his head out the window, his long pink tongue lolling out of his mouth. I'm talking with Martina on speakerphone as I drive; she told me to call her at *any* time if I felt tired. She remembers, all too well, the time I was driving us both home from a school dance junior year and fell asleep, driving Granddad's pickup into a telephone pole. Luckily neither of us was hurt, but we were both pretty shaken up.

"Tell me your plans for tomorrow," Martina says, which is a welcome change of topic from the past thirty minutes she's spent telling me how much she loves being married. She and Ricky are adorable, but they also make me feel deeply, distressingly single.

I haven't dated anyone in a few years, and most of the time, I'm fine with that. Between nannying and visiting Granddad, I don't have time for much else.

"I'm meeting with the real estate agent tomorrow," I tell Martina. "She's going to tell me how much we can sell it for, and then we'll get it listed ASAP."

I searched online for real estate agents in the Destin area and found several that looked promising. I didn't know how to decide which one to call—until I saw the name Harriet Beaver. I snort-laughed so hard I choked, then immediately called her. Any woman with the confidence to put that name on her business card is a woman I want in my corner.

"Let's hope she can get you a couple million, since you have to split it in half," Martina says.

I laugh. "That would be fantastic, but let's not get ahead of ourselves."

Last I spoke with Harriet, she told me that a three-bedroom beachfront house could get at least a million. It's such a staggering amount I can hardly grasp it, even if half of it goes to Kat.

I've never had more than a couple of hundred dollars in my bank account. My grandparents lived that way, too, always just barely making it through.

My life is about to change forever.

"Speaking of the other heiress," Martina says, "have you heard from her?"

"No," I say, somewhat abruptly.

I don't plan to speak with Kat at all. I'm going to work completely through Mr. Callahan. I *have* been checking her Instagram—a bad habit, I know, but I have a bizarre fascination with her. She's the type to overshare on social media, posting daily on her feed and constantly blabbing in her stories. It feels weird to know the intimate details of her life—like what she eats for breakfast or the brand of vitamin C serum she uses—when she knows nothing about me.

But strangely, she's made no mention of her father's death online. Zero. She hasn't missed a beat, staying busy with her shopping hauls and organic smoothies. Any sympathy I had for her has dissolved. I've never seen a more self-centered person in my life.

"You should've seen her post today," Martina says. She's joined my semi-obsession with the #KatWalk. "She was showing off this denim jumpsuit that costs two *thousand* dollars. That girl is so high-maintenance it's hard to believe you ever got along with her, even as a kid."

I know what she means—Kat radiates luxury. Expensive clothes and shoes, dewy skin, shiny chestnut hair. Even the supposedly casual shots are too perfect, too put together. I can't imagine the time and energy Kat must spend in order to look like that—the eyebrow waxing (and probably upper-lip waxing—even at twelve Kat had peach fuzz there), the manicures and pedicures (I have had exactly two pedicures in my life, both forced fun when I was in a bridal party), the spray tans and lash lifts (I didn't even know that "lash lifting" was a thing until Kat posted about it, and I'm still horrified that people put those chemicals near their eyes). Even the pictures she posts with her shopping hauls, floral arrangements, and foodie shots look like something out of a magazine.

In contrast, I'm so low-maintenance that the last guy I went out with called me a "bruh girl," and he did *not* mean that as a compliment. Currently, I'm wearing a free T-shirt I got from a fun run at the Vanderhaaven kids' school, cutoff jean shorts that I cut off myself, and flip-flops I bought for one dollar at Old Navy. I'm not wearing any makeup, but when I do, it's the kind you buy at Target, not at a fancy department store cosmetics counter.

It's not that I don't care what I look like, because I do—in fact, just last week I was staring at myself in the mirror, wondering how I got all the way to twenty-seven without knowing how to properly apply eyeliner. But I don't have the time, money, or skills to hold myself to Kat Steiner's standards.

"She seemed different back then," I say, bringing myself back to the conversation with Martina. The operative word is "seemed." More likely, she was exactly the same but was slumming it with me during those weeks at summer camp.

Then I look around and notice my surroundings, and gasp. "Holy shit."

"What?" Martina asks.

"I wish I could show you," I say, taking in the beauty in front of me. I'm driving across the long Mid-Bay Bridge that leads from the mainland to the little strip of land where Destin sits. Water stretching on all sides, dotted with boats, the sun setting in the western horizon. "It's beautiful. Breathtaking."

"You deserve a little beauty," Martina says.

"I'll only be here for a couple days," I remind her. "How's my granddad doing?"

"Great. He was watching *True Grit* when I came by with his lunch."

"The original?" It's Granddad's favorite movie, and I love it, too. John Wayne earned that Oscar for his portrayal of crotchety old Rooster Cogburn.

"Obviously," Martina says, a smile in her voice. "Gotta go—Ricky just got home from work. FaceTime me later? I want to see this amazing beach house!"

And there it is again, that voice in my head: *My life is about to change forever.*

. . .

I MAKE IT across the bridge, allowing my GPS app to lead me onto Old 98, toward the address Mr. Callahan gave me. My stomach flutters with excitement and nerves. My father spent so much time here as a child and as an adult, and yet I have no memory of him telling me about it. It makes me realize, once again, how little I knew about him; his presence loomed so large in my childhood, but in reality, he played only a small role in my life.

I *lived* for his visits when I was a kid. The rest of the world ceased to exist when he showed up; my mom would take off work and all her usual stress would fade away. At bedtime, he'd make up stories for me about a brave princess who saved the kingdom from attacking dragons, then tuck me in and say, *I love you so much, Blake. Never forget that.*

I have one distinct memory of sitting on the couch between my parents long after a movie ended, snuggled under a blanket, pretending to be asleep so I could stay right there. I remember opening my eyes a sliver and seeing my father press a gentle kiss to my mother's mouth, gazing at her like she was his entire world.

It was all such absolute bullshit.

The voice on my GPS tells me that I'm only a mile away. Shaking off those memories, I roll down the windows and inhale the salty air. Behind me, the dog runs back and forth across the back seat; he's excited, too.

Palm trees line the two-lane street, and every so often, there's a gap between the hotels and condo complexes, giving me a glimpse of the striking green waters of the Gulf. As I get closer, the street becomes lined with gigantic beach houses in white or pastel, many of them three or four stories tall, gleaming in the setting sun.

Granddad would've loved to see this; since he specialized in home renovations, one of his hobbies was to drive around neighborhoods and look at the houses. He would've gotten a kick out of this place, so different from the practical midwestern architecture of the homes back in Minnesota.

I slow as I approach the address given to me by the estate lawyer: 3466 . . . 3472 . . . 3478. Each house is nicer than the one before. I hold my breath as the beach house, *my* beach house, comes into view.

"Your destination is on the right," the GPS voice tells me, and I slow and turn into a driveway.

I park and look at the house.

And blink.

And blink again.

DILAPIDATED. RAMSHACKLE. BROKEN-DOWN.

Those are the best words to describe this place. It's a two-story pale yellow house with worn-out siding desperately in need of paint. The porch steps are practically falling off. Weeds have overgrown the flower beds. One of the upstairs windows is broken and boarded up.

This can't be the right place.

Shaking my head in disbelief, I pull up the email from Scott Callahan to check the address. I must have entered it incorrectly into the GPS. But no, it's the same.

My heart falls like a brick into my stomach. This cannot be happening. Mr. Callahan overnighted me a package with the keys, and I pull those out of my canvas tote and head to the door. The steps wiggle in a frightening way as I walk up them, and I'm half worried they might crumble under my weight.

I say a silent prayer that my key won't fit, but when I slide the key into the keyhole, it goes in smoothly. Holding my breath, I walk in, hoping the inside is nicer than the outside. But as I flick on the lights, the dog scampering past me into the house, my heart drops all the way to my toes.

Somehow, it's even worse.

The walls are covered with old-fashioned wallpaper, a hideous seashell print, peeling at the corners. The living room has mint-colored carpet and old wicker furniture that looks like it hasn't been moved in fifty years. The kitchen is cramped and ugly, with dark wood cabinets and a yellow linoleum floor.

Well. I guess I should have expected that my father's final gift to me would be nothing more than a big heap of trash.

THE NEXT MORNING, after a long, depressing night spent sleeping on an ancient mattress that smelled like mold and stale peppermint, I'm standing in the kitchen as Harriet Beaver confirms my worst fears.

"I'm really sorry," she says, giving me a grim smile, "but you're not going to get much for the house in this market."

As soon as the real estate agent walked in, dressed in her sharp blue suit with her blond bob teased to perfection, her smile froze. I knew it wasn't going to be good news.

"You have two options," Harriet continues. "You can either sell the place as is, basically selling it for the land, or you can renovate and get a much better price. No one is looking for fixer-uppers right now—buyers want a home that is vacation-ready."

This doesn't surprise me. The one good feature of the house is its location—a pristine white-sand beach just out the back door, leading to the glistening waters of the Gulf.

I look down at the kitchen table, where Harriet has written her estimate of what the house could sell for now. It's a depressingly small amount, especially when divided in half. Despite Grand-dad's memory issues, his body is as healthy as a horse. He could live for five or ten more years. My lungs tighten with panic and desperation; I need to get more out of this house.

"Realistically," I say to her, "what do you think this house could get if it was in better condition?"

Harriet twists her pink-lipsticked mouth to the side, thinking. "The kitchen needs to be completely redone. You see how there's no natural light in the living room? It needs to be opened up—buyers want open concept. All the wallpaper and carpet need to go. Bathrooms redone. New light fixtures. It would be a huge job."

"But if all that was done, what could I get for it?"

She spits out a high six-figure number that makes me suck in a breath. I need that money. I *need* it.

I turn around, this time trying to see it through my grand-father's eyes. I imagine how the place would look without the wall separating the living room from the kitchen. You'd be able to see right out the windows to the beach; it would feel open and breezy. The kitchen cabinets can be painted—a big job, but an inexpensive way to make a huge impact.

Next, I go into the living room, where I bend down and pull up a corner of the carpet. There's a hardwood subfloor under-neath. I personally helped Granddad refinish a similar floor in their house when I was a teenager.

And just like that, I know what he would say about this house, if he were here: *It needs work, Blakers, but it has good bones.*

"Maybe I could fix it up," I say, standing.

Harriet gives me a surprised smile. "That would be lovely. This place has tons of potential. Just needs a little love and elbow grease! Well, maybe a lot of love."

Now that I've seen the house, I'm sure Kat won't want it—it doesn't fit with her lifestyle. Even if she does, she can buy me out *after* I fix it up. Some of these projects are above my skill level, but I'm willing to learn, and it's the only way I can turn my dad's crap "gift" into something useful.

The bigger problem is the time this will require. I'll have to convince the Vanderhaavens to let me stay here with their dog. If I can get them to pay me my entire summer salary now, I can use that as my budget to fix up the place. Kat can pay her share when she buys me out.

I turn to face Harriet, a smile growing on my face for the first time since I pulled my car up to this hunk of junk. "I'm going to do it. Is that crazy?"

"Not at all," she says. "I think it's a wonderful idea, if you can swing it. How about you get back in contact with me when you're ready to talk about selling—"

"WHAT THE ACTUAL FUCK?"

My heart seizes and I spin around.

It's Kat. Standing in the middle of the kitchen, looking like she's walked off the runway for a summer fashion show, all glossy brown hair and long, tanned legs. Even though I've seen her on Instagram plenty of times, it's surreal seeing her in person. She's tall and hourglass-shaped, the kind of woman who oozes confidence and style.

In a heartbeat I'm back at Camp Chickawah, standing on the dock in my bathing suit, holding Kat's hand and counting to three before jumping. Icy lake water closing over my head, her fingers still clasped in mine, then resurfacing, gasping and laughing in the sunshine.

Blinking, I take a deep breath. "Hello, Kat. The real estate agent and I—"

"Why is there a real estate agent here?" Kat demands, taking her sunglasses off. Fury burns in her eyes. It's terrifying.

I glance back at Harriet, who has a stiff smile on her face.

"Well," I say, "we're discussing how to get the most value out of the house—"

"The most *value*?" Kat says, her voice rising. "You can't sell it out from under me."

My stomach clenches; I hate conflict, always have, and part of me wants to run out to my car and drive away rather than face this fiery, wrathful warrior princess standing in front of me. But I need to stand up for myself.

"I wasn't going to—"

"How dare you waltz in here like this is *your* place," she says, steamrolling right over me. "This is *my* grandparents' beach house—I spent my childhood here, and I'll be damned if I let you steal that away from me."

That makes me straighten up, indignant. "I'm not *stealing* anything. In case you've forgotten, you're the one who ended up with everything."

"Don't talk to me about what I ended up with—you have no idea!" Kat's voice is now a shriek. "You're slithering back into my life, trying to take the last thing I have left, my *grandparents'* house, and—" She turns her blazing eyes onto the dog, who has stupidly run up to her, wagging his tail. "And dogs are not allowed!"

Whirling around, she storms down the hall and into the bathroom. She slams the door behind her, rattling the house, and a framed picture falls off the nearest wall, the glass shattering with a spectacular crash.

The dog scrambles behind my legs and cowers there, trembling. I'm shaking, too, though in my case it's from frustration, not fear.

I glance at Harriet Beaver, whose mouth has fallen open.

"So . . ." I say. "She's the other owner."

CHAPTER FIVE

KAT

MY HANDS ARE LITERALLY SHAKING FROM ANGER, WHICH makes washing them difficult. I cringe as water splashes from the sink and lands in giant droplets on my silk peasant blouse. I turn off the faucet and grab one of the hand towels monogrammed with a blue *S* for "Steiner," clutching it as if it's proof this house belongs to me.

Dabbing at the wet spots only makes them worse, and I wish I could get a do-over of the last five minutes. My father would be disappointed at the way I barreled in. As far as he was concerned, emotions were a sign of weakness, and they had no business being at the table in a negotiation—a fact he drilled into my mind from a very young age.

While other dads were reading fairy tales to their little girls, mine taught me to hold my cards close to my chest, to never let anyone see how much I wanted something. The goal, he'd say, wasn't to play nice or make friends, but to get what you wanted and come out on top.

Not great advice for the playground in third grade when I wanted to be captain of the dodgeball team, but it would have come in handy today. I wonder if this was the moment he'd been training me for my whole life—and once again, I let him down.

Exhaling a deep breath, I look in the mirror. I hardly recognize this angry version of myself—my shoulders are stiff, my jaw is clenched, and my heart hasn't stopped racing since this morning when I got the text that sent me hurrying to Destin to stop Blake.

I was enjoying a little self-care, getting a mani-pedi on Briarcliff, when my phone buzzed with a text from Nicole "CoCo" Rooney, one of my oldest and closest friends.

The Rooney family owns one of the largest underwear companies in the world, almost as big as Hanes or Fruit of the Loom. When we were growing up, Rooney Undergarments were synonymous with granny panties and supportive underthings for women of a certain age, but a few years ago they launched Under-Rooneys, a line of hip and fun bras, panties, and boxers for millennials. One of my first brand partnerships was with Under-Rooneys, thanks to CoCo.

We don't see each other often since she lives in Boston and I'm in Atlanta, but her family has a beach house—well, more like a beach mansion—down the road from ours.

This morning, I'd been sitting at the salon with my right hand under the blue light, OPI Cajun Shrimp polish hardening on my nails, when I saw CoCo's name pop up on the screen. I smiled until I read her message: Damn, I wish I knew you were in Destin this week!

I borrowed my hand back from the manicurist long enough to text back a single question mark.

A few minutes later, another message popped up saying she'd seen a car parked at my grandparents' beach house and assumed it was mine.

At first, I was confused—no one had used the beach house

in years—and then it hit me with a sudden, blinding rage. *That bitch.* Callahan had mentioned Blake was going to get an appraisal, but I never expected she would go gallivanting around like she owned the place.

I left the salon before my toes even dried and sped through two yellow lights on my way home. I was there just long enough to throw some clothes in a bag before I hit the road.

I'd hoped the five-hour drive would calm me down—I even blasted old-school Kelly Clarkson and scream-sang along with the windows down, trying to release my rage. But it didn't help. If anything, it made it worse.

The music triggered a memory from camp. Our counselor, Rainbow, loved angsty rock and was teaching herself how to play "Since U Been Gone" and "Miss Independent" on guitar. Blake and I thought she was the coolest. Of course, my judgment was shit back then—I also thought Blake was best friend material.

It still makes my head hurt to think about that last day at camp. I'd already been out of sorts, sad about my grandfather, sad about leaving camp and Blake. She hadn't just been my best camp friend—she'd been my *best* friend. The girl who killed a spider so I wouldn't have to, who didn't tell anyone I was scared of the dark, who stayed in the shallow end of the lake with me because I got nervous when my feet couldn't touch the ground.

But she was also the girl who lied to my face every single day that summer. Our entire friendship had been built on a lie; she used me to try to get to my father.

The quiet murmur of voices on the other side of the door reminds me that the real estate agent is still out there, talking to Blake as if she's the rightful owner.

I lock eyes with my reflection and remind myself I am not twelve years old anymore, and I am not going to let Blake O'Neill take what's mine. It didn't work fifteen years ago when she tried to break up my family, and it's not going to work now.

One more deep breath, and I grab the monogrammed S towel, clutching it like it's a tallit, a Jewish prayer shawl. I've never been very religious, but I have a feeling I'm going to need the help of a higher power to stay calm out there.

I open the door and step back into the hallway. With my head held high, I try to exude the confidence that comes with knowing that you're right. I walk past Blake, who's standing in the living room with her wispy blond hair and the same lost-puppy look she had on the first day of camp before I asked if she wanted to share a bunk. She's wearing cheap flip-flops, and I'm glad I didn't change out of my heels so I have a few inches on her.

"Thanks so much for coming," I tell the real estate agent, my voice dripping with false cheer, "but we won't be needing your services."

"Wait," Blake says. "You can't just—"

I turn and give Blake a conversation-ending look. Her face goes slack, and if we didn't have all this history and bad blood between us, I might feel bad for her. But we do, and I don't.

"Thanks for coming," Blake says to the woman, an apology in her voice. "I'll be in touch."

The real estate agent gives a pained smile, then bolts out of the house faster than if she'd found out the place was infested. Which I suppose it is. Only instead of roaches or ants, there's just one unwelcome pest.

AS SOON AS the door closes behind the woman, I take a deep breath and turn to face Blake O'Neill for the first time since that fateful day in 2007.

"Who the hell do you think you are?" I ask, but I don't stop to hear an answer. "You have no fucking right to be here." The words keep coming, building momentum and gaining fury as I go. "It's bullshit. I don't care what my dad or the lawyer or anyone else says. This is not your house. You cannot steal what belongs to me!"

My voice is getting louder, and I curse myself for failing once again to remain calm. But I can't help it. These words haven't just been building up over the last five hours in the car, or even the last few weeks. They're full of the hurt and heartbreak I've been carrying around for more than a decade.

"It's un-fucking-believable," I yell. "This house belonged to my grandparents—you didn't know them! They didn't even know you existed, and they wouldn't want you here. You or your stupid dog."

I pause to let my words sink in, but Blake just stands there in her cutoff jean shorts and some kind of sporty T-shirt with her hand on her hip like she's exactly where she's supposed to be.

My cheeks flush with anger. She seems unaffected by the whole situation, and I need her to hurt like I am.

Before I can stop myself, I narrow my eyes and lower my voice to deliver one final punch. "It didn't work the last time you tried to steal something from me," I remind her. "My dad didn't want you then, and I don't want you now. You don't belong here."

Silence settles between us, and the only thing I hear is my heart pounding in my chest and the dog, panting as it watches us.

"Do you feel better now?" Blake asks in a smug tone that matches her expression.

I clutch the monogrammed towel tighter in my hands. I hate that she's acting like the bigger person, the kind of person my dad always wanted me to be. I wonder if she grew up hearing the same lectures, only with her, the lessons stuck.

"You were very rude to Harriet," Blake says when I don't answer.

The way she so casually mentions the real estate agent re-ignites the spark of anger, but this time I manage to keep my voice steady. "She had no reason to be here in the first place—you can't sell this house without me, and I don't want to sell. It's half mine," I say, even though I hate to admit, even by default, that the other half is hers.

"I don't care about this damn house," Blake says.

"Exactly!" I yell, grateful she made the point for me. This house means nothing to her, so she has no reason to stake a claim on it unless she just wants to hurt me again, which I wouldn't put past her.

Blake's blond hair falls in her face, lifting slightly as she exhales a quick breath.

The gesture instantly takes me back to a day we were at the archery range and a boy from the other side of camp started picking on Blake, saying the only reason she could hit the bull's-eye was because she didn't have boobs yet. Instead of fighting back, Blake untucked her hair from behind her ears so it hung in front of her face, but I could still see her cheeks burning bright red as she turned and walked away.

"Listen," I say, hoping we can find a way to meet in the middle.

"It's my turn to speak now," Blake says, cutting me off.

I take a step back, surprised and a tiny bit impressed. I'm not a fan of conflict, but when it can't be avoided, it helps having a sparring partner who's willing to fight back. The Blake I used to know would have caved right away to avoid conflict like she did at the archery range.

"As I was saying," she continues, "I don't care about this house, but I need the money." Her eyes narrow and I know she's thinking that I have plenty of it, but she's mistaken about that. "You're welcome to buy me out, but on the house's future value."

"The future value?" I ask with a laugh. What, is she psychic now?

"This land is worth a lot," Blake says, and she's not wrong. "But the house isn't worth much in this condition."

I frown and look around the living room. Sure, the white wicker furniture went out of style a few decades ago, and I wouldn't exactly call the seashell wallpaper on trend—but it's on-brand for a beach house. The dusty blue carpet is the same as it's always been, and there's an old-fashioned phone on the side table. I still know the number by heart: 850-555-1005.

"It could use a little face-lift," I admit.

Blake laughs. "I'm thinking more like reconstructive surgery," she says. "All the carpet, the wallpaper, the kitchen. New lighting, knocking out this wall," she says, nodding toward the kitchen wall.

I fold my arms in front of my chest and keep my expression neutral even though the spark of an idea is formulating. I should be offended at all the major changes she's suggesting, but if the rumors are true about the Worthington brand expanding into the home décor space, a little home renovation project could give me an even bigger advantage than I already have.

Surely my eye for fashion can translate to home décor. If I take before-and-after pictures and document the process, a stylish renovation could be the cherry on top for my application.

I can feel Blake watching me, but I don't want to give her the satisfaction of knowing I'm on board, and maybe even a little excited about this prospect.

Channeling my high school drama instructor, I let out a long-suffering sigh. "Be my guest if you want to make a few updates. But I'm not going to let this house leave my family."

"That's fine," Blake says. "Once we get it in selling condition, we'll get another appraisal, and you can buy me out for half. Then you can go back to pretending I don't exist."

The hurt behind Blake's voice catches me by surprise. I feel a pang of guilt but quickly remind myself that I'm dealing with someone who hurt me once and wouldn't think twice about doing it again.

"Before you so rudely stormed in," Blake says, giving me a look that I assume is supposed to carry a warning, "Harriet was giving me an estimated value of what the house might be worth after a major renovation. If we get her back, she can give us an official estimate, and you can decide if you want to buy me out now or later."

My stomach sinks with the realization that I couldn't afford to buy Blake out now, even with the house in its current state. I wish my dad were here to tell me whether it would be a sign of weakness or strength to let Blake know I'm no longer the rich girl she thinks I am.

"I can't," I tell her, before I can stop myself. "I don't have money."

Blake tilts her head and looks at me curiously before letting out a laugh. She thinks I'm joking.

"I'm serious," I tell her. "My dad's the one who had money, and he . . ." My voice trails off. It feels like a weird betrayal to tell her his secrets even though she was one of them. And while my sponsorships are enough for me to live on, it's not like I have any savings. My parents were always my safety net.

My head spins with the strangeness of this situation and I wonder again what my dad was thinking when he left the house to us both.

I look back up at Blake, who's giving me a suspicious look like she's worried about *me* stealing from *her*, which is hilarious.

"I may not have gone to your fancy private school"—Blake looks me up and down, and I can practically see the dollar signs in her eyes as she judges my outfit—"but I wasn't born yesterday."

"I didn't say you were," I snap back, feeling like a preteen version of myself engaged in a playground battle of the frenemies. But I'm an adult now, and I don't have to have defend myself. Not to her. "I need some air," I say, turning and walking toward the back of the house.

As I walk through the kitchen, I can't help but see it through Blake's eyes. Without the rose-colored glasses of memory, it looks run-down and abandoned. But the view out the window still takes my breath away.

I unlock the sliding glass door and step outside. The beach instantly calms me, and I exhale a cleansing breath, letting the salty air fill my lungs. I didn't realize how much I'd missed this place with the tall sea grass, white-sand beaches, and emerald-green water.

I lean against the railing and look out at the beach, feeling a surge of loneliness being here without my family or friends. I think of CoCo and realize she's just the distraction I need. I reach for my phone and pull up our text exchange from earlier.

Hey, just got to town

A few seconds later, my phone buzzes and a photo of CoCo's smiling face pops up on my screen. With her dark-brown hair and sparkling green eyes, we looked similar enough to be cousins when we were kids. Of course, I'm Jewish and she's Irish, but that didn't stop us from pretending.

"Hi," I say, answering the phone.

"Kitty Kat!" Hearing her voice and my childhood nickname makes my eyes well with tears. The unexpected wave of emotion surprises me, and I realize how much I could use a friend right now. "How the hell are you?" she asks.

"Oh, you know," I say, forcing a smile even though she can't see me. "Any chance you're free to meet for a drink?"

"I wish," CoCo says, "but I landed in Boston an hour ago."

"And you can't come back?" I ask. For anyone else, it would be a ridiculous proposition, but CoCo has done crazier things.

"I can't tonight," she says, "but I might be back soon. Our housekeeper up and quit this morning before I left, and my parents are making me deal with finding a replacement."

"Oh no," I say. While we usually had a cleaning service come in and tidy up after every trip, the Rooneys had a full live-in staff at their eight-bedroom house in a gated community down the road.

"I know," CoCo says through a sigh. "I can't believe she walked away from such an easy job—we're barely there, so it's not like she had to work a lot. At least the groundskeeper's still there so we have someone at the house."

"Thank goodness," I say, allowing a hint of sarcasm in my voice. Although I always used to appreciate the hot men the Rooneys hired to maintain the landscaping.

"Let me know if you know of anyone who's looking for a cush job that comes with a free place to stay on the beach," CoCo says. "Oh shit, my mom's calling. Probably more drama with Junior."

The thought of CoCo's older brother makes me smile. Junior Rooney was my first kiss a million years ago, when I was thirteen and he was fifteen. It was the last week of summer, so nothing ever came of it. I'd been hoping we could pick up where things left off the next summer, but he had a girlfriend. Last I heard, he was engaged and working for the family business.

"Good luck," I tell CoCo before she hangs up.

I look back down at my phone, wishing there was someone else I could call. I may be up to seventy-eight thousand followers online, and I have a handful of acquaintances back in Atlanta, but there's no one I can really talk to.

The sound of families laughing drifts up from the beach below and my heart constricts. I miss my dad, and I wish I could call and hear his voice, even if just to say he's running into a meeting and can't talk.

I wipe a stray tear from my cheek, feeling pathetic and more alone than ever. But being alone beats being with Blake. I can't stomach the thought of staying in this house with her even a minute longer. I really need that drink. Just because CoCo isn't here to join me doesn't mean I can't take myself out for one.

I breathe in one more cleansing breath of the Gulf air and slip back inside the house, grab my purse and keys, and walk out the door. Blake is nowhere in sight, so I'm thankful for that. She doesn't deserve to know where I'm going or when I'll be back.

CHAPTER SIX

BLAKE

WHEN I COME DOWNSTAIRS, THE HOUSE IS EMPTY AND
Kat's Audi isn't in the driveway. All she's left behind is a wake of
confused, upset feelings inside me. The Vanderhaavens' dog is
sprawled out on the ugly wicker couch like he owns the place,
and the sight makes me perversely happy. Kat would pitch a fit if
she saw him there.

So. It's clear Kat is going to make it difficult for me to sell
this house. No surprise—Kat has always made things difficult. I
have a vivid memory of one day at camp when our cabin was
supposed to go on a nature hike to the other side of the lake.

Kat couldn't find the expensive hiking socks her mother had
special ordered for her. She made a huge fuss, saying she absolutely *needed* to wear those socks or she'd end up with blisters. It
took so long to find her socks (she'd left them in the communal
bathroom to dry) that she made us all late. By the time we returned and got to the mess hall for dinner, the food was mostly
gone, and *then* we had to do the dishes as punishment.

At the time, I'd stood up for Kat when the other girls blamed
her for ruining their day. But now I realize that that whole expe-

rience was a perfect encapsulation of Kat's personality: high-maintenance and self-centered.

It took every bit of self-control to keep myself from crumbling when she was yelling at me a few minutes ago, and if I didn't have Granddad to think of, I probably would have. But I can't let my fear of confrontation keep me from getting what I deserve.

I head out the door that leads toward the beach. The deck wobbles under my weight, and I hold my breath, hoping it doesn't collapse in a pile of worm-eaten wood.

If I'd been here under any other circumstances, I'd probably be dazzled by the glistening bluish-green waters of the Gulf, but my mind is elsewhere, the weight of the past on my shoulders.

There's a special kind of shame that comes from knowing your father was a cheater, that your mother was the other woman, and that you are the product of their terrible decisions. I'm not sure which one of them should carry the blame, but it's harder to be angry at my mother—maybe because she isn't the one who left me on purpose. She was stolen from me by a college kid texting on his phone who ran a red light and T-boned her car.

But my father? He left me of his own volition.

I was so young when my mom died that my memories of her are spotty now. I remember she was tired a lot and we never had much money, but she somehow made my childhood feel magical. She'd cut my sandwiches into stars using cookie cutters, and she'd always turn the music up loud in the car so we could sing along with Madonna, Whitney, and Dolly.

She was beautiful, too. Curly golden hair, a tiny waist, and cleavage that must have helped her get better tips at her waitressing job. I'm like a two-dimensional version of her: thin blond hair, body like a prepubescent boy.

My mom had wanted to be a singer—that's how she met my

father. It took me a lot of prying to get the story out of my grand-mother, but she eventually told me they'd met at a bar in Nash-ville where my mother sometimes sang with a cover band. My father owned several commercial properties in Nashville, so he had reason to keep visiting my mother even though he lived a few hours away in Atlanta.

Per my grandma, when my mom found out she was pregnant with me, my father tried to convince her to have an abortion, but my mother wouldn't do it. I sometimes wonder if that was be-cause she wanted *me* or because she hoped it would make *him* stick around.

And I guess it did get him to stick around, sort of. He'd visit a couple of weekends a month, sometimes longer, which makes me wonder how he explained it to his wife. At the time I be-lieved what my mom told me: that Daddy had to travel a lot for work. Now I wonder how long those visits would have lasted if my mother hadn't been killed. If she'd still be his side piece, all these years later.

I'm not sure how my father found out that she'd died. Maybe they had mutual friends who reached out and let him know. Or maybe he figured it out because my mother wasn't responding to calls and he eventually found her obituary online, weeks after her death.

That's how I imagine it: my dark-haired father sitting in his office at some big walnut desk, realizing that his mistress hadn't returned his calls in a while, then searching her name on the internet and finding out what had happened. I wonder if he can-celed the rest of his day's meetings, or if he shrugged it off and carried on with business as usual.

There's no way for me to know because he never returned to my life. Not one phone call or letter or visit. The woman he had carried on an affair with for more than a decade had *died*, and he couldn't even reach out to the child they created together. There's no excuse for that. None whatsoever.

The worst part is that I spent the first nine years of my life believing he loved me. But you can't love someone and then walk out of their life.

I assume he must have loved my mother—or at least, he loved the idea of her, the ability to take a break from his real life and indulge in a fantasy with a woman who was good enough to fuck but not good enough to marry.

But he didn't really love *me*.

As I remember all this, my heart aches with a familiar mixture of anger and betrayal. I need to talk to my granddad, the one person I have left who loves me unconditionally. I pull out my phone and FaceTime Martina, knowing that she's working today.

Martina answers right away; she's in the supply closet where they keep the adult diapers and urinals.

"Hey," she says in a gentle voice. We talked last night, so she knows about my disappointment with the house. "How are you?"

"I'm okay," I tell her, because I don't want to get into everything that happened with Kat. "Can you help me talk to my granddad?"

"Sure thing," she says, and I'm ever so grateful for this friend of mine.

Soon she's out in the garden with Granddad, where he likes to sit and watch the birds. She reminds him how to hold her phone so he can see me, but I only see the top of his head.

"Hi, Granddad!" I say, trying my best to sound cheerful.

"Hello there, Blakers," he says.

"Want to see my view? It's gorgeous here." I flip the camera and pan across the beach. When I turn the camera back to my face, he's smiling.

"Well, France sure is pretty, isn't it?"

My smile falters. "I'm in Florida, remember? I didn't go to France after all."

I'd debated whether to tell him about the inheritance and decided against it. I didn't want to dredge up all the anger he has at my father. Plus, when I do sell this place, I don't want Granddad to suspect I'm using the money to pay for his care—he'd hate that.

"Ah, that's right," he says, nodding. "Are you having a good time?"

"Who wouldn't be having a good time here?" It's the best I can manage without an outright lie.

I ask him what movies he's been watching lately, and he tells me about a Clint Eastwood one that I don't remember seeing. Clint comes in a close second to John Wayne in Granddad's eyes.

"Next time I visit you," I tell him, "we should watch that one together."

"You're going to visit me?" he says, sounding surprised.

"Of course!"

"Well, it'll be nice to meet you. Remind me your name?"

I blink. "It's Blake, Granddad."

"Now, what's a girl like you doing with a boy's name?" He laughs, and my breath catches.

This is the first time he hasn't recognized me, and even though the Alzheimer's has been slowly stealing his memory of other people, I had hoped he wouldn't forget me. I tell myself it's even more confusing for him on FaceTime, but even still, my eyes fill with tears.

"Oh dear," he says. "Please don't cry, pretty lady."

Of course, that makes it worse. The tears roll down my face, and I quickly wipe them away. I'm about to try to explain that I'm his granddaughter when I hear a sound behind me. The door at the back of the house, opening and closing, then the stomping of feet.

It's Hurricane Kat, coming in like a Category 5.

"Hey, Martina?" I say. "I gotta go."

I hang up as Kat barges out onto the deck, her jaw set in the stubborn way I remember from camp. Like the day she'd been determined to conquer the rock-climbing wall, even though she was terrified of heights and had fallen three times already.

Right now, I'm pretty sure Kat sees me like that wall: as a problem to be conquered. I stand, determined not to let her look down on me more than necessary.

"Like I said," Kat says, brisk and businesslike. "I can't buy you out now, but if you give me to the end of the summer, I'll figure it out. And in the meantime, I've decided that I'll let you update the house."

I struggle mightily not to roll my eyes. "Great, thanks so much for letting me do something I have every right to do."

She shoots me a withering glare, then continues. "I want to make sure you don't change anything without clearing it with me first. I have certain standards for my house."

"It's half mine, so maybe I'll just fix up half of it," I snap, then bite my tongue. It's not just that I hate confrontation; I also hate getting emotional in front of other people. After my mom died I was overly emotional, lashing out in anger or crying too easily. It caused problems at school, and I had to talk with the school counselor twice a week to work through my "issues." I was embarrassed to be singled out that way, and the kids teased me even more. After that, I learned to keep my emotions inside until I know I can trust someone.

And I definitely can't trust Kat.

"The house belongs to both of us," she says, her tone implying that she isn't happy about that, "so we should both be involved in fixing it up."

"You're welcome to stay here all summer and work alongside me."

I'm calling her bluff; the thought of Kat with safety glasses on her face and sawdust in her hair is laughable. As unlikely as me getting dressed up in designer clothes and doing the #KatWalk for Instagram likes.

"I'm not staying here if you're here," she says, as expected. "We'll have to trade off. I get a week, then you get a week."

"I'm not going to waste money on a hotel when I own half a beach house. And I can't drive back and forth to Minnesota each week."

"That's not my problem," Kat says.

"Yes, it is, because you're the one who doesn't want to stay here together." I assume this will make her back down; I'd love it if she would go back to Atlanta until I'm done.

Kat's eyes light up, like something has occurred to her. It's the same look she got when she talked me into sneaking out of our cabin one night to take a canoe out on the lake. I was terrified that we were going to be caught and punished. It ended up being fun—magical, actually, staring up at stars, the boat rocking with the waves—but I'm not in the mood to entertain positive memories of Kat Steiner. My shoulders tense in anticipation of what she's going to say next.

"Since you don't appear to have a problem with a little construction," she says, "how do you feel about cleaning? My friend lost her housekeeper. You could stay in their casita—they won't even be there until the Fourth of July. They need someone to tidy up the main house, make sure it's clean and dusted when they come back. They'd even pay you. It'll be easy money and you can stay there the weeks I'm here."

I bristle. Kat thinks of me as *hired help*? Someone she can farm out to her rich friends? I open my mouth to spit out a retort, but then close it again. I refuse to spend the summer allowing Kat to get under my skin.

It wouldn't be a good idea for us both to be here at the same time; there's too much tension. Plus, I could use the extra money, and my weeks away could be a chance for me to make plans, buy supplies, and learn how to tackle the renovation. As much as it irks me, I need to swallow my pride and play the long game here. I'm determined to get what I deserve out of this inheritance.

I take a deep breath and nod. "We can trade off weeks. During the weeks you're here, I'll stay at that casita and clean your friend's house. During my weeks, you'll leave."

I don't mean for my words to sound so abrupt, and I catch a flash of surprise in Kat's eyes. "Fine," she says. "Since I'm already here, I'll take this week."

She says this as if it's a done deal, which makes me bristle again. Is this how it's going to be all summer long, Kat bossing me around, and me allowing it? *Play the long game*, I remind myself. I also need to work on growing a backbone; I'm going to need one with Kat around.

Without another word, I go inside and head upstairs to pack. Halfway up the stairs, I turn and look behind me at the living room, the old carpet, the dated furniture, and I'm suddenly overwhelmed with the magnitude of what I've taken on.

My head spins. Sure, I've helped my granddad with projects, but I've never spearheaded anything myself. I don't actually *know* how to demo a wall or replace light fixtures by myself. I don't even have any tools. Not to mention, I don't know how I'm going to work with Kat when we can barely speak to each other without arguing or one of us running away.

But I do know one thing for sure: it's going to be a long summer.

CHAPTER SEVEN

KAT

UPSTAIRS, I HEAR BLAKE MOVING AROUND, PACKING UP HER suitcase.

I just got off the phone with CoCo, who was beyond thrilled I'd found someone for her—I left out the fact that it's someone who shares half of my DNA—and she forwarded me an email with all the information Blake needs to get in the house and the casita.

When CoCo asked if Blake would mind getting paid under the table, I agreed on her behalf. I figured if she was okay being the "other daughter" of a married man, accepting a little tax-free cash wasn't too big a stretch.

Blake didn't seem too happy about the whole arrangement, but I'm sure she'll change her tune once she sees the Rooneys' mansion. It'll be like living in a luxury hotel every other week—hell, maybe she'll want to stay there all summer. I know it's a long shot, but if a girl can't dream about her estranged half sister running away and never coming back, then what can she dream about?

My shoulders are tight with tension from all these bad memories that've been stirred up. I honestly thought I'd dealt with my feelings around Blake O'Neill more than a decade ago, but seeing her here, in this place where she doesn't belong, brought everything back up.

The sense of betrayal—both from Blake and from my dad—feels so fresh. I can still remember the way my stomach dropped to my toes in that moment: standing in front of the lodge at Camp Chickawah when I realized my "best friend" had been lying to me, and my dad had, too.

I'm sure I'll feel better once Blake's out of the house. Maybe spending time in one of the few places I was truly happy will help me find a little bit of that happiness again.

I grab my suitcase from the car and head upstairs to get settled in my old room. I pause at the top of the stairs, and before I realize what I'm doing, I turn and look toward the guest room. The door is open, and I see Blake carefully folding her clothes and placing them in the suitcase.

A shiver runs down my spine as I remember the night all those years ago when I was the one packing my suitcase to leave. I'd been so distraught, I was just throwing things from my drawer into my suitcase, but Blake had taken my crumpled clothes, folding them one at a time like each T-shirt was precious.

She didn't just help me pack that night—she stayed with me and asked me questions about my grandpa. Somehow, she knew I needed to talk about him, to keep him alive in that moment and for as long as I could.

It's nearly impossible to reconcile that girl from my memory with this cold, money-hungry, house-and-inheritance-stealing bitch.

Blake must hear me, because she turns and glares in my direction. Her eyes are shining with tears and I instantly soften. Maybe I had this whole thing wrong. Maybe she's not just here for the money; maybe she's as lost and alone as I am. I'm about to tell her I'm sorry, that she doesn't have to go, when she snaps at me.

"I'll be out of your hair in two minutes," she says, pulling a ratty old teddy bear out of her duffel bag.

I gasp. *It can't be.*

I walk into the room. Sure enough, it's Beary, the old teddy bear I gave Blake on that last morning at camp, making her promise she'd give him back to me in person.

"You still have Beary?" I ask, my voice wavering with emotion.

"Here," she says, tossing him toward me. "I was planning to leave him here for you."

I catch Beary and look down at his discolored fur, the missing eye and worn button nose. He's clearly been well-loved over the years, when she could have easily thrown him away.

I look back up at Blake, her blond hair hanging in front of her face, her expression still fiery. "I don't have anything else of yours," she says. "Search my bag if you want."

She turns away, folding and refolding the same clothes she'd already placed in her bag. I can tell I'm making her uncomfortable, so I leave her to pack in peace.

After dropping my bag in my room—the pink-and-purple floral wallpaper I picked out in second grade really hasn't aged well—I head back downstairs and sit on what used to be my spot on the couch.

The cushions have lost their fluff and I can feel the braids of wicker under my butt, and I add a new couch and love seat to my mental list of potential sponsored deals to secure once I'm back in Atlanta. They may not pay for the placement, but it's a good way for me to break into the home décor content stream, and it could help give me the edge I need to score the Worthington sponsorship.

I shift on the couch, trying to find a comfortable position

while I wait for Blake to leave. If she doesn't hurry, it'll be dark by the time she gets to the Rooneys'.

At the sound of steps on the carpeted stairs, I pretend to look engrossed in something on my phone. There are a few hundred likes and comments I might as well respond to while I'm waiting.

I try to reply to individual comments when I can. It's good for engagement, and it helps my followers feel like they know me—even though they have no idea what's really going on in my life. Especially now. I haven't even posted anything about my dad dying.

The day of the funeral, I recycled some old content that I'd saved for a rainy day—a picture of a recent manicure and a question about nail polish colors.

While I stood silently next to my mother at the temple and then at the graveside, my followers were debating whether or not it was better for the nail polish on your hands to match the polish on your feet, or if different colors were better.

The post performed well—different colors came out on top even though I'm still a fan of matching or at least complementary colors—but instead of making me feel proud, the high numbers just made me feel more alone.

After that, I thought about sharing the news about my dad. I went as far as pulling photos together, but when I went to write something, I couldn't find the right words. It's probably for the best; I prefer it when people look at me with admiration, not pity.

Blake walks into the room, sounding out of breath. I look up and realize it's not her; it's the dog. I accidentally make eye contact and the big, dopey fur ball lopes toward me.

"Down, boy," I say, even though I don't know if it's a boy or a girl.

The dog mistakes my outstretched hand as an invitation to come closer. He nuzzles his fuzzy head underneath my hand, trying to get me to pat or rub him. The gesture reminds me of several men I've dated, so I assume my instincts were right and the dog is a boy.

He tries again, nudging his head between my lap and my arm, looking up at me with those puppy dog eyes, and suddenly I understand the root of that phrase. But his canine charm won't work on me.

As I pull my hand away, I swear the dog frowns before flopping in a big, furry ball at my feet.

A few minutes later, Blake comes downstairs, duffel bag in hand. Her eyes go wide when she sees the dog cuddled up near me, which gives me a sudden fondness for the animal.

"Come here!" she says to the dog, as if he's in trouble.

The dog lifts his head lazily before laying it back down on top of my feet.

"Come here *now*," she says, putting extra emphasis on the last word.

This time, the dog doesn't react at all.

Blake huffs in frustration and stomps over to the couch. She grabs the dog by its collar and tugs. The dog reluctantly follows her and looks back at me in the most human way, like he's begging me to let him stay. Part of me wants to, even though I don't know the first thing about taking care of pets. I'm not even good with plants—all the ones at my apartment are fake. I call it my faux forest.

Blake is clearly struggling to hold the bag, the door, and the dog. Before I can decide whether or not to offer my help, she says, "Want a treat?"

The dog sits up straight, tongue and tail wagging. Blake releases her hold on his collar, grabs the duffel bag, and opens the door, and the dog obediently trots outside.

"Let me know if you have any trouble getting in the house," I tell her.

She turns and glares at me as if I insulted her outfit (which isn't great) instead of offering my help.

"I'll be back on Sunday," she says, before closing the door.

Moments later, I flinch at the sound of her trunk slamming shut. Apparently, I'm not the only one with anger issues—although I'm not sure why she's so upset. Blake barely knew my dad, and she didn't know my grandparents at all. It's not like her memories are being divvied up and sold.

I stand up from the wicker torture couch and watch out the window as she turns left out of the driveway, heading in the opposite direction from the Rooneys'. For a split second, I wonder if she's heading to a bar or something first, and I wish I could join her for a drink. Not *her* exactly, but the adult version of the girl I used to know.

Before the shadow of sadness can fully sneak up on me, I see Blake's blue Subaru wagon pass by in the correct direction. I laugh and forget to be sad for a moment. But when the sound of my laughter fades, I realize just how quiet the house is.

I've never, not once in my whole life, been at the beach house by myself. When I was a kid, it was crowded and full of laughter and love, with my grandparents, my parents, and me. In later years, it was just my parents and me, and more recently—although not recently enough—I came down with a few friends. The last time I was here a few years ago, I brought Greg, an ex-boyfriend who never should've made it to boyfriend status.

The only reason I put up with him as long as I did was because my dad seemed to like him, and I thought maybe he saw something I'd been missing. But my dad didn't have to listen to his pillow talk about the stock market or watch him clip his toenails in bed.

I always meant to ask my dad what it was he liked about Greg. What he thought I should look for in a life partner. Why he chose to marry my mom, or if he wished he'd married Blake's mom instead. What was so special about her anyway? And why did he stay if he wanted to go? All the questions I thought I'd have forever to ask.

Of course, I'd give up knowing all the answers if I could know one thing—what in the world was he thinking by trapping us with the beach house? I can't imagine why he threw Blake and me together like this without a word after all those years of keeping us apart. Why couldn't he have just given the house to me and left something else to Blake, like his tie collection?

Although, come to think of it, he had some pretty nice ties.

I might be able to do something crafty with them—turn them into a skirt or a blanket. That could be a good project to do at the Peachtree Center. Sewing is a good life skill, and so is learning how to repurpose old materials.

Hopefully Mom hasn't already put Dad's ties in the "donate" pile. I should let her know I'm in Destin, anyway, so I head out to the back porch to call her. The chairs might not be any more comfortable than the wicker couch, but the view can't be beat.

My mom answers on the first ring.

"Hi, darling," she says.

Hearing her voice so far away while I'm standing in the middle of all these memories causes another seismic shift. My whole world feels out of balance, and I realize my mom should've been my first call when I needed someone to talk to.

After all, she's the only other person on the planet who understands what I'm going through. Sooner rather than later, she'll be making some of the same decisions about the Buckhead house as I am with the beach house. Of course, that's not just a vacation home; it's her *home* home.

"This is so hard," I say, before unloading it all. I tell my mom about seeing Blake after all these years, how the house hasn't held up the way it did in my memories, how I don't want to let go but I can't afford to hold on.

By the time I finish talking, my throat is scratchy and my cheeks are stained with tears. There's nothing but silence on the other end of the line.

"Mom?" I ask, wondering if the call dropped.

"I'm here," she says softly.

"Well?" I ask.

When she speaks again, it sounds like a long-suffering sigh. "I'm not sure what you want me to do, Kat."

Even though I'm two decades too old for such a reaction, I pout. Sometimes you just want your mom to make you feel better, even if she has to lie a little to do it.

"You were in that lawyer's office," she says. "You heard as well as I did, the money's gone."

"I know," I say. And I do know, in theory. But I've never not had money. We were never mega-rich like the Rooneys, but money wasn't something I had to worry about. If I wanted to go out to dinner, I went. If I wanted a new pair of Tory Burch sandals, I bought them.

"I know you don't want to hear this," my mom says, "but I think you should sell the house, take your half of the money, and move on with your life."

My jaw literally drops. This, coming from a woman who lives in a four-thousand-square-foot home by herself and, as far as I can tell, has no plans of downsizing.

"I know you have some money coming in," she says, "but if something happens . . ." Her voice trails off and she doesn't finish her thought. She clears the emotion from her throat and continues. "It's good to have a nest egg. Security. It's important."

"I know it's important," I say, my voice sounding snippier than I'd like. "But so is my career. I believe in myself—"

"I'm not saying I don't believe in you," she says gently. "I'm just saying—"

"—that I should sell this house," I say, finishing her thought. "I'm sorry, Mom, but I'm not going to. This is the last piece of Dad I have left."

Tears fill my eyes and I hear a sniffle on the other end of the line. I can't handle this, not right now.

"I have to go," I tell her. "I'll call you soon."

I hang up, feeling worse than before I called. Next time I'm looking for comfort, I'll just turn to Ben & Jerry's Phish Food. I mentally put a pint on my grocery list for tomorrow and open my phone to check Instagram.

Engagement is down, but that's my own fault. I haven't been as active as usual since I'm out of my daily routine. But I can't let a personal catastrophe get in the way of my job if I don't want to prove my parents right.

I take a deep breath and open the camera, switching it to selfie mode. I frown at the image I see reflected back at me—the siding of the house is too shabby to be chic. As much as I love this place, it's not on-brand, so I turn and lean against the railing, ignoring the way it creaks under my weight.

This angle is much better. My makeup isn't perfect, but the light from the setting sun makes up for it.

I snap a few shots, then load the best one into a separate editing app. I make a few small adjustments, softening the glare on my face to a golden glow and adding my signature preset so my grid feels cohesive. When I'm satisfied, I go back to Instagram and start a post with the caption Life's a beach when you remember to #KatWalk.

I don't usually ad lib posts on my feed—my grid is planned

out at least a week in advance and I carefully select the most advantageous times to post based on my followers' activity—but sometimes you happen on a magical picture that demands to be posted. And to be honest, I could use some support right now, even if it's from people I've never met.

A few seconds after I hit post, hearts and comments start flooding in. While they make me smile, I can't help but think of what the camera couldn't see. A house that's seen better days, and a girl who has, too.

CHAPTER EIGHT

BLAKE

THE DOG IS WHINING.

I peel my eyes open, wincing against the sunlight streaming in the windows. Last night was my first night at the casita, where I'll be staying every other week to clean up after Kat's rich friends. I talked to Mrs. Vanderhaaven yesterday, and she agreed to pay me up front and let me keep the dog down here this summer.

A glance at my phone tells me that it's almost ten o'clock, and I inwardly curse. I'd planned to get up early, but the dog kept hopping on my bed last night, trying to sleep on my feet, which meant I kept waking up to remind him that he has a very nice dog bed on the floor. Now he needs to go out and I've overslept. I can imagine Granddad's voice: *Come on, Blakers, we're burning daylight!*

With a sigh, I haul myself out of bed. The casita is colorful and bright, with its own small kitchen and bathroom, but I'm too bleary-eyed to appreciate it. I shove my feet into my flip-flops, brush my messy hair out of my face with one hand, and head to the door.

The dog is off like a shot before I can even get the door all the way open, running to the grass on the other side of the pool to do his business. I step outside and stretch, thinking about getting some coffee. I saw a Keurig in the kitchen and a few pods to get me started.

The Rooneys' house is all gleaming and white in the morning sun, three stories high with big windows and tall pillars. The courtyard contains a pool surrounded by lounge chairs and blue-and-white-striped umbrellas that are currently in a closed position. The space is bordered by palm trees and flower beds filled with plants I've never seen before, and—

I jump. There's a man here, too. He's kneeling next to the flower bed across the pool from me, his back toward me. He's wearing a wide-brimmed straw hat and a threadbare T-shirt. I assume he's the groundskeeper Kat mentioned.

His shirt has ridden up to show a few inches of golden skin on his toned lower back. His shorts are riding low on his hips, and I find my eyes drifting downward until . . .

"You done ogling me yet?"

His voice startles me; he hasn't even turned around, so I'm not sure how he knew I was looking at him.

"I wasn't—"

"No matter how hard you stare," he says, cutting me off, "my clothes aren't going to suddenly fall off."

My cheeks heat. "I didn't—You just surprised me. I didn't know anyone else was here."

Turning, he gives me a quick, dismissive glance, his face shadowed by his straw hat. "Clearly," he says.

I am suddenly aware that I'm wearing pajama shorts that barely cover my ass, a tank top, and no bra.

Quickly, I fold my arms across my chest. "You must be the groundskeeper," I say.

"That would appear to be the case," he says in a dry voice as he turns back to the flower bed.

I roll my eyes. Apparently, he's one of *those* guys, the kind who think they are hilariously deadpan but are actually kind of douchey.

"Nice to meet you," I say, determined not to let him get to me. "I'm staying here every other week this summer to do some light housekeeping."

He snorts. "They told you it was *light* housekeeping?"

Yikes. That sounds ominous. This family is wealthy enough to employ two full-time staff members year-round—they've probably never cleaned up after themselves in their entire privileged lives.

"Imagine having a gorgeous vacation home like this," I say, looking around, "and only visiting a few weekends per year."

He picks up his bucket and moves down a few feet, and my eyes are drawn to his forearms, all ropy and muscular. "Believe me, you should be grateful for that. My recommendation is that you clear out when they come for the Fourth of July. I'm going to."

I'm curious about these people—I found out that these Rooneys are the Rooneys of the eponymous underwear company, purveyors of undergarments for old and young. I'm about to ask what he knows about them when the dog bounds toward him, his tail wagging in anticipation of meeting a new friend.

I lunge for the dog's collar, not wanting him to mess up the groundskeeper's work, but I'm too late. The dog trots up to him, and to my surprise, the groundskeeper sets down his trowel and looks up.

"Hey there, buddy," he says, using a totally different voice than the one he used to speak to me. He scratches the dog's ears, neck, and down his sides. "What's your name?"

I go blank for a moment, because I only think of him as "the dog," and then it comes to me. "His name is Max. I'm dog-sitting him for the summer. And I'm Blake, by the way. Blake O'Neill."

I extend my hand, then remember, too late, that I'm not wearing a bra. To his credit, the groundskeeper looks up at my face, not my chest, which means I see his face for the first time. He's probably around my age, but it's hard to tell since he's sporting a scraggly light-brown beard that goes all the way down his neck. It gives me Tom Hanks–in-*Castaway* vibes, after the part when he knocks out his infected tooth with an ice skate blade, but before he starts having conversations with a bloodstained volleyball.

"Noah Jameson," he says, not shaking my hand. He turns his attention back to the dog, who has rolled onto his back in a blatant attempt to solicit belly rubs. "I'm staying in the room over the garage this summer, so I'm sure I'll see you around."

I awkwardly return my arm to its folded position, hoping he hasn't noticed that I'm free-boobing it. "I'm just going to—I'll be right back. Can I leave the dog out here?"

Noah doesn't answer; he's too busy scratching the dog's belly with two hands, and the dog's eyes are closed in pure bliss.

WHEN I COME back out, dressed in my usual denim cutoffs and a tank (with a bra), ready to start on my duties in the Rooneys' house, Noah is back to weeding the flower beds. Max is next to him, curled up in the shade created by Noah's body.

And I have to admit that, objectively speaking, it is a rather nice body. Noah Jameson is lean and toned and tan, and when he reaches forward to pull a few weeds, I see taut muscles stretching and tensing under his T-shirt. He drops the weeds in the bucket, then takes off his gloves to scratch the dog's head, murmuring something I can't quite catch.

I take a few steps closer.

"Hey, Max," Noah is saying in a soft voice. "You're such a

good boy, little Maxie, Maximus Decimus Meridius. Yes, you are, little Maxi-pad."

I stifle a snort, but it's too late; he looks back at me.

"What?" he says, defensive.

"You really just went from *Gladiator* to sanitary napkins," I say, laughing.

"And you really just went back to ogling." His eyes are bright blue, peering out between the brim of his hat and the scruff of his beard. "Don't think I couldn't sense you standing there, undressing me with your eyes."

"Congratulations on having such a high opinion of yourself," I say, refusing to let him fluster me. I head toward the door that'll lead me into the main house to get started with the cleaning.

"While you're working in there," he calls, "maybe you can also work on learning how to not objectify other human beings."

"I'll add that to my to-do list."

"I'm not here to be eye candy for the housekeeper, you know."

I roll my eyes. "You do realize that your facial hair looks like a small, furry animal has been shot, skinned, and taxidermied onto your face, right?"

He barks a surprised laugh, then says, "Pretty sure that wasn't my *face* you were staring at."

"See you around, Noah," I say, turning away so he won't see my blush. I punch in the lockbox code that Kat's friend emailed me and pull out a key. "Max, come on, buddy. Let's go."

The dog perks up—it's the first time I've called him by his name in days, and the first time I've ever called him "buddy"—and trots after me, gleefully leaving Noah behind. I can't help feeling a teensy bit triumphant.

But as soon as I walk into the house, all sense of triumph drops to the floor and shatters like an expensive crystal vase.

It's a huge, gorgeous place—and it's also a total mess. So much worse than I imagined. There's sand scattered on the travertine floors, wet towels draped across expensive-looking furniture—which explains the hint of mildew I smell.

When I walk into the kitchen, I gasp in horror. The sink is full of dishes; the counters are covered with empty wine and liquor bottles; the trash cans are overflowing. The smell is worse in here, and it makes me wonder if some animal crawled in to munch on the trash, got poisoned, and died.

For an instant, rage boils inside me, hot and liquid as lava, and it's all directed toward Kat. She's the reason I'm here, having to clean up after the underwear royalty, when I have a perfectly adequate beach house just a short walk down the road. My fists clench and I consider storming out and telling Kat she's just going to have to deal with me staying with her because there's no way I'm going to clean up this disaster.

But then I take a few breaths and stifle the rage. There are three things I need to keep in mind: (1) I don't actually want to be around Kat; (2) I need the extra money; (3) my grandparents raised me to never be afraid of hard work. And even though it's going to be a hell of a job to get this all cleaned up, once it's done, I won't have to do much other than occasionally dust.

"All right, Maximus—I mean Max," I say, looking at the dog. He nudges my hand with his wet nose, like he wants me to pet him. "Yeah, we're not gonna go that far. But you can hang around me if you don't get in my way, okay?"

In response, the dog tilts his head, and I take that as a yes. When I head down the hall to find the cleaning supplies, he follows, and I have to admit it's nice to not be alone.

IT TAKES ME four days to get the Rooneys' vacation home in order. I run countless loads of laundry full of towels and sheets.

I scrub the kitchen, vacuum the rugs, polish the countertops, straighten and dust knickknacks and picture frames. Every so often, my rage at Kat threatens to boil over, but I tamp it down and focus on the task at hand.

I distract myself in the evenings by doing some online digging about the Rooneys. When I was growing up, Rooney underwear was mostly sturdy, supportive stuff my grandma wore, identified by their signature *R* on the tag. But a few years ago, they launched a new line called UnderRooneys, with trendy, affordable pieces for people of my generation. I own several items, in fact; my favorites are a matching bra and boy shorts featuring smiling pineapples on a hot pink background.

But about a year ago, according to an article I found on Forbes.com, a huge scandal erupted when it was revealed that their underwear was made in sweatshops in underdeveloped countries with unsafe conditions for workers. After that, Target stopped carrying the brand and several other distributors followed suit. There were boycotts, too, which I probably would've known about if I paid attention to business-related news.

I guess I should stop wearing my pineapple underwear—or maybe not, since that would mean those workers' efforts went to waste. It's not like anyone else has seen my underwear in many, many moons. Anyway, the whole mess is a reminder that wealthy people are willing to walk over anyone to get what they want—so it makes sense that Kat's family has been friends with them for years.

By Thursday, the house is sparkling clean and I'm exhausted. Finally, I get to turn my attention to my real project for the summer: renovating the beach house.

It's evening, and I head out to the beach in front of the Rooneys', where I'm planning to sit and make a list of all the projects I want to tackle next week. I've decided to start with painting the kitchen cabinets. Not only will it make a huge positive difference for a relatively small expense, but it's also something that I feel confident doing.

Max follows me, and when he bounds away, I'm pretty sure I know why. Yep, there's Noah, the groundskeeper, parked in a lounge chair. It's become apparent over the past several days that this is his routine: he does a few hours of work on the grounds every morning, then spends the rest of the day lounging on the beach or next to the pool with a bottle of beer or four.

We haven't talked much since that first day, except for him chastising me for ogling him—which I am not doing right now, by the way. He's just . . . a striking figure, his long, tanned legs stretched across the lounge chair like he owns the place. If he weren't sitting in front of a multimillion-dollar beach house, he might be mistaken for a passed-out homeless guy.

When Max runs up to Noah, he puts down his beer and hauls himself upright, and they greet each other like they've been separated for months, rather than just a few hours.

"Hey there, Maxie," Noah says, scratching the dog's ears, chest, and then belly when the dog rolls over. "Such a good boy, little Maxie-Waxy. Wax on, wax off, wax on, wax off."

He's doing the wax-on-wax-off motions as he rubs Max's belly like Daniel LaRusso on Mr. Miyagi's car. I press my lips together to stop myself from grinning. He's ridiculous, which makes it even more irritating that he also manages to be so attractive. At least, from the shoulders down; the whole scruffy-caveman/neck-beard thing doesn't do anything for me.

Although he might just seem attractive because he's very, *very* tall—around six foot five, I'm guessing—and there's something interesting about his body, all lanky and angular. His clothes never seem to fit him; his ratty old T-shirts aren't long enough to cover his torso, and his shorts are always sliding down his hips, which feels quasi-obscene whenever he bends or reaches for something.

Like now, as he picks up Max's slobbery tennis ball, my gaze is drawn, against my will, to his exposed lower back, the muscles alongside his spine, the jut of a hip bone, the dimples above his waistband. He stands and tosses the tennis ball down the beach, sending Max chasing after it.

Noah hitches his shorts up, then turns and gives me a side-eye. "Can you dial down the staring? I mean, I know it's probably difficult for you, since I'm out here looking like a snack."

That last part is delivered with a cheeky wink, and I shake my head as I sit, cross-legged, on the soft, white sand. "My idea of a 'snack' isn't a guy who wears T-shirts so worn-out even Good-will wouldn't want them."

"I like my clothes broken in," he says.

"Yeah, well, that shirt is so broken in it's practically see-through."

He runs a hand over his scruffy beard, narrowing his eyes. "Maybe you should stop trying to see through it."

"Maybe you should buy yourself a belt," I fire back, then re-alize, too late, what that comment just revealed about me.

He grins, giving me a flash of white teeth. "Watch it, perv. Or I'll report you for workplace harassment."

"Right, because our employers seem so concerned about what we do here. Do they realize you spend most of your day lounging in the shade, drinking beer?"

"Do *you* realize you killed yourself cleaning a house that's just going to get trashed again when they come back?"

Max returns with the tennis ball and drops it at Noah's feet, and he lazily picks it up and sends it flying with a flick of his wrist.

"In all seriousness," he says, "the one good thing about this gig is that the owners are rarely here. Don't waste your time or energy giving A-plus effort for people who won't notice or appreciate it. Learn to do C-minus work and you'll be a lot happier."

After that cynical statement, delivered in a sardonic tone that rubs me wrong for some reason, he settles back into his lounge chair and takes a long swallow of his beer. Noah reminds me of the guys Granddad used to hire for seasonal construction work. Easygoing but a smidge lazy, they'd put in the bare minimum to get a paycheck for a few weeks or months before drifting somewhere else.

Granddad wasn't like that, and I'm not either—the O'Neills have always taken pride in a little thing called work ethic. Noah has a point, though; if I'm going to give an A-plus effort, I want it to be on the renovations I'm planning, not cleaning up after spoiled millionaires. From now on, I tell myself, the bulk of my efforts will go toward that goal.

I turn my attention to the list of supplies in my notebook: painter's tape, paintbrushes and rollers, primer, sandpaper. Noah continues tossing the ball, and Max chases after it and returns. The breeze ruffles my hair, and the waves lap lazily against the shore.

I sketch out the floor plan of the beach house, trying to imagine how it might look with the wall between the kitchen and dining room removed. I'm so absorbed that I hardly notice when Noah appears next to me. I look up, startled, and he settles beside me on the sand, folding his long legs under him.

He hands me a beer, condensation dripping from the bottle. "Here—got you a cold one. You deserve it after this week." He nods toward the house behind us. "I took a peek inside. The place looks great."

I gasp in mock surprise. "Is Noah Jameson being *nice* to me? I thought you were only nice to creatures with four legs and a drooling problem."

"I am *occasionally* nice to human beings," he says, and I'm pretty sure he's grinning at me again from under that beard. "What are you working on?"

I show him the notebook. "This is my real reason for being here this summer. I inherited a beach house from a distant family member, but it's a total pile of crap. I'm going to fix it up over the summer and sell it."

It sounds so simple when I say it like that. Just fix it up and sell it, no big deal. But the knot in my stomach reminds me that it *is* a big deal—not just the work I'm doing on the house, but all that stuff in my past that I've spent the past fifteen years trying to forget about. Keep the emotion out of it, I remind myself.

"So why are you here, then?" he asks. "Staying in the house-keeper's quarters when you have a beach house down the road?"

I hesitate, not wanting to go into my life story with this guy I barely know. "It's . . . complicated," I say.

He nods and takes a sip of his beer. "I understand complicated."

As he says that, all the joking and sarcasm in his tone fade away. His eyes look tired and, dare I say, sad. I'm tempted to ask what his story is—he's obviously down on his luck to end up working here—but then I remind myself that I wouldn't want him prying into my life, so I shouldn't pry into his.

"I'm going to spend every other week at my beach house, fixing it up," I tell him. It's weird to say the words "my beach house," but I like how they feel on my tongue. "I'm going to start with the kitchen and work my way through the place."

"If you need help, let me know," Noah says.

Ah. So that's why he's asking about this. He's angling for a job. "Sorry—I'm doing this on a shoestring budget and I can't afford to hire anyone."

"No, I didn't—" He clears his throat. For the first time, he looks uncomfortable. "There's not enough work to keep me busy here full-time—as you so kindly pointed out. I'd be happy to help out."

"I might take you up on that," I say, still surprised he's being nice. "The sooner I get this renovation done, the sooner I can get out of here and on with my life."

Noah gives a slow nod, his gaze fixed over the horizon. "I can drink to that," he says, lifting his beer. "To getting on with life."

I clink my bottle against his, and we sit like that, silent and pensive, watching the sun go down.

CHAPTER NINE

KAT

IT'S BEEN FOUR DAYS SINCE I GOT TO THE BEACH HOUSE, and I've barely stepped foot on the sand. Hopefully there will be plenty of time for that later—as in many, many years later if everything works out the way I want it to. The way I need it to.

My first call after my mom was to get Wi-Fi installed because internet is like air, and it would've been impossible to get anything else done without it. The second those beautiful signal lines appeared on my laptop I started reaching out to people in my network, crowdsourcing advice and connections.

In the past forty-eight hours, I've spoken with so many estate lawyers and real estate agents and financial advisers that it feels like I'm at some god-awful speed-dating event for business school grads. I probably would've had more success if it was a date I'd been after.

While everyone I talked with had sympathy for my situation—I spoke in vague terms whenever possible—their answers were all the same: there are no loopholes, and contesting the will would be a losing battle that might end up costing me four times

the amount my dad left me. In every single one of their professional opinions, my best and only bet is to buy Blake out.

Which is why I'm sitting in a freezing cold air-conditioned
office, sharing my sob story with Steve Everett, the mortgage
broker CoCo recommended. For some reason—maybe because
he has kind eyes and doesn't know me or my family—I find myself telling him everything.

"So now I need to buy Blake out so I can keep the house
that's been in my family for generations," I say, finishing.

Steve nods and my heart lifts with hope that he'll be the
knight on a white horse I so desperately need—handing me a
loan that will be enough to send Blake on her merry way.

But then his mouth twists and he furrows his eyebrows, and
I watch as my last whisper of hope vanishes into thin air.

"I feel for your predicament," Steve says, "but without a steady
source of income or any equity, I'm afraid the math just isn't in
your favor."

The math or anything else. I sink back in the chair, and Steve's
face softens. Normally, I hate anyone feeling sorry for me—I
like to portray an image that's strong and powerful, not weak
and weepy—but I'm running out of options.

"Do you have anyone who could cosign the loan?" Steve asks.

My father's face comes into focus in my mind—and he's
scowling, disappointed in me like always. It's hard to believe it
was only a few months ago we had a conversation about financial stability. I'd just reached seventy thousand followers on Instagram, and I'd hoped he'd finally be impressed. I even looked
up the stats so I could tell him the number in baseball terms—
which was almost twice as many people as could fit in the Braves'
stadium.

I remember the way his eyebrows lifted momentarily before

he scowled again. "What would you get if you took those numbers to the bank?" he'd asked.

Clearly, nothing.

I shiver, wondering if my dad's response was a prophecy or self-fulfilled curse. Either way, I'm broke and have nowhere else to turn.

"Thank you for seeing me," I tell Steve as I stand to leave.

"I really am sorry for your loss," he says.

I nod and wonder if he's talking about my father, the beach house, or both. They're tied together in my mind, but there's only one I have a fighting chance to keep.

A sob rises in my throat, but I swallow it down and slip my sunglasses on, grateful for the cover to hide the tears welling in my eyes. I may not have money or equity or enough credit, but I still have my pride.

Taking a deep breath, I hold my head high, push my shoulders back, and #KatWalk out of his office. Like I tell my followers, if you walk like you're confident, that's how the world will see you.

Outside, the heat is oppressive and the warm air instantly fogs my lenses. I rip them off, annoyed that even my sunglasses are letting me down. Out of the corner of my eye, I notice a man stopped in middle of the sidewalk. He doesn't even pretend not to be staring as I walk past.

Attention from men comes with the #KatWalk territory. Normally I don't mind; sometimes I even flirt back—but I'm not in Destin to have fun. I'm here to save my family's beach house.

My lower lip trembles with the sense of my impending failure, and I pick up the pace. I'm almost to my car when I hear the man's voice.

"Kitty?"

The once familiar name stops me in my tracks. I started going by Kat at summer camp because I thought it sounded more "sophisticated" and continued it when I got home, but for a different reason.

At the time, my mom thought I'd abandoned the nickname because my bat mitzvah was approaching and according to Jewish law, I would be a woman soon. No longer a little girl. Of course, in reality, it wasn't a religious ceremony that ended my childhood.

The weight of the secret I carried for my dad changed me, along with the knowledge that my family could fall apart if I said or did the wrong thing. The old nickname didn't fit me anymore. Kitty was gone. I was Kat.

I turn and glare at the man, who's still unabashedly staring. I squint to get a better look, but the sun is shining directly behind him. I lift my hand to shield my eyes and walk toward him, propelled by curiosity.

The man is tall and broad shouldered, with wavy brown hair that's on the long side, tucked behind his ears. It's not on trend, but he pulls it off. His outfit is even less on trend, unless "Construction Chic" is a new style. He's wearing a short-sleeved plaid shirt and jeans that look naturally worn, not like they were bought that way.

I can't put my finger on why he seems so familiar. He looks like he works with his hands—maybe he's one of the guys who used to work at the Rooneys' house, although then he'd know me as Kat, not Kitty.

"Henry Alexander," the man says with a half wave.

At the sound of his name, the past and present versions of my childhood friend merge into one. "The boy with two first names," I say, as if I'm solving a puzzle on *Wheel of Fortune*.

Henry pushes a lock of hair away from his face and smiles. I don't know how I didn't see it before. With those deep green eyes and the single dimple on his cheek, the man standing in front of me is so clearly a grown-up version of the boy I used to spend summers and spring breaks with.

The two of us and the Rooneys—CoCo and Junior—had been inseparable when we were kids. I don't remember when or why we stopped hanging out, but I know it's been years. More than a decade.

"I can't believe you recognized me," I say.

"I'd know that smile anywhere," he says.

"I wasn't smiling."

"Well then," Henry says, his own smile faltering. "Maybe it was that look of determination on your face."

That gets a laugh. When "resting bitch face" became a thing, I heard it a lot—but I'm not a bitch unless someone deserves it. I did a whole post on Instagram about it, how just because I'm not smiling doesn't mean I'm angry or a bitch. It's my look of determination and overall badassery.

Henry seems like the type who doesn't even have an Instagram account, so I'm sure the phrase is just a coincidence. And when he saw me just now, I was determined—not to lose my shit in public.

The dark cloud hanging over my head seems to have passed for the moment, and I wonder if it's the return of Henry Alexander, or if there's something about him that reminds me of the way I used to be.

"What are you doing here?" I ask, no longer in a rush. Henry's eyes dart over to the bank, then back at me. "In Destin, I mean."

What he's doing at the bank is none of my business, just like what I was doing isn't his or anyone else's business. CoCo doesn't even know why I needed a contact for a mortgage broker. She didn't question me when I asked, which is good since I still haven't told her what's going on.

She probably assumed I'm looking to upgrade to a bigger place—or more likely, she was too focused on whatever's going on in her own life to think about mine. In her defense, it sounds like the drama with her brother has gotten pretty out of hand.

"I live here," Henry says. "Never left."

I nod, remembering that Henry was a year-round beach kid. "Must be nice living where other people only get to come for vacation," I say.

"You're here for vacation?"

I shrug and make a noncommittal noise. "Not exactly."

Henry tilts his head and keeps his eyes locked on mine—this man I knew in another lifetime when I was another person looks like he genuinely cares. Even though he and I are virtual strangers now, there's something about him that makes me want to share all my secrets.

Which is ridiculous, I remind myself. He's just being polite. Henry was always well-mannered, even as a kid. Not only did he go out of his way to say *please* and *thank you*, but he'd have actual conversations with my parents and grandparents, asking how they were. They adored Henry, and my mom not so subtly told me I could learn a thing or two from him.

When I don't elaborate, Henry nods and puts his hands in his pockets. It looks like he's about to walk away, and for some reason, I don't want him to go just yet.

"Do you work?" I ask, realizing too late how terrible that sounds. Of course the man works. "I mean, what do you do?"

Henry smiles and runs a hand over his face, which I notice is covered with the growth of a few days' stubble. "I've got my own business."

"Oh," I say, hopefully with a polite amount of surprise. He doesn't strike me as a business owner with his casual, weekend grandpa look in the middle of the week.

"I do odds and ends," he explains. "Everything from light construction work to changing lightbulbs and running errands for the elderly."

"That's awesome," I say, realizing that my first assessment of him as someone who might very well work for the Rooneys was accurate.

"It pays the bills. And the flexibility is nice."

That I can relate to. "Free time is a major perk in working for yourself," I agree. "Especially in Destin—I'd be down at the water all the time if I could."

"I don't have that much free time," Henry says. "But every once in a while, I help a buddy out and sell boiled peanuts out on Crab Island."

"Ah, Crab Island." I have a lot of great memories of being out there on my grandfather's boat—sunny days anchored in the warm, shallow Gulf, people watching and playing Frisbee from boat to boat. "I'll have to find a way out there while I'm here."

Henry's face lights up but falls again as his phone chirps. "I'm sorry, I have to get to my meeting." He pauses and looks at me, the smile lighting up his face again. "But it was great running into you."

He reaches into his back pocket and pulls out a well-worn wallet. It's adorable how old-fashioned it is. These days, I pay for everything with credit cards linked to my phone.

"Here," he says, handing me a card for his business, Henry's Helping Hands. "Give me a call if you need help with anything, or just want to grab a beer."

I slip the card into my own pocket and smile. "It was good running into you, too, Henry Alexander." His phone chirps again, and I turn to go, leaving him to his meeting—which I hope will be more successful than mine was.

As I walk to the car, there's a lightness to my step and a smile on my face. My car automatically unlocks as I approach, and before I climb inside, I look back, where Henry Alexander is still staring, getting later for his appointment by the second.

THE NEXT MORNING, I wake up even more tired than I'd been the night before when I finally went to bed around one a.m. I never sleep well when I have too much on my mind, and right now, it's like the whole world is rattling around in there.

During the little time I did sleep, I had a dream that might've been a memory. I was young, maybe nine or ten. I was coming back home after the beach when I heard my parents fighting out on the back porch. I stopped halfway up the stairs, out of sight, as they argued in hushed, angry voices.

I'm not sure how much of what I heard is influenced by what I know now, but I swear my mom said, "your whore" and "that illegitimate child." I was terrified they'd turn their anger on me if they knew I'd overheard, so I ran off, hoping to run into CoCo or Junior. Instead, I ran into Henry, who was standing outside the convenience store his father owned.

He asked what was wrong, but I didn't say anything. I couldn't—my parents had a very strict rule about not airing dirty laundry. Henry didn't push me to talk; he just said, "Hang on, I'll be right back." Then he disappeared into his father's store, coming out a few minutes later with two Popsicles—a red one for me and a purple one for him.

We sat on the curb of the parking lot, eating our Popsicles and not talking. By the time we were left holding empty wooden sticks, I felt better. I thanked Henry and walked back to the beach house, where I found my dad watching baseball and my mom cooking dinner as if nothing had happened.

Taking a page from my parents' playbook, I brush the memory

away and force myself to get out of bed. I only have two days before Blake comes back, and I have to make the most of this time. But first, coffee.

Down in the kitchen, I open the cabinet for a mug and the door practically falls off in my hands. "Shit!" I say, jumping back.

The bottom hinge is hanging on by a bolt. Or a nail. Maybe a screw? I know less about this home renovation business than I do accounting, or whatever degree mortgage brokers have. I give the cabinet door a tentative tug, but it doesn't budge, so I leave it resting against the counter and grab a smug LIFE'S A BEACH mug.

Fifteen minutes later, I'm on the back porch with my coffee and a 'Gram-worthy plate of avocado toast. I snap a picture and upload it to my stories, promising myself that I'll do better about preplanning posts when I'm home next week. Now is not the time to get complacent.

Speaking of which, I open my laptop and pull up the Worthington application. With her Southern style, billions of dollars, and millions of followers, Rachel Worthington is my only hope for being able to buy Blake out.

The application starts out easy, and I fill out the basic information: my name, Instagram handle, location, and number of followers, which has just passed eighty-seven thousand. I'm confident and optimistic as I scroll to the second page and read the first question under the getting-to-know-you section.

Question 1. *In 1,000 words or less, tell us your "why."*

My stomach twists and I have the same queasy feeling I got when I had to write essays for my college applications. I'm not a bad writer, but my pithy and clever style is better suited to the small bites of content on Instagram—not essays that have my whole future riding on them.

Even if I was a better writer, I have no idea what my "why" should be. I have a brand moniker with #KatWalk and the "Life is a fashion show" line, but that feels too shallow for someone like Rachel, who's down-to-earth, authentic, and classy.

If Rachel Worthington is going to pick me to represent her brand, I'll need something with more depth. I think back to my early days on Instagram. It started as a fun way to show off my shopping hauls. But one post went viral after I went on a tiny rant about how it should be okay to wear white after Labor Day—hello, "winter white!"—and I got more and more followers. Brands started reaching out to me to feature their products, and I did that for more than a year before I realized I could turn my hobby into a legitimate career.

Four years later, it *is* my career, and I'm proud of how I've turned nothing into something. A big something. I'm within reach of one hundred thousand followers, yet I can't come up with a thousand measly words on why I do what I do?

Maybe I should ask my followers for their opinion: why they follow me, what they get out of the content I put out in the world. It strikes me again that while some of them feel like friends, they have no idea they're getting a curated version of me. My life isn't that photogenic, and I'm not nearly as together as they think I am.

I'm sure Blake would be more than happy to set them straight and tell them all I'm a superficial, selfish snob. There's so much hate in her eyes when she looks at me, it's hard to imagine there was a time when we loved each other.

The truth of who I am is probably somewhere in the middle. Between the superficial girl Blake and my followers see, and the broke and broken girl I feel like who doesn't have a why in the world.

CHAPTER TEN

BLAKE

TODAY'S THE DAY! MY FIRST DAY WORKING AT THE BEACH house. It's been a long week at the Rooneys' casita and I'm excited to get going. Which is why I'm here bright and early in the kitchen of the beach house, my good friend Taylor Swift singing in my earbuds as I take the doors off the cabinets. One of them is already hanging by a half-broken hinge. Leave it to Kat to treat our house as cavalierly as the Rooneys treat theirs.

The most important step for any painting project is prep, prep, and more prep, as Granddad would say. Sanding, cleaning, and taping will take most of the day. Later, I'll prime everything and get these babies ready to paint the next week I'm here.

Even the dog seems excited, pacing underfoot, watching everything I do with laser-sharp focus as if I'm going to accidentally drop one of these cabinet doors on his tail.

"I'll be careful," I promise him, then return to singing along with TayTay. I don't have an amazing voice, nothing like my mom's, but I'm alone in the house—a house I technically own—so I allow myself to let loose.

I'm fully in my feels when I see something out of the corner of my eye—there's a person standing in the doorway.

My heart seizes. For a split second I'm convinced that I'm about to be brutally murdered with one of the dull knives in the butcher block on the counter. But then I realize the person is Kat, though she doesn't look anything like the glossy, polished influencer I've come to expect.

She's wearing matching pajama shorts and a top with a polka-dot sleep mask pushed up on her forehead. Her hair is a wild, tangled mane, and she's got mascara smudges under her eyes and pillow creases on her cheek.

Also, she's yelling at me.

I yank the earbuds out of my ears and catch her mid-shriek: ". . . in the actual hell are you doing here at the crack of freaking dawn, singing—badly—and banging around like a construction worker?"

My heart is still spasming from shock, but I force myself to speak calmly. "Morning, Kat. I didn't see your car parked outside."

"It's in the garage—you know, the place where cars are placed to protect them from the elements?" She folds her arms. "You didn't answer my question—what are you doing in my kitchen so early?"

"It's my week. Sorry for interrupting your beauty sleep"— she obviously needs it—"but I have work to do to get *my* kitchen remodeled so I can sell this shithole and return to a life that does *not* include having to deal with your temper tantrums."

Okay, so that last part was not delivered very calmly, but I do feel proud of myself for delivering a zinger. I'm normally not the zinging kind—I'm the kind to slink away in shame and spend the next eight hours replaying the conversation in my mind. Maybe fifteen years of built-up anger has made me a little spicy.

I brace myself for another barrage of shouting, but instead, Kat blinks a few times and I'm terrified she's going to burst into tears. What am I supposed to do with that? I can handle a raging, entitled Kat—but not an emotional, sobbing one. I'm not great at handling my own tears, let alone someone else's.

But then she throws her hands up in the air and yells, "Ugh!" before stomping back up the stairs.

Replacing my headphones, I remind myself to not allow her to derail my progress. I have a job to do, and I'm going to do it.

AN HOUR LATER, I'm removing the fronts from all the drawers when Kat returns downstairs pulling a suitcase the size of a small coffin. She's wearing a gauzy summer dress that hits mid-thigh on her golden-tan legs, her hair piled in a perfect messy bun, her sunglasses in place so I can't see her eyes.

"I'll be back in one week," she says, her voice brisk. "And I'll be sure not to arrive until standard hotel checkout time so you don't have to rush out the door. That's eleven o'clock, bee-tee-dubs."

Something about the way she says this makes me unreasonably irritated. Maybe it's the haughty tone of her voice, or that stupid abbreviation for "by the way" that doesn't actually save any syllables. Or maybe it's the insinuation that I'm some kind of backwoods hick who's never stayed in a hotel before.

I bite back a snarky retort and give her a thumbs-up and a big, bright smile. "Rightio," I say.

That earns me an exasperated huff as she stalks out the door, hauling that gigantic suitcase behind her. Pretty soon I hear the sound of the garage door opening and her fancy car pulling out of the driveway.

The dog nudges his wet nose against my hand, and I absently

scratch his head before turning back to my task. Still, I'm un-settled; I'm not proud of the way I acted toward Kat. She's raw with grief after losing her dad, and I remember that pain, the hollow feeling in my chest that nothing could fill.

My sinuses start to burn, and I clear my throat. No time for tears. In go the earbuds, up goes the volume, and soon enough I'm singing along to *Lover*, grateful that no one is around to hear my voice falter as I try not to think about my parents and the giant hole they left behind.

BY THAT EVENING, I'm exhausted. I make myself a sandwich—peanut butter with a sprinkling of brown sugar, my favorite—and plop down on the kitchen floor to eat. The dog curls up next to me, and I break off a piece and give it to him.

"We got a lot done today," I tell him. "Maybe we should celebrate by taking a walk?"

He perks up and tilts his head.

"All right, let me finish eating," I say. While I chew, I peel up the edge of the linoleum flooring to get a sense of how difficult it's going to be to remove. The wood subfloor I saw under the carpet in the living room extends into the kitchen, too.

I pop the last bite of sandwich in my mouth and grab a hammer, using the claw end to pry up a couple of square feet of the linoleum. Yep. Hardwood. It's stained and a little warped, but it looks salvageable.

Excitement bubbles through me. It's a lot of work to refinish floors, but there's nothing like the warm, lived-in feeling of old wood. I reach for my phone, hoping Martina can help me Face-Time with Granddad. I'd love to show him the subfloor and get his advice on refinishing it.

But then I remember that she's not working tonight. *Later*, I tell myself, but my heart drops with disappointment. I miss him intensely—his warm hugs, his comforting voice—and for the second time that day, I'm close to crying.

Clearing my throat, I stand. "Ready for a walk, dog?"

BY THURSDAY, my body aches from five long days of manual labor, but I'm proud of what I've accomplished. I've gotten most of the linoleum floor up, but there are globs of glue or resin left behind that I haven't figured out how to remove. I've finished prepping the cabinets and now it's time to start priming. The guy at the paint store said I could get away with one coat of primer but two would be better, so that's what I'm planning. I've laid all the cabinet doors out on two-by-fours in the garage, and I head out there with a paint pan and a can of primer.

The dog follows me; he's been my constant companion, either flopped at my feet or watching my every move. I wonder if he feels abandoned by the Vanderhaavens and he's worried I'm going to leave him, too. Because of that, I've given him a few extra pats and treats, though I draw the line at letting him sleep on my bed.

I'm prying the top off the can of primer when the dog trots off, tail wagging. I look up to see none other than Noah Jameson standing in the driveway, a plastic sack in each hand. He's tall and angular and scruffy, dressed in his usual low-slung shorts and threadbare T-shirt. My stomach does a weird little swoop.

"You ogling me now?" I ask, walking out of the garage. "I'm here to work, not to be eye candy for some groundskeeper."

He flashes me a grin. "Don't flatter yourself. I'm here for the dog." He sets down the bags to greet the dog, who rolls over for the obligatory belly rub. "Hey there little Waxy man, wax on, wax off, little Daniel-san."

He's using that dopey voice he saves for the dog, and I laugh and shake my head. "That dog is going to be so confused about what his actual name is. You know it's Max, right?"

"His name is Daniel-san," Noah says to the dog. "Little Danny. Such a good little Danny boy. Oh Danny boy, the pipes, the pipes are callin'."

The last part is delivered in an Irish accent that blends into the melody sung by every middle school choir ever. At my school there was always one soprano who ended up crying by the end, which made me roll my eyes, much like I'm doing right now.

"How've you been?" I ask. "Enjoying your life of leisure while I bust my ass, as per usual?"

It's a humid, sunny day, and I shield my eyes with my hand and look up at him as he stands to his full height. Oh my heavens, he is *so* damn tall.

"Doing my best. It's easier when I don't have to worry about being gawked at all day by the housekeeper." He looks over at the beach house and whistles, rubbing a hand over his shaggy beard as he surveys the place. "This is the place you inherited? It's—"

"A dump, I know." I motion to the garage behind me, all the cabinet doors laid out. "But I'm making progress. I was about to get some primer on these babies when I was so rudely interrupted by a dude flirting with my dog."

The corner of his mouth lifts—or at least I think it does; difficult to tell under all that beard. "*Your* dog, eh?" he says.

"*The* dog. The dog I am responsible for." I fold my arms and give him a cheery smile. "Run along now, Noah. I have work to do."

He raises both hands. "Sorry, sorry. I'll take my eight delicious shrimp tacos and extra-large order of guac with freshly made chips and head on home."

My mouth waters. I've been living on a diet of peanut butter sandwiches and cold cereal, cheap food I can shovel into my mouth so I can get back to work as quickly as possible.

Also: Did Noah come here specifically to run into me, or was he just passing by? I told him the general area of this house, but I didn't tell him which one is mine. The thought makes my stomach do another swoop.

"Eight tacos sound like a lot for one person," I say. "I'd be happy to take some off your hands."

"Eh, I don't know if you can handle these tacos. They're legendary. Probably the closest thing to an orgasm you've experienced in a long, long time."

"Or the closest thing to an orgasm you've *given* anyone in a long, long time." The words are out of my mouth so fast they bypass my usual filter.

Noah bursts out laughing, and I can't help feeling triumphant.

"Well, damn," he says when he recovers. "You just earned yourself some tacos, Blake O'Neill."

THE TACOS ARE pretty close to orgasmic, and I have to hold myself back from moaning as I take my first bite. We're sitting on the lawn in the shade of the garage, the dog between us, and when we finish, I stand, feeling a sense of urgency to get back to work.

"Thanks for lunch," I say. "I owe you one."

I expect him to head back to the Rooneys' to spend the afternoon lounging in the shade drinking beer, as is his custom, but he surprises me.

"You want some help with those?" he says, nodding at the cabinet doors on the garage floor.

I give him a skeptical look. "I don't want to interfere with your afternoon plans. Priming is kind of a miserable task."

"My baseline is miserable," he says, giving me a wry look. "I'll be fine."

SOON, IT'S APPARENT that Noah is not a good painter—he's messy and drippy, and even though I've given him the easier task of rolling the flat surfaces while I do the detail work, I have to keep stopping to remind him of proper technique: not too much paint, only a thin layer. Still, it's nice to have someone to talk to after so many days on my own.

There's an old eight-track player in the garage, and we take turns choosing music—ABBA, Fleetwood Mac, Aretha Franklin. It takes hours to prime both sides of the cabinet doors, plus the cabinet bases in the kitchen, but we're finished by dinnertime.

Noah suggests we order pizza, which I insist on paying for because he got lunch—though it makes me cringe when I realize I'm spending an entire week's worth of grocery money in one fell swoop. But it's worth it; the pizza is delicious—feta cheese, banana peppers, and red onions—and we eat sitting out on the deck that faces the beach, watching the sun go down.

"So," Noah says, picking up another piece of pizza. "How did you end up here with a dog you don't like and a house you don't want?"

"The dog is easy to explain," I tell him. "I've been a live-in nanny for a family in Minneapolis for a couple years, and he belongs to them. I was supposed to be in France watching their two kids this summer, but at the last minute they hired a French nanny and stuck me with the dog."

"That sucks," he says, and takes a bite of pizza, chewing thoughtfully. "Doesn't explain how you came to be here in Destin, though. You said you inherited this house from a relative?"

That part's tougher to explain, but I take a deep breath and

ALI BRADY

dive in. "From my father," I say. "He wasn't really a part of my life, and I guess he felt bad about that, because when he died, he left me half of this place."

"Half?"

"He left the other half to his *other* daughter—the legitimate one. The one he raised." My cheeks grow hot. "My mother was the other woman. His, um, mistress. She died when I was nine, and after that, I never saw him again."

Noah's eyebrows shoot up. "Wow. I'm sorry. That's . . ."

"Ancient history," I say, waving a hand. "I'm going to sell the house once it's fixed up and use the money to pay for my grandpa's care facility. He's got Alzheimer's." I clear my throat, feeling uncomfortably exposed, wondering why I'm telling this to a guy I hardly know. "What about you? Why are you here?"

He exhales a long breath. "Over the past year, I've screwed up every single aspect of my life. I came here to hide from the world for a while. Figure out my next step."

He sounds defeated, and my heart goes out to him about whatever happened to put him here, living above a garage and wearing clothes he might have found in a dumpster. I wonder if that's what the unkempt beard is about; another way to hide from the world.

"Are you having any luck?" I ask. "Figuring out your next step, I mean?"

"I don't know. I want to do something to add a net value to the world." It's an oddly introspective response coming from him, and it makes me wonder if he has a background in business. I get the sense that there's more to Noah Jameson than I've seen so far. But it's clear there's a big pile of hurt beneath his words, and I figure it's time for me to change the subject.

"Well," I say, trying to sound upbeat, "you added a net value to my kitchen remodel today, but just barely."

He gives me a quizzical look, eyebrows cocked. "Just barely?"

"Have you never painted anything in your entire life? The drips! I'm going to spend most of tomorrow sanding those out and scraping blobs of primer off the garage floor."

"Maybe I wanted to give you a little something to remember me by," he says, smirking.

He's flirting, and although it's fun, I'm not sure if that's where I want things to head. I have a lot to accomplish this summer and I don't need distractions. Plus, he clearly has his own issues.

That's when I notice that he's looking at my mouth. Almost immediately, his eyes flick away.

"You gave me the lip look," I blurt, then clap my hand over my mouth. "Sorry, ignore that. I'm tired. It's been a long day."

"No, no, please explain," he says, amused. "What is this lip look?"

His gaze drops to my mouth for another brief moment, and there it is again: that flip in my stomach.

"It's something my friend and I used to talk about when we were kids," I say, then stop myself. It was Kat, actually. We talked about it at camp, in our bunks when we stayed up long after all the other girls were asleep. We shared the names of the boys we were crushing on, and who we'd like to have our first kiss with. Shaking that off, I continue. "In romantic movies, the characters always look at each other's lips before going in for a kiss. Next time you watch a movie, you'll see. It's totally true."

He sits forward, his eyes crinkling at the corners. "Interesting. I guess I want to know . . ." He glances at my mouth again, then raises his eyebrows. "Would that be a bad thing, right now, in this moment?"

I swallow. He's close enough that I can smell him, and he smells *very* nice. A little sweaty from working outdoors, but it's a clean sweat. Spicy and musky and masculine. My hands feel tingly, and I know if I lean toward him, he'll close the gap and kiss me.

But I don't. Instead, I give an awkward laugh and lean back on my hands.

"Well, this whole scruffy face-pubes thing"—I motion to his beard—"makes it difficult for me to know what's going on under there."

"Ah. Understood." His voice sounds strained, and his expression is unreadable as he stands. "Better get going, anyway. Tomorrow is pool-cleaning day."

I feel like I've done something wrong.

"See you in a few days," I say, "and thanks for the help."

But he's already walking away, tossing a goodbye over his shoulder.

MY FINAL NIGHT in the beach house, I can't sleep. My body is so tired it's practically twitching, but I can't seem to relax. It's definitely *not* because of Noah and the fact that I'm still replaying our last conversation, wondering if I should have made a different decision.

To distract myself, I head to the bookshelf in the living room and look for something to read. The dog follows me, keeping an eye on me in the darkness. There are a whole bunch of old paperbacks there, Nora Roberts and Stephen King and Tom Clancy. I'm about to pull one out when I see what's on the lowest shelf.

Photo albums.

I choose one, then settle cross-legged on the creaky wicker sofa and flick on a lamp. Soft yellow light falls across my lap as I open the album. The first page is a picture of a chubby toddler with big brown eyes and curly pigtails. Kat. She's sitting on the beach, a sand shovel in one hand, laughing at the camera.

Quickly, I turn the page; the image of Kat as a tiny, vulnerable child makes my heart hurt in a way I don't want to analyze too closely. I continue turning pages, seeing more pictures of Kat that must have been taken that same summer. I identify her mother, because she looks a lot like Kat does now, and her grandparents, who look sweet.

But what draws my attention are the pictures of my father. *Our* father. I've known for fifteen years that he's Kat's father, too, but this photo album drives that home.

Every picture is another burst of pain in my chest. He looks like I remember him, handsome and smiling, but it's all wrong because in these pictures he's here, on this beach, with a woman who isn't my mother, and a little girl who isn't me.

Anger bubbles inside me, hot and sharp, and I slam the album shut. He was a *married man*. Kat is only six months older than me. While her mother was home alone, dealing with morning sickness or heartburn or swollen feet, he was wining and dining my mother. And just a few months later, when my mother was pregnant with me, alone and scared in our shitty apartment in Nashville, he was back in Atlanta with his wife and newborn baby girl.

How convenient for him. How nice that he could skip back and forth between two lives, between two women, never caring enough about either of them to commit to one. Until my mother died, and he didn't have that option anymore. Did he ever think about me, after she died? Did he ever feel guilty about abandoning me?

And did Kat realize how lucky she was to have him? I immediately squash that thought. I do *not* wish I'd had more time with him—he was a liar and a cheater, and I'm ashamed of everything he stands for. Ashamed of who I am, too, and that's his fault. It's all *his fucking fault.*

I need to hang on to this anger, because beneath it is a deep, yawning emptiness that frightens me. Anger is easier, cleaner. That's what's going to get me through this summer, through all my interactions with Kat, through fixing up this house and selling it.

Selling this house won't compensate for a fraction of the pain he's caused me. It'll never balance out the scales—not even close.

But I'll take what I can get.

CHAPTER ELEVEN

KAT

AS I CROSS THE MID-BAY BRIDGE TOWARD DESTIN, MY SHOUL-
ders relax and a smile settles on my face—a far cry from my
normal state the past six weeks since my dad died and my life
imploded.

My spirits dim slightly when I realize I'm stuck in pre–
Memorial Day traffic. It takes three times longer than it should
to get to my stretch of Old 98—and I'm about to pee my pants
when I pull up to the house. At least Blake's old clunker is nowhere in sight.

I hop out of the car, not even bothering to pull into the garage or grab my suitcase. Inside, I make a beeline for the downstairs bathroom, pulling down my bolero pants as I go. The house
smells musty—more like an old attic than a house on the beach.
I'll have to open the windows and get some of that fresh, salty
air in.

I've got a feeling this is going to be a good week. I don't have
to worry about Mom—she got invited to three different Memorial Day parties—and while I have an agenda, it's not so full that
I won't have room for downtime. Plus, I'm excited about what's

on my to-do list, things like doing research on potential vendors for furniture partnerships and taking "before" pictures around the house to maximize the impact of the "after" shots for the Worthington application.

As I wash my hands with the decade-old seashell soap, I start redecorating the bathroom in my mind. Wallpaper is making a comeback—the designs are practically high fashion. It might be nice to have a highlight wall with deep-blue textured wallpaper so it feels nauticalesque without hitting you over the head with an anchor.

The other walls can balance it out with a cool shade of white. My followers can help choose the exact color—engagement always skyrockets when I let people help me pick shades of lipstick or nail polish. So why not paint?

If I can show the Worthington team that my home décor content is just as compelling as my wearable fashion posts, they'd be crazy not to pick me.

Feeling parched from the long drive, I head to the kitchen for an ice cold Pamplemousse LaCroix. Last week, I stocked the fridge with my favorite sparkling water, spiked seltzer, and canned rosé. I considered leaving a Post-it note with my name on them but thought that might be a little extra. I didn't count the cans either, which I thought was big of me.

I can practically taste the sweet bubbles with an essence of grapefruit when I walk into the kitchen and—"What the actual fuck?"

The room looks like it was hit with a singularly focused tornado. The floor is destroyed. Literally. Every single square of linoleum has been hacked up, leaving a dirty wooden floor beneath. The cabinet doors have been removed, including the broken one. They're all lined up against the wall like headstones, and

Blake has painted them the most boring shade of white on the planet. It's so bright it's blinding, and I start seeing red.

I take a deep breath to try to calm myself but end up inhaling a bunch of dirt and debris. The source, I now realize, of the dank aroma that's settled in the house. Eau de Blake.

I agreed to let Blake renovate the house, not to ruin it, and I explicitly told her that I wanted to be involved in every decision regarding the design of the house. Last I checked, the color of the cabinets fits squarely into the design category—and if *this* is the color she thought would be best, then it's clear I'm the one who inherited all the style genes.

I take a step back and survey the disaster of a room. So much for getting a before picture. It's like Blake is sabotaging me every chance she gets.

For a brief second, I wonder if she's doing this all on pur-pose. Maybe she doesn't really need the money; maybe she just wants to leave me holding the debris of this house the way she left me holding the broken pieces of my heart when we were twelve.

My frosty LaCroix forgotten, I retrace my steps, stopping to open the windows a crack, and get back in my car.

The engine hasn't had time to cool down yet, and I sure as hell haven't either. Which is probably good. Blake deserves my full fury, not a watered-down version.

I'M ABLE TO sweet-talk my way past the front gate attendant at the luxury community where the Rooney estate is, and my mem-ory leads me to the circular driveway that is just as perfectly tended as it always was.

With the well-manicured front lawn, palm trees waving in

the Gulf breeze, and exterior paint that looks like it was recently touched up, I'm more aware than ever of the differences between my house and the Rooneys'. Every aspect of their property has been well cared for and maintained, and the comparison makes me realize just how much we have to do at the beach house. Even more now, thanks to Blake's errant disregard for other people's property.

With my fury simmering, I slam the car door and march around back toward the pool and the casita where she's staying. My fists are clenched, ready to bang on the front door so she knows I'm not messing around.

"Blake O'Neill is going to be sorry she came back into my life," I mutter in an attempt to pump myself up. I might talk a good game, but the fact that conflict should be dealt with as discreetly as possible has been ingrained in me from a young age.

I flex my fingers before balling them back up again as I walk up to the casita. I square myself in front of the door and I'm about to knock when it opens.

"Oh," Blake says, stepping back as if she didn't expect to see me standing right outside. At her feet, the dog spins a circle and wags his tail as if he's happy to see me.

There isn't time to be annoyed that I didn't get the pleasure of banging on the door, so I walk past Blake and into the little house—which is even smaller than I remember it.

Rosa, the housekeeper who lived in the casita when we were young, always kept a candy jar in her kitchen that CoCo and I used to sneak wrapped pieces of chocolate from. For a moment, I wonder what ever happened to Rosa—until I realize this isn't the time for a stroll down memory lane. It's the time to protect what's mine.

"What are you doing here?" Blake asks. She sounds more confused than annoyed, which somehow gets me even more riled up.

"What am I doing here?" I repeat in an attempt to buy more time. I hadn't thought much past pounding on her door.

I take another step back, bumping into the table where Blake's laptop is sitting open. I accidentally read the title of the YouTube video she was watching, and just like that, I know exactly what to say.

"What are *you* doing here," I say, motioning toward her cheap computer screen, "watching a tutorial on how to finish floors! If you have to look up how to do something, you shouldn't be doing it. Especially to a house that doesn't even belong to you!"

My hair falls into my face and I brush it away, irritated at the way Blake seems completely unaffected by my outburst. Her wispy blond hair is hanging casually in front of her face, her wide brown eyes focused on me as if she's waiting for me to finish. But I'm not finished. I'm just getting started.

"I should've known not to trust you," I say, my voice rising. "You lied about who you were when we met at camp, so I shouldn't be surprised you lied about knowing what the hell you're doing. Or not doing. Because I am not going to let you lay another finger on my house."

Blake isn't even looking at me now—which makes me even more irritated.

"Max, no," she says, a reprimand in her voice.

Who the hell is Max? I'm about to ask when her dumb dog squats and pees at my feet. Dog urine splashes on my brand-new Kate Spade flip-flops and I think I might vomit.

"You made him do that," I yell at Blake. My toes curl in disgust, and as much as I want to step out of the shoes, I don't want to have to pick them up and touch them with my bare hands.

"I did not," Blake says, crossing her arms in front of her chest. "I was about to take him out to go to the bathroom when you barged in here and started yelling. You made him nervous."

I let out a nonsensical string of vowels and carefully step past Blake and back out the door.

I step—soiled flip-flops and all—onto the first step in the shallow end of the pool. The water is only ankle-deep, and I hope the chlorine will disinfect the shoes enough that I won't have to toss them. They're my favorite pair—zebra-print bottoms and black straps with the signature Kate Spade logo on top. But shoes can be replaced, I remind myself. The beach house and all the memories it holds can't.

I turn around to face Blake—there isn't so much as a smirk on her face, even though I know I must look ridiculous. If the roles were reversed, I'd be laughing hysterically.

"Why did you come here, Kat?" Blake asks, sounding more resigned than angry.

"Because you destroyed the kitchen," I say, keeping my voice calm and steady.

"It's part of the process," she says. "I left you a note."

"Where?" I ask. "I didn't see anything."

"On the kitchen counter. In *our* house. It's half mine, you know."

"I didn't see a note," I tell her, ignoring the remark about her half ownership of the house—that's just a technicality. It's mine in all the ways that matter.

I step out of the pool. I don't want Blake to be taller, looking down on me when I say this to her. "If we're going to do this renovation thing, we're going to do it right and hire help."

"I don't need—"

"If you need a YouTube video, you shouldn't be doing it on your own."

"What, are *you* going to help?" Blake's eyebrows are raised as if she's daring me.

"No," I snap, annoyed. "We'll get someone who knows what they're doing. A professional."

"I know what I'm doing," Blake says, her eyes flashing with anger.

"The kitchen floor would beg to differ."

Blake rolls her eyes. "We can hire someone for the big stuff like plumbing and electrical work," she says, "but I can handle the small stuff."

I'm about to question her definition of "small stuff" when she makes one final point.

"It'll save us a lot of money," Blake says. "And I've done it before."

She's not wrong about the money. A renovation is expensive, and even though Blake's experience seems sketchy, we can't afford to pay for all the help we'll need.

I think of Henry's "helping hands" and wonder if this is the type of project his business handles, and if there might be a friends-and-family discount. I'd feel better if we hired someone I knew I could trust to keep an eye on Blake. God knows I can't leave her to her own devices. The kitchen floor is proof of that— and the hideous paint on the cabinets. Which reminds me . . .

"Whoever does the work," I say, "I need to weigh in on all design decisions."

"Fine," Blake says, a little too easily. But I want to make sure she knows I mean *all* decisions.

"That includes anything that affects the aesthetic of the house," I say, and Blake nods as if she hadn't already made a pretty big design decision on her own. "I want to make sure everything aligns with my brand."

Blake's face cracks into a lopsided smile, and I know she's stifling a laugh—just barely. There are a lot of things I can tolerate, but being the punch line of someone's joke isn't one of them.

"That includes anything you paint," I tell her, trying to get the conversation back on track. "Like the kitchen cabinets."

"Have at it," Blake says. "You can pick the color."

"Good. Because the one you picked won't work."

"I haven't picked a color yet."

Now it's my turn to laugh. "I saw the cabinets—they were painted."

"Oh," Blake says, recrossing her arms in front of her chest. "That's just the primer—you do know what primer is, don't you?"

"Of course," I tell her. And it's not a total lie. I know a lot about the kind of primer you put on your face before applying concealer. "But this primer is ugly."

Blake shrugs, not disagreeing with me. "It exists to be covered up, so it's not meant to be pretty."

"Everything has the potential to be pretty," I inform Blake, who could be a lot prettier herself if she put an ounce of effort into it—if she got a good conditioning treatment on her hair, wore some lipstick and maybe mascara.

But good for Blake if she's okay getting her hands dirty and doing manual labor. She can do that, and I'll make it all look good. Not just good. Runway-worthy.

After all, life is a fashion show.

CHAPTER TWELVE

BLAKE

IT'S HALFWAY THROUGH MY SECOND WEEK AT THE BEACH house, and despite Kat's insistence on approving every single minuscule change, it's going okay. Better than I expected, to be honest. Partly because Kat's handyman friend, Henry, is helping out.

He came over today to look at the plumbing and electrical work I need done in the kitchen, and I'm sitting at the kitchen table making a list of supplies to refinish the floor. Contrary to Kat's assumption last week, I didn't just YouTube how to do it. A few days ago, I FaceTimed Granddad and he talked me through the whole process. He's surprisingly sharp when it comes to remembering construction-related details. Unfortunately, the same can't be said about remembering my name.

A lump forms in my throat and I clear it away.

"Can I ask you a question?" I say to Henry.

He straightens up and retracts his tape measure. "Sure."

Henry Alexander was a surprise when I met him. Kat said he was an old friend of hers, so I expected someone like her or the Rooneys—rich and entitled. But Henry seems down-to-earth, a soft-spoken, thoughtful guy who weighs his words before he speaks. In fact, he reminds me of a younger version of my grand-dad, especially in his jeans, plaid shirt, and work boots.

"I don't think this is load bearing," I say, pointing to the wall between the kitchen and dining room, "but can you confirm?"

Henry looks up at the ceiling, hands on hips, then walks around to the other side of the room. When he reappears, he smiles. "Not load bearing."

I'm relieved. "Great. I'll demolish it whenever I get up the courage to take a sledgehammer to it. Oh, and I guess I need to buy a sledgehammer."

"I have one you can borrow. I'm happy to lend you anything you need." Henry's phone pings, and he pulls it out of his pocket. "I have to be somewhere, but I'll drop off a sledgehammer later this week?"

"No rush," I say. "I'm renting a sander tomorrow to get started on the floors. That'll keep me busy for a few days."

He smiles. "Good luck. Call me if you need any help."

THE NEXT DAY, I've started the grueling job of sanding the sub-floor. It'll take a few days since it covers the entire main level of the house. The dog is scared of the noise, so he's hiding upstairs, leaving me to work in peace. Yesterday, I went to the thrift store and bought a couple of pairs of jeans and some long-sleeve shirts; Granddad was all about safety, and my cutoffs and tank tops won't cut it for the heavy-duty work.

With my eye and ear protection on and the floor sander vi-brating in my hands, the rest of the world fades away. It's almost a meditative feeling. All I have to focus on is this floor, this mo-ment. I block everything else out—the tension with Kat, the worry about Granddad, the simmering anger toward my father.

Out of the corner of my eye, I see the dog bounding down

the stairs toward the door. I turn off the sander and yank my ear protection off, worried that something's wrong.

But then I hear it:

"Hey, little Danny boy. Little Danny DeVito. Danny Dorito, my little Cheeto puff."

Noah.

A smile tugs at my lips. He's brought me lunch a couple of times this week. Without him, I might've succumbed to scurvy from malnourishment. I look forward to his visits more than I should; pretty sure he comes mostly to visit the dog.

"Hi," I say, walking into the kitchen. He's looking particularly scruffy today, his shorts covered with grease stains. Somehow, he also manages to look *damn* sexy, neck beard and all, which is annoying. *It's just because he's tall*, I remind myself. Tall men are my kryptonite.

Unfortunately, he doesn't appear to have any food with him today. No big deal: I can eat peanut butter and brown sugar sandwiches for lunch, just like I did every day in elementary school. *Cheap and delish*, as my mom used to say.

Noah's eyes widen as he sees me. "Whoa. You look like you escaped the dust bowl and are about to head to California on a jalopy with the Joad family."

"Ooh, somebody took AP English." I look down at my sawdust-covered self and lift my safety goggles over my head. "What are you up to? Already done for the day at"—I glance at the digital display on the oven—"2:37?"

"Just taking a break. I've been busy washing the windows—"

"Busy? You?"

He shakes his head. "Hush. As I was saying, I was *very busy* today, and I realized that I'd worked through lunch. I figured you might've done the same. I thought I'd see if you wanted to grab dinner later."

"Sure." I blow on my safety goggles, getting rid of the coating of dust. "I can pick up the food this time, since you usually do. What do you want?"

"I was thinking we could go somewhere. Get out of here for a couple hours."

I shake my head, replacing the goggles over my eyes. "Can't. Too much to do."

"You've been working sixteen hours a day," he says. "You deserve a break, even if I don't."

I sigh. A break does sound nice. I've been sanding the floor for so long my body feels like it's still vibrating. "Okay, sure. Let's do dinner. Want to meet somewhere?".

"I'll come get you. Seven o'clock?"

"Sure."

He says goodbye, gives the dog another pat, and saunters off.

It's only when I turn the sander back on that it hits me: Did Noah Jameson just ask me out on a date?

SEVERAL HOURS LATER, I'm still stressing about that question. I've showered, dried my hair, and put on makeup for the first time in weeks—I followed a tutorial Kat did on her IGTV, adapting my drugstore products to imitate the "natural beachy look" she was demonstrating. It actually looks decent, not that I will ever admit that to her.

But now I'm standing in my bedroom and staring at my limited selection of clothes. When I packed to come to Destin, I only expected to stay for a few days. I have nothing appropriate for a date. Not that I know it's a date. But if it *is* a date, I don't want to wear the same clothes I wear to clean the Rooneys' house.

It's six thirty, so I don't have time to run out and buy anything, and even if I did, I don't have money to blow. I turn around, trying not to panic, when my eyes land on the closet. The other day I was rummaging around in there and noticed it was full of garment bags. At the time, I had no use for them. But now, I walk over and open the door, curious.

I pull out several bags and lay them on the bed, unzipping them. Inside are an assortment of vintage dresses; handmade, by the looks of them, probably by Kat's grandma. Several from the eighties and early nineties, with poufy sleeves and lace, but a few look like they date back to the seventies. Old enough to look cool and vintage, and in great shape although they're a little musty. One in particular catches my eye: a halter dress in a yellow floral print. Hesitating, I hold it against my body. Kat would have a fit if she knew I was considering wearing one of these dresses. Which makes me want to do it even more.

The dress goes on easily, and I tie the halter straps behind my neck, then turn to look at myself in the floor-length mirror next to the closet.

Stunned, I blink at my reflection. The dress looks like it was made for me. The empire waist and neckline give me the illusion of curves, and the skirt hits a few inches above the knee, making my legs look slim rather than stubby. I get an eerie feeling, almost like déjà vu, and bolt downstairs to the built-in bookshelf in the living room, pushing aside the drop cloth I hung to protect it from dust.

I yank out a photo album and leaf through a few pages until I find it: a picture of Kat's grandmother wearing this exact dress. She's a few years older than I am now, and she's standing on the deck that faces the beach. Her coloring is like Kat's—dark-haired and dark-eyed—but there's something familiar about her.

It's the curve of her smile. The way her chin comes to a slight point. The arch of her brows, the shape of her eyes. It's not that I've seen her before—it's that she looks like me. I look like her.

And it's more than her face; we have the same straight figure that Jackson Franklin in ninth grade compared to a ruler wearing a wig.

All of a sudden it hits me, like a shovel to the forehead: this is *my* grandmother. For some reason it hadn't sunk in until now. She isn't just Kat's grandma; she's mine, too.

The image of my grandma O'Neill flashes into my mind, the woman who raised me after my mother died, who made me a healthy snack every day after school, who went to my parent-teacher conferences, who helped fill out my applications for college. She was short and soft, with sparkling blue eyes and a big smile. I adored her.

I suddenly have the itch to get this dress off me, like it's disrespectful to her that I'm wearing it, pretending to have any connection to this *other* grandmother, who may not have even known about me. Her son's illegitimate child.

There's a knock on the door behind me, and I jump.

"Hello?" I call out.

"It's me," Noah says.

Shit. My existential crisis went on too long and now I don't have time to change.

"Come in," I say. "I'll be ready in two minutes."

The front door opens as I race upstairs. Behind me, I hear Noah and the dog reuniting with their standard greeting of tail wagging, belly scratches, and silly nicknames.

I pull on a pair of leather sandals and do one more quick check of myself in the mirror. The yellow sundress looks good on me, I realize, and I have every right to wear it. Just like I have every right to be here, in this house, despite what Kat seems to believe.

I belong here. The realization rushes over me like a warm breeze. I'm still angry and hurt—but I also feel somehow tethered. Like a few small threads have anchored me here for the first time.

But I need to go; Noah is waiting for our dinner that might or might not be a date. My stomach flutters as I head downstairs, hoping I'm not overdressed. He's in the kitchen, his back to me, petting the dog and murmuring in his silly voice. I take a moment to admire the view: he's definitely upped his clothing game for tonight—nice shorts and a button-down shirt, the sleeves rolled up—and I exhale in relief. At least I won't look out of place.

"Sorry for the wait," I say, and he stands and turns around.

I gasp.

It takes a moment for my brain to catch up to what I'm seeing: the man standing in front of me is not the scruffy drifter I've come to know the past few weeks. The neck beard is gone. He's not completely clean-shaven, but he's trimmed the bush down, cleaned up the edges, exposing a sharp jawline and cheekbones.

He's done something to his hair, too, swooping it off his forehead in lovely chestnut waves, and my stomach bottoms out as I realize what this means: Noah dressed up. He trimmed his beard. I did my hair, put on makeup, and put on a dress.

We're going on a date.

"You look—different," I blurt out, then wave in the general direction of his face. "This didn't have anything to do with my comment, did it?"

The one where I shut him down after he'd basically told me he wanted to kiss me?

"I can neither confirm nor deny." He says this straight-faced, in that dry tone I've become accustomed to. But now, with him looking like *that*, it hits differently.

"You ready?" he says. "I have reservations for seven thirty, and the place is about thirty minutes away."

I blink a few times, feeling thrown off-balance. Making

reservations is a normal thing to do for a date, but it's such a change from the lazy, lackadaisical Noah I've gotten to know over the past few weeks.

"I'm ready," I say, but as we head toward the door, I stop. The dog is pacing at my feet, like he's reluctant to let us leave. "Do you think he'll be all right by himself for a few hours?"

Noah glances at me, a cheeky smile on his face. "Well, bless my soul, Blake O'Neill. You're not worried about the dog being lonely, are you? The dog you don't like at all?"

I give him what I hope is a withering glance. "He's seemed nervous lately. What if he pees all over the floors I just sanded? He peed on Kat's shoes the other day."

Noah bursts out laughing. I've told him a bit about Kat, about her expensive clothes and stuck-up attitude. "That's a good puppy." He kneels and gives the dog a few scratches around the ears. "Hey, little Dorito Cheeto. You'll be okay while we're gone, won't you?"

The dog gives a sad whine, and my heart gives a reluctant squeeze.

"He'll be fine," I say, mostly to reassure myself. We can't take the dog to a restaurant. "We should get going, right?"

Noah looks up and shrugs. "I know a place we can go and take the dog with us."

"You're okay with that?" My shoulders drop in relief.

"Sure, why not. I'd hate for you to spend the evening worrying about your dog."

"Worrying about the dog ruining my floors, you mean," I say, grabbing the leash from the kitchen counter. The dog's tail starts wagging immediately.

"Uh-huh. Sure." Noah winks at me, making me feel off-balance once again, then says to the dog, "Okay, Cheeto puff, let's go."

Outside, Noah opens the back door of his car so the dog can jump in. When he shuts the door, I look at him.

"Was this your plan all along?" I say. "To hang out with the dog? Because I would've let you take him anytime."

Noah takes a few steps toward me until he's only a foot away, close enough that I have to tilt my head up to meet his eyes. My heart pounds. I can smell the clean laundry scent of his clothes, feel the warmth of his skin, see the flecks of green in his blue eyes.

Damn it all to hell, he's not *just* tall. He's a highly attractive man, and my body likes his body way too much.

"I didn't do any of this"—he motions at his face, his clothes— "for the dog. Maybe I haven't made my intentions clear, so I will now: you look beautiful, Blake, and I'd like to buy you dinner and spend the next few hours getting to know you better. Is that acceptable?"

I take a shaky breath. "Yes," I manage to spit out. "Of course. Let's go."

NOAH DRIVES US to Seaside, a picturesque beach town about twenty-five miles east of Destin. In the center of the town is a plaza surrounded by palm trees and shops, bustling with people. With the dog on a leash, we walk under twinkle lights strung through the trees, past a line of food trucks in vintage Airstream trailers. Noah buys me a hot dog and gets himself a gourmet grilled cheese, and then we meander through Sundog Books, where he buys me a classic edition of *Little Women* so I "have something to think about besides demolishing houses."

After that, he gets us each an ice cream cone—pralines and cream for me, mint chocolate chip for him—and we wander down toward the beach, the dog trotting along on his leash, happy as a clam.

The sun has set, and the stars wink on overhead, so much brighter than they seem in Minneapolis. We sit and chat as we finish our ice cream, the cool sand beneath us, listening to the waves crashing on the shore.

"So you know why I ended up here in Destin," I say, "but how about you? I'm guessing you haven't always been a grounds-keeper."

"You guessed right." He rubs at the stubble on his face, as if he's still getting used to it. "A year ago, I went to an office every day. Wore a suit. Gave presentations in boardrooms."

"Sounds boring," I say, which makes him laugh. I'm not joking, though. It's easier to imagine this cleaned-up version of Noah having a job like that, but it still doesn't fit him. "What happened?"

He takes a bite out of his waffle cone. "I made some mistakes. Hurt people I care about. People who now want nothing to do with me."

He's speaking in generalities, like always, trying to cover the hurt with a flippant remark. I did the same thing every year for the Dads and Donuts breakfast in school. Granddad would take me, and I loved him for it, but it always felt awkward, and I'd have to pretend like it didn't matter to me that my *actual* dad hadn't come.

"You don't think they'll forgive you?" I ask.

"I don't know—I haven't asked." He glances at me. "And yes, I know it's cowardly to run away from my problems. I just . . . I need some time to figure out what *I* want. I've spent my entire life doing what other people expected of me, and I'm honestly not sure what I expect of *myself*." He takes another bite of his cone. "I'm feeling sort of stuck."

I nod and lick my ice cream. "I can understand that. I'm stuck, too."

I tell him how my grandparents paid for my college educa-
tion but that I didn't finish because my grandma got sick. I came
home to help out, but also because I knew from losing my mom
that once someone was gone, you'd give anything for just one
more day with them.

"Not that I regret leaving school," I say. "But I do wonder
how things might've turned out if I'd finished college."

"What were you studying?"

I shake my head, crunching into my waffle cone. It occurs to
me that I'm being more open with him than I have with anyone
else in a long time, but it feels easy. Comfortable. "I changed my
major three times. Couldn't settle on anything. So maybe it's
good I didn't finish—still, it feels like I wasted their money. I
could've become a nanny without college."

"If you like being a nanny, there's nothing wrong with that."

I'm not sure I actually do like it. I love the kids, but I can't see
myself doing it long term. "There's nothing wrong with being a
groundskeeper," I say to him, "but do you want to do it forever?"

"Definitely not," he says flatly. Then he clears his throat,
knocking his shoulder into mine. "Anyway, this has taken a depressing turn. Change of subject?"

"Good idea," I say, laughing. "What do you want to talk
about?"

He's finished his cone, and I give the last of mine to the dog,
who scarfs it down like he's been waiting his entire life for the
opportunity.

Noah turns to face me. "Hmm, let's see. Rapid-fire questions—
you say the first thing that comes into your head. Favorite Dis-
ney animated movie?"

"*Beauty and the Beast.*"

"Bzzzzt, wrong." He gives a thumbs-down. "The correct answer is *Tarzan.*"

"Phil Collins went *hard* on that soundtrack," I agree, nodding. "Who's your favorite Avenger?"

"Loki."

I snort. "He's not an Avenger, but it doesn't surprise me that you'd like that smarmy, sneaky little shit. The correct answer is Thor—specifically Thor in *Ragnarok*, with short hair and a beard."

His eyes glint with amusement. "With a beard, eh? Who's the best Obi-Wan—Alec Guinness or Ewan McGregor?"

There's a fleck of ice cream on the corner of his mouth, and for a moment I imagine leaning forward and licking it off. Instead, I force myself to answer the question: "Alec is wiser, but Ewan is hotter."

"Hold on—did you just give me the lip look?"

My eyes snap up to meet his. Just like that, the energy between us has shifted from playful to something completely different.

"Um. Sorry." My cheeks warm as I point. "You have a little ice cream right there."

He holds my gaze as he licks the corner of his mouth. "Did I get it?" His voice has dropped an octave.

"Yeah," I say, a little breathless.

"Too bad. I thought maybe you were going to . . . you know."

There's heat in his eyes, glinting in the moonlight, and I squeeze my thighs together. "Maybe I was hoping *you* would."

"I wanted to do that a couple weeks ago, but you said the beard grossed you out."

I scoff. "I didn't say it grossed me out!"

"You said the beard made it 'difficult to know what was going on under there.' Now you *do* know. So . . ." He raises his eyebrows, challenging me.

"That's not—I didn't—" I shake my head, exhaling. "Oh, fine."

And I lean forward and press my mouth against his.

He gives a small, surprised grunt. I'm flooded with embarrassment and pull away, my heart pounding. But then his hand comes up to cup my face and he draws me back in.

It's a gentle kiss, like a question, his lips soft against mine, testing the waters. His fingers skate along my jaw, sending goose bumps racing along my neck and shoulders.

I lean into him, answering the question by deepening the kiss, parting my lips, letting my tongue meet his. He tastes exactly like ice cream eaten on a beach, sweet and a little salty. I run my palm against his cheek, feeling the rough stubble, then slide my hand up into his wavy hair. He hums in appreciation and his hand tightens on my neck, like he's holding himself back from doing more.

When we part it feels too soon, but we *are* sitting on a public beach. The dog lays his head on my lap, and I stroke his fur absently.

"I want to make something clear," I say, and Noah tilts his head, listening. "I wasn't being superficial when I made that comment about your bushy beard. I was genuinely concerned about what could be hiding under it. Like, yesterday's breakfast? A family of field mice? A contagious skin disease?"

He throws his head back and laughs, and I'm convinced that Noah's laughter is my new favorite sound in all the world. When he catches his breath, he interlaces his fingers with mine.

"Let's do this again sometime," he says.

I smile, my chest warming. "I'd like that."

CHAPTER THIRTEEN

KAT

THE DRIVE FROM ATLANTA TO DESTIN NEVER USED TO bother me—but I've never driven there and back every other week. And it's getting old, fast.

What kills me is that I'm pretty sure Blake feels put out by having to stay at the Rooneys'. She has no idea how good she has it, having to move less than a mile down the road. Sure, she has to do some light housekeeping, but the Rooneys' place is always spotless, and she gets to spend all summer at the beach.

I mean, I wouldn't want to do it—but she obviously doesn't mind doing dirty work. Besides, I have responsibilities back in Atlanta. My mom, for one. She looks forward to our weekly dinners like I'm the light of her life. And I look forward to my afternoons volunteering at the Peachtree Boys' and Girls' Center like they're the light of mine.

Last week, I accidentally told the girls about the Worthington application. I usually make an effort to keep the conversations focused on what's going on in their lives, not mine—but they got so excited, I'm glad I told them.

Luna had a good idea about creating a time lapse for each

room as it evolves, and when I said I was going to do it and give her credit in the post, her face lit up. I can't remember the last time I saw her genuinely smile. I know all her problems will still be there when she goes home, but for an hour, she was happy.

When I finally pull up to the beach house, I'm thrilled to see that the only car in the driveway is a blue truck with a Helping Hands logo on the side. I haven't seen Henry since the day at the bank, but we've been texting since he agreed to take on the job helping Blake.

I unfold the visor and look at my reflection in the mirror. My hair is a mess from having the windows down, so I run my fingers through it and apply a quick layer of my Hourglass sheer lip gloss.

I'm not trying impress him or anything—if I was, I'd put on lipstick, not gloss. Henry's a great guy and he's not bad to look at, but I'm more into white-collar men than blue.

Still, I've got to stay true to my brand and treat every walk like it's a #KatWalk. Even if that walk is through a house that's "going to look a lot worse before it gets better"—which is what Henry said when I told him my theory about Blake sabotaging the project. I'm trying to be chill and trust the process as if I haven't been burned before. But I have been burned, and I've got the scars to prove it.

After the shock of walking into the shitstorm last week, I'm a little nervous about what I'll find inside. Hopefully things aren't *that* much worse. I'm getting some of the new furniture delivered this week from a few of the product placement deals I secured back in Atlanta. I might be crazy trusting Blake not to damage it in the renovation process, but my ass can't handle another week of that wicker furniture.

As soon as I'm out of the car, I hear music drifting through the open windows of the house. Classic rock. Tom Petty?

I let myself in and follow the sound to the kitchen, where Henry

ALI BRADY

is standing on a ladder, singing along to "Free Fallin'." Not the wisest lyrical choice when you're standing three feet off the ground.

His arms are up, fiddling with lights on the ceiling, and my eyes are drawn to the taut muscles peeking out between the top of his jeans and the hem of his plaid shirt. The baby fat is long gone, and somewhere over the last decade, Henry got buff.

I'm about to knock on the doorframe—which is now missing the door—to get Henry's attention when he looks down. He startles at the sight of me and almost topples off the ladder.

"Hey," he says, stabilizing himself, brushing a lock of brown hair behind his ear. "I didn't hear you come in."

"I didn't mean to interrupt the jam session," I tease.

Henry steps down off the ladder and lowers the volume on his old-school boom box. Someone needs to get that man into the twenty-first century. Bluetooth speakers that connect to his phone would be a lot less cumbersome to cart around, and the sound quality would be much clearer.

"Helps the time go by," he says. His cheeks are flushed, and for a brief moment, I see him so clearly as the boy I used to know. It's strange how he can seem so familiar and unfamiliar at the same time.

Without the music, the silence between us feels awkward, and I don't do awkward. Henry doesn't either, judging by the way he's shifting his weight back and forth on his feet.

"What are you working on?" I ask, nodding toward the ceiling.

His face relaxes and he breaks into an easy smile that brings his dimple out. "Took out the old fluorescent box lights and I'm replacing them with can lights. It's going to look like a whole new room. Blake has a great—"

"Ugh," I say interrupting him.

Henry furrows his brow, looking confused.

144

"Just hearing her name sends my anxiety through the roof," I tell him.

Before I can stop myself, the words start tumbling out. Words I haven't been able to say to my mom because she's already so broken and I don't want to cause any more damage. Words I haven't said to CoCo because I'm genetically programmed to give a shit what people think about me and my family. And even though Henry counts as "people," something about him makes it easier to open up.

"Blake's not even pretending this isn't just about money for her," I tell Henry. "But I wonder if there's a part of her that wants to twist the knife in my heart, you know? It's not enough I lost my dad; now she's trying to take this house away from me, too. It's like she resents me for being the one who got to grow up with him—but let me tell you, being David Steiner's daughter wasn't all sunshine and roses. He was—"

I stop myself before I say something I'll regret. My dad wasn't perfect, but he was my dad, and like my mom says, his memory should be a blessing. Everyone has flaws, but no one wants to be remembered for them.

Yet another reason I need Blake O'Neill out of my life: she reminds me of the worst of my dad when I want to remember the best.

"She's trying to ruin my life," I tell Henry, who is looking at me like he's afraid I might break. But I'm not fragile. I'm strong, damn it. As if to prove it to myself, I take a deep breath and square my shoulders, standing like a woman who's confident in her place in the world.

"So, the lighting," I say, in what might be the least subtle subject change in the history of conversation. Luckily, Henry seems equally desperate for a new topic.

"It's going to look great in here," he says. "And your, uh, evil sister left some stuff for you to look at."

"My evil *half* sister," I correct him. I follow his gaze to the kitchen table, where there's a note written in the neat, slanted writing that hasn't changed over the years. If anything, it's gotten even more precise.

Seeing my name, *Kat—*, written at the top of the page instantly takes me back to the dozen letters she sent. As part of the whole keeping-my-dad's-deep-dark-secret thing, I hid the letters inside a shoebox, inside a Tupperware box that was covered with a bunch of old T-shirts under my bed. Throwing them in the trash was too big a risk; my mom might find them and ask questions I couldn't answer about this girl from camp who kept sending me letters.

Looking back, I realize she was the one who got the mail every day, but at twelve, I wasn't exactly a critical thinker. I just knew I needed to protect my family, and the only way to do that was to keep my mom in the dark.

Of course, now, I know she already knew, although I don't know how or when she found out.

I pick up the paper and read Blake's note:

Kat—

Here are a few color options for the stain on the wood floor (for the kitchen and the rest of the main level) and also for the cabinets.

I picked a few colors I thought would be nice—but if you don't like them, you can find rows and rows of them at Lowe's.

Let me know what you think. I'm going to start painting next week.

—Blake

The colors she picked aren't awful, and suddenly I feel like the evil sister. I didn't think she would stay true to her word, but she's letting me make the call.

To someone like Blake, white is white is white. But I have an elevated understanding of the depths that define color, how there are warm whites and cool whites and crisp whites and even off-whites.

I pick up the stack of paint chips and study the colors. Vanilla Milkshake and Moonshine, White Dove and Paper White. Now I just have to decide which shade of beautiful to choose—this one decision will set the tone for all the others to come.

I'm creating not just the aesthetic for a room, but the backdrop for future memories—provided I can get my shit together and convince Rachel Worthington I'm the perfect influencer to represent her brand.

I clear a space on the kitchen table—the warm wood will make a perfect backdrop for the shades of white—and arrange the paint chips into the shape of a heart. To get the perfect shot, I need some height, so I pull out a chair and step up, holding my phone over the table.

Just when I have the heart perfectly positioned in the frame, my chair starts to wobble. Before I can decide whether to catch my balance or capture the shot, Henry is there, keeping the chair steady.

He doesn't say anything, just smiles and waits patiently as I take the picture from a few different angles and heights.

"Thanks," I say, stepping down from the chair once I'm confident I have one that will work.

"Might want to add some new chairs to the reno list," Henry says.

"Maybe something with a pop of color," I agree. I'm leaning toward a cool, bright white for the room that would look great against shades of blue and green. Just like the view outside the window—the signature white sand and emerald-green water of Destin.

"I was thinking something a little sturdier," Henry says, heading back to the ladder to get back to whatever he was doing with the lights. "But color would be nice, too."

"Color is always nice," I say, taking a seat on the chair, hoping it's sturdy enough to hold me. I pick the best photo and bring it into an editing app, then add text that says **Color Wars** to the middle of the heart before I write the post copy:

All right, pretty people. Let's talk about home décor. It's basically fashion, but for a room, right?

I'm in the early stages of a big home reno project, and I'm going to need your help picking the perfect color for the kitchen cabinets.

Every day for the next week, I'm going to post a color battle in my stories and you can vote on which shade will move forward until we have a winner.

This is going to be fun! Thanks for playing along—and remember, every room is a runway when life's a fashion show.

Tell me your favorite shade of white in the comments and check out my stories for the first battle!

I post the first battle between two cool tones—I learned early on that there's a way to give my followers a say while still having control of the outcome. The votes and comments start coming in right away, and it warms my heart to know how many

THE BEACH TRAP

people out there care about me. I need to remember that the next time I feel sad and lonely, like when I got back to Atlanta last week.

Henry steps down off the ladder and walks to the switch on the wall. "Let there be light," he says, turning it on.

"Beautiful." The light cans, or whatever he called them, give the room a warm glow that's much more forgiving than the old fluorescents. This room is going to be so 'Grammable by the time we're done with it!

"I think all this hard work deserves a drink," I say. "Any interest in walking down to the Crab Trap?"

"I can't," Henry says abruptly, turning the lights back off as if he's emphasizing the point.

"Oh," I say, taken aback at how quickly he shut me down. I hope he doesn't think I was coming on to him—if I was flirting, he'd know it. Not that I would flirt with Henry Alexander.

Maybe my outburst earlier scared him off. Men aren't good with handling emotions, and I let them all out when I went on my little Blake rant.

He probably thinks I'm a spoiled brat—talking so much shit about Blake. God, I hope they didn't become friends over the past week. I should have warned Henry that she is not one to be trusted.

An awkward silence settles between us, until he breaks it, saying, "I have to pick up my daughter."

"Oh," I say again, like a moron who can only speak in vowel sounds. "I didn't realize you had a daughter."

Henry's face lights up. "Sunny's six. She's a handful—but she's the best thing that ever happened to me."

My eyes drift to his left hand, confirming his ring finger is empty. I realize I've been doing most of the talking, and there's a lot I don't know about adult Henry.

149

"And her mom?" I ask.

Henry's lips dip into a slight frown, making his dimple disappear. "She's not in the picture anymore."

There's a story there, but I sense it's one he doesn't want to talk about, so I don't push.

Quiet settles between us again, but this time it's slightly less awkward. Henry glances at his watch like he can't get out of here fast enough.

"I've got to pick her up from camp," he says. "But if you like burgers, you're welcome to come over for dinner."

"I love burgers," I say, even though what I really mean is that I'd love to find out more about adult Henry, the daughter who makes him light up like the sun she's named after, and the ex-wife who doesn't have custody.

A FEW HOURS later, I'm walking up to the address Henry texted me, wearing a floral print sundress from an up-and-coming Belgian designer.

His house is on a side street between Old and New 98, not far from where his parents' convenience store used to be. It's a one-level bungalow, painted pale blue, with a small front porch. Not that I'm an expert, but it looks like it could use some of the love he's giving to my beach house.

Armed with a bottle of rosé in one hand and a sparkling bottle of grape juice tucked beneath my arm, I knock.

The door opens, and a little girl with blond hair in spiral curls looks up at me. "Hi!" she says, and her giant smile reveals a missing tooth. "You're my dad's old friend who he used to know when he was a kid!"

"I am," I say, laughing. "And you must be Sunny."

"That's me," she says, beaming. "I'm six and a half, my birthday is in November just like Thanksgiving, and my dad says he's the most thankful for me than anything else in the whole world."

I nod, instantly enamored with this little girl. "I bet you're pretty thankful for him, too."

"Sometimes," she says with a shrug. "Except for when he snores."

"Hey now," Henry's voice booms from inside. "That's supposed to be between you and me."

"Oops," Sunny says with a giggle. "I forgot." The girl really is sunshine embodied.

"Come on in," Henry says, opening the door wider.

"This is our living room," Sunny says, holding her arm out to the cozy room. "It's where we watch TV. I love cartoons. Do you like cartoons?"

"I do," I tell her.

She beams and I wish adults were this easy to win over.

"Want to see my room?" she asks, reaching for my hand.

"Later," Henry tells Sunny, a slight warning to his voice.

Sunny shrugs it off and plops in front of a toy box that's overflowing with trucks, dolls, and colorful building blocks.

"Want something to drink?" Henry asks, and I follow him into the kitchen, where the refrigerator is covered in Sunny's art.

"She's adorable *and* talented," I say, admiring a drawing of what looks like Sunny and Henry out on a tiny boat.

As if she senses the compliment, Sunny is instantly by my side again. "Purple is my favorite color. What's yours?"

"Cerulean blue," I tell her.

"Ooh, what's that?"

Henry shakes his head and takes the bottle of wine from my hand to open while Sunny and I continue to talk about all things color, art, fashion, and ice cream.

The girl's chatter is constant and continues all through dinner.

I wonder if Henry doesn't say much because he can't get a word in edgewise, or if the reason Sunny talks so much is to fill the silence that seems to surround her dad. Either way, they are one hell of a dynamic duo.

After we eat the most incredible cheeseburgers I've ever tasted—Henry said the secret is ranch seasoning and crumbled blue cheese—I insist on washing the dishes.

Sunny "helps" by standing next to me, regaling me with stories about her and her dad and their life together. I notice none of the stories include her mom, which makes me more curious than ever. But I can't exactly ask a six-year-old where her mommy is.

"Say good night, Sunshine," Henry says, walking back into the kitchen as the day turns to dusk.

"Good night, Sunshine," Sunny parrots. "Can Kat tuck me in?"

Henry's eyes dart toward mine and I nod. "I'd love to," I tell them both.

That's all Sunny needs to hear. She leads me down the hallway toward her bedroom, where she takes me through her bedtime routine: picking out pajamas, brushing her teeth, and choosing a bedtime story.

I meet Nuh-Nuh, a stuffed bunny that has seen better days. He or she only has one eye, and its left ear seems to be hanging on by a thread. It reminds me of Beary, and I'm still not sure what to make of the fact that Blake kept him for me after all these years.

After I read Sunny a story about Morris the Moose and tuck her in, Henry comes in to kiss her good night.

"I love you to the moon and back," he says, bending down to kiss her forehead.

"I love you to Jupiter," Sunny says. "Or to Mars? Which planet is farther away?" She looks at me when she asks the question, and I look at Henry, hoping he knows the answer, because I have no clue.

"We'll look it up tomorrow," he says, pulling the covers tighter around Sunny.

"Careful!" Sunny warns when Henry accidentally jostles her bunny.

"I'm always careful," Henry says. "But, sweetie, Nuh-Nuh isn't going to last forever. One day, you're going to have to give him up like a big girl."

"I don't want to be a big girl," she says, squeezing the bunny tighter.

I want to tell Sunny it's okay, and tell Henry to delay this life lesson as long as he can. Sunny will have plenty of chances to learn that the world is a big and lonely place, full of disappointments and broken promises and lies. For now, let her be little enough that she can find comfort in a well-loved stuffed animal, the way I did with Beary.

But it's not my place to tell either of them any of that.

Instead, I say, "Good night," and awkwardly stand to leave. Henry and Sunny don't need an audience for this conversation, and I'm suddenly missing my own dad, wishing he was here to tell me everything will be okay.

Even though he's the one who created this problem I'm living in the first place.

CHAPTER FOURTEEN

BLAKE

WELL, BUTTER MY BISCUIT, AS GRANDDAD WOULD SAY: AC-
tual progress has been made on the beach house during my week
at the Rooneys' casita. The ugly box light on the kitchen ceiling
has been removed, and in its place are sleek LED can lights.
That was all Henry's doing, of course. Kat's contributions remain in the superficial realm, but I'm trying to practice gratitude. Her followers have chosen paint for the walls and cabinets
in the kitchen and beyond, and I have to admit that the colors
are pretty.

I also have to admit that I *may* have voted in several of the
polls. Trying to sway them a little, because I didn't want the living room to be painted avocado green. Let's just pray that Kat
doesn't analyze the list of respondents too closely, because I don't
need her to know I was participating in her silly games.

But I do appreciate that she went to the paint store and bought
the paint rather than leaving me a list and assuming I'd take care
of it. It was nice to walk in and see the cans lined up, labeled in
Kat's swirly handwriting. *Kitchen/dining/living room walls; Kitchen
cabinets; 1st floor bathroom walls.*

I'm walking into Lowe's right now to pick out new baseboards for the main level. I removed the old ones—little two-inch strips, warped and unsightly—in preparation for sanding the floor, and I want to replace them with something more substantial.

On my way into the store, I take out my phone and send Kat a text, extending an olive branch:

Thanks for getting the paint

I'm oddly nervous while waiting for her reply, which comes a few seconds later.

You're welcome

I stare at the words for a few moments, then pocket my phone, satisfied. We can be civil to each other. It's a little thing, but it feels like a big deal. Maybe because she never responded to my letters after camp; even though that was a long time ago, deep down, I'm still that sad little twelve-year-old, waiting every day for the mail to come, never receiving anything.

I head to the area of the store where the baseboards and trim are located, and when an employee walks by, I stop him.

"Excuse me," I say. His name badge says KAVIN, which is weird. "I have a question. I'm planning to use a miter saw to cut my baseboards, but do you recommend coping as well?"

I read a home reno blog yesterday that suggested using a coping saw to back-cut the corners for a cleaner line on the inside corners.

Kavin is short, just an inch taller than me, and he has curly hair that reminds me of ramen noodles. He looks me up and down, his lip curled in an expression halfway between a smile and a sneer. A smear, if you will.

"Who's helping you?" he says, looking around. "Your husband? Boyfriend?"

My face heats with indignation. I hate being underestimated. Henry lent me his miter saw and I am perfectly capable of using it, thank you very much. "I'm doing it myself. And I just need to know a little about coping—"

"You sure you can handle that? That's not exactly a *beginner-level* cut." He says it like I'm a kindergartner trying to learn calculus.

Flames of anger lick the sides of my face, and I force myself to speak evenly.

"I'm not a beginner," I say, biting off my words. Granddad taught me to use a miter saw when I was eleven years old. The coping is new to me, but I can figure it out with a little help.

Kavin rolls his eyes. "You want the numbers of some finish carpenters in the area? We have a list at the front desk. Probably better to leave something like that to the pros, sweetie."

And then he's gone and I'm seething, with no desire to spend money at this place.

I'M STILL MAD when I get back to the beach house. Just because I'm a small blond woman doesn't mean I'm incapable of making a few simple cuts with a saw. It's ridiculous and sexist and so dismissive.

Anger churns in my chest like shark-infested waters, and when my gaze lands on the sledgehammer Henry dropped off a couple of days ago, I know exactly how I'm going to channel this feeling.

I'm taking the wall down, baby.

Grabbing the sledgehammer, I walk over to the wall between the kitchen and living room. I like the weight of the hammer in my hands, solid and heavy, and I swing it like I swung a bat when

I played softball back in middle school. With a grunt, I slam it into the wall.

There's a satisfying crunch as the sledgehammer goes through the wall, sending dust and debris flying. Only then do I realize that I'm not wearing any safety gear—I'm in my cutoff shorts and a tank top, with nothing protecting my eyes. I'm too revved up to go upstairs and change clothes, but I do grab a pair of safety goggles and jam them on my face.

Then I swing the sledgehammer again. "This is for you, *Kavin*, with your stupid noodle hair and your stupid sneering smile." *Slam.*

This hit is even more satisfying than the last, and I swing again, harder.

"And this is for not helping me with the baseboards." *Slam.*

I keep going, settling into a rhythm. Every time I hit the wall, chunks of plaster fly off, hitting the exposed skin on my legs and shoulders. It stings, but I don't care. I am a powerful woman. A wrecking ball of destruction. Nothing can stop me now.

In a flash, my father's face fills my mind, and I'm filled with a rage so hot and intense it might boil over.

"This is for making my mother your weekend side piece," I say, and slam the sledgehammer into the wall. This time I hit a stud, and the wood crunching beneath my blow sends a shock wave through my body. It's painful, but that only makes me swing harder.

"This is for not coming to her funeral," I say, louder. Another slam, more flying pieces of wood and plaster.

"For never calling me after she died." *Slam.* "For never writing me." *Slam.* "For never once reaching out. For ignoring me because it was easier for you. For pretending like I don't even fucking exist."

I'm breathing heavily, and hot tears fill my eyes. Angrily, I swipe under the goggles. No time for weakness.

"This is for recognizing me at camp and doing nothing about it," I shout, slamming again and again and again, letting the wall disintegrate around me. "For looking right at me, saying my name, then getting in the car and driving away. For choosing Kat over me. For choosing *your* comfort over mine, again and again and *again*."

With all my strength I swing that sledgehammer into the wall, but when I pull it back, the hammer gets stuck on a chunk of plaster before coming free. This sends me off-balance and I fall backward, my butt hitting the wood floor and the sledgehammer falling next to me with a solid *thump*.

"You okay?"

I whip my head around to see Noah standing in the doorway.

I scramble to my feet, my cheeks hot with embarrassment. "I'm fine. Just . . . doing a little demo."

Today, Noah is wearing a trucker hat and aviators that look like he bought them at a gas station. Luckily, the beard hasn't returned to its previously feral state.

Noah takes off his sunglasses. A wrinkle of concern forms between his eyebrows. "You're sure you're okay?"

Horrified, I realize that my eyes are probably red from crying, my cheeks smeared with dust and tears. I clear my throat and turn away from him.

"How long were you standing there?" I ask, praying he didn't hear my emotional outburst.

He hesitates. "Um. I walked in when you fell."

He's lying, but I appreciate the effort. Luckily for me, the dog bounds down the stairs and runs to Noah, his tail wagging. This gives me a moment to collect myself, swiping under my eyes for any rogue tears before I turn back around.

"Hey there, little Cheeto puff," Noah says as he scratches the dog's ears. "Puff daddy. Puff the magic dragon."

He sings the last line, and I can't help smiling, even though I still feel awkward. And not only because of what Noah just witnessed.

Things have been weird since our kiss on the beach the other day. I don't know how to act around him, so I've mostly avoided him. Childish, I know, but it's a bad habit of mine. Allowing people to get too close makes me uncomfortable.

"So . . . what brought that on?" Noah asks, nodding at the wall.

"The guy at the lumber store treated me like an idiot," I say, shrugging. "His name was Kavin and he kept insinuating that I didn't know what I was doing. It made me mad."

His eyebrows shoot up. "Remind me not to piss you off."

"Har har," I say, which is not my wittiest comeback. But I'm still feeling a little vulnerable, emotionally. "What brings you by today? You missed the dog?"

"I did, yeah," he says. "But I mostly wanted to talk to you. Can we sit somewhere?"

My muscles tighten; that sounds ominous. "Sure. Let's go outside on the deck."

We head out, and I'm happy to notice the deck doesn't wobble beneath our weight, thanks to Henry's work last week, reinforcing the support structure. It still needs to be sanded down and stained, but at least it won't collapse under us.

"What's up?" I ask as we sit, several feet apart.

The dog comes between us and lays his head on Noah's lap. He scratches the dog's ears before starting to speak.

"You've been avoiding me," he says, matter-of-fact. "Which is fine—you're not obligated to go out with me again or even to talk to me. But maybe you could let me know what's going on in your head so I can respond accordingly."

I exhale. I've never been great at communicating. Plus, I have overall trust issues with men—not a huge surprise, given what my dad did. My emotions have become increasingly raw the longer I stay here in Destin, as evidenced by my rage-filled attack on the wall moments ago. It's easier to keep my distance, to avoid catching any pesky feelings for him.

"I'm really sorry," I say.

Noah slides me a grin. "You didn't crush my soul or anything; it's just weird being ignored and I wanted to make sure there wasn't anything else going on. That's it."

I bite my lip, trying to decide how much to tell him. How much of myself to expose. "Okay, you're right. I've been avoiding you because my focus is on getting this renovation done. I don't want to get distracted."

It's not the entire truth, but it's not a lie, either.

"Fair enough," he says, nodding. "Thanks for telling me."

He seems like he's about to stand up and leave, and I suddenly want him to stay, so on impulse I reach out and grab his forearm. "I'm not great at opening up to people, just so you know. Nothing to do with you, specifically."

Martina said once that she thinks I leave people before they have a chance to leave me. This is why I rarely go out with anyone more than once or twice. She calls it *preemptive abandonment*, which makes me roll my eyes. But she's not wrong.

"I guess I'm glad it's not *specifically* me," Noah says, an amused smile on his face. "Why aren't you great at opening up to people?"

I blink, surprised; I feel like that should be obvious. Also: Who is this emotionally intelligent man, asking thoughtful questions and being all mature and communicative? It's weird.

"Well," I say, "I told you my dad disappeared from my life after my mom died. I guess I have abandonment issues or whatever."

"Which you took out on that poor wall in there," he says, angling his head back toward the house.

"I *knew* you heard all of that." I cover my face with my hands. "Ugh, so embarrassing."

"Why are you embarrassed? From where I'm sitting, your dad is the one who should've been embarrassed. He was the asshole in the situation, not you."

"I know, I know. It's just that I've become pretty good at keeping my feelings about him locked away, but being here is forcing me to deal with all of it and I *hate* feeling all these *emotions.*"

"Yeah, emotions suck," he says, smiling.

"They do! They're so inconvenient!" My eyes fill with tears, and I wipe them away with one hand.

He laughs, not unkindly, and knocks his shoulder into mine. "You're doing a good job with the house, you know. I'm impressed."

That makes me smile. "Thanks. The dude at the store shook my confidence a little."

"Don't let the Kavins of the world rattle you, Blake O'Neill," he says, nodding sagely.

"His hair looked like ramen noodles. You know, like 1990s Justin Timberlake?"

"It may shock you to hear that I haven't tracked Justin Timberlake's hairstyles over the past several decades." He stands and takes my hands, then hauls me to my feet. "What can I help you with tonight?"

I think about the giant pile of broken wall debris in the kitchen. "You want to help me clean up the mess I made?"

"Sure."

I hesitate. Now that we have that awkward conversation out of the way, I don't want him to leave. "And maybe after that you could hang out for a little while. Guess what I found in the master bedroom closet."

He strokes the stubble on his chin, thinking. "A box of old toupees?"

"Ew. No."

"A dildo from the 1970s?"

"Gross, Noah. They were my *grandparents*." It's the first time I've called them that out loud. The word feels stiff, like putting on a pair of jeans for the first time. But it fits. It feels right. "No, there are hundreds of old VHS tapes in there. It's like a treasure trove. Want to watch a movie after we clean up? I have popcorn and four different kinds of Haribo gummies." I tick them off on my fingers: "Frogs, Happy Cola, Gold Bears, and Peaches."

"Dibs on the Peaches," he says immediately.

My chest warms. "Deal."

IT TAKES TWO hours to clean up the demolition mess, then I pop a frozen pizza in the oven while I take a quick shower and change into a T-shirt and my clean pair of cutoffs. We eat the pizza standing up in the kitchen, then make popcorn. It's then I realize my mistake: the only TV that's hooked to a VCR is in the master bedroom, so the only place for us to sit is on the bed. I grab extra pillows from my bedroom so we can each prop ourselves up, plus two throw blankets.

We're just two friends who kissed once, sitting on a fifty-year-old mattress that squeaks every time one of us moves, sharing a bowl of popcorn and various gummies while watching a movie. No big deal.

We decided on the original *Jurassic Park* because neither of us has seen it since we were kids. The movie holds up surprisingly well and within a few minutes I'm wrapped up in the story. Jeff Goldblum is sexy and quirky, Laura Dern is a badass who knows a lot about ancient plants, and Sam Neill is a freaking icon as he saves the two kids from being eaten by the T. rex.

Still, I'm hyperaware of the fact that Noah is sitting next to me on a bed. In the dark. Only inches away. I can hear him breathing, can hear his soft chuckles when I flinch at the scary parts. Somehow, I manage to stay relatively chill until the scene in the kitchen at the end, when the velociraptors are tracking the kids. My muscles are so tense I'm shaking, hugging my knees to my chest.

Then the raptor lunges and we both let out identical shrieks of terror. In a flash, Noah pulls me against him.

"This scene is fucking *scary*," Noah says, gasping.

I'm laughing so hard there are tears in my eyes. "I think my heart stopped beating for a second."

His arm is still around me, and I realize that I have no desire to move. I relax against his chest and we finish the movie like that, the dog curled at our feet.

By the time the helicopter lifts off the island to the stirring strains of John Williams's score, I reluctantly start to pull away.

Noah's arm tightens around me. "You're fine where you are," he says in a low voice. I feel it against my skin like a vibration.

I tilt my head to look up at him. His blue eyes glint in the darkness. He is most definitely giving me the lip look.

Oh, what the hell. It's not going to hurt anything if I allow myself to have a little fun. Why do I have to decide between getting my to-do list checked off and enjoying myself? Why does it have to be either/or? Why can't it be *and*?

With that thought, I roll over until I'm pressed flush against his side, my top leg looped over his. Still making eye contact, I say, "How about this?"

His breathing goes shallow, his eyes dark and focused. "That's good. But this would be better."

With his hands on my hips, he shifts me so I'm right on top of him, my chest on his chest, my thighs on his thighs. My body goes tingly and hot. We just moved into dangerous territory.

"What about this?" I whisper, and rock my pelvis against him.

He lets out a sharp exhale. There is definitely something stirring in his pants, and my body responds with another rush of heat.

"That's good. Very good." His voice is strained. "But this would be even better."

He leans toward me and I'm right there with him, ready to feel his lips on mine again. This kiss is hungrier than the one on the beach, and when his tongue meets mine a soft groan escapes my mouth.

We kiss in that position for what feels like an eternity, his hands on my hips, holding me in place, the intensity growing between us until I think I might die if he doesn't touch my skin. Finally, his hands slide under my shirt to my rib cage, his fingers warm and greedy. He stops before he gets to my bra, though, and I bite at his lower lip, frustrated. Then I bring my knees up so I'm straddling him. Just to make my intentions clear.

"Jesus, Blake," he gasps, then pulls away slightly. "This might be a stupid question, but you're good with this, right? After what you said earlier, I want to—"

In response, I grind against him. "I'm more than good with this."

"Let the record show," he says, his voice shaky, "that the lady is in favor of proceeding. All in favor, say aye."

"Aye," I whisper, and then he's kissing me again, fierce and breathless. His body is lean and strong, and I run my hands up his arms to his shoulders, down his torso, then slide my hands under his shirt to his chest. "Can this come off?" I say, tugging at his shirt.

"You've been wanting to do that since the day you first saw me," he says, smirking.

"Yeah, yeah, I was ogling you. Now take it off."

He laughs, and then his voice dips lower. "You have no idea what I've been thinking about every time I see you in these little cutoff shorts. Dirty, dirty thoughts. You would blush if you knew."

"Tell me." My hands are fisted in his shirt, ready to yank it over his head, but I pull back so I can see his face.

His cheeks are ruddy, his hair disheveled. "First off, I've been wanting to do this." His hands slide into my shorts until he's cupping my butt. I suck in a breath as his fingers slip under the hem of my underwear. "And then I want to—"

There's a popping sound outside and the dog leaps from his spot at the foot of the bed, barking hysterically.

We spring apart. "What's wrong?" I say to the dog.

Then I hear another scattering of pops. It's fireworks—the ones people set off in their driveways. The dog yelps again, whimpering.

"Seriously, people?" I mumble, irritated. The Fourth of July is a week away. I pull the dog toward me. He's trembling with fear, and I pat him gently.

Stupid people, scaring my dog.

I glance back at Noah; he's flopped against the bed, breathing heavily. His hair is messy, his shirt twisted to the side, and he has a stunned look on his face.

I can't help laughing. "You look like a horny teenager who was getting busy behind the bleachers and got interrupted by the principal."

He puffs out his cheeks, then exhales slowly. "That's pretty much how I feel." He blinks a few times and runs his hands through his hair, then sits up and leans toward the dog. "How's my P. Diddy? You okay, little guy?"

The dog inches toward Noah until he's snuggled between us. Noah runs his big hands through the dog's soft fur, slow and soothing, until he stops trembling.

"All right," Noah says quietly, then looks at me. "I'm going out of town for a while. Leaving early tomorrow morning."

I nod, remembering he said he'd be gone when the Rooneys came for the Fourth. "We better call it a night, then."

Probably for the best.

CHAPTER FIFTEEN

KAT

THE CALENDAR IS NOT WORKING IN MY FAVOR THIS WEEK.
I'm supposed to be driving back to Atlanta tomorrow—two
days before the Fourth of July, which happens to be one of my
favorite times of the year in Destin.

I have so many wonderful memories of the holiday weekend
here—golf cart parades down Old 98, my grandma's famous
Jell-O salad, watching fireworks on the beach. I hate to miss it
all, especially knowing there's a chance—albeit a very small one—
that this might be the last summer the beach house will be in the
Steiner family.

It wouldn't be so bad if I wasn't already down here, but since
I am, I don't want to leave. If Blake had half a heart, she'd invite
me to stay for the holiday. It's not like I'd be putting her out—
she could just stay at the Rooneys' casita a few more days.

I sigh, wishing there was a way I could tell her that I want to
stay without telling her I want to stay. We've been texting a bit
about house stuff, but nothing beyond that. But I do know she's
following me on Instagram.

I noticed her name the other day when I was scrolling through the votes for the shade of blue we're going to use for the tiled backsplash in the kitchen.

Her handle is just her name and birthday—not very original, although neither is her content. There's no rhyme or reason to her grid; she's got unfiltered pictures of food, photos of herself without a drop of makeup on, and a few scenic shots around Destin. I'm pretty sure she's been going around town with some guy.

Not that I was snooping. When I looked at her feed, I noticed a picture of the food trucks in Seaside, and I scrolled to see where else she went—the bookstore and the beach. At sunset, the most romantic and photogenic time of day. In the corner of her picture of the sun going down, you can see a man's legs stretched out in the sand beside her, feet crossed at the ankles.

The composition would've been better if she'd cropped him out, but maybe she included him on purpose, a subtle way to let the world know she's getting laid.

That gives me an idea—since I know she's following me, I can post something about how much the holiday down here means to me, and when she sees it, she'll feel guilty and let me stay.

I'm not supposed to post until tomorrow morning, but this is worth going off-grid. I pull a chair over to the porch railing and rest my feet on the ledge. My signature OPI Cajun Shrimp polish looks perfect against the backdrop of the beach.

I take a photo and put my preset filter on it, then post it with a subtle SOS to Blake.

Kicking up my feet and taking in this gorge view. There is seriously no better place to #KatWalk than the white-sand beaches of Destin, Florida. Growing up, I used to spend every Fourth of July here with the fam. I'm supposed to be heading back to Atlanta on Sunday, but part of me wishes I could stay and watch the fireworks over the beach.

What do you think, pretty people? Should I stay or should I go?

Three hours after I posted my plea, there are five thousand hearts and more than eleven thousand accounts reached, but I can't tell if Blake was one of them. With literally no other choice, I pull up my text thread with Blake.

Kat: Hey! Any chance I can stay at the house for a few more days? Just until after the Fourth?

If she says no, it doesn't mean I have to go back to Atlanta. I could get a room at the Henderson—except I'm sure the rates will be astronomical on a holiday weekend—and I want to stay at *my* house. This is where all my memories are. It's where I feel close to my dad.

I look down at my phone, where Blake's three dots appear momentarily before disappearing. They do that another two times before a text finally pops up.

Blake: Fine with me, but I'll be there, too

"Ugh." I give the phone a dirty look. I don't get why it matters if she stays here or at the casita. She's probably just being difficult because she knows I want to be here.

Blake said herself she doesn't care about the house—and it's not like she has any special memories here she's trying to hold on to—but beggars can't be choosers, so I text her back.

Kat: okay

Blake replies with a thumbs-up emoji. I like having the last word, so I react to her thumbs-up with a thumbs-up of my own.

With that settled, I feel better. It might even be good for me to be here while Blake is doing work on the house. If I get creative with angles, I might be able to pass off pictures of her manual laboring like it's me, although her unmanicured hands would be a dead giveaway.

It's not like I *need* the photos—I've got a decent amount of content samples for the Worthington application, but what I still need is an answer to "what's your why?"

In the beginning, my brand was all about treating life like a runway—looking good, feeling good, and letting the world see it. But after the last few months, I feel like there has to be more to me than that. Because it definitely won't be enough to stand out from all the other applicants.

And I don't just want that contract. I have to have it if there's any hope of keeping the beach house.

THE DAY BEFORE the Fourth, I'm getting some much-needed sun on the back deck and reading the latest Rachel Worthington book club pick. I've got a post planned for it—and I'm hoping my followers won't point out that this is the first book I've ever shared in my feed.

Blake is inside, banging around doing something constructive. For a quiet person, she makes an awful lot of noise.

It hasn't been as bad as I thought, being here together. We mostly stay out of each other's way—and when we are in the same room, either she's busy tearing something apart or putting

THE BEACH TRAP

something back together, or she has her nose buried in her phone.

I assume she's texting Hairy Legs from her Seaside photo. I'm curious about why her mystery man hasn't been over to the house, but she doesn't know I know about him, so it's not like I can just ask.

"Oof!"

The noise catches me by surprise, and I look up to see Blake through the back window. She's standing on something, a stool or a chair—we got new cerulean-blue ones—and she's got one of the kitchen cabinets in her hands.

It looks like she's struggling, and my LaCroix is almost empty anyway, so I head back inside.

"Need some help?" I ask.

"I've got it," Blake snaps, even though from the looks of things, she most definitely does not "got it." Her face is bright red; wisps of her blond hair are stuck to her sweaty forehead and clinging to her safety goggles. She's got one foot on a stool and another on the kitchen counter as she's trying to hold the freshly painted door at the right angle to drill it to the hinge.

"Let me," I say, helping anyway. I refuse to let her turn me into the bad guy when I'm perfectly capable of contributing.

"Hold it a little higher and to the left," she says.

Someone got bossy over the last two decades.

But she's the one holding the tool, so I comply and stand still while she drills, closing my eyes tight to protect them from the specks of dust. I should get myself a pair of safety goggles like Blake—but cuter, obviously.

It's too bad no one's here to snap a picture of us. It would be Worthington gold. Maybe we can re-create the moment when Henry and Sunny are here tomorrow. I'd have to do an outfit change—I'm going to be wearing an adorable jumpsuit with blue and white stripes and a red belt tomorrow. It's the perfect outfit for a casual beach bash, but not right for home construction, no matter how light.

"So," I say, at the same time she says, "Mind holding this one for me, too?"

"Of course not," I say, reaching for the cabinet door. "Like this?"

"A little to the left," she says, and I realize this might be the first conversation we've had without one of us—usually me—yelling at the other. It's not awful. Maybe we can have a temporary cease-fire for the holiday.

"Thanks," she says after she finishes.

"I'm decent at holding things," I tell her, "but that's about where my handiness ends."

Blake laughs, a series of three quick chuckles that takes me back to the two of us sitting on the bottom bunk talking about the boys we wanted to give us the "lip look."

The ice between us thaws the tiniest bit, and I decide to keep it going. "Got any plans for the Fourth?"

Blake shakes her head, and when her blond hair falls in front of her face, she doesn't brush it away, hiding from the world. From me. I wonder if she knows that she does that, or if it's a mindless tic.

Before I can stop myself, I ask, "You aren't doing something with the guy you're seeing?"

Her head pops up, sending her hair flying back. "What are you talking about?"

I can't exactly tell her I was nosing around her Instagram account, so I say the first plausible thing that comes to mind.

"Henry mentioned you're seeing someone," I say, gambling on the fact that (A) Blake confided in Henry about her love life and (B) she doesn't know Henry well enough to know the man doesn't have a gossiping bone in his body.

If he did know, he wouldn't have told me—he tries to change the subject every time I bring Blake up, except for when he tells me that I'd like her if I gave her a chance.

But that's the problem—I *did* like her. At one point, I even loved her in that innocent twelve-year-old way.

"He's out of town," Blake says, bringing me back to the moment. Her voice sounds sad, and for a brief moment I see a crack in her hard exterior.

For a reason I can't explain—whether it's the sentimentality of the holiday, the memory of the friendship we used to have, or Henry's influence—I say, "You're welcome to join us, if you want."

Blake's eyes widen, like she's as surprised to receive my invitation as I was to give it.

"Henry and Sunny are coming over," I tell her. "Nothing big, we're just going to barbecue—well, Henry is going to barbecue—and we're going to watch fireworks on the beach."

"That sounds nice. Thank you."

I smile, and a silence that's almost comfortable settles between us. I'm relieved when her phone buzzes. Her sad eyes light up, and I assume it's a text from Hairy Legs. The mystery guy she apparently told Henry about, not me.

CHAPTER SIXTEEN

BLAKE

THIS IS THE FIRST TIME IN FIFTEEN YEARS I'VE SLEPT UNDER the same roof as Kat Steiner, and it's . . . strange. When she asked if she could stay through the Fourth, I was irritated—she's the one who was so averse to being around me that she found me a job working as a literal servant—but I also felt like I couldn't say no. I realize this beach house has more emotional meaning to her than to me. I'm guessing she spent many Independence Days here with her family, and since this is her first summer without her father, I feel bad for her.

I'm going to try to not let that become a habit.

We've mostly stayed out of each other's way. I'm working through my long list of renovation projects, and she's taking selfies like it's her job. Which I guess it is. But who would want that job? Exposing yourself to the world isn't my idea of a worthwhile occupation.

Right now, she's outside on the deck, filming "a tutorial about patriotic holiday makeup looks," as she told me this morning while I tried to keep a straight face. She's got a whole palette of blue eye shadows and a dozen shades of red lipstick. I'm inside, using a crowbar to pull off the hideous kitchen backsplash while the dog watches with rapt attention. My phone vibrates in my pocket, and I pause to pull it out.

It's a text from Noah: Who's the best breakfast cereal mascot?

And just like that, even though I'm tired and it's been a long day, a smile blossoms on my face. I haven't seen him since the night we made out like horny teenagers on my long-lost grandparents' ancient mattress, but he's been texting me multiple times a day with these random questions that make me laugh. He still hasn't told me where he's gone or why, so I'm not sure what the constant texting means. But I like it.

Blake: Most people would say Tony the Tiger, but his overconfidence has always rubbed me wrong

Noah: So true. Is Frosted Flakes really GRRRRRRREAT or do we just think that because he's brainwashed us?

Blake: I'm gonna go with Captain Crunch. Gotta respect that he has an actual military rank.

Noah: Fun fact, it's an honorary title. Cap'n not Captain. He's not even in the Navy.

Blake: What?? I feel so deceived.

Noah: I know. So many lies. Btw, Honey Smacks has the best mascot.

I have to google Honey Smacks, and when I see its mascot, I shake my head in disappointment.

Blake: The weird green frog?

Noah: Don't be mean. His name is the Dig'em Frog and he's a little frog with a big voice.

I chuckle as I type a response.

Blake: Okay, I have a question for you. Ready?

Noah: Born ready

Blake: How many five-year-olds could you defeat in hand-to-hand combat? No weapons of any kind.

His three dots are present for a while; hopefully this means he's taking the question seriously. I'll be disappointed if he says something boring like "I would never fight children" or "Do you need a psychiatrist?"

Noah: I'm long-limbed, which would be to my advantage. I could kick several in the face before they got within six feet of me, then I could grab a couple others and toss them into the rest. However, if there was a veritable horde some could sneak up on me from behind. So I'd say I could take 11 of them easily. 12-17 would be a challenge and I'd end up bruised and battered. More than 18 and I'd be a goner.

I'm cracking up, and Kat looks through the open deck door. "What?" she asks. I can't tell if she's genuinely curious or if she thinks I'm laughing at her blue eyeshadow and red lipstick—which does look a little over-the-top.

"Nothing," I say, and try to make it look like I'm concentrating on my task.

Kat shrugs and goes back to posing. I stop and watch her for a minute; I have to admit, it's interesting to see the process and not just the final product she posts on Instagram, all cropped and filtered.

She's got a whole setup out there, a tripod, a ring light, and a remote she uses to take the photos—it's complicated. Right now, she's struggling to keep everything together because there's a breeze. The lipstick tubes keep rolling, and the American flag she's holding in one hand keeps blowing away.

My conscience pricks: *You should offer to help.* I don't want to. My to-do list is endless, but she did help me with the cabinet doors yesterday.

Almost against my will, I call out, "Want some help?"

She looks up, her glossy red lips forming a surprised O. Have I really been that much of a bitch to her that she's shocked by my offer? I feel a little bad.

"Um, sure," she says. "Want to hold the other end of the flag?"

I go outside and take one end of the flag while she snaps a few pictures, keeping my hands out of the shot.

Kat looks glamorous, as usual, wearing a gauzy see-through cover-up over a blue-and-white-striped bikini. Her nails are painted an orangey red, her skin so poreless it looks airbrushed. I feel sweaty and disheveled next to her, like my first day of high school when I walked into class wearing overalls and Granddad's company T-shirt when all the other girls wore makeup and new outfits from the mall.

"Did you always spend the Fourth here as a kid?" I ask, trying to make conversation.

Kat nods, moving the flag a millimeter to the right. "Always. What did you do on the Fourth when you were growing up?"

"My granddad usually grilled hamburgers, then we'd drive to the city park to watch fireworks. Grandma would make caramel corn and bring it in a paper sack, and we'd lie on our backs on an old denim quilt and look up at the sky."

"That sounds nice," Kat says, giving me a brief smile.

"It was."

And it's true. I have lovely memories of this holiday with my grandparents, but the way I answered her question feels like I erased all the years before I went to live with them. Before my mom died.

One summer in particular sticks out in my mind—the summer I turned nine, the last summer we had together. She'd braided my hair with red, white, and blue ribbons, and we went to our neighborhood parade. I have a vivid memory of sitting on the curb, kicking my feet in my jelly sandals. I remember my mom's curly blond hair in a high ponytail, her red halter top, her oversize sunglasses. And I remember looking around at all the families there at the parade, all the kids with their moms *and* dads, and wondering why my father wasn't there.

My mom always told me he had to travel a lot for work, and I was young enough that I believed it. Young enough that I didn't question why he only kept a few changes of clothes in my mom's closet, why he wasn't always around for my birthday, why he rarely came to my school events.

But all of a sudden, my mom's explanations didn't make sense.

I turned to my mom—she was sitting with friends, talking

and laughing—and said, "Why is Daddy gone for work if it's a holiday?"

My mom's smile froze. Her friends went silent and glanced away. I knew I'd said something I shouldn't have, but I didn't understand why.

"He—he just can't be here right now, sweetie," my mom said.

That was the first time I knew there was something embarrassing about my family, something so wrong we couldn't even talk about it. And of course, I had to wonder: Maybe there was something wrong with *me*?

It's painful to realize, now, that he was here in Destin with his real family. Probably not even thinking about the fact that his other daughter was sitting alone on a hot street curb, watching the other kids with their dads, wondering if it was her fault that he wasn't around more.

My eyes sting and I stand quickly.

"Are you good now?" I say to Kat. "I—I need to get back to what I'm doing."

Kat looks startled but nods. "Yeah, I'm good. Thanks for your help."

I rush back into the house before she can see that my eyes are watering.

I GIVE KAT a wide berth after that. She's prepping for an epic, color-coordinated, red-white-and-blue-themed dinner for tomorrow, and none of that is appealing to me. Of course, neither is what I'm currently doing: removing wallpaper in the upstairs bathroom, using a steamer to loosen the paste so I can peel it off. I want to finish before I go to bed, but at my current rate, that'll be past midnight.

Halfway through the first wall, I get a text from Noah: What are you up to?

Setting down the steamer, I start to reply that I've been stripping wallpaper for the past hour. Then I pause, my thumbs hovering over the keyboard. Noah's been walking the line between friendly and flirty with his texts the past few days. Maybe I should meet him halfway.

I type one word and hit send before I can rethink it.

Blake: Stripping

His three dots appear and disappear, like he's trying to figure out how to respond. My heart rate quickens. Then finally—

Noah: Um

Noah: Please be serious

Laughing, I type my reply: Stripping WALLPAPER, Noah. Get your mind out of the gutter.

Noah: It's your fault my mind went there, so now you have to face the consequences

Noah: So . . . what are you wearing?

I stare at the question on the screen and decide to play along.

Blake: You want to see?

Noah: Absolutely I do

I glance in the mirror. I'm wearing a T-shirt I bought at Goodwill that features a purple wolf howling at a glittery moon. My face is shiny with sweat, little strands of hair stuck to my forehead. No way in hell I'm sending him a picture of that.

Instead, I take a video as I remove a strip of wallpaper—showing only my hand grasping the edge, pulling with a slow, sensuous flick of the wrist—and send it.

Noah: Damn, that looks satisfying

Blake: Oh yeah. So long and thick.

I may have crossed a line. When I catch another glimpse of myself in the mirror, my cheeks are so red they look like they've been slapped.

Quickly, I type: The wallpaper, I mean

Then I set my phone on the bathroom counter out of reach and continue steaming the opposite wall. *Focus*, I tell myself. I am definitely not thinking about Noah. Nor am I wondering if he's thinking about me.

I'm such a liar. The instant my phone pings again, I launch across the room and grab it, breathless as I read his response.

Noah: Is it nice and wet?

I don't know whether to burst out laughing or splash water on my face. Noah just pushed right on past flirty into dirty. Putting a hand to my forehead, I take a deep breath and ponder my response. But then another text comes in.

Noah: The wallpaper, I mean

Noah: When you strip it

I stifle a laugh. For heaven's sakes. I am getting turned on, standing alone in a half-demolished bathroom, texting about wall-paper removal. I wonder if he's in bed—shirtless, maybe even naked? Does Noah Jameson sleep naked? Has he been thinking about me, in bed, while he is naked? My Lord.

Grinning and flushing, I type a reply.

Blake: What are you doing right now?

Noah: You want to see?

Blake: Absolutely I do

He sends me a picture of a deep-dish pizza, the top of which is entirely covered by a massive sausage patty.

Noah: Trying to figure out how much I can eat without bringing on a heart attack

My laugh dies in my throat as I study the picture. Next to the pizza are a bottle of beer and a glass of white wine. He can't be on a date, can he? It'd be shitty of him to text me while he's out with someone else, but then again, I don't know him that well. He could be that kind of person. My stomach goes sour.

Is this why he's been so evasive about his past, and about this trip he's on? Because he's got a girlfriend—or God forbid, a wife—somewhere else? Biting my lip, I shake my head. Just because my father did that doesn't mean it's standard practice for all men.

My granddad was loyal and faithful to my grandma for more than sixty years. They were high school sweethearts. They had coordinating shirts, his with the words "She's my sweet potato" and hers with the words "Yes, I yam!" He took care of her selflessly for the last months of her life, barely leaving her side. I know that kind of love exists; it's what I want someday.

Shaking my head, I type a response.

Blake: Have fun at dinner with your friend. Gotta go.

My response is abrupt and a little mean, but that picture sucked all the air out of me. I feel like a deflated balloon, limp and wrinkly, hanging from a string the morning after a party.

Noah: No offense to my college roommate and his husband, but you're more fun

A picture arrives. It's of Noah at the restaurant, sitting across from two men his age, a white guy with sandy blond hair in a ponytail and an Asian guy wearing a Cubs hat. Noah's holding the beer, Ponytail is holding the glass of wine, and Cubs Fan has a cocktail.

Noah: William and Jon say hi, btw. I think they're sick of hearing me talk about you.

My internal balloon inflates, my chest expanding as a smile returns to my face. Noah has been talking about me to his friends? Maybe I've been on his mind as much as he's been on mine, all day long, even in the middle of other activities. Somehow, that's even better than if he were texting me while he's in bed.

Smiling wide, I reply.

Tell them hi from me. And if you do have a heart attack, ask them to please resuscitate you. You and I have unfinished business.

CHAPTER SEVENTEEN

KAT

THE BIGGEST DIFFERENCE BETWEEN THIS FOURTH OF JULY and all the ones in my memory is that there's no one here to do all the prep work. Instead of spending all day at the beach, I spend the day in the kitchen—which is looking pretty good with the freshly painted Vanilla Milkshake white cabinets. The rest of the house is still a disaster, but this room gives me hope.

Dinner doesn't need that much prep, but I'm proud of how on-brand the menu is. I'm making potato salad with red, white, and purple potatoes that look kind of blue, caprese salads with tomato, onion, and blue cheese, my grandma's famous Jell-O salad, and the angel food cake with Cool Whip, strawberries, and blueberries that my dad loved, and Henry's going to grill burgers.

I take one break when the golf cart parade goes by—it's cute in a sentimental way, but not as exciting as I remember from when I was a kid. I head back inside before it's over so everything will be ready once Henry and Sunny arrive.

It feels more like a party as soon as they get here. Sunny looks adorable in a patriotic sundress, red with blue and white stars. And as a bonus, it perfectly complements my blue-and-white outfit with a splash of red. Henry even gives his okay for me to share a few shots of Sunny and me on my Instagram stories.

I'm not purposefully avoiding Blake in the pictures—but her cutoff jeans and gray T-shirt aren't exactly festive or 'Gramworthy. At least Henry wore a blue version of his standard plaid short-sleeve shirt for the occasion.

While he grills, Sunny bounces between Blake and me, talking endless circles about anything and everything.

"I love American food," she says. "The fruit on the cake is red and blue just like the flag! There aren't any white berries, but the frosting is white."

"That makes sense," Blake agrees, and Sunny lights up.

"Know why we had cheeseburgers instead of normal burgers?" Henry asks Sunny, as he sets the blue tray, full of burgers, on the red-and-white tablecloth.

"Did George Washington like them?" Sunny asks.

"Nope," Henry says. "Because the cheese is American."

Sunny scrunches her nose like she's trying to understand the joke.

"American cheese," Henry says, and Sunny erupts in giggles.

I lean back in my chair and watch Henry and his daughter banter back and forth. That girl brings out a playful side of her dad, and I have to admit, I like it.

"Whose turn is it to do the dishes?" Henry asks when we finish eating, resting his finger on his nose.

Sunny gasps and puts her finger on her nose as well. Blake and I exchange a look, clearly on the outside of this inside joke. Sunny giggles, looking back and forth between Blake and me.

Blake puts her finger on her nose, then looks at me and shrugs. I'm about to do the same when Sunny shouts, "Kat's the last one! She's doing dishes!"

"Hey," I protest. "You can't start a game if not everyone knows you're playing."

"Sorry," Henry says. "Rules are rules, but I'll help."

"We don't have to clean!" Sunny shouts, holding her hand up to give Blake a high five. "We can stay out here and play and have fun, because everything is fun if it's not cleaning!"

Blake flashes us a "wish me luck" smile as Sunny grabs her hand and drags her to the other side of the porch, leaving Henry and me alone.

"You can go play, if you want," I say, giving him an out.

"I'll have more fun with you," Henry says. A lock of his hair falls into his face, and I ignore the urge to tuck it back behind his ear.

"We better get moving if we want a good spot on the beach for fireworks," I say, awkwardly changing the subject before heading inside. Henry follows me, and even though I'm the one who lost, he offers to wash while I dry.

"Dinner was good," he says, his hands deep in the soapy water.

"Thanks," I say, even though it would have been just a bunch of sides without his cheeseburgers.

It's quiet as we wash and dry, and my skin buzzes with energy being close to him. My body apparently can't tell the difference between a guy who is dateable and one who should obviously remain a friend.

The sound of Sunny's laughter floats in from outside, and I suddenly feel like laughing, too. "Sunny's adorable," I tell Henry. "Did you pick out her dress?"

Henry shakes his head, then looks out the window, where Blake and Sunny have their heads bent together. "She hasn't let me pick out her clothes since she was three."

"A girl after my own heart."

Henry smiles and goes back to scrubbing a platter. "Things

seem to be going well with you and Blake," he says, handing me a clean dish.

I take it from him and start to dry. "Don't get any ideas; I'm just being nice because it's a holiday."

"Ahh," Henry says, as if he sees my logic. "That makes sense."

"It does?" I ask, surprised he accepted my answer so easily.

"No," Henry says. He hands me another dish and I try to ignore the spark I feel as our fingers brush in the exchange. We both stare at the dish in our hands for a moment until he clears his throat and continues. "But I learned a long time ago that sometimes, I just can't understand women."

This seems like the perfect opportunity to ask about his ex, but before I can get the words out, Sunny calls for him.

"Daddy, come look!"

He leans toward me, trying to get a better look out the window, and I inhale his sandalwood scent. It's not my favorite, but it smells good on him.

"Be right back," he says to me.

I figure the rest of the dishes can wait, so I follow him out to the deck. I don't want to miss whatever Sunny wants to show Henry.

Outside, Sunny is sitting on the table, her face tilted up toward Blake, who is standing before her.

I feel a pang of nostalgia as I realize Blake is painting a red, white, and blue design on Sunny's cheek. She's using what looks like professional face paint, unlike the Sharpies we used back at camp when we gave each other BEST FRIEND FOREVER tattoos.

We'd each drawn a butterfly on the other's wrist in a Sharpie I'd stolen from the arts and crafts cabin. The one Blake drew on my wrist was beautiful—the details on the wings were so intricate. I stuck my arm out of the shower every day that week so it wouldn't get wet. The one I drew on her wrist was decidedly less beautiful, but I've never been great with analog art.

"Do I look beautiful, Daddy?" Sunny asks, striking a pose.

"You're always beautiful," Henry says. "On the outside *and* the inside."

Sunny gives an exaggerated sigh. "You have to say that because you're my dad."

Before Henry can convince her otherwise, a singsong voice drifts up from the beach below us. "Helloooo! Anyone there?"

I walk over to the railing and look down, and sure enough, it's CoCo Rooney.

"Get your ass up here and give me a hug!" I shout.

My old friend squeals and runs up the stairs. She looks fabulous as always, in a white sundress that shows off her tan skin. Her brown hair is cut short with severe edges that make her cheekbones even more defined.

"What are you doing here?" I ask, throwing my arms around her. It feels good to hug someone who knows me, who knew my dad and how much he meant to me.

"The whole family is here for the week," CoCo says. "My parents are in rare form, so Brent and I had to get out for a while. This is Brent," she says, gesturing at the man beside her. He looks like a Ken doll brought to life, with thick sandy hair and an "I summer in the Hamptons" vibe.

"They're still devastated about Junior's little midlife crisis," CoCo says. "If that whole scandal with the manufacturers overseas wasn't enough, he went and called off his engagement, so now *all* their hopes and dreams are focused on me." CoCo laughs at her own predicament. "Don't get me wrong, I love attention, but a girl needs to breathe! Am I right?"

"You are so right," I agree. But my mind is stuck on one detail she hadn't mentioned the last time we talked. "So Junior's single?"

"Very single," CoCo says with a knowing smile. It's not a secret I had a giant crush on Junior Rooney from the time I was seven until I was a teenager. CoCo and I used to dream about my marrying Junior so we could be sisters—we'd definitely have more in common as sisters than Blake and I do.

I'm waiting for CoCo to tell me more about Junior, but her attention is focused elsewhere. I follow her gaze and realize she's looking behind me at Henry, studying him like he's eye candy.

"You remember Henry," I say, realizing I should make introductions. Henry nods and CoCo waves, her eyes growing wide as I imagine mine did when I first recognized him.

"Wow, somebody had a glow up," CoCo says, not bothering to drop her voice to a whisper.

I blush on Henry's behalf and keep talking. "That's his daughter, Sunny, and this is Blake."

"Blake?" CoCo says, tilting her head. "Blake as in our house-keeper?"

My jaw drops, but Blake stays cool and collected. I'm happy to see her hair is pushed back and not covering her face as she says, "Blake as in O'Neill."

CoCo gives Blake a dismissive smile before turning back to me, and I'm suddenly embarrassed—not about Blake, but about CoCo's behavior, treating Henry like a slab of meat and Blake like she's nothing more than hired help.

For the first time since I set this whole arrangement in motion, I wonder if it was the right thing.

"Well, we've got to get going; Brent got us a resi down at 790." CoCo turns and looks adoringly at her boyfriend, who seems to have the personality of a doormat. "Let's do drinks before I go back to Boston."

I nod and give CoCo another hug before she and Brent leave. It might be my imagination, but as soon as they disappear down the stairs, everyone seems to exhale a deep sigh of relief.

. . .

WATCHING FIREWORKS ON the beach is just as magical as I remember. Flashes of color explode in the sky and reflect off the water as they cascade down. Tonight is the closest I've felt to my old self since my dad died.

We found a perfect spot on the beach and laid out three blue-and-white-striped beach towels to sit on.

For a few minutes, I almost forgot I was supposed to be documenting the occasion for the Worthington application. It wasn't until I turned and looked at Henry sitting with Sunny, snug in his lap, her face lit up in wonder, that I reached for my phone.

I got some great pictures of them, and a few 'Grammable shots of the fireworks, including a boomerang I didn't even bother editing before sharing to my stories. I got one shot of Blake but didn't post it. There was something about her body language that made her look like she was lost in her own world. Beautiful but sad.

After the last firework goes off, Henry looks down at Sunny, who is snuggled against her dad's broad chest. "I'd better get this little firecracker to bed," he says.

Sunny yawns and says, "I'm not sleepy," before closing her eyes.

Henry laughs and somehow manages to stand up without waking Sunny.

"Do you need anything from the house?" I ask.

"Nah," Henry says. "I've got everything I need." He kisses Sunny's blond curls and my heart constricts. I miss my dad—and more than that, I realize I miss the dad he never was.

"I'll walk you to the car," I offer, not ready to go back inside quite yet.

Henry says goodbye to Blake, and we walk around the side of

the house, where, when I was nine, I tried selling passes to the public beach. I made a sign and everything: STEINER BEACH ACCESS, $3. Never mind that there was free beach access at almost every street that intersected Old 98. I figured it was a better business plan than selling lemonade since I didn't have to buy or make anything to turn a profit.

Maybe I was smarter than I give myself credit for.

Henry transfers Sunny from his arms to her car seat with the skill of a pro, which, of course, he is. He quietly closes the back door and exhales.

"Thanks for today," Henry says. "Sunny had a lot of fun."

"Just Sunny?" I ask. There were definitely moments today where Henry seemed more relaxed than usual, and I'd hoped that meant he was having fun, too.

"Not just Sunny," he says, lowering his voice. When his eyes lock on mine, goosebumps run up and down my arms. I rub my hands over my skin, telling it—and myself—to calm down. Even if Henry Alexander was my type, he'd never be looking for a casual summer fling, which is all this could be.

"Well," Henry says, breaking the silence after I dropped my end of the conversational volley. "I guess I'll be seeing you tomorrow. Good night, Kat."

He tips an imaginary hat before walking around to get in the front seat, and I sigh, realizing it's just me and Blake for the rest of the night.

After Henry pulls away, I walk up the front steps, already looking forward to the morning, when he'll be back to help Blake on the house. A few more scattered fireworks burst overhead as I open the door, and I almost fall backward at the force of the dog pushing past me, running like a frantic, terrified ball of fur.

"Shit," I mutter, glancing back and forth between the open door and the dog heading down the scenic route toward the

Crab Trap. "Blake!" I yell, hoping she's back from the beach. "Blake!"

Goddamn it.

The dog had been hanging out, chilling, until the fireworks started. After that, he'd vanished somewhere inside, hiding who knows where, and I forgot he was in the house.

"Blake!" I yell again, running down the stairs and in the same direction as the dog.

"What?" Blake says, popping her head out the door, sounding as if I'm interrupting her instead of trying to rescue her damn dog.

"The dog!" I shout, yelling behind me.

The front door slams shut, and moments later, Blake is running beside me, a lot less out of breath than I am. Old 98 is crowded with cars and golf carts in bumper-to-bumper traffic trying to get home after the festivities.

"There!" I shout, pointing at the road ahead, where the dog is running, dodging in and out of dark shadows between the cars. I start to call his name, then realize I don't know it. Blake usually refers to him as "the dog." "What's his name?" I ask, glancing over at Blake.

Her face goes blank for a brief moment before she says, "Max. His name is Max."

"Max!" I yell.

"Max!" Blake echoes, her voice panicky. "Here, boy!"

The dog stops just before a beach-access parking lot and turns, staring as we approach. He's trembling, tail between his legs. I slow my pace, not wanting to scare him off again, when someone—a tourist, no doubt—sets off a pop-snapper firework.

Max darts across the street, narrowly avoiding getting hit by a car.

Blake gasps, and out of instinct, I reach for her arm. I don't know if it's for support or to keep her from getting hit herself.

"If I lose him," she says, "if he gets hurt, I don't know what I'll do."

"He'll be okay," I tell Blake as we run across the street between two stopped cars. I wish Henry were still here; he'd know what to do.

"He's a five-thousand-dollar dog," Blake says, panting.

I stop in my tracks. I'd spend five grand on a lot of things, but a dog?

"Seriously?"

Blake shrugs as if she doesn't understand it, either. When she looks at me, I wonder if she's remembering the same thing I am—the night we played capture the flag at camp and we were the last two left on our team. Just like then, it feels like we're in this together.

"There!" I shout, startling Blake.

The dog has circled back and is heading toward us on the sidewalk. We both start to run but are blocked by a huge family in matching T-shirts walking in the opposite direction.

"Excuse us," I say, trying to elbow my way through.

"Maxy Waxy!" Blake calls, just a few feet from the dog. "Here, Puffball, Crazy Cheeto!"

Blake is in grabbing distance of the dog's collar and almost has him when more fireworks go off. I curse the morons who think this is fun as the dog sprints back across the street again. A car barely misses him and Blake gasps like she's just been punched in the gut.

I take her hand and we run across the street, waving apologies to the cars we weave in front of. The dog runs down one of the side streets, where there's less traffic, and a lot less light.

"You run ahead on that side," I tell Blake, pointing to the other side of the street. "Run past him, then circle back and we can close in on him."

Blake nods and starts to run, but slows in front of a yard where the remnants of a barbecue are scattered on the lawn.

"Cheese," she says.

I look around, confused. "Is someone taking our picture?"

"No. The dog loves cheese." Blake steps onto the lawn, where a fold-out table is full of condiments, and grabs two slices of cheese, handing me one.

Blake takes off, leaving me holding the cheese as a man walks out of the house.

"Hey, that's my cheese!" the man shouts. I shrug in lieu of an explanation and jog off after Blake, who's running with the form of an elite athlete.

I find myself wondering if she played sports in college. If she even went to college. It strikes me that as much time as we've spent orbiting around each other the last few weeks, I have no idea what she's been up to the last fifteen years.

"Max!" Blake calls from the far side of the street, blocking the dog's line of escape. "Here, Maxi-pad!"

"I've got cheese!" I call as I creep closer to him. "Want some yummy cheese?"

I have no idea if dogs understand English, but I'm pretty sure he'll know the sound of the plastic wrap opening.

Blake and I inch closer on either side of the dog. He's frozen in place, trembling with fear.

"Come and get some cheese," I say.

The dog looks at me, tongue hanging out of his mouth, tail wagging.

"Come here, boy," I say, squatting down to his level. I wave the flimsy slice of cheese like a surrender flag and the dog ambles toward me.

I keep my eyes on him, ready to lunge for his collar. "Good boy," I say, trying to keep my voice calm and reassuring. Blake closes in from the other side, so even if the dog attempts a dine-and-dash, she'll be there to get him.

Luckily it doesn't come to that. The dog takes the cheese from my outstretched hand, then curls up at my feet to eat it. Blake swoops in and pulls him into her lap.

Her entire face melts, and tears slide down her cheeks. "You stupid dog," she says, nuzzling her face in his fur. "What were you thinking?"

The dog licks Blake's face as she rubs his belly. For someone who says she doesn't care for the animal, it seems the five-grand price tag isn't the only reason she's so relieved.

"Thank you," Blake says to me.

"Anytime," I tell her, even though I wouldn't mind if I never had to do that again.

BY THE TIME we get the dog safely back in the house, I'm exhausted.

"I could use a drink," I announce.

"Same," Blake says. She looks at me and I smile, and I guess we're having a drink together.

"Want a Truly?" I ask. I noticed earlier she was only drinking the beer she'd bought.

She says, "Sure," and I grab two from the fridge and we both head outside.

As soon as the sweet bubbles slide down my throat, I relax. The earlier panic from Dog-Gate finally starts to dissipate.

Blake and I sit in companionable silence for a while, listening to the waves and the last stragglers clearing out from the beach. Something between our chairs catches my eye and I lean over to pick it up: one of the face-paint brushes Blake used on Sunny earlier.

"Want a butterfly tattoo?" Blake asks, a familiar spark in her eyes.

"You remember." Somehow, it makes me feel less alone to know someone else shares my memories. Even if that someone is Blake.

"Of course," she says. "How could I forget?"

I smile and take another sip of my Truly. The conversation is getting dangerously close to a place I don't want to go. I'm not strong enough to dive back into all the feelings of betrayal I felt that summer, so I try to think of a safe topic—something between then and now.

"So, what have you been up to the last fifteen years?" I ask.

Blake laughs but doesn't call me out on the abrupt change of subject. I'm grateful when she starts to talk. She tells me how she went to college thanks to her grandparents' generosity. She explains how she left school when her grandmother got sick, wanting to spend as much time with her as possible.

I can relate to that feeling and wish I had some sort of clue that the end had been near for my dad, so I could've known to spend more time with him. To create more good memories to counter the less-than-good ones.

Blake's energy shifts as she tells me her grandfather hasn't been doing well. "That's why I want to sell the house," she explains. "I need to get him into the memory unit at his care facility. And it isn't cheap."

"Wow," I say, wondering if there's a graceful way to apologize for misjudging her. I guess she's not just after the money to hurt me.

"When my mom died, my grandparents took me in, no question. I kept waiting for my dad—" She pauses and looks at me. I nod in case she wants my permission to keep going. "I thought I'd just be with my grandparents for a while, that he'd come back for me. But it never happened, obviously. Which was fine—my grandparents filled that role and then some."

There's bravado to Blake's voice, and I know she doesn't want me or anyone else feeling bad for her. And I don't, not exactly. It sounds like she grew up in a home filled with a lot more love than our house.

"I'm sorry our dad was such an ass," I tell her. She smiles, and I know she notices this is the first time I've admitted that my dad was also her dad. "If it makes you feel better, you didn't miss out on much."

Instantly, Blake's smile fades and her face hardens. She bites her lip and shakes her head.

"What?" I ask, not sure what I said or did wrong. Just a second ago, it felt like there was a chance we could start being friends.

Before she can explain, her phone buzzes. Blake glances at the screen, and her lips curve into a faint smile again.

"I'm pretty tired," she says, standing up. "I'm going to call it a night."

I hear her say a soft "hello" into the phone as she walks back inside.

She closes the door, leaving me alone on the deck, which just a few short hours ago was buzzing with energy. Sitting out here with nothing but the moon to light the sky, I realize everybody has somebody but me. Henry has Sunny. Blake has her mystery guy. And I've got a half-empty can of Truly.

"Happy Independence Day," I say, raising my can before taking a sip.

I honestly wonder why everyone cares so much about being independent. I for one like it much better when I'm not on my own.

CHAPTER EIGHTEEN

BLAKE

I'M OFFICIALLY EXHAUSTED. IT TOOK THREE DAYS TO CLEAN the Rooneys' house after they left, then today I stained the wood floor at my beach house. I can't walk on it for twenty-four hours, so I'm back at the casita watching YouTube videos about how to install a tile backsplash. Even though it's only eight o'clock in the evening, I keep nodding off. I'm about to get in my pajamas and go to bed early when a knock startles me.

I open the door to see Noah, and my stomach flips.

"Hey!" I say. "You're back in town."

I'm trying hard not to appear too giddy—although that's exactly how I feel. All those days of increasingly flirty texting have left me horny as hell. And now here he is in the flesh, leaning against the doorframe, all six foot five inches of him, dressed in his typical threadbare T-shirt and shorts, with a smirk on his face.

"How's my puffball after his traumatic fireworks incident?" Noah asks, peering around the door to look into the casita.

I laugh. Of course he's mostly concerned about the dog.

"He's good. Actually, I took him to get groomed today and it didn't cost extra to let him stay at the doggy daycare and play, so I left him there for a few hours. They said he had an amazing time, made lots of friends, and now he's all tuckered out."

So tired, in fact, that at the sound of Noah's voice, all he does is raise his head and give a few weak wags of his tail before falling back asleep.

Noah chuckles. "Want to hang out?"

Again, that flip in my stomach. What does he mean? This man has sent me some borderline dirty texts and now he wants to *hang out*.

"Sure," I say. I slip on my flip-flops and follow him out to the pool area. The sky is dusky overhead and the landscaping lights have turned on, making the pool water shimmer like there's glitter sprinkled on the surface. Noah's brought out a couple of beers, and we sit poolside and dangle our feet in the water.

I catch him up on my progress on the house since Kat left the day after the Fourth.

"Tomorrow I've got to finish painting the main-floor bedroom," I tell him. "I did the first coat this morning, and it took forever—such a pain going up and down the stepstool to reach the top part of the wall."

"Want some help?"

"Typical," I say, grinning. "You waited until I was on the last coat to show up. But yes, I'd love some help. How was Chicago?"

He apparently drove there to visit a friend from college, which seems odd to me. It's a thirteen-hour drive and he's been evasive about his reasons for the trip, just like he's been evasive about pretty much everything in his past.

"It was great," he says. "Stuffed myself with pizza, hot dogs, and Italian beef. How are you? Everything going okay with Kat?"

I'm not sure how to answer that. At times, I've gotten the

sense that something is shifting inside Kat. Not only in person—she was so helpful in getting the dog back safely—but even on Instagram there's a smidge more depth behind her posts. But then she made that comment about how I wasn't missing much by not having our father in my life. As if the fact that he was a workaholic and missed a few of her school functions is equal to being completely abandoned.

I take a sip of beer, trying to figure out how to articulate what I'm feeling. "She has no idea what a privileged life she had. No idea how hard it was growing up without a father. She's so clueless sometimes." It's not Kat's fault that our dad was an asshole, I remind myself. And it can't have been easy for her, knowing that her father had cheated on her mother.

Exhaling, I lean back and look up at the sky, navy blue and speckled with stars. It's easier to say things like this if I'm not making eye contact. "I'm still so angry at him. My dad, I mean. But I'm realizing that being angry at him isn't going to hurt *him*—but it's hurting me. I want to try and let that go."

"Good for you," Noah says, turning serious. "Like, for real. Not sure I'll ever get there."

I glance at him, hesitating. I desperately want to ask what the story is with his family. He's made so many references like this but never follows up with any actual details.

"What happened?" I ask. "You can tell me if you want. No pressure."

"It's a long story."

I shrug. "I have nothing else to do tonight. Can't work in the beach house until tomorrow afternoon."

He looks over at me, and there's so much sadness in his eyes that I wish I could give him a hug. "I've been meaning to tell you for a while, but . . . I'm not exactly proud of myself for how it went down."

"I won't judge," I say, brushing my hair away from my eyes and tucking it behind my ears.

He takes a long swallow from his bottle. "I think I mentioned that last year I was working a boring professional job?" I nod, motioning for him to continue. "Before that, when I was in grad school—wait, let me go back even further. I haven't told you about my family. Let's start there."

"I'm listening," I say.

He winces, like this is hard for him to get out. "My family is—"

My phone rings, and I pull it out of my pocket. "It's Kat," I tell him. "Sorry. Hold that thought."

"Hey," she says when I answer. "Sorry to bother you. I have a quick question."

She sounds a little awkward, and I realize that this is the first time we've spoken to each other over the phone.

"What's up?" I say.

"I got a sponsorship with a local company in Atlanta. They're going to give us rugs for the dining area and living room, but I need dimensions of the rooms. Do you mind measuring them?"

"Oh, sorry—I finished staining the floor and can't go in until tomorrow." I pause. "Actually, I have the floor plan sketched out with dimensions. I'll text you a picture."

"Thanks." There's another awkward pause, and I get the sense that she wants to say something else. But then she clears her throat. "Okay. Have a good night. Bye."

After ending the call, I go into the casita and snap a picture of my floor-plan sketch, then text it to Kat. When I come out of the casita, Noah is standing in the shallow end of the pool, the water halfway up his calves.

"Going night swimming?" I say.

He gets a mischievous look in his eyes. "That could be fun."

The thought of being in the swimming pool with Noah makes my stomach flip again. "Don't get your hopes up. I didn't even bring a swimsuit here."

Noah's mouth falls open; he's aghast. "Wait a second—are you telling me that you haven't been in the pool at all?"

I shake my head. "I've been busy working. I know that's a foreign concept to you, but—"

"So this means you haven't been swimming in the *Gulf*, either?" When I shake my head, he climbs out of the pool. "Okay, no. This is unacceptable. We've got to do something about this. Immediately."

"Huh?"

"We're going swimming. Right now."

I shake my head, alarmed. "I just told you—I don't have a bathing suit!"

His eyes glint. "You don't technically *need* one."

"I'm not going skinny-dipping!" I say, horrified but also a little intrigued. I wouldn't mind seeing Noah in the buff.

He shrugs. "Just go in your underwear. I can't believe you've spent the past six weeks living on one of the prettiest beaches in America and haven't gotten in the water once. How embarrassing for you." He says that in a teasing tone. "Come on, Blake. Don't be boring."

He's daring me. And I don't like backing down from a dare.

"Fine," I say, throwing my hands in the air. "Just a quick swim, in and out of the water. Let me grab some towels."

SOON AFTER, we're stepping across the cool sand in the darkness toward the water. We set our towels on the dry sand, and then it's time to get undressed. Thanks be to the underwear gods, I'm wearing a decent set today—my UnderRooneys bra and boy short set with the smiling pineapples. More modest than a typical bikini, I remind myself as I shuck my clothes.

I slide a glance over at Noah, who is pulling his shirt over his head, revealing a gloriously toned, lean, muscular torso. He unbuttons his shorts and my mouth goes dry. Then he steps *out* of his shorts and I stop breathing. He's wearing nothing but a pair of shorty-short boxer briefs, and dear mother of all that is holy, he looks *damn* good.

"Still with the ogling?" he says, grinning at me. But it looks like he might be doing a little ogling of his own, his eyes drifting down my body. "Nice underwear."

I blush. "Stop. You're the one who said it would be fine."

"No, I mean it. They look nice. *You* look nice." His voice goes husky on that last sentence, which makes my insides go squishy. He holds out a hand. "Let's go."

I take his hand and we run into the cool water until it's up to our thighs, then together we dive into a wave. It breaks over my head, engulfing me in silence for a few seconds. In an instant, all my exhaustion from the past few days washes away. When I resurface, Noah is shaking droplets out of his hair.

"Okay, you're right," I say, spreading my arms out wide. "I should've done this a long time ago."

The water is the perfect temperature, cool but not cold, and even standing half out of the water, I don't shiver. The soft breeze caresses my skin and moonlight dances across the waves.

"I wouldn't steer you wrong," Noah says, before diving under another wave.

We hang out there for a while, kicking our feet and floating in silence. The waves feel like gentle, rolling hills that lift me up and set me back down on the sand. I try to imagine all the worries and stress of the past several weeks dissolving from my body and drifting away.

Noah is stealing glances at me, and I'm doing the same to him, but I don't know what the rules are after you make out with a guy and then he leaves town and you text each other nonstop. Maybe he decided I wasn't worth the trouble and this is just a platonic late-night underwear swim? Maybe I'm misreading all the tension and electricity between us?

Then he reaches out and takes my hand, pulling me toward him until we're less than a foot apart. All the air leaves my body in a rush. He's so much taller than me, I have to tilt my head way up to meet his eyes.

"I missed you," he says quietly. "I just needed you to know that."

My heart pounds. "I missed you, too. I'm glad you're back."

"I'm glad you're glad," he says. Then he kisses me, putting his hands around my waist to lift me to his level. I respond by wrapping my legs around *his* waist, and he smiles against my mouth. The kiss gets deeper, and when he sets me down, I'm breathless and light-headed.

Maybe that explains why I say the next thing that pops into my mind: "Are we ever going to have sex?"

Noah throws his head back, his laughter ringing in the night air. "God, I hope so. Why haven't we yet?"

I'm too relieved—and excited—to feel embarrassed about being so forward. "Not here," I say quickly. Nobody wants salt-water rashes in *those* areas. "And the dog's in the casita. I don't want an audience."

His eyes dance with mischief. "Luckily we have access to a very fancy, very empty beach house."

I grin. "Race you there."

A few minutes later—after rinsing off in the outdoor shower, then wrapping up in dry towels—we're rushing into the Rooneys' dark, empty house. All my previous bravado has worn off and my stomach is fluttering with nerves. Still, I have no intention of stopping.

Noah pulls me into the first bedroom and his mouth is immediately on mine again, his hands cupping my face. His towel falls in a heap to the floor and my brain almost misfires: *Noah is kissing me and he's wearing nothing but a soaking-wet pair of boxer briefs.*

I want him so badly it aches. My towel is still wrapped around me, and I take a deep breath and drop it. Noah steps back and watches, wide-eyed, as I reach behind me and unhook my wet bra, letting it fall to the floor.

He stares for several seconds. "Gorgeous," he finally says. "You're gorgeous."

A beam of moonlight through the window casts silvery shadows on his torso—shoulders, chest, abs—and the trail of darker hair that disappears into his waistband. Lust pools in my belly as my gaze snags on what's going on below that waistband.

"Ma'am," he says, "my eyes are up here."

I force myself to look up at his face and say, "I'd like to apologize in advance for objectifying the hell out of you tonight."

"Back at you." His face breaks into a smile and he scoops me up, making me laugh. I wrap my legs around his waist as he walks us over to the bed.

"New rule," I say, running my hands down his shoulders. "Shirtless gardening from now on."

"Only if there's shirtless housekeeping, too." He tosses me gently on the mattress, then crawls over me until he's caging me in with his arms, gazing down at me.

He's hardly touching me, but this direct eye contact is intense, intimate. In the past, my mind has sometimes wandered during sex, but there's no chance of that happening now. I am locked into this moment, hyperaware of every detail: the slight hitch in his breath, the laugh lines around his eyes, the damp heat of his skin inches away from mine.

"I've been thinking about doing this with you since we watched *Jurassic Park*," he says, still holding my gaze. "Every night. During the day, too. It's been torture. Absolute *torture*."

It's such a relief, hearing those words. "I thought maybe I scared you off."

"Definitely not," he says, and then finally he breaks eye contact and kisses my mouth, my jaw, my neck. Warm and wet and hungry. "I couldn't wait to get back. I was hoping you'd want to do this."

"I really, really want to do this," I say, not even caring how needy I sound. He's touching me everywhere—my breasts, my waist, my hips—and I arch my back and close my eyes and let myself drown in the sensations. My entire existence narrows to this and nothing else: Noah's mouth and hands on my body, his low voice asking if I like what he's doing, his soft chuckles of satisfaction when I gasp.

Then all of a sudden he's gone, the bed rocking as he climbs off. I sit up, alarmed that he's leaving. "Wait—what?"

But he hasn't gone anywhere. He's standing next to the bed, wrapping his big, warm hands around my thighs. He pulls me toward him. His hands go to the waistband of my underwear. And then he kneels down.

Oh.

"Blake," he says gently. "Please, may I? I've been dying to taste you."

What can I do but lie back on the bed as he peels my underwear down, let my legs fall open, and take what he wants to give?

And holy *shit*, does he give it to me. His tongue is warm and skilled and infinitely patient, and he keeps going until my eyes roll back in my head and I let out a sound somewhere between a groan and a strangled shout.

When I finally stop shaking, he pulls himself up next to me on the bed. He's smiling like he just won an Olympic gold medal.

"So smug," I say, brushing his wet hair back from his forehead. I'm floating, feeling boneless and tingly. But then I glance down at his boxer briefs, and I want more. "Take those off," I say, pointing.

"So bossy. Hang on one second." Leaning away, he opens the nightstand drawer and rummages around for a few seconds before pulling out a condom.

"You're lucky those were in there," I say, relieved—my brain is so scrambled right now that I haven't given one thought to protection.

"Damn lucky," he says, but he's looking at me, his eyes glinting in the darkness.

And then the boxer briefs come off and the condom goes on and he's lifting his long, lean body over mine, holding my gaze.

"Ready?" he says, and when I nod he slides inside me. I tilt my hips, inviting him deeper, and he groans. "This feels amazing, Blake. *You* feel amazing."

"As good as you hoped?" I love that he's been thinking about this. *Every night*, he'd said.

"Better."

We move together slowly, learning each other's rhythms, the unique way our bodies shift and slide against each other. I run my hands across his back, then down to his butt.

"Don't mind me," I say, giving him a squeeze. "Just some casual groping."

He laughs softly and kisses me. "Feel free."

I take that as a challenge and see how much of him I can touch, which isn't easy given that he's a foot taller than me. He murmurs in my ear that he enjoys having my hands on him; I reply that I enjoy having him inside of me. A lot.

Then he locks eyes with me, and I can't breathe for a moment. He's completely focused on my face, gauging my reaction to each roll of his hips, making adjustments to ratchet up the intensity. Time seems to slow down. He grabs under my thighs, tilting my pelvis a few crucial degrees, and on the next thrust I practically see stars.

"I'm dying," I gasp. "Noah, I might actually die."

"Good." His voice is rough. The veins on his neck stand out; he's trying to hold off. "Blake," he says, his jaw tight. "Blake, I can't . . ."

"Go for it," I say. "Don't hold back."

At that, he exhales and closes his eyes, like he's finally allowing himself to focus on his own pleasure. Now it's my turn to watch *his* face, the way his brow furrows and his mouth tightens. The tension builds, his breath coming faster until he gasps and shudders and we both ride out his waves together.

When he withdraws and goes into the bathroom, my body feels weightless and grounded at the same time. I desperately hope that he's planning on coming back to bed, because after *that*, I'm not about to sleep in the casita alone. But soon he's sliding into bed and wrapping his arms around me.

"All good?" he murmurs.

In response, I nestle against his warm body. "Just let me know when you're ready to do it again."

. . .

THE NEXT MORNING I wake to the sound of the dog whimpering. Blinking through groggy eyes, I remind myself where I am: in one of the gigantic bedrooms at the Rooneys' house. After having sex, Noah and I fell asleep for a couple of hours, then woke up and did it again. It was even better the second time.

After that, Noah got the dog from the casita, took him out to pee, then brought him into the house, where he slept on the bed with us. And I didn't even care. In fact, it felt perfect, Noah next to me, the dog at our feet.

Noah is currently asleep on his stomach, the sheets an inch or two below the tan line above his butt. I could stay here forever and stare, but the dog whimpers again—he needs to go out.

Carefully, I climb out of bed and take the dog outside so he can relieve himself. On the way back, I duck into the attached bathroom and use the toilet. As I'm washing my hands, I stare at my reflection in the massive mirror. My hair is a tangled mess and I'm wearing nothing but Noah's T-shirt, but my skin is glowing. My eyes are shining. I look like a woman who went swimming in the ocean and then had excellent sex. Twice.

Noah's words from last night float through my mind: *I've been dying to taste you.* And then later, during round two: *That feels so fucking good. Yes, that. Don't stop.*

I'm getting hot all over again, just thinking about it. Hopefully he'll be up for round three soon.

I head into the bedroom, but my eyes catch on something in the walk-in closet. I haven't spent much time in there because it didn't need any cleaning. This entire suite, in fact, hasn't been used either time the Rooneys have been here, which strikes me as odd.

A bunch of framed pictures are leaning against the back

wall, and I wonder if they are pictures of the Rooneys. I haven't gotten over my curiosity about them, so I walk over and lift the pictures away from the wall.

The first one is a giant framed photograph of the Rooneys in front of this very house. I recognize CoCo, Kat's friend, and behind her are a middle-aged, expensive-looking couple. Her parents, of course. But there's someone else in the picture, someone standing next to CoCo.

Noah.

He's a few years younger, clean-shaven, with perfectly coiffed wavy brown hair, wearing clothes so preppy he looks like he just came from a yacht club. But it's definitely him.

Holding my breath, I look through the rest of the pictures: they all include Noah, mostly of the Rooneys together as a family in Destin, out on their boat or at the beach, one with teenage Noah on a paddleboard, another of him and CoCo as children next to a lopsided sandcastle.

It's as if someone went through the house and took down every reminder of him and stacked them in this closet. My chest swells with a deep sadness. Who would do such an awful thing to their only son?

But also: Why didn't Noah tell me? He let me think he was the gardener, that we were in the same boat, both of us broke and stuck here for the summer, working for the Rooneys. He even let me go on and on about how stuck-up and entitled they are. My cheeks flush with a mixture of indignation and embarrassment. Was he laughing at me this entire time?

Behind the pictures is a white cardboard box, and I open it to find a stack of save-the-date cards, announcing the upcoming marriage of Noah Jameson Rooney Jr. to Annalise Cunningham. My stomach feels queasy. I look at the date: they were supposed to be married last month. June 14.

This must be Noah's closet, Noah's bedroom. That's why it's gone unused when the Rooneys have been here. And that's why Noah knew exactly where the condoms were. No luck about it.

Hands shaking, I grab one of the smaller pictures and a save-the-date card and go into the bedroom, sitting on the bed next to Noah. He rolls over and looks up at me.

"Morning, beautiful," he says, giving a lazy smile. "Glad you're back."

I press my lips together and show him the picture and the card. "You need to tell me what's going on."

When he registers what I'm holding, he sits up lightning fast. "Shit. Blake—I'm sorry. I'm so sorry. I was going to tell you last night, but—"

"You should have told me *before* that," I say. My voice sounds sharper than I intended; I do remember that he was about to explain about his family, but Kat called.

He cringes, his forehead creased with guilt. "I know. Just—please let me explain. Okay? Before you walk out and never speak to me again?"

"I told you last night I would listen without judgment, and that hasn't changed," I say. "But I do want to know the truth now. The *whole* truth."

He exhales, clearly relieved and a little surprised. "Okay. Where to start. Let's see—I was groomed my entire life to take over the Rooney underwear company. I started working for my dad after college and continued while doing an MBA. At the time, the company wasn't doing well, and I had an idea to revitalize things. Get a whole new generation excited about buying our products."

"You came up with UnderRooneys," I say, which makes sense.

He nods. "I convinced my father to let me take the reins on the project. I was in charge of it all—the design, the marketing, everything. The product sold better than my wildest dreams. It was exhilarating; we were bringing in more money than any year in the last decade. My dad was thrilled. But then . . .”

“Someone leaked the information about the sweatshops,” I say as it dawns on me. “I read about it online. The company lost a lot of money.”

His reluctance to tell me makes sense now, and I feel myself softening further. He’s embarrassed he was part of something like that. He must have left the company, which caused a rift in his family.

But Noah shakes his head. “No, that’s not—let me back up. About a year ago, I went with some board members to tour our factory in Malaysia. I was horrified at the conditions. They were working fourteen hours a day; the factories were filthy and hot; people were getting hurt. It felt wrong that we were raking in the dough while our workers were struggling. But when I brought it up with my dad, he brushed it off. Said that this was how the world worked, and I needed to get used to it. But I couldn’t get used to it—I felt like the welfare of those workers was *my* responsibility. But since my dad wouldn’t listen . . .”

He trails off, wincing, and it all clicks in my mind in one horrifying instant.

“*You* leaked the information,” I say, putting a hand to my mouth.

“Yes.” His jaw tightens. “I went to the media and reported it. Our stock plummeted. Several huge distributors pulled out; consumers boycotted us. The board fired me. My fiancée dumped me. My parents were furious.”

“They disowned you,” I whisper, thinking about those pictures in the closet, facing the wall.

He nods, then looks away. “It gets worse. A few months ago,

I got a call from the foreman of that factory. The company closed it down and thousands of people lost their jobs. The foreman wanted me to know that it was my fault. That he and every other worker in that factory blamed me—*personally*—for the fact that they couldn't feed their families. And he was right. He was absolutely right."

My heart drops. I can see the pain on his face, the guilt weighing on him.

Noah runs both hands through his hair, looking exhausted and defeated. "I'd been so self-righteous, acting like a goddamn martyr for standing up to the big, bad corporation, when in actuality, I made everything worse." He lets out a long, heavy sigh. "Anyway. After that, I needed to get away from everything. That's why I ended up here, squatting in my family's beach house. I have no idea what to do next. How do I even begin to make amends for what I've done? When you assumed I was the groundskeeper, I just went with it. I shouldn't have lied to you, Blake. But I have to admit, it was nice for a little while. Pretending to be someone else. Pretending I didn't belong to the Rooney family."

I'm stunned speechless. This is what Noah has been keeping inside of him all this time. So much hurt and shame hidden under a veneer of sarcasm. Now he's split himself open in front of me, and he still seems to expect that I'm going to walk out of here, disgusted, and never speak to him again.

That's the last thing I'm going to do.

"I wish you would've told me earlier," I say, "but I understand what it's like to feel ashamed of your family."

He glances at me, eyebrows raised. "How are you not more upset?"

"I am upset. I'm upset with your *parents*." My voice catches. "It's not just the company they kicked you out of—they kicked you out of the family. They took your pictures off the wall, Noah. Who does that to their own child?"

My eyes fill with tears. I'm not just thinking about Noah's family. I'm thinking of mine—of my own father, cutting me out of his life. He never even *had* a picture of me on his walls.

"Sorry," I say, brushing away my tears. This isn't about me.

"No, *I'm* sorry," Noah says, taking my hand. "And I don't blame you if you're angry with me."

I bite my lip, assessing him. He's shirtless, his face scruffy and unshaven, hair messy. There's a softness about him, a vulnerability that makes my throat tighten. I spent hours exploring his naked body last night, but this is the first time I feel like I've actually seen *him*.

Over the past year, he's been stripped of everything that made up his identity. It's obvious he still carries the weight of all the countless workers who were mistreated in Rooney factories, who later lost their jobs. He blames himself. Deeply.

I want to reassure him that he may have made some mistakes, but he should be proud of himself for acting with integrity. But I suspect he isn't ready to hear that yet. There's only so much vulnerability that can be crammed into one morning.

Instead, I squeeze his hand. "I'm not angry. Although part of my reaction may be related to the fact that you gave me several excellent orgasms last night, and I would like more in the near future."

His shoulders drop with relief. "The *very* near future," he says, leaning in to kiss me.

"Wait a minute," I say, as something occurs to me. If Noah's full name is Noah Jameson Rooney *Junior*, that means— "You're the boy Kat had a crush on when we were twelve!"

He rolls his eyes. "Did she? Weird. She always seemed like an extra little sister." Then he wraps his hand behind my neck and pulls me toward him. "I'd rather not talk about her right now—I'm too distracted by the beautiful woman in my bed who's wearing nothing but my T-shirt."

I grin and yank the shirt over my head. "Is this less or more distracting?"

He laughs and pulls me into bed with him, and within a few minutes I'm so happy I could float away.

CHAPTER NINETEEN

KAT

IT'S HOT AS BALLS OUTSIDE, AND EVEN THOUGH THERE ARE plenty of empty air-conditioned rooms inside the Peachtree Boys' and Girls' Center, the girls want to hang out at our usual spot in the courtyard. I managed to grab a seat in the shade, but my skin is still crying sweat, desperate tears sliding down my thighs. But the girls look happy, painting their nails a rainbow of my favorite OPI colors.

In Chelsea's case, she's painting a literal rainbow, from Relentless Ruby on her pinky to Turn on the Northern Lights on her thumb—she skipped yellow because I didn't have it, and she'd need twelve fingers for a full rainbow.

"What do you think, Miss Kat?" she says, holding her hands out for me to admire.

It's a little extra for my taste, not that I'd ever tell her that. Chelsea cares too much about my opinion—more than she probably should. I've noticed lately, especially in the last few weeks, she's been asking what I think about everything from the way she should part her hair (middle) to the way she should wear her shirt (French tuck) and how many pins to put on her backpack (less is more).

At first, I was flattered, but now I'm wondering if it's a bit excessive. A sign that her self-confidence could use a boost.

"What I think doesn't matter as much as what you think," I tell her.

Chelsea frowns and looks down at her colorful hands. When she looks up back up, her eyes are shining. "You don't like them?"

"No," I say, backtracking. "Of course I do. How could I not—they're all my colors."

Chelsea smiles, and I'm relieved she was convinced so easily. I make a mental note to do some googling on ways to improve self-confidence in teenage girls.

"No way," Luna says, crossing her arms in front of her chest. "I don't buy that bullshit."

The girls' eyes grow wide and they look between Luna and me. Cursing is not allowed at the center, but I know she's just testing me.

"Why do you say that?" I ask, keeping my tone light the way they taught at volunteer orientation. Kids pick up what you're putting down, the program director told us. If you keep calm, chances are they will, too.

"Pshaw," Luna says. "They might all be your colors, but you'd never wear them all at the same time like that."

"Not true," I say, even though it's most definitely true. But I figure this is one time where honesty might not be the best policy.

"I saw your story about matching colors on your fingers and toes," Luna says. "You like yours to match."

I cringe and resist the urge to look down at my feet, wishing I'd worn closed-toe shoes that would hide the Cajun Shrimp polish that does in fact match my fingernails. I could tell her that fashion and style evolve, but the post was pretty recent. Three months and four days ago. The day of my dad's funeral.

At the time, I explained away the need to post as wanting to control something in the middle of the chaos, but now I wonder if I was trying to cling to an idealized version of my life that didn't exist.

Luna takes my lack of response as victory. She sits up straight and holds her head high as she tells the girls, "Life is a fashion show, ladies." There's admiration in her voice, but hearing my brand mantra in this context makes me want to take the words back.

If Chelsea's rainbow nails make her happy, then she should wear them that way. Happiness matters more than what someone else—influencer or not—decides is beautiful. Besides, there's more to life than looking good on the outside. Especially if you're just using makeup and clothes to cover up how broken you are on the inside.

My eyes well up with tears and I blink them away as I look down at my own nails. I get them done every two weeks, but I can't remember the last time they brought me happiness.

"Hand me that To Infinity and Blue-Yond," I tell Chelsea.

She hands me the bottle of blue polish. I twist the cap off and carefully paint over the Cajun Shrimp on my pinky finger. I haven't painted my own nails since that summer at camp. I have a fuzzy memory of sitting on the dock with Blake, giving each other manis and pedis. I don't think she'd ever had hers painted before. And maybe not since.

I paint every other nail blue, leaving the coral ones in between. It's not me, but it is fun. When I finish the first hand, I hold it up for Chelsea to see. "What do you think?"

"I love it," Chelsea says, blushing.

"But what do *you* think, Miss Kat?" Jackie teases, a smirk in her eye.

"I love it, too," I tell her as I keep going on my right hand. It's a little more difficult since I'm right-handed. Seeing me struggle, LaTasha takes the brush from my hand and finishes the job for me. It's not perfect and there are a few places where the polish gets on my skin, but I decide to embrace the imperfections.

"This is what we call a teachable moment, ladies," Luna says, her voice dripping with sarcasm. "She's probably going to take it off as soon as she gets home."

"No, I'm not," I tell her.

Luna smirks as she holds her hand up to her face and pretends to talk into a phone. "Hello, nail lady," she says in a high-pitched voice. "I've got me a nail emergency!"

The girls all laugh, except for Chelsea, who's looking down at her rainbow nails with apprehension. I reach for my phone and carefully pick it up, handing it to Chelsea.

"Take a picture for me?" I ask. I position my hands artfully on the table, with my right hand on top of the left, so all ten nails are visible within the square frame.

"She's not actually going to post it," Luna says, watching with a critical stare. "It won't go with her grid."

I eye Luna, impressed and a little surprised that she seems to know what she's talking about. Both the language and the strategy. It's true the clashing, bright colors don't match my carefully curated feed, and I'm not scheduled to post again until tomorrow—but screw it. This is more important. I want the girls to know I mean what I'm telling them. That life doesn't have to be beautiful to be worthwhile.

Maybe that's why I haven't been able to answer that damn "what's your why" question on the Worthington application. Maybe my "why" is changing. Maybe I am, too.

. . .

THREE DAYS LATER, I'm on the road to Destin, staring at my hands wrapped around the steering wheel. The nail polish colors are starting to grow on me, but I haven't gotten any closer to figuring out my "why." It feels like the right answer is hovering just below the surface, and all I have to do is dig deep. Which terrifies me.

I'm hoping something will come to me this week while I'm at the beach house. If not, I might have a bigger problem on my hands. The application is due in less than three weeks.

I've been binge-listening to influencer podcasts, trying to pick up any tips and tricks. They've had some good ideas, but I'm worried that everyone else is listening to the exact same advice, and I want to stand out, not blend in.

As soon as I get past the traffic on 75 South, I trade my driving playlist for a podcast called *Crushing Your Comfort Zone* that showed up on my "recommended" list.

"Hey, friends," the woman says with a slight Southern drawl. "I hope y'all are having a good day today, wherever you are. And if you're having a shitty day . . . well, I hope tomorrow is a little less shitty."

She laughs, and I find myself smiling. I already like her.

"Today we're talking about finding the right people for the message you're putting out in the world. And before you go thinking about personality types and all that bullshit—important bullshit, but bullshit all the same—just hear me out."

I lean in, curious to hear her philosophy. I don't think it'll help me with the application, but if my content's going to evolve, I need my audience to shift, too.

Four hours and episodes later, my head is spinning in the best possible way. The podcaster, "Lou, short for Louise not Loser," had a lot of insightful tips, not just for my brand, but for my life as well. The thing that stuck out the most was that every person walking the planet has an emotional wound they're trying to heal.

The quest to become whole is the subtext for everything we do, buy, or try—and for me, as an influencer, it's the best way to identify "my people." The way she explained it didn't sound opportunistic, more like she was pointing out the ways we could all help one another.

She gave several examples, including one of a woman who'd been the victim of a break-in. Her wound might be not feeling safe at home—a home security system or self-defense class might help, but so would a really plush couch or a puppy to make her feel safe and protected, a lighthearted movie or book to help put her at ease.

As I cross the Georgia-Florida line, I wonder what my wound is. I'm aware I've lived a privileged life—especially compared to the girls at the center. Even compared to Blake. There was no crime or tragedy in my life other than the obvious "my best friend is really my half sister" thing.

Sure, that's a wound, but I realize for the first time that it wasn't Blake's betrayal that stung the most. If I'm being honest, she was just the one who was easier to blame. And if I'm *really* being honest, things with my dad weren't all that great before I knew Blake O'Neill existed.

Even as a kid, I remember thinking I wasn't good or smart enough for my dad. I always tried so hard to impress him, like when I joined the Future Business Leaders of America group freshman year in high school, even though I would have rather joined the yearbook committee. I was like a puppy, greedy for attention or praise. When it didn't come—and it almost never did—my mom would try to make up for it with a trip to the mall.

No wonder I've spent my life trying to self-soothe with retail therapy. I learned from the best. Although, at the end of the day, I don't think my mom is actually happy. And I know I'm not.

I think about all the things my parents bought me over the years, the things I've bought for myself. None of my "valuable" things really bring me joy.

The things that do make me happy aren't the most fancy or expensive, but they have the most meaning. Like the throw pillow I made from one of my grandpa's old sweaters, the brooch from my grandmother, the friendship bracelet from camp that I could never bring myself to throw away.

As I cross the Mid-Bay Bridge into Destin, I realize there's a difference between being materialistic and finding meaning in certain objects—maybe that's what my brand has been missing.

I've been focusing on the physical beauty of things—from makeup to clothes and, more recently, home décor—without acknowledging their emotional impact. Some things are beautiful because of the memories they hold from the past, or the way they make you feel.

In a way, I've already started incorporating that idea in my photos. And if the engagement on my multicolored mani post tells me anything, it's that my followers connect with content that's honest and real, even if it's not classically beautiful.

That post was the first time that I'd mentioned volunteering because I didn't want it to look like I was doing it for the likes—but I couldn't explain the off-brand mani without saying what it was inspired by.

Pulling up in front of the beach house, I realize this is my most valuable possession. Not just for what it's meant to me in the past, but for its future potential.

• • •

BLAKE HAS MADE a lot of progress in the week since I've been gone. The floors seem to be finished, because the new furniture I got through sponsorships back in Atlanta is no longer hiding under sheets in the garage. It's set up just the way I had pictured it, with the soft gray deep-set couch facing the wall, a matching love seat to its left, the driftwood coffee table in the middle, and a blue-and-white rug anchoring it all together.

I wonder if Blake's mystery man-friend helped her carry it all inside. Or maybe Henry? I try to squash the flare of jealousy that comes with the thought of the two of them hanging out without me.

I know I have no right to be jealous—Henry and I are just friends—besides, I'm the one who introduced them for the benefit of the beach house. Which, from the looks of it, was clearly the right decision. Blake has said more than once that Henry's been a lifesaver.

Looking around the transformed room, I'm grateful Blake was so adamant about moving forward with the renovation. There's still work to do upstairs and with the exterior of the house, but the living room is a work of art. With its cozy, classic beachy vibe, it's a far cry from the outdated, retro style it had before.

But it's not just the look of the room that I appreciate, or the fact that the house will be worth more thanks to the updates. What I love about this room is that it feels like a comfortable place where I can see myself spending time, a place to create new memories, not just reflect on the old ones.

For the first time in weeks, I'm feeling hopeful and dare I say confident about the Worthington application. I think this new worldview might be the thing to set me apart. Not to mention, it feels more authentically me. And Rachel Worthington is all about authenticity.

Walking into the kitchen, I notice the sea-glass backsplash I picked out is up, too. And just like I thought it would, the color perfectly complements the emerald-green Gulf water right outside the window.

As I run my hand along the counter, a sense of sadness comes over me. For the life of me, I can't put my finger on what could possibly be missing from this moment. The construction tools and gadgets are no longer strewn in piles around the room, but I certainly don't miss the clutter.

My phone buzzes in my pocket, and the noise that's supposed to be "silent" seems loud in the still room. Maybe that's what feels so off. This beach house wasn't meant to be a solitary escape for one. It was made for family and friends to enjoy together.

Like last week. Having Henry and Sunny around filled the house with so much energy and laughter and noise. I realize that's what's missing. It had even been nice having Blake around—we'd started to get somewhere after the whole dog incident, until I opened my big, dumb mouth.

I didn't realize how insensitive my comment about Blake not missing out on much had been until I heard that podcast earlier today. When I started to imagine what Blake's wound might be, I thought for the first time about her experience. She didn't just miss out on having my dad in her life—she had to live with the knowledge that he'd abandoned her. I can't believe he walked away from his nine-year-old daughter who had just lost her mother.

Every time I've thought back to that summer over the last fifteen years, I've seen it from my perspective. I hadn't thought about it from Blake's point of view, having her father look her in the face, then drive away—never to reach out to her again. All these years, I've been holding on to my own hurt, never stopping to consider that she was hurting, too.

I feel a desperate need to connect with Blake and let her know I understand. While we both lost the same person, our experience was deeply different. But maybe our loss can be a common ground. I reach for my phone and open our text thread.

I look through the messages between us; the brief back-and-forth reads like a conversation between strangers. Almost every message is about the house, updates on the progress, lists of things to buy, questions about decisions that have to be made, and the occasional message that Henry asked either me or Blake to pass along to the other—even though he has both our phone numbers. The man has not been subtle in his attempts to speed up our reconciliation. But some things can't be rushed.

I stare down at the screen, the blank message field practically daring me to make a move. Maybe it's been long enough. And the house really is too quiet.

Before I can talk myself out of it, I type out a quick message and hit send.

Kat: Hey! Just got to the house, the kitchen looks soooo good! Was thinking about testing it out tonight, free for dinner?

The three dots appear and I hold my breath, hoping that I didn't misread the moment between us on the Fourth of July. She might have been thinking about the holiday as a brief cease-fire like I originally had. If she says no . . .

Blake: Sure, that sounds great

The message appears and I exhale, relieved and looking forward to what I hope will be a fun night, maybe even a memory in the making.

A FEW HOURS later, I'm in the kitchen and Blake is sitting outside at the table I set with place mats and an ornate coral centerpiece that I got from a gallery in Buckhead in exchange for an Instagram post.

Blake offered to help, but I insisted that she's my guest tonight, and I don't want her to lift a finger unless it's bringing her wineglass to her mouth. I figure this evening can be a thank-you for all the hard work she's been putting in.

As an extra-special treat, I decide to make my dad's famous fettuccine alfredo. When I was a kid, I thought he was an amazing chef until I grew up and realized he just made this one dish really, really well.

I transfer the pasta from the pot to the cerulean-blue serving dish I bought today for the occasion, and carefully place the shrimp on top because presentation matters. The salad is already on the table, so I just need to bring out the pasta and the bread.

"Dinner's ready!" I call out to Blake through the open window.

She stands and pops her head in the door. "Can I help bring anything out?"

"Sure," I say, taking the pasta dish and nodding toward the tray with the garlic bread. "Can you grab that?"

She smiles and walks behind me, craning her neck to see the dish in my hands. "Fe-tu-chi-ni," she says in the same bad Italian accent my dad used to use when he served the dish. "It smells just like Dad used to make."

Her words hit me like a punch in the gut, and I turn so she

doesn't see the heartbreak on my face. My dad's been gone more than three months, but it feels like I keep losing more pieces of him with every new realization.

"This was the one and only meal he'd cook when he was at our house," Blake continues. "Other than that, my mom barely let him in the kitchen."

I try to manage a laugh, but it sounds more like a choked sob. The dish feels heavy in my hands; the memory I'd been looking forward to sharing with Blake feels tarnished now that I know she has her own version of the same exact one. Just like she had her own version of my dad.

Blinking back tears, I set the dish down on the table and force a happy expression because my mom taught me the most important thing a hostess can serve is a smile to make her guests feel comfortable.

"So," I say, helping myself to a scoop of salad and a slice of bread. "Tell me about this guy you're dating."

"Oh, I don't know," Blake says, her cheeks blushing. "It's still early days, too new to talk about."

Ordinarily, I'd try to get her to spill at least a few details, but with our current relationship status being as fragile as it is, I don't want to risk pushing her away.

Blake picks up the seashell tongs—another of today's purchases—and looks up before she digs into the pasta. "Do you want to take a picture first?"

I'd thought about it, but the dish no longer feels special. It was just my dad's shtick. "Go ahead," I tell her.

Blake smiles and helps herself to the fettuccini.

"Mmm," she says after her first bite. "It's even better than I remember."

"I modified his recipe a bit," I tell Blake, trying to keep things light even though my heart is sinking like a stone. "I added some freshly shredded Parmesan in with the grated Kraft kind he always used."

"It's amazing," she says, taking another bite. She notices I haven't taken any and pushes the bowl in my direction.

It does smell good, and if this is the last time I'm ever going to make it, which I have a feeling it will be, I might as well taste it.

"This is a little weird, right?" Blake asks, acknowledging the elephant who isn't just in the room, but sitting at the table between us. "That he made the same thing for both of us?"

"*So* weird." I never would've brought it up, but I'm glad she did. The tension in the air already feels lighter, even as the silence settles between us.

After a few moments, Blake eases into the conversation we've been circling around for weeks. "What was he like?" she asks, taking a sip of the rosé she brought.

"My dad?" I ask, as if she could be talking about anyone else.

Blake nods, and I take a deep breath, trying to think of how to describe the man I spent so much of my life worshipping. My feelings about him have always been complicated, even more so now that he's gone.

I look up at Blake, whose brown eyes reflect the same trepidation I feel, and I imagine this isn't easy for her, either.

"He wasn't around much," I finally tell her. "When he wasn't working, he was playing golf or watching baseball."

"The Braves," Blake says, and I nod. It's weird knowing we both have memories of the same person in a completely different context. "We used to watch together," she says. "He taught me how to play catch and throw a ball, and how to eat sunflower seeds the right way."

I wince. I didn't know there was a wrong way to eat sunflower seeds, but I would have liked to have learned. I would've played catch or watched the game with him if he'd let me. I look across the table at Blake, sitting there with her easy smile and quiet confidence, and wonder what it was about her that made him be the kind of dad I always wanted him to be.

For some reason, I need her to know that he wasn't always that way. At least, not with me.

"He could be tough," I say, trying to mince my words so I don't speak ill of the dead. "He had high expectations, liked things to be and look a certain way."

"He hated clutter, right?" Blake asks.

This time, I'm the one who nods.

"It drove him crazy that my mom always had stuff everywhere," Blake says. "It was a running joke between them. She always told him if he didn't like it, he could leave her for a tidier woman." She stops talking and clears her throat. "In hindsight, it's not that funny."

I manage a weak laugh, but I can't wrap my head around the idea of my dad joking and being lighthearted with his other family. "Did he and your mom fight a lot?" I ask.

"Oh no," Blake says, answering without giving it a second thought. "They were crazy about each other in that cheesy way you see in the movies. My mom seemed to glow whenever he was there, and he was always touching her, even if it was just a hand on her arm or her leg."

I don't say anything, because I'm afraid that if I open my mouth, I'll just scream or cry. Maybe both. The man she's describing doesn't sound a thing like the dad I had or the husband my mom did.

"Was he like that with your mom?" Blake asks. Her voice is almost timid, and I'm pretty sure she already knows the answer.

I shake my head. "They fought a lot. But only behind closed doors. In public, they acted like an adoring couple with a perfect life."

"It's almost like he was two different people," Blake says, putting into words what I've been thinking.

I sigh and look down at my empty plate. I don't even remember tasting the pasta, but it's gone. "Do you want coffee or something?" I ask, slipping back into my role as hostess.

"I'd love some tea," Blake says. "But I'll get it. Please. I'm not a guest." She doesn't say what she really is—a co-owner of this house. And in some strange way, family.

I follow her into the kitchen and watch as she takes a mug down from the cabinet above the sink. She seems so at home here, which she should after all these weeks, but it still feels unsettling seeing her move around my house like it's hers.

After she microwaves the water and drops in the tea bag, I watch as Blake takes a sugar packet and hits it three times against her palm before tearing the corner and pouring it into the mug.

Goosebumps run up and down my arms. It's the exact same way my dad used to pour sugar into his coffee. I know he was just loosening up the crystals, but I used to tease him about it—would it not taste as sweet if he only tapped it twice? Too sweet if he tapped it four times?

For the last fifteen years, I've known that Blake was my father's daughter, but it hits me all over again, seeing such small similarities between them.

I don't say much while Blake drinks her tea. It's not very hostessy of me, but my mind is swirling and I can't bring myself to make small talk. Not when everything feels so overwhelmingly big.

AFTER BLAKE LEAVES to head back to the casita, I stay out on the back porch and finish the bottle of wine. I think about my dad, and how sad it is that I'll never know which "him" was the real one. The weekend version Blake grew up with, or the weekday one I had.

The stories Blake shared sounded like they were about a completely different man, a man I would've liked to know. A man who would've actually been worthy of the way I worshipped him.

I used to explain away my dad's faults—how cold and difficult he was—by telling myself he didn't have the capacity to love. Now it turns out he had the ability; he just chose to give it to someone else. She got the best of him, and I got the rest of him. And I'll never know how different things would have been, how different I would be, if I'd grown up with the version of our dad Blake had.

I look up and wonder if he's watching. What he'd think of all this, and if, at the end of the day, he had any regrets.

That's one thing I know: I don't want any regrets. I don't want to die and have people realize they never knew the real me. I think about all my followers and the show I've been putting on for them. For myself.

Before I can talk myself out of it, I open Instagram on my phone, search for one of the rare photos of me and my dad, and start a post. I write a few sentences about him, sharing that he passed away a few months ago and that I haven't been strong enough to share with the world yet because it's been too painful.

I want to let my followers know what's really going on in my life. Not all the sordid details, just enough to let them know that in losing my dad, I've lost my footing in the world and the way I see it.

After I hit post, I turn my phone all the way off so I'm not tempted to go back in and delete it. It may not be pretty. But it's authentic. And it's most definitely me.

CHAPTER TWENTY

BLAKE

I WAKE TO THE FEELING OF NOAH'S LIPS PRESSING AGAINST the back of my neck.

"Good morning," he murmurs. "You smell good."

A soft smile spreads across my face. I've already gotten way too used to waking up like this. We quickly migrated to sleeping together in his bedroom at the Rooneys'—so much nicer than either the casita or his room over the garage. The dog sleeps curled up at the foot of the bed, a fluffy ball of happiness.

"Let's stay in bed all day," Noah says in my ear, and I roll over to face him. I love the way he looks in the morning, his hair rumpled, his eyes soft. "My arms are aching from painting baseboards yesterday. You're quite the taskmaster, you know that, right?"

I run my hand down his cheek, his beard soft against my palm, and trace his lips with my fingertips. "Hopefully what I did for you last night made it worth it?"

He tilts his head, his eyes dancing with laughter. "Eh, I'm not sure. You might have to do it again to remind me."

I laugh and snuggle against him, my cheek against his chest and my legs twining with his under the sheets. We've been spending practically every moment together—making breakfast in the mornings in the Rooneys' fancy kitchen, then heading over to my beach house to knock out whatever is on my list for that day. Noah may not be very skilled at home improvement, but he makes up for it by feeding me and making me laugh so hard I nearly pee my pants. And I appreciate having his body at my disposal—not just for the renovation-related tasks that require his height, but also for whatever activities we get up to in bed.

"Have to say, it's weird to sleep in a room where you've slept with a dozen other girls." I say it in a teasing tone, but there's some truth behind it. I'm guessing teenage Noah—or rather, *Junior Rooney*—was a hit with the girls of Destin. I remember Kat talking about how dreamy he was when we were at camp.

"I was way too afraid of my parents' disapproval to have sex right under their noses," he says, trailing his fingers across my stomach. "The only person they *knew* slept here with me was Annalise."

Ah yes. His ex-fiancée. Thinking of her gives me a pinched feeling inside. Jealousy? Or maybe confusion. I found a picture of her, tucked into the top dresser drawer. She's tall and brunette, posh and preppy. Exactly the kind of woman I'd picture a guy like him with. I wouldn't be surprised if there's a building at some Ivy League school with her family name on it. It makes me wonder what Noah is doing with me.

But I'm not going to waste time being insecure. We have a few short weeks left together before the summer ends and we go our separate ways, and I want to make use of every moment.

"The way you say that implies that there were other women your parents *didn't* know about," I say, glancing up at him.

He hums, thinking. "Well, just one when I was seventeen. It was a girl whose family has a beach house in the area. We were both desperate to lose our virginity. My parents had gone to Pensacola for the evening and CoCo had a bunch of friends over. I snuck the girl in my bedroom window and her shorts got torn on the windowsill."

"Sounds dangerous," I say.

He gives a soft chuckle. "Honestly, it wasn't very good. I was nervous and kept awkwardly apologizing, like, 'Sorry, sorry, didn't mean to do that.' But hopefully"—he flips me over on my back, grins down at me—"I've gotten better since then."

I smile up at him. "I'll be the judge of that."

WE SPEND THE day running errands together, picking up supplies for next week. Somehow, we get on the topic of food, and when I admit I've never had oysters, Noah is horrified. He insists that we go to Hunt's Oyster Bar for dinner, so we tuck the dog in my room at the casita with a treat and drive an hour from Destin to Panama City.

The restaurant is a ramshackle yellow building surrounded by a crowd of people waiting. Seashells and oyster shells litter the ground, and a few old guys play cornhole outside. My stomach growls with hunger and excitement. Inside, Hunt's is packed, with people sitting at the bar and around tables, the wood-plank walls lit up with neon beer signs. We order drinks, and Noah orders a whole bunch of oysters, raw and baked.

"My parents never wanted to come here," Noah says, after our waitress leaves with our orders. "Annalise, either. Too much of a dive for them."

"Dives like this are always the best places to eat," I say.

"You look really nice tonight, by the way," he says, smiling at me. "Just in case I haven't told you."

"You've mentioned it a few times," I say. And yet I still feel myself glowing with the compliment. I'm wearing another vintage sundress of my grandmother's that I borrowed from the beach house. This one is red gingham with a keyhole neckline, and once again, it feels like it was made for me. Judging by Noah's reaction—his eyes are drifting over my body right now, a smile curving his lips—he agrees.

"Have you decided what you're going to do when the summer is over?" he asks.

"Just return to my regular life," I say, shrugging. "Working for the Vanderhaavens, picking up their dry cleaning, driving the kids to school, taking Charlotte to dance lessons and Zachary to soccer."

"Is this what you want to do long term? Like, does it fulfill you?"

His question makes me pause—I'm guessing he's thinking about his own life—but fulfillment has never been the point for me. I've never had the financial safety net to consider what I *want*; I've lived paycheck to paycheck my entire adult life. "It allows me to visit my granddad every weekend. It pays fairly well. But . . ." I take a breath. "It's not my dream job."

"What is your dream job?"

I contemplate that. "No idea. I'd have to go back to college to get a 'real' career, but being cooped up in an office, having to say 'yes, ma'am' and 'yes, sir' all day—that doesn't appeal to me. What about you? Now that you're no longer heir to the Rooney Underwear Empire."

He snorts. "I have a couple leads. My buddy in Chicago, the one I visited over the Fourth, has a tech start-up that's doing well. That's why I went to visit him; he wants someone to run the business side of things so he can focus on the rest. But I also heard from someone at my family's company, too."

Our waitress arrives with a platter of baked oysters, and

Noah watches as I try the first one. It's delicious—breaded and cheesy—and I reach for a second one as soon as I finish the first.

"You like it?" Noah says, grinning.

"I *love* it," I tell him. "Now go on—you heard from someone at your family's company?"

Noah finishes his own oyster, then nods. "He said that my dad is on board with improving conditions at the overseas factories. I'm not sure his motive is altruistic—it's all about the bottom line for him, always has been—but it could be a good thing for the workers, and that's what matters."

I give a cautious nod. "Do you think you'd ever work for them again?"

"The company's been in the family for four generations, so I can't help feeling a sense of loyalty. My dad isn't getting any younger; someday he'll have to sell, and that feels wrong. His great-great-grandfather started the business."

That must be how Kat feels about the beach house. That's why she's so desperate to keep it, no matter the cost. And I can understand the feeling, a little; losing the house would feel like losing a connection to my past, too. A past I'm only just starting to understand.

"But on the other hand," Noah continues, "I want to figure out who I am, separate from my family. Write my own story. My own identity."

"As Noah, not Junior," I say.

"Exactly."

Our waitress reappears, this time with a platter of raw oysters. I'm a little nervous about these, but Noah tells me to go for it. I top one with a squeeze of lemon and a little cocktail sauce, take a deep breath, and slurp it down. It's a cool, crisp burst in my mouth, slightly salty, like a bite of the ocean itself.

"Amazing," I say after I swallow it. "That's the best thing I've ever tasted in my life. Present company excepted, of course."

Noah laughs, and I'm already helping myself to another one. After slurping that one down, I realize that he's smiling at me, his eyes soft.

"What?" I say.

He shakes his head, still smiling. "Have another oyster, Blake O'Neill."

BY THE TIME we leave Hunt's, I'm so stuffed my stomach hurts. We drive back to the Rooneys' place, where the dog is overjoyed to see us again. He's practically bouncing off the walls with energy, so we take him on a walk down Old 98.

At one point, Noah glances over at me. "By the way, you're gorgeous. Did I say that already tonight?"

I laugh as he pulls me in for a kiss, and for a moment the rest of the world fades away. Gone is the laughter of tourists on the beach, the cry of seagulls overhead, and the crash of waves on the sand. All I can feel is Noah's mouth, Noah's hands on my hips, Noah's fingers drifting lower on my butt. When the dog tries to weasel between us, Noah laughs and releases me. "I'll try to control myself until we get somewhere private," he says, and gives me another quick peck.

We keep walking, and my mind drifts back to what he said at Hunt's about writing his own story. I can relate to that. My identity has always been tied up in my origins as an illegitimate child. Abandoned and left behind. Raised by grandparents whom I now feel compelled to repay.

I'd love to write a new story for myself.

My phone rings with a FaceTime call, distracting me.

"It's Kat," I tell Noah. "Sorry. Give me one minute."

He nods and motions that he'll take the dog so I can talk. When I answer, Kat's face appears on the screen. She's sitting on her bed at the beach house, and she's wearing a sheet mask that makes her look like a pale pink zombie.

"Hey!" she says. "Quick question. I got us the sponsorship for the bedding—do you prefer down comforters or temperature-control ones?"

I'm momentarily taken aback; Kat is asking *my* opinion? "Um. Down is good."

She smiles, crinkling the sheet mask. "Totally agree. Yay. Also, Henry wanted me to tell you that he's starting the electric on the second floor tomorrow and he won't be finished until the middle of next week. Just so you're aware for your own projects."

She keeps prattling on about the renovation, and I half listen. Across the sidewalk, Noah is approached by a family with a little boy and girl who have asked to pet the dog. Noah smiles and goes down on one knee, helping the dog sit while the kids pat his sides and belly. This is what Noah could look like ten years down the road, I realize, patiently showing his own children how to approach a dog. He'll have a wife, too, someone who isn't me, and although it's totally irrational, my heart constricts with longing. *Ridiculous*, I tell myself. And yet I can't stop watching.

The boy asks what the dog's name is, and Noah responds in a serious voice: "His legal name is Cheeto Puff Ball the Magic Dragon, but he prefers to be called Magic Mike."

I stifle a laugh, then force myself to focus on Kat, who is now awaiting an answer. "Yep, that all sounds good. Thanks."

"Where are you?" Kat says.

"Uh . . . just on a walk." I don't know why I feel reluctant to tell Kat about Noah. It's like I don't want to jinx things by talking about it. Like I want to keep it to myself, shiny and precious like a pearl.

Noah is now holding both of the dog's front paws, doing a weird little shimmy-dance to entertain the kids. "Hey, Magic Mike," he's saying. "Shake that moneymaker."

On my phone screen, Kat's eyes widen. "Wait, are you with your guy? Let me see him!"

Noah glances over at me; he must have heard that. *Your guy?* he mouths, his eyes crinkling with mischief.

I shake my head, my cheeks warming, and lower my voice. "He's not *my* guy," I tell Kat in an almost whisper. "I should get going—"

"Oh my god," she says, her voice dropping. "You're wearing Grandma's dress."

I freeze, berating myself for not asking Kat first. "Is that okay?"

Her eyes fill with tears, and she blinks. "Of course. It's just—I haven't seen that dress in ages. It looks great on you—with my hips I'd never get it on. Grandma would be happy that it's being worn."

But would she be happy her son's illegitimate daughter is the one wearing it? I'm not so sure about that.

"Thanks," I say, my voice thick with emotion. We're having such a normal conversation, but it feels momentous. We're talking about *our* grandmother. *Our* shared past. I suddenly wish I could reach through the phone and give her a hug, which is totally out of character for me, and she probably wouldn't want that anyway. But I make a mental note to spend another evening with her soon. I want to talk more about our father. I want to tell her about Noah, too. We have fifteen years to make up for, and I don't want to waste any more time.

She clears her throat, glancing away. Kat isn't any more comfortable with emotion than I am. "I'll let you go," she says. "Have the best time."

After ending the call, I rejoin Noah across the sidewalk.

"So . . ." he says. "Are things with Kat okay?"

"Yeah. Still a little awkward. Maybe it'll always be that way between us. Sometimes she seems so completely opposite me, like . . ."

"Like how could you be sisters?" he says. "I've wondered the same thing."

"We're not really sisters," I say automatically. We link hands and start walking again. "I know we share a father, but the word 'sister' implies memories, inside jokes. Some sort of intimacy. And we don't have that."

But I would like to, I think to myself. *Maybe I can work on that.*

"I don't think Kat ever had that in her family," Noah says.

My interest is piqued. "What do you mean?"

"I mean, I understand pressure—my parents laid it on, too—but it almost seemed like it was Kat's job to make her parents look good. Like they cared more about how she made them look than they cared about her."

"What were her parents like?" My voice catches on the word "parents," but luckily, Noah acts like he doesn't notice.

"This one time—I was thirteen or so—my parents held a party and invited some families in the area, including Kat's. Everyone was out on the lanai, and I went inside to the bathroom. I overheard Kat's parents arguing in the kitchen. It felt nasty, like the air was saturated with the absolute contempt they had for each other. My parents, for all their flaws, never talked to each other like that."

I'm having a hard time imagining my father behaving like that, even though it squares with how Kat described him the other night. In my memories, he was always so sweet to my mother. And why wouldn't he be? She had no expectations of him. When he came to our place, the stress of his everyday life could melt away.

For the first time, I wonder if I was lucky to only see that side of him. Though I wonder which version was real.

"Anyway," Noah continues, "when Kat's parents came back outside a few minutes later, they were smiling like nothing had happened. It was . . . eerie. Like they'd put on masks or something. Turned into this happy, shiny, perfect couple."

Kat must have seen her parents do the same thing, over and over again, throughout her life. It makes sense, when I think about it, why she'd be obsessed with creating a perfect image on Instagram. She learned it from her parents.

SEVERAL DAYS LATER, Kat has gone back to Atlanta to work her magic with some home décor sponsors, and Noah has a virtual interview about a potential job opportunity in New York. My main goal today is to install the new light fixtures in the dining room and bedrooms—free products Kat drummed up in exchange for placement on her Instagram feed. Have to admit, her influencer prowess has come in handy.

Unfortunately, I gave myself a minor shock this morning trying to wire the new dining room chandelier, so I called Henry. He came over with Sunny an hour ago. And even though he could've installed it himself in fifteen minutes, I asked him to talk me through it so I can learn how to do it on my own.

First, he had me turn off the breaker (rookie mistake), and now we're doing the actual installation.

"That black wire connects to the black wire on the light fixture," he says, pointing. "Remember, those wires are 'hot'—that's where the electricity will come through." I'm up on a ladder and he's standing on a chair, holding the light fixture while I wire it. I follow his directions, twisting the two black wires together.

The best thing about Henry is that he has a way of explaining things that feels supportive rather than patronizing—unlike that noodle-haired jackass at the hardware store.

"Like this?" I say, following his instructions.

"Perfect."

From the living room, I hear Sunny talking to the dog: "If you were my dog, I'd put beautiful ribbons in your hair and I'd brush you every day so your fur would always be shiny and luscious. But my *dad*"—her voice increases in volume, as if she's trying to make sure we hear her—"says I can't have a dog because I'm not 'sponsible enough."

"Sounds like you need to get that girl a puppy," I say to Henry.

He shakes his head, smiling. "She'd have a dozen puppies if I let her. Here, secure those together with this wire nut."

He hands me a red plastic cap, and I twist it onto my two black wires. We do the same thing with the white wires—they carry unused electricity back to the breaker, Henry explains—and then connect the bare copper ground wires together. Then he lifts the light fixture flush with the ceiling so I can secure it to the electrical box.

"So," he says. "Kat's in Atlanta this week?"

I nod, grunting as I tighten the bolts. "Yeah. Working on some sponsorships."

He nods to himself. I've learned that Henry doesn't say much, but he has a lot going on in his head. "Driving back and forth must be hard," he says.

"Probably. Does this go here?"

"Yep, you're doing great. I guess Kat wants to visit her mom, though."

I glance at him. His tone sounds almost *too* casual. "I'm sure she does."

"And she probably has other people to see while she's there, too," he says. "Like friends or . . . something."

I stop, a smile stretching my face. "Are you trying to ask me if Kat's dating anyone?"

"No, no, that's not—" Henry sputters. A flush creeps up the back of his neck as he glances at me. "Is she?"

I force myself to suppress a grin. He *likes* her. I had an inkling that he did, from the way he acted on the Fourth of July. It wasn't that he was staring at her; it was more like he oriented himself toward her, subtly shifting his body in her direction, and when she talked, he stopped whatever he was doing to listen to her.

The bigger question is if Kat likes him. I'm guessing yes. I noticed her staring at his arms on multiple occasions—the man doesn't just have guns; he has *cannons*—and at his butt at least once.

"I don't think she's seeing anyone," I say. "You should ask her out."

He shakes his head. "Oh. I don't—I doubt that would go over well."

"Why not?"

"She's—I mean, I'm definitely not her type."

I study him. He's actually serious? "Henry. You're tall and good-looking; you have your own business; you're smart and kind and reliable. Why wouldn't you be her type?"

The flush on his neck deepens. "It's just that I'm—and she's—" He coughs. "Forget it. I'll go turn on the breaker."

He climbs down from his chair and heads to the utility closet at the back of the house while I finish screwing in the new bulbs. Part of me wants to keep pushing the subject with Henry, but he's so obviously uncomfortable that I decide to show some mercy and back off.

When he returns, all I say is, "Well, if you don't ask her, you'll never know. Want to turn on the light now?"

"You should do the honors."

I climb down the ladder and walk over to the switch. Holding my breath, I turn it on, and—hallelujah!—the bulbs flick on, bathing the dining room in warm light. Once I hang the ninety-five crystals around the chandelier, it's going to be stunning.

"I did it!" I say, delighted. "I mean, with your help."

"No, that was all you." He smiles. "I'm sure you can do the ones in the bedrooms without any problem."

I'm ridiculously proud of myself. Henry calls to Sunny that it's time to head home. She bounds into the dining room, the dog following her. The top of his head is covered in a dozen multicolored ribbons that Sunny has affixed to his fur.

"Look how beautiful he looks!" Sunny says proudly. "I shall call him Ribbon Head!"

AFTER HENRY AND Sunny leave, I carefully extract each ribbon from the dog's fur and give him a few nice scratches. Then I sit down on a kitchen chair and look around, satisfaction creeping over me. My vision is turning into a reality, which means I'm getting closer to my goal of selling the house to help my granddad. I talked with him over FaceTime yesterday, with Martina's help, and he's doing well. Staying busy watching John Wayne movies and playing bingo in the common area.

The only problem was that Martina had to remind him five times that he was talking to me. Blake, his granddaughter. I need to get back to him before he forgets me completely. But for some reason, my stomach clenches at the thought of leaving.

Maybe because I have nowhere to call home. My grandparents' house was sold a few years ago; the Vanderhaavens' house certainly isn't home, even though I've lived there for two years. But I feel a connection to this beach house. It's tied to a family and a past I'm just getting acquainted with—plus, I've put so much of myself into renovating it. Selling it off is bound to be painful.

But that's not all. This house is my only connection with Kat. When this summer is over, we'll have no reason to stay in contact. If she buys the beach house from me, she won't need me for anything. On the other hand, if she can't buy me out and we have to sell it, she'll probably never talk to me again because she'll blame me for losing it. No matter what, our relationship feels too new and fragile to survive without anything to connect us.

Strange how a few weeks ago I was looking forward to leaving here and never seeing Kat again, and now my eyes are filling with tears at the prospect of losing her, too.

I dash the tears away. There's no way I can keep this house— that's ridiculous. I have a responsibility to my granddad, who sacrificed so much for me. Selling this house is the only way to take care of him, and I have to be okay with that. Even if it feels like I'll be carving away a little piece of my soul.

CHAPTER TWENTY-ONE

KAT

TWO WEEKS LATER, I'M BACK IN DESTIN AND THE WORTHING- ton application is more than halfway finished—so when Henry asks if I want to go out to Crab Island with him on his friend's boat, the only answer is obviously hell yeah.

I haven't been out on the water in God knows how long— my dad got rid of my grandfather's boat when I was seventeen. He said it was falling apart and not worth the maintenance and dock-storage fees. I didn't mind—the Rooneys' boat was bigger and nicer than ours.

I loved going out on the Rooneys' boat because I felt like royalty. The fridge was always full of beer and soda, there was a spot out front where we could lay out and pretend to be human hood ornaments—and best of all, CoCo's dad didn't make us spend an hour cleaning the boat after every trip. They had staff for that.

I have a feeling Henry's the type to clean the boat himself like my dad was, but I wouldn't mind helping him. Especially if he's stripped down to his swim trunks.

Henry Alexander may not be my type to date, but the man is

built like a living sculpture. His broad chest and solid arms are hard not to stare at, and I've gotten a few glimpses of what I'm pretty sure is a six-pack while he's been working.

A body like that is made to be admired, and if he asks for help applying sunscreen while we're out on the boat, then it would be my honor to help protect him from skin cancer.

I shiver at the thought of him returning the favor, imagining his big, strong hands and calloused fingers on my bare back. I realize I'm getting way ahead of myself. This is definitely not a date—although Sunny isn't coming with us.

When I asked about her, Henry made a joke about child labor being against the law. I sent back a laughing-so-hard-I'm-crying emoji, because my dad clearly didn't have that same philosophy.

One last look in the mirror, and I'm ready to go. My outfit is nautical inspired, a cute blue-and-white-striped dress and straw hat I bought from Rachel Worthington's website. They were full price, which I shouldn't be paying right now, but I figure it's important to show that I'm an advocate of the brand with or without the sponsorship.

The swimsuit I have on underneath, a gold lamé bikini, is a little extra for my taste, but right now, I'm not in a position to turn down a paid post. I'll do a hell of a lot more than wear a crazy swimsuit if it'll help me keep my beach house.

At the start of the summer, the suit would've looked ridiculous against my pale skin, but between my tan and my filters, I'm ready for it. And the contrast will be great against the emerald-green water if Henry snaps a few pictures of me when we get to Crab Island.

Henry offered to pick me up, but he had to make a few stops before getting on the boat, and ten a.m. was already early enough for me to get ready and pack everything up. I've got a mini cooler (filled with snacks, bottles of water, and cans of Truly) plus my

Rachel Worthington beach bag (which is not only cute, but big enough to hold the rest of my essentials: a towel, the latest novel from Rachel's book club, sunscreen, and tanning spray).

I wonder if this is how moms feel, carrying bags laden with stuff everywhere they go. I laugh at the image of Henry as one of the moms, carting around a diaper bag—maybe a diaper backpack?—when Sunny was a baby. The man seems to put everyone before himself.

I'm glad he's taking a day off and honored that he's spending it with me.

THE DOCK WHERE I'm meeting Henry is farther down in Destin than where we used to keep our boat, and it's less manicured, too. The parking lot is more like an empty dirt patch, with cars parked wherever they please. I grab a "spot" and triple-check to make sure my car is locked before heading to find Henry.

I stop by a wooden sign that says THIS WAY TO THE WATER and snap a selfie in front of it. I post it to my stories with the caption: Ahoy! Ready for a fun day on the water with an old friend!

Then I use my phone's camera to check my hair one last time. It took me an hour to get perfect beach waves—which I know is ironic since I spend a fortune every three months on a keratin straightening treatment, but it is what it is. I snap a picture because you can't fake this kind of happy—my crazy-wide smile shows how much I'm looking forward to this day. I adjust the hat, then throw a bag on each shoulder and follow the sign toward the water.

The path is paved with old bricks, and there are a few big wheelbarrows over to the side. I consider using one to carry everything down to the boat, but I want Henry to see Blake's not the only one who can handle hard things.

As I turn the corner toward the promised water, I stop in my tracks. The dock is a dock all right, but there aren't any boats in sight. At least, not the kind of boats I'm used to. This looks like a graveyard where boats come to die.

For half a second, I hope there was a mistake, that Henry gave me the wrong address. That this is some kind of funny joke and he's going to send me a text, saying he's kidding and he'll give me the real address for the correct dock.

I take out my phone, just in case, when I hear him call my name.

"Kat!" he calls. "Over here!"

My heart lifts at the sound of his voice, then quickly falls when I realize that means I'm exactly where I'm supposed to be. I take a deep breath, slip my phone back in my bag, and keep walking toward Henry's voice.

He's standing in a boat that looks like a blow-up raft with a motor on the back, and I feel like an idiot for showing up dressed for a day on a yacht. Although he could have clarified what kind of boat he was inviting me out on.

"Hey," I say through a big smile that I hope Henry doesn't realize is totally fake. I set my bags down and can't help but wince as I take in the "cabin" of the boat. I'm not sure it will fit both of us, my two bags, and Henry's giant cooler, which looks big enough to hold a mini keg.

"Hey," he says, a question in his voice as he looks me up and down, and not in a flattering way. He laughs but stops abruptly when he sees my steely expression. I'm not amused. Not by any of this. "You look . . . nice," he says.

I manage a smile at the quasi-compliment and look at Henry's outfit to try to return the favor, but he's wearing old cargo shorts and a T-shirt that's seen better days.

"Where's your swimsuit?" I ask.

He raises a questioning eyebrow. "I don't go in the water when I'm working."

"Working?"

Henry laughs as if everything suddenly makes sense to him. "I told you I work some shifts on my friend's boat?"

I shake my head. I would have remembered something like that.

"Selling boiled peanuts out on Crab Island?" he says, as if hearing more information will trigger a memory of something that never happened.

I shake my head again.

"I distinctly remember you saying you wanted to get out to Crab Island while you were here," Henry says. "That day at the bank."

"That may be true," I tell him—that part does sound familiar—"but I wanted to go on a boat."

Henry flashes a bright smile that highlights his cheek dimple and holds his hands out to the boat-like object at his feet. It rocks precariously, like it might tip over if he makes a sudden move.

Henry's smile and his dimple vanish when he realizes I'm not buying it. "Listen," he says after a moment. "You don't have to go."

My shoulders slump, and I deflate at the thought of going back to the empty beach house and posting a jk not really going out on a boat message to my story.

"I should've known this wouldn't be your idea of fun," Henry says.

He sounds sad, and I hate being the cause of that. Especially since I'd have fun hanging out with Henry even if we were doing grunt work at the house. Out here, I can at least get a tan. And this could be an opportunity to show my followers that things don't have to be beautiful to be worthy of love. They're probably picturing me on a fancy yacht, just like I was.

If I show them that I can have a fun day on the water in this . . . thing it could be a turning point in evolving my brand. The vulnerability angle is already working in my favor—the post about my dad had more than triple the engagement of my average fashion posts.

If I can be honest and share the truth of the day—admitting the mishap, maybe modifying my reaction and the time it took me to go from "hell no" to "oh, what the hell!" it might have the same impact.

Of course, I'll have to find another way to showcase this bathing suit. If I ask Henry to take a picture of me posing in a gold lamé bikini, it will just confirm what he probably already thinks of me. And it isn't pretty.

I look back up at Henry, whose face looks poised for disappointment, one side of his mouth on the verge of turning down. He looks like he genuinely wants me to go with him. And who am I to keep Henry from getting what he wants, especially after he's done so much for me and Blake.

"Are you going to help me get on this thing or what?" I ask.

Henry's face lights up again, and he holds his hand out for me to step into the boat. It wobbles beneath my feet, and I'm glad I settled on white flip-flops instead of the wedge sandals that looked cuter with this outfit.

"Shall we?" he asks, grabbing my two bags and wedging them next to the big red cooler, which I assume is filled with boiled peanuts, not beer.

"Let's go sell some nuts," I tell him.

TURNS OUT, I don't have to try very hard to have fun. The tiny boat has its benefits. It doesn't go as fast as the ones I'm used to, but being closer to the water makes it more exciting.

It's too noisy to talk, so I close my eyes and feel the wind in my face and the water spraying pretty much everything as we cut across the sparkling water, the sun shining down on us. With Instagram off my agenda, I can just enjoy the day for what it is.

Henry and I cover every inch of Crab Island—which isn't really an island, just a shallow section of water near the Destin Bridge. On nice days it's like a floating block party, with boats anchoring together or on their own. The water is waist-high so people can walk around, play Frisbee and football, or just float from boat to boat.

Since Henry's boat is so small, we easily maneuver in between the normal-boat-size boats and yachts, which is some of the best people watching I've ever witnessed.

At the first few boats we stop at, I sit back and watch Henry make the sale. He's able to close the whole deal with not much more than hand gestures and a "That'll be five dollars."

At first, the extent of my helping is either making change or handing Henry bags of the boiled peanuts from the cooler. But after about half an hour, he putters past a boat where I see a woman wearing the same Rachel Worthington cover-up as mine. That turns into a conversation, which turns into a sale, and after that, I'm hooked!

By the end of the day, we've switched roles: Henry is handling the money and the nuts, and I'm talking to customers and drumming up sales. Although to hear Henry tell the story, I'm doing less selling and more talking. But we still manage to sell the last bag by two o'clock.

"That was really fun," I tell him as we head back toward the dock.

"And you almost didn't come," Henry says, as if it's fact.

"Not true," I tell him, even though there was a hot minute

when I was considering coming down with a spontaneous stomach bug.

Henry shakes his head. "The look on your face. And your outfit."

"Hey," I say in defense of myself and the great Rachel Worthington. "I look cute."

"You look beautiful," Henry says, which makes me unexpectedly glow inside. "Just not dressed for a day's work."

"Which you forgot to mention," I remind him—even though Henry insisted earlier that I had all the information and simply chose to believe what I wanted to.

"Either way," Henry says, "I'm glad you stuck with it. You made the day a lot of fun."

"And I was a big help," I add.

"You made the day more fun," he says again, a smile cracking on his normally serious face. The smile fades and he's all business as we come in for a landing parallel to the dock. "Watch your hands," Henry says.

He hops out of the boat with ease, even though the dock is a good foot and a half above us. "Hand me the rope?" he asks, nodding toward a thick white rope coiled in the bottom of the boat. He wraps the loose end around a pole, doing one of the knots I'm pretty sure we learned at camp.

Once the rope is secure, I stand, trying to get my balance. It feels like the floor of the boat and the water are moving in different directions. "What's next, boss?"

Henry laughs. "You're relieved of duty. I've got the cleanup; you helped more than enough with the sales."

My ears perk up and I grab Henry's extended hand to help me out of the boat. "What's that?" I tease as I step onto the dock. "Did you just admit I was helpful?"

Before he can answer, my left flip-flop catches between two

wooden slats on the dock, and I fall forward, catching myself on Henry's broad, sturdy chest.

His hands are instantly on my waist, holding me steady. I look up at the same time Henry looks down, and our eyes lock. My heart is racing and I'm as out of breath as if I've just run a mile, not tripped an inch. We hold each other's stare for what feels like forever, until he breaks it, his gaze drifting down to my lips.

My breath hitches and I realize I want to kiss him. Even more surprising: I think he wants to kiss me, too. I can feel his heart beating beneath my palm, heat radiating from his skin. I tilt my head up, ever so slightly, an invitation to cross the friend-zone line.

An invitation he turns down with a hard stop, going stiff and taking a step back. The playful, fun energy we've had between us is gone, replaced by a sinking feeling of embarrassment. I must have completely read that moment wrong.

The only saving grace is that I drove my own car, so I can escape with my head held high and don't have to stick around pretending that Henry Alexander didn't just turn down my accidental advance. I can't even bring myself to look him in the face. Afraid of what I'll see in his striking green eyes.

"You sure you don't need me to do anything?" I ask, hoping his answer will remain no.

"It's okay," he says, hopping back into the boat, as if he can't get far enough away from me. "Thanks again for the help."

I can feel his eyes on me after he sets my beach bag and cooler on the dock, so I force myself to meet his stare and smile. He's the only real friend I have, and I can't afford to lose him over an awkward almost kiss. He was right to shut me down—I'm as wrong for him as wrong can be. He's a grown man with a young daughter and a boatload of responsibility, and I'm a hot mess.

As I head back to the parking lot, a bag on each shoulder, I think of all the ways I'm wrong for Henry Alexander. I'm flighty as hell, for one, I don't have a stable job, and three, he probably thinks I'm a selfish, spoiled brat. Especially after the way our day started.

And what sucks the most is that I'm pretty sure I had more fun on his damn dinghy than I would on the biggest yacht in Destin. But even if I told Henry that, I doubt he'd believe me. He has a picture of me in his mind, and that isn't going to change.

Besides, even if he was interested—which he clearly isn't—it could never be more than a fling since I live in Atlanta. And he's a *dad*. Dads shouldn't have flings.

My stomach twists with the truth I can no longer pretend away. My dad had a fling. More than a fling. He had a second family. A family who got the best version of him. I blink away the tears threatening to fall and load up the car to head back to my empty beach house, feeling more alone than ever.

THE NEXT DAY, I'm sitting out on the back deck, trying to think of the perfect answer for the Worthington "why" question that's still haunting me, and trying not to think about the inappropriate dream I had last night starring me and Henry in the bucket of his little boat.

My cheeks burn with the memory—both of the dream and of his stone-cold rejection. I texted him last night, thanking him for a great day, but he hasn't texted back yet.

As if reading my mind, my phone buzzes, making the table vibrate. My heart sinks at the sight of CoCo's face on the screen, until I realize she's just the person to cheer me up.

Before I can even say hello, she launches into her story.

"OMG, Kat," she says. "I am so glad you answered. I just have to tell somebody." I smile at the thought of being someone's "somebody," until she spoils the compliment. "I swear, you're the only one who answers their phone."

"What's going on?" I ask, even though I'm not sure I can muster whatever enthusiasm or sympathy CoCo needs.

"I called the gardener with a question about the hydrangeas, and the guy is down in Key West!"

"Oh?" I say, not sure why this is a big deal.

"Right?" CoCo says. "Turns out my fuckup of a brother gave the guy a paid vacation—told him to leave town and keep collecting his paycheck. Apparently, Junior has been living in the apartment above the garage and taking care of the property himself."

"Oh," I say, intrigued this time.

"I know, right?" CoCo says, getting more worked up. "I haven't told my parents because they'd die—but you're down there, and he's down there, and I don't know, I was thinking maybe you could talk some sense into him?"

"I'm the wrong person for that job," I tell her.

"You're the only person," CoCo says. "The only person I trust. Besides, my brother loves you. Last time I saw him, I caught him looking at your IG. He said you were hot and that he'd missed out."

My belly flutters with the thought of reuniting with my childhood crush. CoCo has always been angling for us to end up together—plus Junior and I would make sense. A day on the water with him would be on a yacht, which is honestly where I belong.

"What do you want me to do?" I ask CoCo, resigned.

"Omigod," CoCo gasps. "You're my hero."

THREE HOURS LATER, CoCo has somehow found out that Junior is going to Boshamps for happy hour. Since Blake has a date with her mystery man and things are still weird with Henry, I have no reason not to agree to show up there and "accidentally" run into Junior. CoCo promised he'd be happy to see me, which is good because I couldn't take two rejections in as many days.

My outfit is perfectly curated, from a fun and flirty Alice + Olivia dress down to the UnderRooney thong I'm wearing beneath it all. Normally, I'd wear my favorite pair of Hanky Pankys if there was even a chance the night would end in bed—but I thought Junior might appreciate the brand loyalty.

Somewhere on the drive between the beach house and Boshamps, I start imagining a world where Junior and I might actually get together like a second chance love story. CoCo would certainly love that—she thinks a healthy relationship with a good woman from a good family could be just the thing Junior needs to save his reputation and get his old life back.

I find a parking spot right out front of Boshamps, which I take as a good sign. After yesterday, I have a new appreciation for paved parking lots. I brush away the thought of Henry and his strong arms catching me, then pushing me away, and remind myself that Junior is the kind of man I should be involved with.

With my head held high and butterflies fluttering in my belly, I walk through the restaurant and out to the patio, where there's a bar and a beautiful view of the water and the harbor below.

I see Junior as soon as I walk outside. His back is toward me, but I recognize his tall, slim frame, and the light brown hair that used to be blond when we were young. It's a bit longer than I've ever seen it, but he wears it well. Junior Rooney can wear anything well.

I take a steadying breath, smooth out the skirt of my dress, and approach my target.

"Hey, stranger," I say in a high-pitched voice that doesn't sound like my own. Before I can stop myself, I attempt a casual shoulder bump as if we're bros on the football team—forgetting that Junior is almost a foot taller than me.

Junior startles, looking down at me. His normally chiseled face is covered with a beard that's a little much for my taste, but that's why God invented razors. Even with the beard and the lines around his eyes that remind me neither of us is a kid anymore, he's still hot as hell.

"Kat?" Junior says after a pause that's a beat too long. He looks surprised, but not in the good way CoCo promised.

"The one and only," I say, holding my hands out as if presenting myself. "So, what's a guy like you doing alone in a place like this?"

I cringe as I hear the cheesy line coming out of my mouth—it's been so long since I've attempted to flirt in person that I've forgotten how. It's so much easier on the apps, where you can just swipe right if you're interested.

"I'm here with somebody," Junior says, looking over my shoulder toward the door.

"Well, lucky me, I ran into you first," I say, knowing full well that luck has nothing to do with it.

Junior nods but still seems to be looking over my head.

"Aren't you going to ask if I want a drink?" I say, flashing the smile that's usually good for a free vodka soda.

"Uh . . ."

"It would be fun to catch up," I say. "It's been a long time—remember that bonfire on the beach?"

That brings a smile to Junior's face, and I wonder if he's fondly remembering the night when we stayed at the bonfire after everyone else went inside, toasting s'mores. The sticky-sweet kiss was my first. It was over before I realized what was happening and I spent the next four years hoping I would have a chance at a do-over.

Before I can think of something witty to say, a blond woman brushes past me and plants her lips on Junior's. This is not a friendly, "hey, good to see you" kind of kiss. This kiss is a prelude for what's to come later.

I look away as Junior deepens the kiss—he's clearly forgotten all about me—and I curse CoCo for getting her signals crossed. Her brother doesn't seem to be single, seeing as he's in the middle of a bar, kissing—my sister?

My jaw drops as Blake and Junior separate. "Well, hello to you, too," she says, smiling up at him, her hand against his chest. *Too early in the relationship, my ass.*

The two of them are still staring at each other like I don't even exist. I shake my head, and I can't stop the words from tumbling out. "This is why you wouldn't tell me about your boyfriend?" I ask Blake, trying not to raise my voice, but I'm boiling mad.

Blake turns, clearly shocked to see me. Her expression quickly turns to guilt. This isn't some accident; everything about Blake is calculated. She's wearing lipstick, for God's sake. And one of my grandmother's sundresses. She knew exactly what she was doing when she went after Junior Rooney, trying to stake her claim on yet another person in my life.

"Kat," Blake says my name like it's an apology, but I don't want to hear it. My mind is spinning back to all those times I asked about her mystery guy and she played coy. I should have known she was up to something—what other reason would a grown woman have to be so secretive? So many fucking secrets.

"What are you doing here?" Blake asks, acting all innocent and confused.

"Me?" I shriek, my voice well beyond a normal volume. "What are *you* doing here? In my grandmother's dress! You can wear her clothes, but that doesn't make you one of us. And of all the men in Destin, you had to get involved with *him*? You knew I had a thing for CoCo's brother."

"I didn't know he was her brother," Blake says, stepping away from Junior as if that can erase the memory of their lips locked on each other's just a moment before.

I laugh even though there's nothing funny about the situation. "Silly me, I thought you'd be smart enough to realize that the guy named *Junior* living in his *parents'* house would be CoCo's brother."

"Stop calling me Junior," Junior snaps, finally speaking up. "I have my own name."

I don't even acknowledge him; this has nothing to do with him.

Blake's face has gone white. "I thought he was the gardener at first," she says. "And when I found out he was a Rooney—"

"So you *did* know!" I say, giving a bitter laugh. "Did you go after him just to get back at me? That's why you're here, isn't it? You want to sell my grandparents' house just to hurt me. Just because you can."

"Of course not," Blake says. She reaches her hand toward me, but I pull my arm away. If she touches me I'll fall apart, and I want to be angry. It's easier to be angry.

"I had a crush on him for *ten years*," I tell Blake, already so embarrassed I don't even care that Junior's listening. "Why do you have to try and take everything I have left? Everything and everyone I love."

People are staring; Dad would be disappointed in me for making a scene—but it's his damn fault that we're in this mess. His fault, and Blake's.

"I didn't know," Blake says, her voice calm and at a reasonable volume. She's the kind of daughter my dad always wanted me to be. I choke back a sob because I know if I start crying, I won't be able to stop.

"Even if you did know," I say, trying to stop my voice from shaking, "you would've done the same thing because that's what you do. You get people to trust you, then you hurt them."

"I'm sorry." Blake's voice cracks with emotion, but I don't believe it. I don't believe her. There's a reason people say "fool me once, shame on you, fool me twice, shame on me." And I am done letting Blake O'Neill make me look like a fool.

Junior rests a hand on Blake's shoulder and I just can't. I don't give a shit about him, but I thought I cared about Blake. I thought we were getting to a place where we could be like sisters.

Maybe that does make me a fool. But it also makes her a manipulative jerk.

"Save your sad act for someone else," I tell her. "I see through it all. I see the real you, just like my dad did. You're pathetic. No wonder he didn't come back for you."

Blake's face crumples, and I instantly feel sick to my stomach. I just said the worst possible thing to her. But before I can take it back, she runs down the wooden stairs toward the harbor.

Junior looks at me, his blue eyes fiery with anger. "What the fuck is wrong with you?" he says, then runs off after her.

I shut my eyes and try to calm the storm raging in my head. I don't know whether to scream or cry; I just know I have to get the hell out of here. People are staring and whispering, and I hope like hell that none of them recognize me.

CHAPTER TWENTY-TWO

BLAKE

MY EYES ARE SO FULL OF TEARS I CAN HARDLY SEE, AND I nearly run into a group of people on the boardwalk in front of Boshamps. Dodging them, I keep moving, desperate to be away from the crush of bodies, the smell of fried food wafting from the restaurant. My chest feels like it's been wrapped in barbed wire. I can't breathe; I need space.

Noah is somewhere behind me, calling my name, but I don't stop or turn around. I need to get away from them—both Noah and Kat—so I can process what just happened.

My phone buzzes in my pocket, and I pull it out: a call from Noah. I don't think I'm capable of speech right now—my throat is so thick and swollen it hurts to swallow. I silence my phone and brush tears from my cheeks with the back of my hand. A sweet elderly gentleman asks me if I'm all right, and I nod even though it's obvious that isn't true.

I head past rows of gigantic deep-sea-fishing boats to a less crowded spot, where I find a place to sit down. My phone vibrates again—another call from Noah. Just thinking about him makes my eyes tear up again, so I don't answer. I'm about to turn off my phone when a text comes in from him: At least tell me that you're okay.

That, I know, is the right thing to do. I reply, I just need some time alone. I'm okay. If you could keep an eye on the dog for a few hours I would appreciate it. Then I turn my phone off.

The message was partially true: I do need time alone, but I don't know if I'm okay. My emotions are so tangled up I can hardly sort them out—embarrassment and anger and a deep, aching sadness. Kat's words are still ringing in my ears, and all I can see when I close my eyes is the disgust on her face. Just when we were finally, finally forging a connection, everything has been blown to bits. I wrap my arms around myself, rest my forehead on my knees, and try to focus on the sound of the water, the feel of the breeze, the squawk of seagulls in the harbor.

I had no idea Kat still had feelings for Noah. We were twelve the last time I heard her talk about him, and every girl in our cabin had a crush on some ridiculous boy; we'd giggle about them at night after lights-out. Mine was Timothy Bottsweiler, a boy with adorable dimples and hair like a young Zac Efron, who slow danced with me to James Blunt's "You're Beautiful" at the sixth-grade promotion party. All summer, I practiced writing *Blake Bottsweiler, Blake O. Bottsweiler, Blake O'Neill-Bottsweiler,* in the margins of my camp journal. But now? I probably wouldn't recognize him if he stood up in my soup. Definitely wouldn't give two shits if Kat started dating him now.

However. From what Kat said in the bar, her feelings for Noah are more than just a middle school crush.

My stomach drops. Was Kat the girl Noah lost his virginity to? The one he snuck in through his bedroom window, the girl who tore her shorts on the windowsill? He said it was a girl whose family had a beach house in the area. It makes me sick to consider it, but it makes a horrid kind of sense. If I'd known that, I never would've gotten involved with him.

What is he even doing with me? Noah's a decent human being—that I know—so I can't believe he's been intentionally playing me this summer. But it's obvious I'm not the kind of woman he'll end up with long term. He comes from a vastly different background than mine. A world like Kat's, full of wealth and privilege that I frankly don't want to be part of.

This summer has just been a nice break for Noah, a chance to slum it for a few months while he figures out the next move in his real life. But my feelings for him *are* real. And they're stronger than I've allowed myself to admit—the sharp ache in my chest makes that clear.

Tears burn my eyes and I blink them away. I've fallen hard for Noah over the past few weeks; he's sweet and funny and sexy and I never stood a chance against those ridiculous nicknames he makes up for the dog. But how he feels about me isn't so clear. He enjoys being with me; I make him laugh; we have a great time together. But deep down, I suspect that he thinks of me as a fun summer fling. A break from his real life.

Just like my mother and I were for my father.

And that cuts to the heart of it. I curl my knees into my chest and put my forehead on my them, letting myself cry silently, my shoulders shaking in stiff, jerking sobs. For the first time in years, I don't try to stop them, don't try to stuff them back down and bury them under a shell of indifference. I let it all roll through me: the day of my mother's funeral, when I searched the face of every man walking through the door of the church, believing my father would be one of them. The long, lonely weeks after I moved in with my grandparents, when I woke up every morning believing today would be the day he'd pull in the driveway and take me to live with him. The crisp summer morning at camp when he came to get Kat; when he recognized me, said my name, and for one shining moment I believed that he would run to me, put his arms around me, tell me that he'd been searching for me all these years and that he would never, ever let me go.

But instead, he turned and walked away.

Those moments are scraped into my soul, like initials carved into a tree, marking me forever. I'm easy to walk away from, easy to leave, easy to forget. Not worth fighting for. How else could my own father have abandoned me? And if he would do that, how can I expect anyone else to stay?

CHAPTER TWENTY-THREE

KAT

AFTER LEAVING BOSHAMPS, I DRIVE AIMLESSLY AROUND
Destin, heading nowhere because I don't have anywhere to go.
My face is damp with tears and my ears are still ringing from my
confrontation with Blake. I'm desperate for someone to talk to,
but I don't have anyone to call. Which is pretty pathetic for someone who has almost one hundred thousand "friends."

I can't call CoCo—she has no idea what's going on with me,
or her brother, apparently. I can't call my mom. I wish I could
talk to Henry, but we haven't really cleared the air about what
happened the other day.

And Blake . . . I never should've opened the door for her
again. She was literally the person who taught me that people
you love could hurt you. When will I learn people don't change
and I shouldn't expect anything different from them? Isn't that
the definition of insanity? Doing the same thing and expecting
different results?

It was insane to let my guard down, to trust Blake. My eyes
sting with fresh tears as I think of the way she walked right past

me and into Junior's arms as if I wasn't even there. Their embrace is burned in my mind, the way his hands trailed down her back toward her butt. I shake the image out of my head, knowing it won't do me any good.

As I pull up to the light at Crystal Beach Drive, the familiar opening chords of "Build Me Up Buttercup" come drifting through my speakers. The song stirs a memory and tears stream down my face as I picture Blake and me in the dining hall at camp, practicing our lip-sync dance routine when that hippie counselor walked in and told me about my grandpa.

At the time, I had no idea that wouldn't be the only terrible news I'd be getting that week. But I can't help but wonder if Blake had known what was coming. If that was why she'd offered to wait at the lodge with me that morning. If she'd just pretended to be sad I was leaving, while in reality, she couldn't wait to be reunited with her dad. My dad. Our dad.

Behind me, a car honks. The light has turned green, but instead of continuing straight, I turn right, not allowing myself to think about who I'm heading toward, and why he's the only person I want to see.

A FEW MINUTES later, I pull in front of Henry's little blue house. The sun has started to set and the sky is an orangey pink. It would make a beautiful #NoFilter photo for my stories, but I don't have the heart or the energy.

Henry's sitting on the front porch, his nose buried in a book. He doesn't look up until I close the car door.

I watch as the expression on his face transforms from surprise to delight, then concern at the sight of my tear-streaked face. I thought for sure the well of my tears had run dry, but at the tilt of Henry's head and the slight dip in the corner of his mouth, they start again.

"Kat?" Henry says, standing up. "What's wrong?"

"What isn't wrong?" I laugh, but the sound turns to sobs.

He's by my side instantly, helping me up the porch steps as if my leg is broken, not my heart. As we walk, he rubs my back in the way I imagine he does for Sunny. She's so lucky to have such a good dad. I would have given anything for my dad to have done that, to try to comfort me just one time when I was sad.

The thought makes me come undone, and a new wave of grief washes over me.

"Shh," Henry says, still rubbing my back as we sit side by side on the front porch swing. "What happened?"

I manage to tell him most of the story—pretending I'm talking to my old friend Henry and not the Henry I almost kissed. I tell him about how excited I'd been after the call from CoCo, the shock of seeing Blake and Junior together, and how the pieces of the puzzle finally clicked, why she's been so secretive about the guy she's been dating.

"I'm just so tired of losing everything that matters to me," I say, standing up. I start pacing, too upset and anxious to sit. "And I'm so mad at Blake. I'm mad at myself for being in this position again—it's just like when we were twelve, but instead of trying to take my dad, she's trying to take my beach house. And now Junior? She wants to take everything I love!"

"You don't love Junior Rooney," Henry says. The first words he's spoken in more than ten minutes.

"I could have," I say, turning around to face him. "But Blake ruined it, like she ruins everything." Out of words and out of energy, I lean against the railing, holding on to the pole for support. It buckles under my weight and swings loose.

"Oh!" I jump back, bringing on more fresh tears. *Where do they keep coming from?* "Now *I'm* the one ruining everything!"

"It's okay," Henry says, leading me back to the porch swing. "It's been broken for ages—you know what they say about the fix-it guy's house being the last thing to be fixed."

"Do they say that?" I ask, wiping away the tears I'm tired of crying.

"If they don't, they should," he says, holding my elbow as we sit.

It's quiet save for the sound of my sniffles and the TV inside, where I imagine Sunny is watching cartoons. I hope I didn't scare her with my emotional outburst. It was selfish of me to come here. I should've gone to the outlets and found solace in a sale.

"Want to talk about what's really bothering you?" Henry asks.

I turn and look at him, wondering who the hell I've been pouring my heart out to for the last twenty minutes. "I just told you," I say, dumbfounded. "Were you not listening?"

"Of course I was listening. Both to what you said, and what you didn't say."

I slide over, putting space between us as I wait for Henry to tell me what I'm thinking. I really didn't think he was the mansplaining type.

"I don't think it's Blake you're angry with," he says.

I laugh, a sound that's sharp and hard-edged. "Oh yeah? Who am I mad at, then?"

"I think you're mad at what Blake represents," he says.

I shrug, considering the thought. At least it's still Blake adjacent.

"But"—he pauses—"I think the person you're really angry with is your dad."

My shoulders slump as my defenses fall away and I lean back into the swinging bench. Henry's not wrong. I mean, I'm still

270

mad at Blake, but I'm fucking furious at my dad—and somehow, that's even harder than missing him.

"I hate being mad at him," I admit. I spent my life idolizing the man, and now that he's gone, it doesn't seem right to have all these thoughts about his flaws. "I also really miss him. So much."

The tears are back, silently spilling down my cheeks. "I want to give him a bear hug, then yell at him until I'm blue in the face. My feelings are so conflicted and I don't know how they can even exist together. And do I even have a right to be mad at him when he's not here to defend himself?"

"It's like a one-sided fight you can't win," Henry says.

"Exactly." I turn and look at Henry, amazed that he managed to put exactly how I've been feeling into words.

"I have similar feelings toward my ex," he says. "Sunny's mom."

My ears perk up. I've been dying to know about Henry's ex since the moment he said she wasn't in the picture. There hasn't been a right time to ask him about her, and this hardly seems like it—but he's the one who brought her up.

"You're mad at her?" I ask.

"Oh, absolutely," he says. "I knew she was a free spirit when I met her—that was part of what attracted me to her, and I didn't want her to change. I just wanted her to be here. Not for me, but for Sunny. A little girl needs her mom."

"At least she has an amazing dad," I tell him. I don't add what else I'm thinking, that having his love and attention makes up for the absence of her mom.

If my dad had been even half the dad Henry is, I'm sure I wouldn't be feeling this way. But I wonder if Sunny will still grow up feeling abandoned the way Blake does. I don't understand how a parent can just walk away from their kids.

I cringe with the memory of what I said to Blake about Dad

not coming back for her. I may be mad at her—but that was cruel.

"I try my best," Henry says, bringing me back to the moment. "And like you said, there's a lot of conflicted feelings. I wouldn't trade Sunny for the world, and I love that she's got her mom's zest for life."

"Where is she now?" I ask. "Your ex?"

He shrugs. "We get postcards every few months. Last one was from Bali."

"So, she's out there living her best life while you're doing the job of two parents?" I ask, getting riled up on Henry's behalf. It's a lot easier to be mad at someone you don't know, who you don't love. "I'd be furious."

"Yeah," Henry says, and I can tell there's a "but" coming. "But it takes so much energy to be mad, and I'm the only one it hurts. Instead, I try to be grateful—she gave me the greatest gift in Sunny. Kind of like how your dad gave you the gift of a sister."

I harrumph at his attempt to get me to forgive Blake. I'm not ready for that. Not yet.

"If he wanted me to have a sister, then why did he wait so long to bring us back together?" I say, asking the big question I haven't stopped thinking about. "I hate that I'll never know what he was thinking—if he wanted us to get along or if he wanted us to battle it out, one daughter against the other. None of it makes sense."

"Maybe it's not up to him," Henry says. "Maybe the choice is yours."

"It's never been my choice," I tell him, shaking my head for emphasis. "It was my dad's choice to have another family—and it was Blake's choice when she came to camp and tricked me into being her friend so she could get close to my dad and try to steal him back."

"You think Blake was that manipulative at twelve? That she would have been able to plan, much less execute, all that? Do you think she arranged to be in your same cabin?"

"I wouldn't put it past her," I say, even though I'm not so sure anymore. But after fifteen years of telling myself this story, it's hard to imagine it any other way.

"Have you asked Blake about it? Heard her side of things?" Henry asks. He hasn't said this many words together this whole summer, and I don't think I like the way he keeps pushing my buttons.

"I . . . I . . ." I'm not sure what to say, or why he cares so much about Blake. He's been trying to get us to reconcile since he first met her. My stomach twists in a knot at the realization: Henry has a thing for Blake.

It guts me. Everyone seems to prefer Blake over me, and why wouldn't they? She's beautiful in an unassuming way, she listens when people talk, and it seems there's nothing she can't do.

She's the one my dad taught how to spit sunflower seeds; she's the one Junior has fallen for—so of course, Henry would, too. She's definitely more his type than I am. She doesn't mind getting her hands dirty, no one would ever think to call *her* a spoiled snob, and Sunny adores her.

It shouldn't matter—Henry already made it clear he isn't interested in me—but I'm just so tired of being second place.

I turn and look at Henry, whose green eyes are full of concern and focused on me. There's a speck of brown in his left eye I haven't noticed before. He breaks the stare and looks at his hands, folded in his lap. I summon the courage to put it out there and ask. It's better to know than to wonder.

"You like her, don't you?" I ask. "Blake? You've got a thing for her, too?"

Henry looks up, and as his mouth settles into a frown, I know I'm right. For once, I wish I wasn't.

"No," he says. "I've got a thing for her sister."

I frown, too, until I realize what he said. As far as I know, I'm the only sister Blake has.

The knot in my stomach loosens as I think back to the last few months. Seeing Henry outside the bank, the fact that he even recognized me, then watched as I walked away. How patient he was helping me choose between colors for the kitchen backsplash when I know he doesn't give two shits about color. The way he lingered after fireworks on the Fourth. The invitation to go boating. Alone. Just the two of us. That moment after I fell. He hesitated. I could feel his heart beating beneath my palm, and I knew I wasn't the only one who felt something. I've been assuming he'd never go for someone like me, but maybe he's been thinking the same thing about me.

For the second time tonight, I take a risk and put my heart out there. "I've got a thing for you, too," I tell him.

Henry shakes his head, and it takes everything in me not to crumble in a million little pieces. "Two minutes ago, you were crying about Junior, the underwear heir."

"You were right," I say, hoping desperately that he'll believe me. "It wasn't about him."

Henry nods. He knows it's true; he's already said as much. But he's still painfully far away from me on the other side of the bench. I want to close the distance between us, feel his strong hands on my back, his soft lips on mine. They look like they'd be soft.

"You've got a lot in your head right now," he says. "I can't just be something you use to make yourself feel better."

Then, without a word, he stands up, making the bench and my heart rock with his absence. He can't just leave me out here alone. There's a storm brewing inside me, and he's the one who stirred all these feelings up.

"Where are you going?" I ask, torn between hurt and dismay.

"Relax," Henry says. "I'll be right back."

The door closes behind him, and I sit, stewing in my feelings and trying to make sense of it all. How can he say he has a thing for me, and then just walk away?

A few minutes later, the door swings open again, and Henry smiles at me from the doorway. He's holding two Popsicles, just like in my dream of us as children. My heart lifts, and I'm certain it was a memory.

"Do you still like these?" he asks.

I nod, even though I can't remember the last time I had a Popsicle. Such a simple, sweet treat, synonymous with childhood.

He hands me one, and I unwrap it. Red. My favorite flavor.

Henry sits down on the bench beside me and opens his grape one. The two inches of air between us are charged with electricity, and this time, I know it's not my imagination.

I bring the Popsicle to my lips and taste it. It's cold and sweet, and just like back then, it makes the sting of my troubles melt away—although I'm not sure if I can give that credit to the Popsicle or the man who knew it would do the trick.

"Thank you," I tell him. "I already feel better."

Henry nods and twirls the grape Popsicle in his mouth. My stomach flutters, and I can't believe I'm jealous of frozen fruit juice on a stick. It hurts my heart that Henry would think that I'd just use him. Even if he never kisses me, I need him to know that I wasn't just looking for a distraction.

I take a deep breath, then say, "I may have more than just 'a thing' for you." He looks at me, and a lock of thick chestnut brown hair falls in his face and I want more than anything to reach over and tuck it behind his ear. But I have more to tell him.

You've gotten under my skin, Henry Alexander. It's amazing how patient you are. You're such a good listener that you even hear the things I don't say. I love what a good dad you are to Sunny, and most of all . . ." I stop, unsure how to put this feeling into words. "You're the one person who's been able to make me feel grounded and safe and real. But if you don't feel the same—"

Before I can finish, Henry's lips are on mine. They're just as soft as I imagined, but colder, and sweet like artificial grape flavoring. I open my mouth, inviting him to deepen the kiss. This time, he accepts. The kiss is tentative at first, but then his hand slips behind my neck and pulls me closer. I shiver at the cold rush of his tongue brushing against mine, and I'm pretty sure I'll never think of Popsicles the same way again.

A sound at the door startles us both, and we pull back like teenagers up to no good, straightening up just as Sunny pops her head out the door.

"Kat!" she exclaims, bounding toward us and climbing in my lap.

"Hi, sweet girl," I say, giving her a kiss on top of her head. My heart surges with love for this man and his daughter and this moment. Never in a million years would I have thought this was what happiness looked like: a run-down porch, a man with holes in his jeans, a girl with a ratty old bunny and a stain on her shirt. The feeling of belonging.

It hits me that I've had it all wrong. I've been looking for beautiful things to bring meaning to life, when it's moments like these—vulnerable, authentic, imperfect—that make life beautiful.

Suddenly, I know what I have to do to finish the Rachel Worthington application. It's due end of day tomorrow, so I've got to hurry. Even if I don't win the sponsorship, at least I'll know I've created something that's authentically me.

"I've got to go," I tell Henry.

Sunny crawls from my lap to his, and I wish I could lean down and give him another kiss, but I don't want to be presumptuous in front of Sunny.

"Thanks for the Popsicle," I tell him. "I'll call you later?"

He smiles and nods, pulling his little girl closer.

"Say 'good night, Kat,'" he says, and Sunny echoes his words in a singsong voice.

I bound down the stairs, feeling like there are clouds beneath my feet. I turn back before getting in the car and give Henry a "let's pick up where we left off soon" smile.

CHAPTER TWENTY-FOUR

BLAKE

I'M NOT SURE HOW LONG I SIT NEAR THE HARBOR BY MY-self, but the sun has fully set and my body feels stiff by the time I stand up. When I pass a group of people heading into a bar, I let my hair fall in front of my face to shield my puffy red eyes. I'm several miles from the Rooneys' place, and I know I could call Noah to pick me up, but I need to sort through my thoughts first. I can't talk with Kat yet; after the way she yelled at me, I'm not sure I'll be ready for a while. But I do need to talk with Noah.

It takes me nearly two hours to walk back to the Rooneys' house. By the time I get there, all the emotion has drained out of me. I'm a dried-up sponge with sore feet. Near the pool, Noah is asleep on a lounge chair, and for a moment I'm transported back to the first few weeks I knew him, when he was just the sexy, sarcastic groundskeeper, fun to tease and undress with my eyes. The dog is asleep on the ground next to him, one of Noah's hands resting on his furry head.

I take a few steps forward, and Noah sits up at the sound. The shimmering water of the pool reflects the glow of the landscaping lights, casting shadows on his face, deepening the lines on his forehead and around his mouth. He's still wearing the button-down and shorts he wore to the bar, but they're wrinkled and disheveled now.

"Did you walk here?" he asks quietly.

I nod. The dog perks up and trots over to greet me, and I kneel down and give him a scratch around his ears, appreciating the comfort of his soft warmth.

"That's got to be five or six miles," Noah says, shaking his head. "Why didn't you call me?"

"I needed to clear my head." My excuse sounds weak and flimsy, which is exactly how I feel.

Noah's eyes track my face, like he wants to say something but doesn't know how. He looks worried and exhausted, and my throat tightens when I realize that it's my fault for running out on him.

I walk over and sit on the lounge chair next to his, facing him, our knees a few inches apart. The dog sits between us, tail wagging happily. Oblivious to the tension in the air.

"Please talk to me," Noah says.

The quiet concern in his voice sparks fresh tears in my eyes, and I blink to clear them. Noah reaches for my hand, but I keep it on my lap. I'm not strong enough to touch him. If I do, I won't be able to go through with this.

"I—I need you to explain some things," I say.

"Of course. Anything."

"Kat's the girl you lost your virginity to, right?"

His eyes go wide. "Oh my god—no. No. Absolutely not. Blake, I would never, ever—she was like a little sister to me."

My body goes slack with relief. But still: "She had a crush on you for years, though. She made it sound like you two were—"

"We kissed once," Noah says. "I think I was sixteen? It was

a stupid teenage kiss, but I never had any romantic feelings toward her. My sister's always had this idea that Kat and I should end up together, but I was never part of that. Never, Blake. Please believe me."

I do believe him. But that only makes it harder for me to say what I need to say. "Kat has feelings for you, though."

He waves a hand. "I don't know why that matters."

"You heard her! You saw how crushed she was."

"What are you saying?" He stares at me, his eyebrows pulling together in confusion.

I'm having trouble getting out the words, so I run my hands through the dog's fur to help me focus. "We—we have to end it."

"End it?" Noah repeats, his voice flat. "End what?"

I motion weakly between us, unable to meet his eyes. "End whatever this is. Things between us."

"Wait—what?" He sounds incredulous. "I can understand why you're upset about how Kat treated you, but I don't see what that has to do with you and me."

I squeeze my hands together, frustrated he's not getting it. "She has feelings for you."

"So?"

"So I can't do that to her!"

He stares at me again, speechless, for several seconds. "Please tell me that I'm misunderstanding you. I can't believe you're bending over backward for that selfish, entitled, spoiled brat—"

"Hey!" My voice is as sharp as a knife. "Careful who you call entitled—and don't talk about my sister like that."

I stop, shocked at the words that just came out of my mouth. *My sister.* Kat's face appears in my mind, and I see it clearly: all the loneliness and grief she's been carrying all summer, an invisible armor. She's my sister, and right now she's devastated and alone.

And so am I. The weight of everyone I've lost seems to press down on me. My mom, my dad, my grandmother, and someday in the not-so-distant future, my granddad, too. I can't lose Kat. I've had a glimpse of sisterhood, and I can't let it go.

"So that's it?" Noah says. His eyes are sharp, his jaw tight. "Kat throws a temper tantrum, and you end things between us? I thought we had something good, Blake."

I take a shaky breath. "It's been wonderful, Noah, but you know we weren't going to last beyond the summer."

"Why?" There's challenge in his voice, and it makes me sit up straight and take stock of him. His eyes are blazing.

I falter. "Because neither of us lives here. I'm going back to Minneapolis—"

"Why do you think I'm considering the job with my friend in Chicago? I'm trying to figure out how to be as close as possible to you. I don't want to say goodbye when the summer ends. I want to keep seeing you."

I'm stunned. I had no idea he was thinking this. "You—you do? You did?"

"How is it not obvious that I'm crazy about you? I want to be with you constantly. You're all I fucking think about!" He runs his hands through his hair, then leans forward, his eyes locked onto mine. "Just last night I was looking at flights from Chicago to Minneapolis. I could fly out to see you on a Friday night and spend the weekend with you. Every weekend, if you wanted me."

My mouth falls open. I'm speechless, fighting warring emotions. On the one hand, I'm elated that he's been planning a possible future for us, scoping it out. But on the other hand, I'm thinking of my father, showing up for the weekend a couple of times a month, then disappearing back to his regular life.

Yes, it was fun for him, fun for my mom, but there was no commitment, no real intimacy, no mutual support through good times and bad. Real life doesn't just happen on the weekends; it's the weekday mornings when you're out of milk and someone needs to run to the grocery store, the weeknights when you don't have the energy to make dinner, when you're sick or lonely and just want someone to help shoulder the burdens of life.

I'll never know if my mother was happy about the arrangement—maybe she was; maybe she liked her independence; maybe it was exactly what she wanted.

But it isn't what I want.

"I—I can't be your weekend girl," I say. The words feel like acid in my mouth.

"My *weekend* girl? That's not—" Noah shakes his head. "I've been trying not to freak you out by coming on too strong, so maybe I haven't been clear enough. I want to be with you, Blake. I want to see where this can go between us."

My heart feels like it's going to burst. He's so earnest, so lovely and sweet, and I can't take it. I squeeze my eyes shut so I don't have to see the hurt on his face, because now I'm waffling. I'm eight years old again, sneaking out of bed to find my parents slow dancing in the kitchen, their foreheads pressed together. Watching him take her face in his hands and kiss her like she was the most precious thing in the world. I thought they were the paragon of love. And yet he would get in his car and drive away, every time.

He would always, *always* leave.

"You come from a completely different background from me," I say. Tears overflow my eyes and spill down my cheeks. "A different world. And I know you're angry at your family right now, but at some point, you'll reconcile. You'll return to that world, and that's not what I want—"

"I don't want it, either—"

I hold up a hand. "Don't say that. You can't turn your back

on your family. No matter how imperfect they are, they're irreplaceable." I meet his eyes, needing him to understand this. "Noah, you have to stop hiding out here; go and talk with your father. You need to confront him, tell him how you feel. I wish I'd been brave enough to do that while my dad was still alive."

"Brave enough?" His voice is gentle, but his eyes are fierce. "Don't talk to me about being brave. You're doing this because you're scared. You're leaving me before I can leave you, so you can be the one walking away instead of the one left behind."

His words hang between us, caught in the night air like moths flitting around a porch light. I want to disagree with him. I want to tell him he's wrong. But somehow, he's learned more about me this summer than most people I've known for years. He's seen *me*, and that's damn scary.

"Maybe I am," I whisper. "Maybe that is playing a role in my decision. But bottom line, I choose my sister."

His eyes are red, and he rubs a hand over his face. "Okay," he says. That one word sounds like a surrender. Like defeat. "I'll stop trying to change your mind."

He stands, looking down at me from his full height. "But I need you to know one more thing. If we'd had more time together, I could have loved you."

I inhale as his words hit me. They're too heavy, too significant. I can't hold them right now.

"I could have loved you, Blake," he says again. His voice is soft and so very sad. "Maybe forever, if you would've let me."

Before I can respond, he turns and walks away, up the stairs to his room above the garage, and shuts the door behind him.

AFTER NOAH LEAVES, I go into the casita and call Kat—figuring I should, at the very least, reach out—but she doesn't answer.

I'm not surprised, since it's nearly midnight, but it only adds to my overwhelming sense of loss.

I change into pajamas, wash my face, brush my teeth, and get into bed, going through the motions like a sleepwalker. I haven't slept in this bed for weeks—I've been with Noah every night since our first night together—and it feels somehow wrong. I did the right thing, I remind myself. Tomorrow I'll find Kat and we'll talk. I'll tell her I ended things with Noah. That she's too important to me to lose over some guy.

A sob catches in my throat, because that's such a lie. Noah isn't just *some guy*. But Kat's my sister. And like I told Noah: I choose her. I need her.

The casita is dark and quiet. Loneliness wraps around me like a vise, and I'm about to start crying again when I feel the bed jostle.

The dog. He's jumped on the bed, and he's coming toward me like he knows exactly what I need. I've gotten used to him sleeping at the foot of the bed between me and Noah, but I've never done this.

"Hey, buddy, come here," I say, patting the spot next to me. "Good boy."

He curls up with his back against my hip, like he's been waiting for this moment. And maybe I have, too. I bury my fingers in his soft fur, listening to his steady breathing.

Now that he's next to me, I can finally relax, all the way down to my toes, and sleep.

CHAPTER TWENTY-FIVE

KAT

TWO DAYS LATER, MY BAGS ARE PACKED FOR THE DRIVE back to Atlanta. I'm exhausted but energized after submitting the Rachel Worthington application last night under the wire. It was due by midnight and I literally pressed submit at 11:58.

Other than one walk on the beach with Henry and Sunny, I've been working nonstop. And the walk turned out to be just what I needed. Henry snapped a perfect picture of me and Sunny on the beach. My hair is a mess, windblown and curly, and Sunny has on my Rachel Worthington straw hat. There's sand on her swimsuit and my tan lines are showing—but our smiles are as bright as her namesake, the sun. I added that photo to the final section of the application, and it felt complete.

It turns out that my "why," kind of like Henry, was hiding right under my nose the whole time. I took my brand tagline, "Life is a fashion show," and modified it to be "Life isn't just a fashion show."

On paper, it's a small difference, but in practice it's revolutionary and hopefully right up Rachel Worthington's alley.

So many women hold themselves up to an unattainable level

of beauty, thinking that once they achieve it, then they'll be happy. But the point of life isn't to look beautiful or even to be happy all the time—that's impossible. The point of life is to be *alive* in the world, to feel every emotion, even the messy and painful ones. To challenge yourself, to take risks, to find beauty in the imperfections and be grateful for the opportunity to experience it all.

I'm feeling so good about everything—the only cloud hanging over my head is that I haven't talked to Blake yet. She called twice, but I was rushing to finish the essay and was at a point where I couldn't stop or I'd risk losing inspiration.

And deep down, I knew I couldn't be distracted when we had this conversation. I need to focus on Blake when we talk, which wouldn't have been possible until I hit send on the application. I'm hoping this whole mess will be something we laugh about in the not-too-distant future.

I grab a sheet of paper from my grandmother's old desk, which Blake refinished, and write my sister a note—just in case she thinks my silence is because I'm still upset about Junior.

Blake—

I'm sorry for the way I reacted at Boshamps. I'm happy for you and Junior, I really am. My behavior wasn't about him, or even about you. I'd love to talk about it so I can explain and really apologize. Give me a call this week?

xx
Kat

I grab my bag and make one last stop in the second upstairs bathroom. It's become a source of pride that I don't have to stop once on the five-hour trip.

After I wash my hands, the toilet is still running. I jiggle the handle, but it won't stop. I shrug and assume either it will stop on its own, or Blake will figure it out when she comes back later today. Thank goodness she knows what she's doing with all this stuff.

One last glance in the mirror to make sure my lipstick is still fresh for a quick stop at Henry's, and I head downstairs.

I leave the note on the dining room table, where Blake will be sure to see it, and take one more look around, burning the room into my memory in case my days here are numbered.

I've done all that I can do, I remind myself as I lock the door behind me.

CHAPTER TWENTY-SIX

BLAKE

THE MORNING AFTER THE WHOLE DEBACLE WITH KAT, I sleep until the dog's whining at the door finally forces me out of bed. After I let him outside to pee, I flop back in bed and check my phone. It's 10:17 a.m. And there's a text message from Noah.

> Left early this morning. The regular groundskeeper will be here on Wednesday.

A hollow sensation fills my chest, a feeling I recognize all too well from my childhood. Abandonment. I have no right to feel this way—I'm the one who ended things—but still.

Just yesterday morning I woke up in bed with him, his arm heavy across my waist, his fingers tracing sleepy circles on my bare skin. And now, he's gone.

Noah's words from last night return to me: *If we'd had more time together, I could have loved you.* Did he mean that? For a split second I consider calling him, telling him I made a mistake. But then I take a breath. And remind myself that it's better this way.

I have a house to finish renovating, a relationship to mend

with Kat, and my granddad to take care of. That's where my focus needs to be. Not on some guy who could have loved me—but also could have broken my heart.

I should probably reach out to Kat again. She hasn't returned my call from last night, but after what happened at Boshamps, it's my job to set things right. I only hope that it isn't too late, that something can be salvaged between us.

But when I call her, the phone rings and rings until her voice mail picks up: "Hi, bestie! It's Kat. You know what to do."

Beep.

I clear my throat. "It's Blake. I'd really like to talk before you head back to Atlanta. Call me, okay?"

After that, there's nothing to do but start the day with a bang, as Granddad always says.

THE NEXT TWENTY-FOUR hours are full of errands to get ready for the week ahead. I'm changing out all the light switches and outlet covers, installing the new kitchen sink faucet, and replacing a faulty float valve in the main-floor toilet. As I go from store to store, I keep checking my phone, hoping Kat will return my call.

After my third trip to Home Depot, I'm on my way to the beach house when my phone rings.

I'm relieved until I see the caller ID: *Shaky Oaks Assisted Living.*

My pulse quickening, I answer. "Hello?"

"Is this Blake O'Neill?" The man's voice is vaguely familiar.

"Yes."

"Ms. O'Neill, this is Vincent Jung, the facility director here at Shaky Oaks. I hate to be the bearer of bad news, but unfortunately your grandfather has gone missing again."

It takes me a moment to catch up; my first impulse had been to assume the worst, that he'd passed away, and the twisting nausea in my stomach turns to panic. "Wait, what?"

"Ellis O'Neill, your grandfather, has wandered away. Again."

He says this like it's all a big hassle, like Granddad is nothing more than an inconvenience in his busy day of dividing the cups of Jell-O into red and green, or whatever important things he does. I bristle like a porcupine.

"Where's Martina?" I ask. She'll set things right.

"She's on vacation," Vincent says.

Shit. I knew this; I just lost track of time.

"But even if she were here," Vincent continues, "it wouldn't change the facts of the situation. As you know, this isn't the first time your grandfather has done this."

I feel like a kid called to the principal's office, and I remind myself that I'm a twenty-seven-year-old woman who has single-handedly refinished a wood floor, removed a sixty-year-old bathtub, and demolished a wall with a sledgehammer.

"My grandfather is missing," I say, forcing my voice not to shake. "He could be in danger. What are you doing about that?"

"We're following protocol," Vincent says. "Which includes notifying next of kin and the police. But, Ms. O'Neill, this is precisely why your grandfather must be transferred to the memory care building as soon as possible. Understand?"

My body goes rigid with anger. "At this moment, all I care about is getting my granddad back safely. Understand?"

He's silent. "Of course. Just know we'll continue this discussion in the near future."

I'M SICK WITH dread as I set the phone down. I wish I could call Noah, but he can't be my support system anymore. Selfishly, I hope Kat is still at the beach house when I get there—and that she's ready to talk to me again.

I'm desperate for someone to hold my hand and reassure me that everything is going to be okay. Unfortunately, when I open the garage, her car isn't inside.

After grabbing my purchases from the back of my car, I climb the stairs, thinking I should've probably made two trips with all these bags. When I unlock the door, the dog dashes inside, and I hear a strange sound as he runs through the house.

Splashing.

I push the door open and walk in. The floor is covered with at least an inch of water. Gasping, I set my bags down on the table in the entryway and look around. The dog is bounding around like he's at a splash park, and I can hear running water in the dining room. I head in to see a stream of water coming from the ceiling, right through the beautiful chandelier Henry helped me wire not long ago, soaking the wood table we tried so carefully to preserve. A sopping-wet piece of notebook paper is on the surface of the table, but whatever was written on it—maybe a shopping list?—is unreadable, the ink blurred to the point of illegibility.

"Fuck!" I shout, then race for the stairs, sloshing through water up to my ankles. Upstairs, I run into the second bathroom, which is located above the dining room.

And there it is: the toilet tank is overflowing and there's water all over the tile floor, leaking into the hallway. My eyes fill with tears of horror and desperation, and I reach behind the toilet to turn off the valve.

How the hell did this happen? I'd left a sticky note on the toilet that said *DON'T USE* even though there's no reason Kat would ever come in here; as far as I knew, she always uses the bathroom attached to her bedroom or the one downstairs.

Maybe I should have posted the note on Instagram and tagged her in it. *Then* she would have paid some attention.

Panicking, I clench my fists as I look around the bathroom. There's *so much water.* Hundreds of gallons throughout the house, maybe thousands. The damage is going to be astronomical. Not to mention all the time I put into the beautiful floors, washed away with her reckless mistake.

I really hope this was a mistake, that Kat just didn't see my note, but a nasty little voice whispers that maybe she did it on purpose. That she wanted to punish me, to sabotage my progress so we couldn't sell the house. That she really does hate me that much.

Shoving that thought away, I remind myself I need to take care of this situation before I start assigning blame. *Crying over your spilled milk won't fill your glass up again*, as my grandma would say.

There's no insurance policy on this beach house—it's just been sitting here decaying for years—which means no one else is going to clean this up for me. Kat has run back to her perfect life in Atlanta. Noah has vanished like he couldn't get away from me fast enough. I'd call Henry, but he clearly has the hots for Kat and I don't trust myself not to say something horrible about her right now. I have no other friends here in Destin, and I can't afford to pay anyone to help me.

I sit on the closed toilet seat, my eyes blurring with tears. What was my dad thinking, giving me half of this house, trapping me in this hellhole? I wish he hadn't. I wish he'd gone to his grave pretending like I don't exist. I think back to the day I drove into Destin the first time, the words that echoed through my mind: *My life is about to change forever.*

A bitter laugh escapes my lips. Fuck that. I don't want this. I don't want any of it. I wish I could rewind time back to the day I got the call from the estate lawyer; I'd tell him he had the wrong number. Then I'd rewind all the way back to when I was twelve years old; I'd tell my grandparents I'd changed my mind, that I didn't want to go to Camp Chickawah. I want to erase it all, scrub it from my memory, bleach it away. To live free from the suffocating weight of my past.

Tears roll down my cheeks, and I dash them away, furious that after all these years, I'm still allowing him to hurt me. Why can't I stop caring about what my asshole father did or didn't do?

The dog nudges his way into the bathroom and stares up at me with his liquid brown eyes. The smell of wet dog permeates the room, which snaps me out of my pity party.

Standing, I put my hands on my hips and survey the bathroom. First step: I need to get rid of all this water. Then get everything dried out. And finally, figure out how to repair the damage.

None of it will get done unless I do it. I'm all I've got.

I SPEND THE next several hours vacuuming up water—thank goodness Henry left his Shop-Vac here the other day—then emptying the tank over the deck railing, over and over until my back is aching. I open all the windows and grab a couple of fans from the upstairs closets, then turn them on to get air flowing through the house.

Every hour or so, I call Shaky Oaks for an update on Granddad. They haven't found him, but they assure me the police are looking for him and they've given them a list of places I thought he might go.

I'm scared, feeling helpless, and I even look up plane tickets online, thinking maybe I'll ditch this flooded beach house and go back to Minnesota to join the search for Granddad. But last-minute tickets are ridiculously expensive—thousands of dollars—and I'd be equally helpless in the air.

So I keep working. Keep vacuuming up water, my phone within arm's reach at all times. I've felt lonely many times in my life, but this may top them all. No one to talk to, no one to turn to. Hours pass and finally my phone rings with a call from Shaky Oaks.

"Hello?" I say, breathless.

"It's Vincent. We've found your grandfather."

My knees go limp with relief, and I collapse on the wet wood floor in the middle of the living room. "Where was he?"

"He was found at the movie theater," Vincent says. "Somehow, he sweet-talked the ticket taker into believing that his wife was already in the theater ahead of him, and they let him in. He's been watching movies all day. Happy as a lark, though he did say he was disappointed there were no John Wayne movies showing."

My eyes fill with tears. "Thank God. And thank you for calling me."

As much as I hated Vincent a few hours ago, I could kiss him right now.

Vincent pauses, then clears his throat. "Ms. O'Neill. I hope you know that I'm concerned about the welfare of every member of our community here at Shaky Oaks. I want your grandfather to be safe."

"I know," I say, taking a deep breath. None of this is Vincent's fault. Granddad has needed a higher level of care for months now. We're lucky that nothing worse happened.

"We have an opening coming up in the memory care building next week," Vincent says. His voice is kind, and I realize he was so sharp with me earlier because *he* was scared, too. "We either need to move your grandfather into that room, or you need to find another placement for him. The choice is yours."

I don't hesitate: "I'll take the room."

I'll have to empty my bank account to pay the first month's

fee. I'll survive on peanut butter and brown sugar sandwiches until I get back to the Vanderhaavens, then figure out some way to make extra money for the next month.

I could take on an extra job, something in retail so I can work on the weekends and evenings when I'm not nannying. I could sell plasma. Donate my eggs. Maybe walk other neighborhood dogs while the Vanderhaavens' kids are at school? Whatever it takes.

"It would be ideal if you could help him move to the new room," Vincent says.

I bite my lip. It's a nearly twenty-hour drive there, but Vincent is right. Granddad will be disoriented and frightened transitioning to a new place. I can't let strangers get him settled in.

"Of course," I say, hoping the dog won't mind another road trip. "I'll be there."

AFTER I END the call with Vincent, I take a look around the beach house. I've been so wrapped up in my worries that I haven't allowed myself to pause and take in the damage yet.

It's bad. Really bad. The wood floor is already warping, and it's only going to get worse the more it dries out. Best-case scenario, it'll need to be sanded down and refinished; worst-case scenario, torn up and replaced. The bottom few inches of all the drywall is soaked through and might need to be removed; same with the baseboards.

The chandelier in the dining room that Kat got from a sponsorship is a goner. I'm not sure we'll be able to save the table or chairs, but the living room furniture should be salvageable if I clean the upholstery.

But the worst part is that weeks and weeks of backbreaking labor have been for nothing.

For the first time in weeks, I feel like I can't leave Destin soon enough. The connection I thought I had with this beach house was just wishful thinking. I didn't grow up in this family. I never knew my paternal grandparents, and if they ever knew about me, they didn't care enough to seek me out. Like Kat said that first day she came barging in like a hurricane, I don't belong here.

I'll spend the next week getting the house cleaned up, then head back to Minnesota to get Granddad settled. Once that's done, I might need to return here to finalize things—either to sell the house to Kat or list it with that real estate agent if Kat didn't scare her away. Either way, I shouldn't need to stay long.

It's time for me to get back to my real life and put all this behind me.

CHAPTER TWENTY-SEVEN

KAT

THE DRIVE TO DESTIN IS JUST AS LONG AS IT ALWAYS IS, BUT today, time seems to fly. The traffic is normal and so is the weather—but this is the first trip where I've had Henry to keep me company on the phone. Granted, I've done most of the talking while he works and listens to me on speakerphone, but it's been nice. He's nice. And a damn good kisser based on the few kisses we've been able to sneak when Sunny was distracted.

It seems Henry Alexander is full of surprises. We've talked every night this week after he's put Sunny to bed, and it's mostly helped me keep my mind off the fact that I haven't heard back about the Worthington application. Or from Blake.

She never responded to the note I left, and I can't say I blame her. I said some pretty hurtful things, and Henry's helped me realize I've been taking most of my grief and anger out on her. It was wrong of me, and I'm hoping she'll talk to me face-to-face. That's the best way to apologize, anyway.

"What do you think?" Henry asks.

"Shit," I curse under my breath. The man says a dozen words

and I missed half of them. "Connection dropped for a second. What'd you say?"

Henry laughs and I'm pretty sure he knows I'm full of shit. "I was asking if you wanted to come by for dinner tonight."

My heart does a little dance at the thought of seeing Henry in a few short hours.

"Sunny really wants to see you," he adds.

I smile, knowing that Sunny has nothing to do with it. It's been more than a week since we've been alone together, and I have a feeling he's as anxious as I am to pick up where we left off. My lips tingle with anticipation, but I know there's something else I need to do first.

"I've got to try and see Blake when I get in," I tell him, knowing that if I go to Henry's house, I won't want to leave. And I need Blake to know she's important enough that I wouldn't wait to talk to her.

Henry exhales loud enough for me to hear, and I can't help but smile at his disappointment. I feel it, too, but I know I have to do this.

"I'll come by after," I tell him. "Maybe Sunny will be asleep . . ."

That gets a laugh out of him, and we both agree that a few more hours won't kill us.

"I should get back to work," Henry says.

"Okay," I tell him. Neither of us moves to end the call, and I feel like a teenage girl with a giant crush, not wanting to be the one who hangs up. Twice in the last week, we talked until I fell asleep, which I'm pretty sure means he now knows that I snore, too.

"I'll see you tonight," he says. "And in the meantime, I'll be admiring your Instagram."

"Liar." I laugh. Henry might be the last adult alive who isn't on social media. He says he'll join and follow me to be my lucky one hundred thousandth follower, which is getting closer and closer. It's such a huge milestone, and as excited as I am to reach it, part of me is sad that I'm a few months too late. In my head, 100k was the magic number that would make my dad proud of me. That it would be enough for him to realize that what I was doing mattered. That I mattered.

"What's your count now?" Henry asks, bringing me back to the moment.

"Ninety-nine thousand seven hundred and thirty-two–ish," I tell him.

He laughs the deep belly laugh that makes me feels like I won a prize. "Ish," he says, a teasing lilt to his voice.

"I've been driving and on the phone with you," I remind him. "It's not like I could check in the last few hours."

"I'll let you get back to driving," he says. "Good luck with Blake."

He ends the call, and I drive the last stretch of highway with a smile on my face.

As I cross the Mid-Bay Bridge, my phone buzzes. My heart lifts at the sight of Blake's name on the screen.

I hope this means she's been waiting for me to get back to town, that the reason for her silence wasn't hurt or anger, but that she also thought it would be best for us to talk face-to-face.

As traffic slows at the tollbooth, I reach for my phone and read her message. It's long, which isn't like her.

Blake: There was an issue with the house last week. I'd hoped to have it cleaned up before you got here, but the floor took too long to dry out, so please avoid the area that's blocked off underneath the upstairs bathroom. I had to leave town for a family matter, but I'll be back to finish the work next week.

Behind me, a car honks and I realize it's my turn at the toll. I drive through, my head spinning from Blake's message. There's so much to unpack, starting with her tone. It's cold and distant, the way we were in the beginning. Like we're nothing more than strangers. I wonder what the family matter might be, and I hope her grandfather is okay. He's all she has left. Other than me.

I step on the gas, hoping against hope that I can catch Blake before she leaves town and I miss my chance to make things right.

THERE'S NO SIGN of Blake by the time I pull up in front of the beach house. I grab my phone to text back, to ask her if we can talk, when a part of her message catches my attention. She mentioned the area beneath the upstairs bathroom.

My stomach feels queasy as I remember how the toilet was running before I left, and I hope that had nothing to do with whatever issue Blake didn't have time to fix. I tuck my phone back in my purse and head inside.

Outside the front door, I pause, my hand resting on the handle. I think about how important this house has always been to me, but how its meaning and significance have started to change.

At the beginning of the summer the beach house was a link to my past, a way for me to hold on to all the things that felt like they were slipping away. But now it's also full of potential for new memories, and most important, a connection to Blake. I really hope I didn't screw it up.

I hold my breath as I push the door open, exhaling as I survey the room. It's not as bad as I feared, but it doesn't look good. The furniture has all been pushed to the edges of the room, covered with old sheets, and the floor looks warped. My eyes drift up to the dark circle on the ceiling where I imagine the toilet leaked. All the hard work Blake put into these beautiful floors over the past few months, flushed down the toilet. Literally.

My stomach sinks as I realize that even if I wanted to help make this right—and I do—I wouldn't know where to begin. Blake's the one who knows how to work with her hands, how to do hard things. I grew up learning how to throw money at problems—which I can't afford to do.

I reach for my phone and stare at Blake's message. Now there's one more thing on the growing list of things I owe her an apology for. And this one needs more than words. It needs a big gesture. A gesture I won't be able to pull off on my own.

Henry answers on the first ring. "Hey," he says, a smile in his voice. "Did you change your mind about coming over?"

I wish I could stay in this moment where I'm just a girl excited to see a guy who's excited to see her—but hopefully there will be time for that later. For now, I need his help.

"I kind of screwed up," I tell him.

"Kind of?" Henry asks.

"Kind of majorly," I admit.

I tell him everything: the running toilet, the flood, the text from Blake, and that I need to try to make it right.

"Can you come over?" I ask, trying not to sound desperate as I finish the story.

"Sunny and I are on our way to Fort Walton," he says. "I didn't think you'd be free until later, so—"

"Don't worry about it," I say, interrupting him. He doesn't owe me an explanation.

"I'm not worried about *it*," he says. "I'm worried about *you*. But we've got a week to make it right. Send me some pictures of the floor and the ceiling before the sun goes down, and I'll be there tomorrow morning with everything we'll need."

I exhale, and it's like my whole body relaxes with the realization that for the first time in a long time, I'm not alone.

THE NEXT MORNING, I spend a good five minutes staring into my closet, waiting for the perfect outfit to miraculously appear. I want to look hot, but I also want Henry to know I'm taking this seriously, that I'll be ready to help however I can. Even if that means getting lunch, holding a flashlight, or whatever task is at my nonexistent skill level.

I settle on a pair of distressed Lucky jean shorts and a white tank from Topshop that brings out my tan and has a cute flutter detail around the arms. I throw my hair in a messy bun that hopefully doesn't look like I meticulously picked which strands to untuck so they fell perfectly framing my face. Which, of course, I did.

The doorbell rings right at ten, and I apply another layer of my go-to Charlotte Tilbury lipstick before running down the stairs.

"Hi," I say, before the door is all the way open. So much for playing it cool.

"Hi," Henry says back. He looks effortlessly handsome in a version of the same outfit he wears every day—worn jeans and a short-sleeve plaid shirt. This one is green, and it brings out the warm tones in his eyes.

The corner of his lip twitches into an adorable half smile, and I smile back. We're just standing there, smiling, until I realize his hands are full, and he probably wants to come inside.

"Oh," I say, stepping back and holding the door open. "Come in."

Henry walks through the door, setting down his toolbox and a carry tray with two iced coffees from Dunkin' Donuts. The man clearly knows my love language.

"Hi," I say again, taking a timid step toward him. He's still the Henry I've known for years, I remind myself. The Henry who has been my touchstone, my friend, and my support the last few months. Just because we shared a few kisses doesn't mean things have to be uncomfortable.

"Hi," he says back, taking a step toward me. There are now mere inches between us. I inhale the familiar scent of his cologne and wonder if he thought of me this morning when he was putting it on.

I tilt my head up and Henry closes the distance between us, his lips finding mine. He tastes like peppermint and coffee and I want to drink him up.

There's nothing tentative about our kiss this time—it's hungry and impatient, like we've both been waiting more than a week to do this again. I feel myself melting into him and I wish we could spend all day doing this, but we've got work to do.

Breathless, I pull back just the slightest bit, my nose still grazing his. He gives me one more kiss.

"I've been wanting to do that for a long time," he says.

"Me, too," I tell him. "It's been a long week."

Henry shakes his head. "I'm talking about that first day I saw you at the bank. Maybe even before then."

I don't know what to say to that, so I slip my hand in his and thank him with another kiss.

"Let's see this mess you made," he teases, pulling back, but not letting go of my hand. I lead him toward the offending spot on the ceiling.

Henry blows out a long, slow breath and shakes his head. "It's not pretty," he says.

My heart drops and I realize I didn't even consider the possibility that Henry wouldn't be able to fix this.

"Is it beyond repair?" I ask.

"No such thing," Henry says. He squats down and I try not to stare at his adorable ass as he runs a hand on the dark, mottled wood floor. "It's almost dry; Blake did all the right things."

I frown at the implied comparison, knowing Henry got stuck with the wrong half sister to help with this project. Then he glances back at me with a smile so warm that I know for certain I'm not his second choice.

"You ready to get to work?" he asks.

I put my hand out and haul him up. "Let's do this."

OVER THE NEXT four days, I discover muscles I never knew existed. They all ache, making even the smallest movements a struggle. But I finally understand the phrase "hurts so good." There's something satisfying about not just seeing the results of your hard work, but feeling them, too.

And I've been working hard. Harder than I've ever worked before. Although I'm sure Henry could've done it all faster and more efficiently on his own, he seems to know how much it means for me to help. He has the patience of a saint—a sexy saint—as he teaches me how to work the sander, and the difference between painting with and against the grain while we're staining the floor. And after a couple of days, I feel more confident in my abilities.

He comes over every morning and stays all day until it's time to pick Sunny up from summer camp. The two of them come back here until dinner—I cooked the first night; after that we've ordered in—and they go home before Sunny's bedtime.

I want more than anything to go back to the cute little blue bungalow with them, but Henry wants to take things slow around Sunny, which I respect. He puts her first like the good dad he is. Still, I'm starting to wonder if we're ever going to take this beyond a few stolen kisses.

This morning, we added a layer of clear coat over the stained wood, and all that's left to do is wait. I suggest heading down to the beach and taking a well-deserved break, but Henry Alexander apparently doesn't believe in relaxation.

After I've followed him around like a puppy dog, "helping" as he fixes other odds and ends around the exterior of the house for what feels like hours, he declares the floor dry and the room ready to put back together.

"You're going to have to remind me where all this furniture goes," he says, folding up the sheet that had been covering the couch.

I have every intention of helping him, but the couch looks so soft and inviting that I can't help myself. I collapse onto it, letting my body sink into the plush cushions.

"First, come sit," I say, reaching toward him.

Henry frowns, but luckily accepts my outstretched hand, and I give him the tiniest tug I can muster.

"Every muscle in my body aches," I tell him.

He squeezes in behind me, a leg on either side of me. "Let me help you out with that."

I sigh as he starts kneading the muscles of my neck and shoulders, then squirm as he reaches a particularly sore area. "I'm such a wimp."

"No, you've done great this week. I've been impressed. Really." He pulls me closer toward him, the little spoon to his big one, wrapping his arms around me in the warmest, gentlest hug I've ever experienced. I love how he makes me feel small and safe, curled up against his broad chest. But I really hope this isn't all he wants to do before he has to go.

Then he moves his hand to my bare thigh, and I hold my breath.

The calluses on his skin are rough, but his touch is gentle as he wraps his hand around my thigh, massaging. My skin flushes under his fingers, and I push back against him, feeling his heartbeat getting faster in time with mine. So maybe he does want to take things further.

I tilt my head, exposing the curve of my neck. He takes the hint, pressing his lips to my skin. Heat spreads to my center at the mixed sensations—his rough stubble, his soft lips and warm breath. His grip on my thigh gets tighter, more urgent, as his hand moves up my leg, teasing the hem of my shorts.

No surprise, Henry Alexander is good with his hands.

Every cell in my body is alert, craving his hands, his lips, his touch. I moan in gratitude, and Henry responds with a playful bite on my neck that threatens to undo me.

He pulls me even closer so I'm practically sitting in his lap. I can feel he's just as worked up as I am, and we're getting dangerously close to the point of no return. I should've known better than to start something we can't finish.

My body apparently doesn't have the same concern. I swivel my hips, grinding against his lap as I ask, "What time do you have to be home?"

"Tomorrow," Henry says, his breath tickling my neck.

I twist around to face him, grimacing as my sore muscles react to the sudden movement. Henry's got a smirk on his face. I knew Sunny had a playdate after camp, but I assumed he'd have to get her at some point.

"Sunny's having a sleepover," he says.

"And you?"

He kisses me, long and slow, and I turn to putty in his arms. Henry's hands slide under my butt and he repositions me so we're sitting chest to chest, my legs wrapped around him. "I thought we could have a sleepover, too," he says, lowering his head to kiss the other side of my neck. "If that's okay with you."

"It's more than okay," I say, my fingers fumbling to undo the buttons on his plaid shirt. If he was wearing a T-shirt, it would already be on the floor.

Henry smiles through our kiss and helps with the buttons, starting at the bottom until our hands meet in the middle. I pull back so I can admire the view: shoulders, chest, abs. This man is built like a statue. He's unreal. I run my hands over the contours of his muscles.

"Your body is . . ." I shake my head. "Damn, Henry Alexander."

His lips quirk up in a grin, and I lift the hem of my shirt, grimacing as I raise my arms over my head.

"You okay?" Henry asks, his voice tender.

"Just a little sore," I tell him, letting my fingers trail down his chest, toward the button of his jeans. I can feel him straining against the fabric.

"Do you want to stop?" Henry asks, pausing, even as his hands are positioned and ready to slide his jeans down over his hips.

"Hell no," I say, and he laughs as I help tug off his jeans.

His fingers trace up my back, unhooking my bra. I shrug it off as Henry's hands continue roaming down to my waist and up to my breasts. He cups them, gently at first, then leans down, following his fingers with his mouth. He gently bites my nipple and I think I might spontaneously combust.

"You are the most beautiful woman I've ever seen," he says, gazing at me.

I pull back slightly. "You're crazy—"

"I'm not." He kisses my forehead, my cheeks, my mouth. "Do you have any idea how many times I've imagined this moment?"

"How many?"

"I can't count that high," he says, smiling against my mouth.

"Every day, sometimes every hour. All summer long. You made it hard for me to focus."

"Then why didn't you make a move?" Insecurity is bleeding out of my voice; I can't help it. "That day we went to Crab Island, you didn't want to—"

"Oh, I wanted to," he says. "But you've always seemed so out of my league, Kat. Even when we were kids, I thought you were the prettiest girl. Not just pretty—sassy and fierce; creative and sweet. My crush was out of control, but I knew you didn't feel the same way."

I frown, because he isn't wrong. I was stupidly fixated on Junior Rooney and didn't see what was right in front of me. But does Henry have any idea that he's out of *my* league now? He's the kindest, most generous human being I've ever met. "Henry, I'm sorry—"

"Shh," he says. "I'm living out a fantasy here, Kat. Don't interrupt."

We continue to kiss, discarding clothing as we go, exploring each other in a languid way with hands and lips and the occasional bite. I'm struck by how comfortable this is; usually when I'm with someone for the first time, I get nervous, or I feel like I have to perform in some way. But it's so easy with Henry, almost like we've done this before. His hand reaches between my legs and when he finds the perfect spot I sigh.

"Talk to me," he says. "Tell me what you like."

"I like this. I like it a lot."

He touches me slowly and deliberately, taking his time until I can't take it anymore and I ache with the need to feel him inside me.

"Do you have a condom?" I ask, praying the answer is yes. I brought some with me from Atlanta, but they're upstairs in my bedroom, which feels too far away.

Henry smiles a guilty smile and reaches down for his discarded jeans, where he fishes one out of the pocket.

I take the foil package from his hands and rip it open with my teeth. It makes my heart sing that he thought ahead, that he planned for this. For us to have all night.

He leans back into the couch and watches as I slide the condom on him. I shift on his lap until we're perfectly positioned. There's a little fumbling, a little teasing, and he enters me. We both let out identical sighs of relief.

I lift my eyes to meet his, our faces inches apart. "I like this."

He smiles. "I know."

His arms wrap around me, and together we begin to move. In this position, straddling his lap with my knees on either side, I'm in control, and I love it. Henry lets me set the pace, but he matches me, going deeper when I ask for more, slowing down or speeding up when I need it. His eyes are impossibly dark, so deep I could sink into them and never hit bottom. I've never felt so safe, here with Henry's arms around me. He's gazing at me like I'm special, like I'm precious, like he never wants to let me go.

My eyes fill with tears and I bury my face in his neck; I couldn't talk now if I tried. This emotion I'm feeling—it's overwhelming. It's like I'm caught in a riptide, being tugged into a vast, unending sea, and I don't fight it. I let myself be dragged under the waves, relinquishing all control. He takes over, holding my hips and grinding me against him until I'm frantic with the need to come.

And then, when I'm hovering on the edge, ready to shatter in a million pieces, Henry lays a gentle kiss on my forehead and whispers, "You were worth the wait."

My heart explodes, and I think I might just be falling for Henry Alexander, the boy—the man—with two first names.

CHAPTER TWENTY-EIGHT

BLAKE

SEEING MY GRANDDAD AGAIN HAS BEEN THE BEST FEELING ever. Worth the insanely long drive from Destin to Minnesota with the dog in the back seat, worth the money I had to spend on a pet-friendly hotel room.

It took two days to move Granddad into his new room in the memory care building at Shaky Oaks, and during those two days he was agitated and confused. He had a few outbursts, and there was one painful moment when he didn't recognize me. But it's been three days since then and he's doing well.

The staff have been friendly and professional, Martina has visited him every day, and I can already tell that he's going to be safer here.

But leaving him again is going to tear my heart out.

"Oh, Blakers," he says, enveloping me in a bear hug. "You're gonna come visit again soon, right?"

Tears squeeze from my eyes as I nod. "Of course. I'll be back before you know it."

The Vanderhaavens will return from France in three weeks, so my plan is to drive back to Destin and finalize things, then return to Minneapolis and get the Vanderhaavens' house ready for their return. I wonder if the dog is going to want to sleep in my bed still; it'll be strange sleeping without my personal foot warmer.

"You have a great drive back to France," Granddad says as we separate from our embrace.

I try not to let my smile falter. Being away from him this summer has made me realize how quickly time is passing, how little I have left with him before his memory goes completely.

"Florida, Granddad," I say.

An employee of Shaky Oaks pops her head in the room. "Ellis, the movie is starting in the common room. Would you like to join us?"

Granddad's eyes light up. In an effort to make him feel welcome, the staff has played John Wayne movies every afternoon. Today they're watching *The Man Who Shot Liberty Valance*—always a winner because it also features the handsome and talented Jimmy Stewart.

"Ready as I'll ever be!" Granddad says.

"Have fun," I tell him, and wave as he walks down the hall. I watch, heart aching, as my only remaining family member shuffles away.

WHEN I REACH my car—where the dog is waiting, windows rolled down—my phone dings. It's a voice text from Noah. My heart does a strange gallop in my chest, painful and sharp; it's the first I've heard from him since he left Destin. I take a deep, steadying breath before pressing play.

"Hi, Blake," he says. *"I just wanted to send you a quick message and I figured this was easier than typing it out. I— Well . . ."*

He clears his throat. There's a pause long enough that my heart starts climbing in my chest, hoping he's going to say something about me, about us, and I swear to myself that if he does, I'll call him back and tell him I miss him, that I made a gigantic, stupid mistake and I want to figure out a way to be with him.

"*I'm in Boston with my family,*" he says, and my heart plummets. "*I was nervous to reach out to my parents, but . . . it's been okay. Not perfect, but okay. I'm not sure what that means for the future, but we're talking about possible job options with the company. Anyway, I—I wanted to tell you thanks for giving me the nudge to do this.*"

There's another long pause. "*I hope you're doing well. Take care of yourself, Blake.*"

The message ends and I stare at my phone.

Carefully, I type a reply: I'm happy for you. I'm in Minnesota helping my granddad move into his new place. Good luck, Noah.

Then I pocket my phone, exhale slowly, and get in the car.

THE NEXT AFTERNOON, I'm driving into Destin, like I did all those weeks ago. Just like then, I can't help appreciating the beauty of this place. But unlike the last time I drove across this bridge, now I know what's awaiting me at the beach house.

As I head down Old 98, a heavy weight descends on my shoulders. I'll have to finish the repairs on the house as soon as possible so I can sell it; I won't have the money to pay the second month of Granddad's facility until I do. The dog starts racing back and forth across the back seat in excitement when I pull up to the beach house.

"Hate to break it to you, bud," I say, "but this isn't going to be super fun."

I still haven't heard anything from Kat, so at this point I'm assuming she either didn't come back to the house last week, and therefore has no idea about the flood, or she took one look at it and turned around and drove back to Atlanta. Away from all the mess.

To be honest, that's exactly what I'd do if I could. Still, my stomach aches with the realization that she abandoned me, without a word.

Shaking that off, I mentally run through a list of the tasks I need to accomplish this week—refinish the floor, reinstall the baseboards, touch up the paint. Redoing it all for the second time will feel like torture.

But when I walk into the house, I gasp.

It's *gorgeous*.

The floors are gleaming, golden honey. The kitchen is staged and shining, with fresh flowers on the counter and a delicate citrus scent in the air. The living room looks like something out of a magazine—throw pillows on the couches, a soft blanket draped across the accent chair, an assortment of vintage books about Destin on the coffee table. The original dining room table has been salvaged and polished, set with woven place mats that bring it a beachy vibe, white and blue stoneware that I recognize from the kitchen cabinets, with polished silver candlesticks and more fresh flowers as a centerpiece. It's the perfect blend of classic and modern, cozy and inviting.

All the weight drops from my shoulders. Kat has done an amazing job. I can hardly believe she got all this done in a week—she must have worked nonstop.

There's a noise behind me and I jump, startled. It's Kat, walking down the stairs.

"You're here?" I say, stupidly.

Kat stumbles forward as words pour from her mouth: "I am so, so sorry for leaving the toilet running—I promise I didn't mean to do it."

It's hard to be upset about that, because looking around now, you'd never know it even happened.

"I'm sorry for what happened with Noah," I say. "It's over, by the way. It was over that night at Boshamps."

Kat's eyes flash with shame. "You didn't have to—"

"It wouldn't have worked out with us," I say.

Silence descends again, and Kat glances at the ground. We're both dancing around each other, dancing around the history between us, a legacy of lies and miscommunication.

"Well," Kat says, clearing her throat. "I'll clear out and let you have some space."

"We should probably talk about next steps for the house, right?"

Kat nods but doesn't meet my eyes. "It might be time to call the real estate agent."

That must mean that she doesn't have the ability to buy me out. My stomach bottoms out; Kat must be devastated. She's about to turn and go upstairs when I speak.

"You don't have to leave tonight," I say. "You're welcome to stay, unless you have other plans."

Kat turns, a cautious smile on her face. "I'd like that."

WE ORDER TAKEOUT from Camille's and eat on the back deck, watching the sun go down. The days are getting shorter, a reminder that summer is coming to an end. Just like our time here.

"I'm sorry we have to sell the house," I say as we finish eating our seafood pizza and sushi. We've settled side by side on the top step, looking out over the beach.

She nods and sets her plate aside. "I'm still hoping something might work out, but there's no guarantee. My dad—" She stops, clears her throat. "*Our* dad made some bad financial decisions, so there's no money and my income isn't stable enough to qualify for a mortgage."

Her voice is shaky, and I tread carefully as I speak again. "It's got to feel like losing the last piece of him."

"Yeah," she says, nodding. I steal a glance at her; her eyes glisten with unshed tears. "This was one of the only places where he relaxed and spent time with me, where I felt like he might actually love me. We didn't have an easy relationship, so the memories here feel extra special."

"I'm really sorry," I say, wishing with my entire soul that I had the money to snap my fingers and buy this house for her. For me, too. I might not have grown up coming here, but I can't deny I feel a connection to this place.

Kat leans back on her hands, her eyes fixed on the horizon. "You know that last day at camp, when he came to pick me up?"

"Of course." As if I could forget the defining moment of my adolescence.

"Before that day, Dad was perfect in my eyes. My hero. But after—" She shakes her head. "It shattered my view of him, of my family—of myself, too. We never talked about it—it was this big secret I felt like I had to keep to protect my family. But now I realize it wasn't a secret at all. I'm not sure when my mom found out about you, but she knew."

I ball my hands into fists, not trusting myself to speak. Knowing you were someone's dirty secret and hearing it are two different things, and I'm not sure what to make of the fact that Kat's mom knew.

Kat wipes her eyes. "I idolized him so much growing up that I couldn't blame *him* for any of it. So I blamed you. I'm sorry for that. Sorry for the way I treated you, and I'm sorry I never responded to your letters."

I've never imagined that Kat Steiner could be this vulnerable.

Her hair is loose and slightly frizzy in the ocean breeze, almost no makeup on her face. I can see a few freckles on her cheeks, the beginnings of some lines on her forehead, a tiny scar on her chin from some long-ago injury. It's like I'm seeing her, unfiltered, for the first time.

I'm about to speak, to tell her how sorry I am for judging her so harshly all these years, when I realize she's crying. Silent tears roll down her cheeks; she's trying to keep herself from falling apart.

Feeling awkward, I scooch over and carefully put my arm around her. At my touch, her shoulders shake and she puts her face in her hands, letting herself sob.

When Kat catches her breath, she glances over at me, her face tear-streaked. "How do you get through it?" she asks, pleading. "The grief? All this pain? I feel like I'm walking around with a knife sticking out of my stomach. One wrong move and it hurts so badly I can't breathe."

Tears fill my own eyes as I remember the months after my mom died—not only losing her, but the pain of realizing that my dad wasn't coming for me. I was so young that I hardly had words to express how I felt, but I remember that pain she describes. I felt it again a few years ago, when my grandmother passed. Even though she'd been sick for a while, I wasn't ready to let her go.

"Time does help," I tell her, which sounds trite. "Crying helps, too. Having someone to talk to helps." That was one of the hardest things after my mom died; I had no friends in my new town, and my grandparents were going through their own terrible loss, so I had to keep my grief to myself.

"I probably need therapy," Kat says, giving a sad laugh.

"Maybe," I say. "But you can talk to me, too. Whenever you need to. I can't do much, but I can listen."

She shakes her head. "I can't lay that on you. I feel like I need to spend the next fifteen years apologizing to you for what he did—"

"I have an idea," I say, breaking in. "How about we stop apologizing for our father's mistakes?"

She swallows, takes a deep breath, and nods. "And let's stop blaming each other for his mistakes, too."

"Deal," I say, giving a tentative smile. Then I pause, thinking about something else that's been weighing on me. "I have good memories of him, too. Of our dad. But sometimes I worry that remembering the good means I'm excusing the bad things he did, and I refuse to do that. I can't pretend like the scales are balanced."

Kat thinks on that for a moment. "Maybe the scales don't need to be balanced. Maybe the good and the bad can just exist, side by side. Dad made some serious mistakes, but Henry reminded me the other day that he gave us a gift. And I don't just mean the beach house. I mean the chance to get to know each other again."

I smile. "I can get behind that." Then I nudge her shoulder with mine. "So . . . you've been hanging out with Henry?"

Her cheeks go pink. "Well, yeah. He helped me a lot with getting the house ready."

"That's *all* he helped you with?" I ask, teasing. Her blush deepens, but her smile widens. "I'm happy for you," I say.

And I am. The only problem is that seeing her smile—that flush of first infatuation, heading toward love—reminds me of what I've lost.

Kat must be thinking the same thing, because she says, "I heard from CoCo that Junior is back in Boston. I'm sorry—I was awful that night. I can't believe you ended things with him."

"Of course I chose you—you're my sister."

"Sisters?" Kat repeats, like she's testing out the word.

"That's what I'd like to be, if you're okay with it."

She nods, smiling. "But if you care about Junior, about Noah . . ."

"Like I said, there's no way it would work between us." I pause, overwhelmed with longing, wishing I could rewrite our story so we could, somehow, have a future together.

If we'd had more time together, I could have loved you. That's what he said. But then he left the very next day, drove back to Boston, back to his real life. So maybe he didn't really mean it. Maybe it was just a line.

My eyes fill with tears again and I blink them away. I am *not* going to waste my tears on Noah Rooney. But there's something about Kat sharing her deepest vulnerabilities with me that makes me feel comfortable sharing mine.

"Sometimes I worry that"—I take a deep breath—"that there's something about me that makes me easy to leave behind. Not just our dad, but also Noah. He didn't try very hard to change my mind."

Kat puts her arm around me—no hesitation—and pulls me close, her bare arm warm against mine. "That's his loss," she says, her voice urgent. "But I want you to know something. Other people may come and go in your life—men might come and go. But *I* will never leave you again. I can promise you that. You're stuck with me from here on out."

"Thanks," I whisper, afraid to say anything else because my dam is perilously close to breaking.

I lean against her and she leans against me, and together, we watch the sun set.

LATER THAT NIGHT, Kat leaves to visit Henry, grinning from ear to ear. I'm still out on the deck with the dog, wanting to soak up every minute at the beach, even in the dark. Tomorrow, after meeting with the real estate agent, I'll need to spend the day prepping the Rooneys' vacation home for their visit over Labor Day weekend.

Noah will be with them, I realize, as he should be. I'm happy that he's reconciled with his family, but I can't help feeling wistful over what might've been if we'd had more time together. Not everyone is meant to be together forever, and I don't regret the time I had with Noah.

Still, I do regret not being honest with him about how I felt. I don't want to protect my heart in a glass case anymore; after my conversation with Kat tonight, I've realized that being vulnerable can be freeing.

I pull out my phone and decide to send him a voice text, like he sent me a few days ago. Nervous, I walk down to the beach so I can pace as I talk.

"Hi," I say when I start recording. "I'm so glad that you've been able to reconnect with your family. It probably wasn't easy, but I'm happy for you. Things here have been strange—there was a flood at our beach house that took a while to get sorted out—but everything's okay between Kat and me. Better than okay, actually. We still have a lot of lost time to make up for, but I think we're going to end up with a strong bond after this."

I hesitate, then push forward. Might as well bare it all.

"So, um, you know what you said that night, the last night we saw each other? About if—if we'd had more time together?" Another deep breath. My heart is pounding, telling me to stop talking, but I'm determined to see this through. "Ditto from me. I mean, I feel the same way. I know that's not how it worked out between us because life had other plans, but I want you to know that you weren't alone in—in your feelings. If we'd had more time, I could've loved you, too."

I end the message. My eyes fill with tears, but instead of trying to stop them, I let them run down my face.

There's no one here but the dog padding gently next to me as I walk, and even though I should feel alone, I don't. I believe Kat when she says she won't leave me. Ever. That feels like the biggest, best gift I've received in my entire existence.

I walk into the water, letting the waves hit my ankles, then my knees and thighs, wetting the bottom of my cutoffs. Tonight feels like a goodbye—not just to the beach house and to the summer, but to the old me.

But I'm also saying hello to a new chapter in my life; I have a sister now. I'm not alone in the world.

In one swift motion, I yank off my T-shirt and toss it and my phone on the dry sand. Then I dive forward into a wave, letting it roll over me, pull me in a somersault underwater. I stay under until my lungs are screaming for air, and when I burst out of the water I suck in air and roll my shoulders back and let the water wash everything away.

I STAY OUT there, treading water in my bra and shorts, until I realize the dog is gone. The beach is empty as far as I can see in either direction, and the dog isn't visible near the house, either.

"Shit," I mutter under my breath. I don't have the energy for another search-and-rescue mission like on the Fourth of July.

I scramble out of the water and pull my dry T-shirt over my sopping-wet bra as I scan the darkness. No sign of the dog.

"Max!" I call softly. "Max, buddy, where are you?"

There's a rustle of leaves from the walkway on the left side of the house, so I take a few steps in that direction. Then I hear a voice and stop. At first I can't make out the words, but when I do, I realize it's *my* voice. My words, too.

320

"... *everything's okay between Kat and me. Better than okay, actually.*"

Confused, I take a step forward. I'm not sure where my phone landed; did it somehow start playing the message I left Noah? Then I freeze as I see a tall silhouette coming toward me.

My voice continues: "*So, um, you know what you said that night, the last night we saw each other? About if—if we'd had more time together?*"

I blink and realize it's Noah walking toward me in the shadows, his phone in his hand; he has it on speaker.

"What are you doing here?" I ask. He's supposed to be in Boston.

He doesn't answer, just walks closer until he's about ten paces away from me, his face shadowed so I can't read his expression. The dog dances around his legs, begging for attention, but Noah ignores him; he's focused on me. Holding my gaze with such intensity I can hardly take a breath.

I don't know what to do, how to react, why he's here—so I just stand there shivering, a puddle collecting at my feet, as I listen to myself bare my soul to him:

"... *I want you to know you weren't alone in—in your feelings. If we'd had more time together, I could've loved you, too.*"

My message ends and we're left with silence and darkness and so many questions filling the air that it's difficult to breathe.

Noah breaks the silence. "I've listened to this three times. The first time, I could hardly register what you were saying. The second time, I realized this meant you were here, in Destin. I thought you were in Minnesota."

I'm frozen, unable to move or speak, not sure what to expect from him next.

"And then I ran to my car and drove over here," he continues. "I saw your car parked in the driveway, but when I knocked no one answered, so I stood out there for a while and started your message the third time. The dog came around the side of the house and I followed him . . ."

He stops. Lifts the phone. "Did you mean this? Or did you just say it because you thought I was in Boston and we'd never see each other again?"

"I meant it," I say, just above a whisper. "Every word."

And then he's crossing the distance between us, and his arms are coming around me, and he's scooping me up to his height, squeezing my ribs so tightly that for a moment I think they might crack. Noah is holding me, he's kissing my wet cheeks, whispering in my ear that he missed me, that he couldn't stop thinking about me, that he wants the chance to make me fall in love with him.

That isn't going to be difficult. Because I'm already halfway there, my defenses down as I fall, plummeting into love.

CHAPTER TWENTY-NINE

KAT

EVEN THOUGH I'VE LIVED IN ATLANTA MY WHOLE LIFE AND my apartment was designed to be an Instagrammable sanctuary, it didn't feel like coming home this week.

The two extra days I spent in Destin with Blake filled my heart with something I didn't realize I'd been missing. As much as I loved my weeks alone at the beach house, there's something about being there with someone else. With family.

And now I'm on my way to my weekly dinner with the other living member of my family. My mom.

The dinners are never exactly "fun," but I'm particularly not looking forward to this one. Ever since my conversation with Blake the other night, I've been thinking about the role my mom played in all this.

I know she knew about Blake—but I need to know when she found out. It matters whether it was something she found out in recent years, or if she'd known all along. I really hope she didn't know the whole time.

Even though my mom isn't the most warm and fuzzy woman, I can't imagine she'd be okay with letting a child be practically orphaned.

But there's another piece of the story that doesn't make sense. From all the stories Blake's told me of the way Dad was when they were together, he clearly loved her—so how could he just walk away?

I know what's done is done and there's no changing the past, but I feel like I can't move on if I don't know the whole story and whatever part my mom played in it. Which I hope was that of an innocent bystander.

As I pull into the driveway, I look up at my parents' house. My mother's pride and joy—two stories and more than four thousand square feet. It was too much house for the three of us when I was growing up, so I can't imagine how lonely it feels for her now.

"Hey, Mom!" I call out as I let myself in.

"I'm in the kitchen," she answers, her bright and cheery voice echoing through the house.

I set my purse on the entry table and remind myself that if the law presumes people are innocent until proven guilty, I should, too. I walk past the aptly named "piano room," where the Steinway has sat silent since I gave up lessons in third grade, past the formal family portrait from before I discovered the magic of keratin, and through the arched doors of the kitchen.

"Something smells good," I say, giving my mom a kiss on the cheek.

"It's rosemary lemon chicken," she says, and waves of love and loss swell inside me.

"Dad's favorite," I say.

She turns and gives me a shaky smile, and I realize beneath her smiling exterior, my mom is still grieving. Not just for her husband, but for the life she thought they had. For the financial stability she never had to worry about until now. Another reason she should let this house go.

"Would you believe I miss cooking for him?" my mom asks, her voice cracking just the tiniest bit.

Maybe this isn't the best time to bring up the issue of Blake. I spent fifteen years not knowing the truth; there's no harm in waiting a little longer. A few more weeks, another month or two. Forever?

"The man only liked a handful of dishes—you'd think I'd be thrilled to have the freedom to make anything I wanted," she says.

"I miss him, too," I tell her, my eyes filling with tears. I think about something Henry said the other day, how emotions are complex and that it's okay to be angry with a person and still miss them at the same time. To miss the person they were, but also the person they had the potential to be.

I'm not sure how my mom would feel about my recent revelations, and now doesn't seem like the time to bring them up, so instead I ask, "Can I help set the table?"

TWENTY MINUTES LATER, Mom and I are sitting at the dining room table, quiet other than the occasional clang of silverware against the good china as we eat.

Since Mom has already filled me in on the latest gossip from the club—Lyn's son got engaged, Robin's daughter made partner at a law firm, and one of the Carols is getting divorced—there's not much left to talk about.

Everything in my life that's worth sharing with my mom—Henry, the house, the Rachel Worthington sponsorship I still haven't heard back about—all comes back to Blake.

As the silence continues past the point of being comfortable, I realize that if I don't talk about Blake, I'll be doing the same thing my parents have done my whole life, pretending problems away.

If I want my mom to be real with me, I've got to start being real with her. Life isn't perfect. It's messy and it's hard, but I don't want to be left with regrets about our relationship the way I am with my dad.

Before I lose my nerve, I say, "Things at the beach house are going really well."

Mom looks up at me with surprise. She knows I'm in Destin every other week, but other than a few things about sponsorships I've secured in Atlanta, it's a topic we've both managed to avoid.

"That's nice," she says.

"It really is," I tell her. "I've mostly been helping with the décor, but this last week I helped refinish the floors."

Mom nods and continues to chew, quiet and thoughtful.

"You'd hardly recognize the place," I tell her, letting myself imagine her coming down with me to spend a week just like the old days. Of course, it might be awkward if Blake is there, too. A living, breathing reminder of my dad's decade-long affair.

But Blake isn't a secret anymore. She's part of my life, and I'm not going to pretend she doesn't exist. And as we've learned this past year, sweeping something under the rug doesn't make it disappear.

Besides, I don't want to pick and choose which parts of my life to share with my mom. I take a steadying breath, then look up at my mom. "Blake has really done most of the work," I tell her.

My mom's face remains stoic. She doesn't so much as flinch as I say the name I've avoided speaking or even thinking about for the last fifteen years.

"It's amazing how handy she is," I say, wondering how far I can push my mom until her porcelain mask cracks. "Her grandfather who raised her was a contractor, so she knows what she's doing."

Mom clears her throat and takes a sip of water.

"Blake is really—"

"I'd rather not talk about that," she says, cutting me off. I cringe at my mom's choice of words. Not "her"—a living, breathing person—but "*that*"—a thing, a nuisance, something that could be ignored. Not anymore.

I try again: "If she's going to be a part of my life—"

"That's enough, Kat," my mom says, a note of finality in her voice. It's a tone and a phrase I've heard throughout my life, but usually when we're in public and my mom doesn't want to make a scene. But there's no one else here to pretend or put on a show for. It's just us.

I exhale a slow breath and pick up my fork, cutting a hunk of chicken off the breast. Such a big bite might not be ladylike, but I'm ready for this meal to be over.

The silence between us has gone to full-on awkward as we both stew in our separate thoughts.

I have no idea what she's thinking since she never lets it show. It strikes me that my mom is as much a stranger to me as my dad was. It feels almost like my entire life has been like a mirage—beautiful and shimmering from a distance, but when you get up close, it vanishes and all you're left with is a dry, empty desert.

While that might describe my past, I don't want to let it be my future. If my mom won't talk to me about this, then there's really no point in my being here at all. I spear the last bite of chicken on my plate, preparing for a speedy exit, when Mom finally starts to speak.

"I'm smarter than you give me credit for," she says, her voice halting.

I freeze, unsure where this is going.

She continues speaking, not meeting my eyes. "I knew your father was unfaithful—all those business trips and weekends away. But he got it out of his system and came home to be the father and husband he needed to be."

That part is debatable, but I keep my mouth shut. For one thing, I'm still chewing the too-big bite, and for another, now that my mom is finally talking, I don't want her to stop.

"It was all fine until *that woman* died," she says, shaking her head as if the memory still stings. "He lost all sense of dignity, grieving for her as if he'd lost half of his heart. And he kept talking about the child—how the girl was his responsibility. That he couldn't just walk away."

I swallow, the chicken barely making it past the lump in my throat. My parents, the people I've spent my whole life looking up to, suddenly seem like victims of their own making. My dad, quietly grieving a woman he loved. My mom, standing by and doing nothing.

"I reminded your father about his real responsibility—to this family." She punctuates her words by tapping her freshly manicured nails on the table. "To me, his wife, and his *legitimate* daughter. I told him I wouldn't let him destroy this family, the life we built together. It's one thing to ignore what you can't see—but I was not about to let him bring that girl into our house."

That girl.

My heart hurts for Blake—not the strong and admirable woman she's become, but the nine-year-old girl who was left grieving her mother and wondering what happened to her father.

I wonder what it would've been like if she'd come to live with us. If my parents could've handled being whispered about instead of being the ones doing the whispering. If Blake would have been able to thrive, or if the pressure of this house and this family would have snuffed out her light.

We'll never know. The past can't be changed, but I can do my best to change the future.

Across the table, my mother delicately dabs the corners of her mouth with a cloth napkin before setting it beside her plate.

"I told him it was his choice," she continues. "If he wanted to be a father to *her*, he was going to do it on his own. I was not about to raise another woman's daughter. And your father was a lot of things, but he wasn't a stupid man. He knew he couldn't raise a child alone. He made the smart choice, the right choice. He gave the girl's grandparents some money, and he chose his real family."

He chose us. He chose me. The realization should make me happy—I've always wanted to feel wanted—but instead, it breaks my heart and makes me ashamed of both my parents.

Ashamed of my mother for putting him in the position to choose—for thinking it was acceptable to leave a motherless girl without her last living parent. And my father for not being strong enough to stand up to her, for throwing money at the problem— and it clearly wasn't even enough. I can't believe he could walk away from Blake. From my sister.

I could've had a sister.

My eyes well with tears for Blake. For all the years she spent alone, wondering why her father never came back for her. Wondering why I never answered a single one of her letters.

The letters.

I push my chair back and walk out of the dining room, leaving my mother exposed and alone. If I stay here any longer, I'll say something I can't take back.

Upstairs, my bedroom is just the way it was in high school. The Tiffany blue accent wall, the framed family photos, the four-poster bed, and the Tupperware storage box beneath it.

I sit on the floor and slide the box out. As I open the lid, the musty smell of memories hits me. Mementos from a life that used to feel so important and worth protecting: my bat mitzvah invitation, an old photo album, a newspaper article I wrote for the *Atlanta Jewish Times* about my experience at a high school program in Israel, a Beanie Baby, and Playbills from every musical I was ever in. And beneath it all, a shoebox that holds my letters from Blake, ironically tied with the same blue string we used to make friendship bracelets.

I carefully slide that first letter out of its envelope and look at the words written in Blake's twelve-year-old handwriting.

Dear Kat,

I don't know what to say. We're sisters. I guess you know that by now.

My dad always told me stories of his summers at Camp Chickawah—he said it was a magical place surrounded by trees and a glistening lake where he spent days swimming and sailing and nights roasting marshmallows and singing songs by the campfire.

I thought if I went to camp there, I would be able to find him in a way. To feel close to him in a place he loved. I never imagined I'd actually find him there. That I would find you. My sister.

I've always wanted a sister. Write me back, okay?

Love,
Blake
Cabin 10 Forever!

The words I once read as a confession take on new meaning now. In my memory, she'd gone to camp looking for her dad. For my dad. I thought she sought me out and used me to get close to him.

Of course, now I know that's nothing more than the ridiculous idea of a twelve-year-old girl with a big imagination, whose mind was reeling with shock and betrayal.

My friendship with Blake wasn't part of some big manipulative plan, but maybe it was part of a bigger plan. Maybe we were drawn together because we recognized a piece of ourselves in each other. And the reason our friendship formed so fast and felt so deep wasn't the magic of camp, but our innate connection. She felt like my sister even before I knew she was my sister.

A tear slides down my cheek and falls on the paper, making the blue ink blur. I carefully fold the letter back up and slide it into the envelope. I want to read the others, and I will eventually, but now I need to let Blake know how sorry I am.

My phone buzzes, and I hope it's a text from Blake—that she somehow knew I was sitting here, thinking of her. But it's not. It's an email.

From Rachel Worthington.

Not Rachel Worthington's assistant, but *the* Rachel Worthington herself.

With shaking hands, I tap to open the email thanking me for my thoughtful and honest application, offering me the six-figure year-long contract to represent her brand.

Tears fill my eyes all over again. I can keep the beach house. I can afford to buy Blake out. My heart soars for a beautiful moment, until I realize that's not what I want. I want to keep the house *and* keep our relationship.

I'm not sure if there's a way to have both, but if I have to choose, I won't make the same mistake my dad made. I will choose my sister. I will always choose Blake.

CHAPTER THIRTY

BLAKE

EVERY ONCE IN A WHILE, A RARE MOMENT OF PERFECTION happens. A magical instant when your heart feels perfectly at home. Waking up in my room at the beach house, sunlight streaming through the curtains, and Noah next to me in bed is that kind of moment.

I roll over and see him sprawled out on his stomach, bare from the waist up. He murmurs, "Morning, gorgeous," and pulls me in for a sleepy kiss on the cheek. I stay there for a few minutes, curled up next to him, until his breathing slows, and I know he's drifted back to sleep. Then I pull away carefully and climb out of bed.

The dog follows me, waiting at the top of the stairs, then trailing behind me. As I head into the sun-dappled living room, I'm filled with a sensation of déjà vu so strong it makes me dizzy; I had a dream last night that I was here on a morning just like this. But instead of being empty, the house was full.

There were people in every room, making breakfast and playing games, the air ringing with laughter and the sound of children's feet on the hardwood floor. The dream felt like abundance. Like an overwhelming sensation of *belonging*.

Now, as I walk through the empty house, I'm struck with a bittersweet feeling. The room is gorgeous, pristine and staged like Kat left it, but it feels vacant. There should be board games spread out on the dining room table, people reading and lounging on these plushy couches, sandals lined up by the door, beach towels hanging out on the deck to dry.

My dream felt so vivid it's almost like I'm in the wrong dimension now, and I have to shake myself back into reality.

Heading out to the back deck, I grab a beach towel and make my way down the stairs and out onto the soft white sand. This has been my routine for the past week, soaking up every second because I know it's ending soon. I spread out the towel and sit, the dog resting his head on my thigh, and I lean back on my hands and relax.

There's a hint of a breeze and a few seabirds fly past, making a keening sound that echoes in my chest. I'm filled with a longing to stay, to put down roots here like the palm trees on either side of the house, and I remind myself that this place isn't mine. Not permanently. And even though I know Kat wants to buy me out, it doesn't sound like she'll be able to.

As much as it hurts, my guess is that when the real estate agent comes later today, we'll have to discuss putting the house on the market.

And with that, my mind is pulled back to the dream.

All my life, I longed to be part of a big extended family like the ones the other kids had. A whole passel of cousins, a bunch of aunts and uncles, two sets of grandparents. As an only child of an only child, raised by my mom's parents, I knew it wasn't possible to have that. It's not that I didn't feel loved—I did, unconditionally—but I was always aware that I didn't have layers of family. I knew how fragile my foundation was.

I take a deep breath of salty air, trying to replace the lonely feeling that has settled around me with gratitude for the bond I've forged with Kat this summer. I hope we can find a way to stay connected even without the beach house.

Maybe whoever buys this house will fill it with all the love and laughter I imagined in my dream. If nothing else, I can be proud that our renovation—my structural work, Kat's eye for design—created something beautiful, a place where memories can be made for a new family.

A noise behind me makes me turn; Noah is walking down the stairs to join me. My heart warms at the sight of his tall, angular body, clad in only a pair of low-slung sweatpants, his hair rumpled from sleep. He's holding a mug of coffee in each hand, carefully making his way across the sand so he doesn't spill a drop.

The dog races over to him and Noah says in his dopey voice, "Sorry, little Mike 'n' Ike, can't pet ya right now. Hands are a wee bit full."

I have no idea how the dog's name morphed into that one, but it makes me laugh. At the sound, Noah looks up at me, his smile as warm as sunshine.

"Hey, beautiful," he says when he reaches me. "Care for some company?"

He hands me one of the mugs, then sits behind me, his legs on either side of mine. Then he wraps his free arm around my waist and pulls me flush against him.

"Random but very important question," he says in my ear. "You ready?"

"Born ready."

"Who is the villain: Tom or Jerry?"

"You mean the cartoon cat and mouse?" I ask. When he nods, I chuckle and lean against his chest. "Well, Tom is trying to *eat* Jerry, so I think that makes him by definition the villain."

"See, that's exactly what Jerry wants you to think. Big evil cat, cute little mouse. But you gotta realize that Jerry was trespassing in Tom's house." Noah's voice is dead serious. "And Tom's owner is constantly threatening to throw him out unless he gets rid of the mouse. What's he supposed to do?"

I nod. "I hear you—Tom is acting under duress. And little Jerry is kind of sadistic."

"*Kind of?* He injures and degrades Tom on a daily basis, subjecting him to all sorts of humiliation and abuse, and he does it with a smile. Poor Tom is just defending his home."

"I'll help you start a campaign," I say, lifting my mug. "Justice for Tom!"

Noah pulls me tighter and presses a kiss to my neck. "You know I'm obsessed with you, right?"

I smile. "I might be a little obsessed with you, too."

For the past week, he's been saying stuff like this: *You're stunning, you're my favorite, I can't get enough of you.* All the adoration made me a little uncomfortable at first, but now I realize this is just *Noah*, the real him. He's dropped the sarcastic armor he had at the beginning of the summer when we first met. I want to crawl into his chest and live there, like a happy little hermit in a cave. The thought of it ending—this summer, these moments between us—breaks my heart.

"I made my decision about the job," Noah says, and my body goes still. He's been going back and forth on this all week, trying to decide between returning to work for his family in Boston and taking the job with his friend's tech start-up in Chicago.

I've been giving him space to work out what's best for him, but I'm rooting for Chicago. Boston feels so much farther away—

and not just because it's a three-hour flight to Minneapolis versus just over an hour from Chicago, but because Boston is where his family is, with all their wealth and expectations. I can't help worrying that if he goes back there, it'll be the end of us. I won't fit in with that life, long term.

"Oh yeah?" I say, as casually as possible.

"I'm taking the job working for William."

I take a sip of coffee, trying hard not to whoop in happiness. "You're sure?"

"I just sent him an email accepting it. And"—he kisses my neck again, his free hand running up my torso to my rib cage—"I let him know that I'll be leaving work every Friday at three to catch a flight to spend the weekend with my girlfriend in Minneapolis."

My heart warms. He hasn't called me that before. "Is that what I am? Your long-distance girlfriend?"

"I hope so," he says, "although I want to put a time limit on it."

I spin around, not liking the sound of that. "What do you mean, a time limit?"

"Not on the *girlfriend* part," he says, smirking at the look on my face. "On the long-distance part. In six months, we reevaluate. If you still like me by then, I'll start looking at jobs in the Twin Cities area or convince Will to let me work remotely."

I'm speechless for a second. "You'd move just like that?"

"Of course." He says it like it's no big deal. "I would do it now, but I have a feeling you'd freak out."

He's not wrong; a couple of days ago he brought up the possibility of looking for a job near me and I started spiraling into a panic. It seemed like a lot of pressure if he moved for me and things didn't work out between us. I'm still struggling to overcome my distrust that men will stick around. *Thanks for that, Dad.*

"I like your plan," I say. "We'll see each other every weekend—"

"And when we're not together, we'll have hot phone sex every night," he finishes.

I laugh, because that does sound fun. But it also scares me a little, allowing him in like this. I do like his idea; it's a way to take things slow for a few months, allowing room for our relationship to grow, with the understanding that we're not doing long-distance forever.

"Will your parents be okay with that?" I ask, settling against him again, my back to his chest. "You not coming to work for the family again?"

He takes a sip of his coffee before answering. "They won't be thrilled, but it's my decision. I don't want to be part of the Rooney business, but I do want to be part of the Rooney family, so hopefully they'll understand. Honestly, what I enjoyed most about developing the UnderRooneys line was getting it off the ground, and that's what I'll be doing with Will at his company."

I can hear the excitement in his voice, and it makes me smile. "It sounds like a perfect fit."

"What about you?" he asks. "If you could do anything for a career, what would your perfect fit be?"

I've spent plenty of time thinking about this since the first time he asked, and I'm still having trouble coming up with an answer.

"What I've done this summer has been the most enjoyable work I've experienced," I say. "Renovating this house, making things with my hands, seeing the result of my efforts in real time. I just can't figure out how to turn that into an actual job."

My granddad loved being a general contractor, but I don't have the skills to do that and I don't have the foggiest idea how to get there. Plus, I need a job with a reliable salary; I don't have the luxury of spending months without a paycheck while I figure things out.

"The house looks amazing. It's too bad you can't keep it." Then he straightens up, his voice sounding excited: "Hang on. My dad owes me some of the UnderRooney profits—I haven't accepted it because it feels tainted somehow, but I would love to use that to help pay for your grandfather's place. I'd feel like the money was going to something worthwhile."

My heart swells almost to bursting. It's the sweetest, most generous thing he could say, even though there's no way I can let him do that.

"I appreciate the gesture," I tell him, linking his hand in mine, "but it's my responsibility to take care of my granddad, like he always did for me."

He kisses my cheek. "I figured you'd say that. But still. I know you don't need me to take care of you—you're one of the most independent people I've ever met—but you matter to me. If I can take some weight off your shoulders"—he kisses my shoulder, then my neck and jaw, making my skin flush and tingle—"that'll mean you have more energy for the bedroom, and I have a *lot* more things I want to do to you."

Laughing, I set my coffee down on the sand and twist around, expecting to see a smirk on his face. But he's gazing at me with so much tenderness that my own eyes prick with tears. I'm imagining lazy mornings like this stretching into the future; long walks after work where we both decompress from a stressful day; movie nights and home improvement projects; holidays and birthdays. A dog—our *own* dog. And maybe, someday, a little boy or girl with Noah's cheeky grin.

That all seems too good to be true. Permanence, stability— I've been longing for that since I lost both parents in one fell swoop. I'm worn out from years of guarding my heart, trying to prevent it from being bruised and battered again.

"I hope you still like me in six months," I say. It's the closest I can come to telling him how I feel. The intensity of it scares me.

He shakes his head. "The six months is for you, not for me. I'm so far gone, Blake. I'm not coming back from this. I'm all yours."

His words fill me to the brim, and I shift my weight so I'm nestled in the crook of his arm. He kisses the top of my head and holds me as I soak it in: Noah's warm skin, the soft breeze, the rhythmic waves against sand.

I close my eyes and tell my weary heart that it can finally, finally rest.

CHAPTER THIRTY-ONE

KAT

THE NEXT WEEK, I'M SITTING IN MY NEW FAVORITE PLACE: next to Henry, wherever he happens to be. At the moment, that's on his front porch swing, my legs resting on his lap. He's got one hand on my knee and the other holding a book he's reading on toxic masculinity, while I read the mountain of paperwork comprised of the Worthington contract and everything for the transfer of funds.

At the sound of the floorboard creaking just inside the front door, I slide my legs off Henry's lap, and Sunny steps outside.

My smile falls at the sight of her sad little face. She's carrying Nuh-Nuh. Henry told me the well-loved bunny had been a gift from her mother, which explains the sentimentality.

"Daddy," Sunny says, her voice wobbling as she holds Nuh-Nuh out toward Henry. The bunny's body is in one hand, and its ear is in the other. "I think it's time for me to give Nuh-Nuh up."

I suck in a breath, sad for both Sunny and her bunny. This feels like a moment where I don't belong, but I'm afraid to move and call attention to myself.

"Are you sure?" Henry asks.

I shake my head no as Sunny nods yes. Her lower lip quivers and her eyes fill with tears. Beside me, Henry stiffens. His eyes dart toward me, and I decide to take that as an invitation to butt in.

"I can fix him," I say.

Sunny turns and looks at me, a glimmer of hope in her sad eyes. "All I need is thread and a needle," I tell her. "Do you have that?"

Sunny nods and looks from me to Henry as if asking for his permission to keep her bunny for a while longer.

"You don't have to give him up yet," Henry says. "You're not even seven. Kat still has her old stuffed animal and she's *a lot* older than seven."

I elbow him playfully in the side—he knows Blake was the one who kept Beary and brought him back for me.

Sunny hands me the broken bunny and I take Nuh-Nuh carefully, holding him as if he's as precious to me as he is to Sunny.

"Let's go save this bunny," I say, and Sunny leads me inside to find the lifesaving craft supplies.

FIFTEEN MINUTES LATER, Nuh-Nuh has an ear that's as good as new, and I have a friend for life in Sunny. There was a lot more than needles and thread in the craft kit, so while I was at it, I added a little fashion flair. Not only did the purple ribbon make the bunny more stylish, but it covered the lopsided stitches I did my best to make secure.

"Daddy!" Sunny calls, running back out to the front porch, the new and improved Nuh-Nuh tucked beneath her arm. She launches into Henry's lap, knocking the book out of his hands. "Kat saved him!"

"Let's see her handiwork," Henry says. Sunny looks as proud as if she'd sewn the ear on herself as she hands it over. "Very nice," he says, pulling Sunny closer to his chest and kissing the top of her head. "What do you say we take Kat out to lunch to thank her?"

"Can we go to LuLu's?" Sunny asks.

"I wish I could," I tell them both. LuLu's has become one of my favorite spots—it has a tiny beach for kids to play on, and drinks and live music for adults to enjoy—but there's somewhere else I have to be. "The real estate agent's going to be at the beach house in about an hour."

"Want some company?" Henry asks.

I nod, overcome with gratitude. It's amazing how much my world has changed in the last few months. At the beginning of the summer, I was grieving and reeling and all alone. I'm still grieving—I have a feeling I will be for a while, especially since my feelings toward my dad are so complicated—but I'm no longer alone. And that gives me the strength for what I'm about to do. No matter what happens today, I'll be okay.

"I would love that," I tell him.

"But what about lunch?" Sunny asks.

I smile at her. "I think we've got stuff to make PB and J?"

"With or without the crust?" she asks, posing the question as if this is a win-or-lose detail.

"Without, obviously," I say, hoping I picked the right answer.

I'm rewarded with a bright smile as Sunny holds her bunny tighter. "Let's go!"

WHEN WE GET to the beach house, Blake looks nervous. She won't stop fidgeting and playing with her hair.

At first, I assume it's because Noah is there, and this is the first time he and I have seen each other since "the incident." But I'm a grown-up about it, and he is, too. If anything, Henry seems the most uncomfortable. He shakes Noah's hand stiffly and says, "Been a while," then stands to the side, arms folded.

When Noah and Blake go out back to show Sunny the new sidewalk chalk they bought for her, I tug Henry's hand to stay back, pulling him out of sight and against the wall for a kiss to remind him he's the one I want to be with and that Junior— *Noah*—was just a temporary lapse in judgment.

Seeing Junior and Blake together, I realize they're perfect for each other. They're both glowing, constantly touching each other—not in a PDA way, but like they can't bear to be separated by even a foot of distance. It's the same way I feel about Henry.

At the sound of the back door closing, Henry and I pull apart and take a seat on the couch. *Our* couch. He smirks as he pulls me closer, and I can't wait until the next time we're alone in the house again.

I realize with a sinking feeling that our days of owning this house might be numbered. Depending on what happens in the next few minutes, there's still a chance I'm going to lose the house.

When Blake and Junior come back in, they sit on the love seat across from me and Henry. The room is heavy with tension and the significance of the real estate agent's imminent arrival. This is the moment the whole summer has been leading up to.

Blake's leg starts tapping, stilling for a moment when Junior rests his hand on her knee. The quiet only lasts a moment, and Blake is moving again, adjusting the decorative bowl on the coffee table for the third time since we walked in.

Junior glances at me and we share a quick look of understanding and love for Blake, then I stand and take my sister's hand.

"Come with me," I say, leading her toward the kitchen. If her hands are going to be busy, then she might as well put them to work on something productive.

"What's wrong?" she asks, the concern on her face deepening.

"Nothing," I tell her, grabbing the loaf of white bread from its storage spot inside the microwave. "I just need some help. I promised Sunny a PB and J."

Blake winces as if I was talking about making a peanut butter and dirt sandwich. "What?" I ask. "You go through like a jar of peanut butter every two weeks."

"Peanut butter, yes," she says. "But never with jelly. Here, let me."

She takes the bag of bread from my hands and I watch her work. She already seems calmer than she'd been just a few minutes before, and I realize she's got that in common with our dad. He never seemed comfortable in his skin unless he was actively doing something. I apparently didn't inherit that trait, because doing nothing is my specialty.

I lean against the counter and watch as Blake spreads the creamy peanut butter on one side of the bread, then sprinkles it with brown sugar.

Blake cuts the sandwich diagonally, and because self-control has never been my strong suit, I grab a piece and take a bite. The brown sugar gives the peanut butter a crystallized crunch and I realize I've been eating peanut butter wrong my whole life.

"This is amazing," I say, with my mouth still full.

"I thought this was for Sunny?" Blake asks, a smile stretched across her face.

"She wouldn't like it; there's crust on the bread," I tell her, my mouth already full of another bite.

"Ahh," Blake says. But she humors me and happily takes two

more slices of bread from the bag. This time, she cuts the crust off.

As she plates the second sandwich with a few apple slices for Sunny, there's a knock at the door. We both freeze and Blake inhales a sharp breath.

"I'll get it," I say, loudly enough for Henry and Junior to hear in the other room.

Blake follows me to the door, still holding Sunny's plate. I'm loosely aware of Junior taking it from her; then he and Henry head outside to bring Sunny her sandwich. I exhale and open the door.

Harriet Beaver, her hair still bleach-blond, her oversize teeth still gleaming white, flinches when she sees me. After the way I behaved the last time we met, I don't blame her.

I offer her a smile so she knows I've matured in the last few months, and step aside. "Come on in," I say.

She gives me a polite smile, but her face transforms as she takes in the new and improved space: the floors that were refinished not once, but twice; the fresh paint on the walls; the baseboards and the crown molding; the new furniture and accent pieces.

I knew it was impressive, but her expression confirms it.

"Wow," Harriet says. "You ladies have been busy."

Blake and I share a smile.

"Let me show you around," Blake says to Harriet, who looks relieved that Blake will be leading the tour. I hang back, listening to Blake point out the work she's done throughout the house— the new light fixtures, the remodeled bathrooms. Blake looks and sounds like a pro, and I'm bursting with pride for my sister.

Twenty minutes later, we circle back to the living room, where we started.

"You've really outdone yourselves," Harriet tells us both.

"Blake obviously did most of the work," I admit.

"But the aesthetic is all my sister," Blake says, and I smile.

"I'll need to crunch some numbers and look at comps," Harriet says, "but with the work you've done, this house can be priced on par with the others on this block. You'll be able to get a pretty penny for it."

Harriet's eyes shine like she's already counting all the pennies she'll collect from the commission.

"Of course, that's if you still want to sell." She looks at me when she says that, but I don't meet her eyes. I can't. Because of course I don't want to sell. And I hope with every fiber of my being that Blake doesn't want to, either.

After what I did yesterday, I wouldn't be able to afford to buy Blake out even at the "before" price.

Blake's ringing cell phone interrupts my train of thought, and I watch her expression go from embarrassment to panic.

"I'm sorry, I have to take this. It's my grandfather's care facility," she says, scurrying out the kitchen door to the back porch just as Junior and Henry are walking back inside.

Once Blake is out of earshot, I ask Harriet the question that's been on my mind the last week.

"I'm curious," I say, as if the thought just came to me. "If we don't sell, would renting the house out be a viable option?"

"Absolutely," Harriet says. "Rental houses in this area are filled all year long—not just in season—and you could charge a premium price being on the water."

"If we went that route," I say, "would we be able to block off certain dates where the house wouldn't be available? Like holiday weekends?"

I know I might be getting ahead of myself, but I have a clear vision of all the Fourths of July Blake and I could spend here together, creating new memories.

The sound of the back door closing echoes and we all turn to see Blake. Her eyes are red, her face as white as a sheet.

"Is everything okay?" Junior asks, stepping toward her.

"I think so?" she says. Her hands are shaking, and I worry something terrible happened in the last forty-eight hours that wasn't part of the plan. "Apparently an anonymous donor gave a grant to the memory ward to cover expenses for families who needed a little help, and the director thought of me and my granddad."

"What does that mean?" I ask, playing dumb.

It was Henry's idea to make it look like a general donation to the facility rather than something specifically earmarked for Blake's grandfather. Henry knows Blake almost as well as I do by now, and he pointed out that if Blake knew it was me—well, Rachel Worthington, by extension—who was paying for her grandfather's care, she might refuse to accept the money.

But I need her to take it. Not just so we can keep the house— I know there's still a chance she'll want to sell—but because it feels like the least I can do.

Last week, Blake and I agreed to stop blaming ourselves for the things our father did, but that doesn't mean I can't compensate for some of the hurt he caused. Blake's grandfather put his life on hold to raise Blake when our father took the coward's way out, and now it only seems right to help Blake help him.

"It means . . ." Blake stops and looks at me, her mouth hanging open. I don't know how to read her expression—she seems shell-shocked.

And then her face crumples and she's sobbing, tears running down her cheeks. She covers her face with both hands, like she's embarrassed at the outburst of emotion but can't control herself. Her shoulders shake and her chest heaves as she slides down the wall until she's sitting on the floor.

I watch, terrified that something has gone wrong with my plan. I've never seen Blake lose control like this before. Junior comes over to her, looking concerned, but she motions him away, still crying so hard she can't get any words out.

My shoulders tense. "Are you okay?" I ask.

Blake's gasping for air, trying to speak. "I've been so worried," she says between sobs. "So worried about Granddad—how to pay for his care. I didn't know how I would do it. And now . . ." She hiccups, wipes her eyes. "Now he'll be safe."

My heart aches for her; until this moment, I hadn't realized how heavily this responsibility has been weighing on her. She's weak with relief—I can see it in the way her body relaxes as she leans her head against the wall behind her, tears sliding down her face. And I know that no matter what she says next—even if she doesn't want to keep the beach house with me—I did the right thing.

Still, I hold my breath as I wait for her to speak again.

"And it also means . . ." Blake stops, a sob caught in her throat. "It means we don't have to sell the house."

I suck in a breath. "We don't have to sell?" I ask, a cautious question in my voice.

Blake looks up at me from where she sits on the floor. Her brown eyes are impossibly big, shining with tears. Slowly, her mouth breaks into a huge, radiant smile. It's like the sun coming out after a storm. "We don't have to sell," she repeats.

I rush over to her, grabbing her hands and pulling her to her feet, throwing my arms around her in a huge, impulsive hug. She feels small and fragile in my arms, but she squeezes so tightly it takes my breath away.

When we separate, I'm crying, too. I laugh and wipe away tears.

"Call me if you decide to go the rental route," Harriet says behind us, reminding me that we aren't alone.

We thank her for her time and she says goodbye. Junior and Henry have stepped to the edge of the room, giving Blake and me space to talk.

"What are you thinking?" I ask Blake.

Her face is streaked with tears, but she's grinning. "I'm thinking I can't believe this is my life. What are we going to do with this house?" She spins around slowly, awestruck, like she's seeing the place for the first time.

Or like she's realizing it's ours. No one can take it away from us now.

"We have options," I tell her. My cheeks hurt from smiling. "I was thinking maybe we could rent it out sometimes—let other families create memories here."

"We could do that," Blake says, nodding.

"And we could block off certain weeks just for us," I say.

"For our family," Blake adds.

Her words catch on something deep in my chest—a longing I've had all my life, even as a little girl who didn't understand why I felt so lonely in my fancy house in Atlanta. This was why we connected all those years ago, at camp. Because we saw in each other a need for belonging. And maybe, deep down, we recognized our missing piece.

Blake throws her arms out wide. "This is *our house!*" she shouts, jumping in excitement. "I can't believe it! We get to come here whenever we want!"

I laugh and put my arm around her, pulling her against me for another hug. "It's our house," I whisper.

As we separate, I get the strangest sensation, a prickling on the back of my neck. Like our grandparents are here with us, like our father might somehow be here, too. As if the past and the future are colliding and everything in our lives has led us here, to this moment, with each other.

Two sisters—no *half* about it—with one whole house, and our entire lives to fill it with memories.

EPILOGUE

FIVE YEARS LATER

THE FOURTH OF JULY DAWNS HOT AND HUMID IN DESTIN, the glittering emerald water and white-sand beaches a perfect backdrop for the throngs of holiday visitors. A parade of golf carts takes over Crystal Beach, each one decked out with streamers and flags in raucous red, white, and blue.

The Gulf is alive with boats, the beaches crowded with sunbathers. As the day rolls toward evening, the air fills with the crackle of amateur fireworks and the unmistakable scent of backyard barbecues.

Down Old 98, tucked between two larger and arguably nicer vacation homes, a small yellow beach house is abuzz with activity. It may not be as fancy as its neighbors, but the siding is freshly painted, the flower beds carefully maintained. And in the kitchen, two sisters work side by side, laughing and singing along to their official Fourth of July playlist as they prepare their grandmother's famous Jell-O salad and all the other fixings for dinner.

In the past five years, Kat and Blake have stayed at the beach house often, both together and alone. They sometimes rent it out for extra income or invite other friends to join them. Every year, their lives become busier and more complicated, and most of the time, they both feel pulled in a million directions. But the week spanning the Fourth is sacred. Nothing—absolutely nothing—can stop them from being here, at their beach house. Together.

A new song starts up on the playlist, this one so familiar that by the end of the first bar of music, Kat squeals.

"Yes!" she shouts, grabbing a wooden spoon to use as a microphone.

Blake grabs her own microphone—a whisk—and strikes a pose, ready to go when the vocals start.

Kat sings the first line of "Build Me Up Buttercup," and Blake echoes, "Build me up!"

They continue on, piecing together the long-ago routine they'd worked out as twelve-year-olds at camp, singing along with the Foundations.

"Mommy's singing!" a tiny voice shouts in excitement, followed by two sets of feet pounding on the wood floors into the kitchen, ready to join the show.

Kat scoops up Emma—three years old and dark-haired like her mama—and spins her around. Two-year-old Jameson runs to Blake and they twirl together, until Blake bumps her belly on the kitchen counter.

"Oof," Blake says, groaning. At eight months along, this will be the last vacation she'll take before the baby comes. "I keep forgetting I'm this big."

Kat smiles at her. "You look great. I love Grandma's dress on you."

Blake beams. She's wearing one of the oldest dresses their grandmother left behind—a handmade floral maternity sundress from the sixties. Their grandma must have worn it while pregnant with their father, and when Blake put it on that morning, she was overcome with the same combination of emotions she always feels here at the beach house: gratitude, grief, and love.

A tall, willowy blond eleven-year-old walks into the kitchen. "Dad says the hamburgers are ready," Sunny announces, then rolls her eyes when she sees what's going on in there. "So embarrassing," she mutters, but she's fighting a smile.

Kat and Blake shoo their little ones out with Sunny, then gather up the side dishes to head out to the deck, where Henry and Noah are manning the grill. As they reach the door, Kat pauses and glances at her sister.

Her sister. Those words still sometimes make Kat giddy. Even her mom, who sold the big house and moved into a two-bedroom condo, has reluctantly come around to accepting Blake as a part of their family. She won't outwardly admit it, but it comes through in questions and compliments, and most recently, the old baseball mitt she gifted Jameson that had belonged to Kat and Blake's dad.

"I'm so glad we're here together," Kat says.

Blake's eyes fill with tears—pregnancy hormones have made her extra emotional. "Can you believe it's been five years?"

Indeed, it's sometimes difficult to believe all that happened in the past five years. When that first summer ended, Blake went back to Minnesota, but since she didn't have to worry about paying for her granddad's facility, she decided to take a leap of faith and follow in his footsteps by becoming a general contractor, one of the few women working in that industry. She apprenticed under a friend of her granddad's for a couple of years, then studied and passed the licensing exam.

Meanwhile she and Noah tried the long-distance thing but didn't even make it the six months—he moved to Minneapolis after three. They adopted a scruffy rescue dog they officially named Loki, but they call him a growing collection of nicknames.

A year later, they were married. When Blake's grandfather passed away two years ago, they moved to Atlanta to be closer to Kat.

With Kat's connections, the woman-only crew of O'Neill Construction grew quickly. Noah runs the business side of the company, plus he launched a nonprofit to support victims of sweatshop injuries, using the money owed him from the Under-Rooney sales.

Kat, for her part, has been just as busy. Her Instagram following is now nearly one million, but in her eyes, that's the least important thing she's accomplished. Following her year-long partnership with Rachel Worthington, Kat permanently joined forces with Rachel to develop an accessible brand of home décor and fashion that has a mission of giving back to the community, providing jobs and training for women from underprivileged or marginalized backgrounds. Luna, one of Kat's girls from the Peachtree Center, works as a designer on the apparel side of the business, having sharpened her skills from the tissue-paper-headband days.

On a personal note, Kat and Henry live in Atlanta most of the year, after getting married four years ago due to an unexpected—but definitely not unwanted—pregnancy. Henry was happy to take over as stay-at-home dad extraordinaire to allow Kat to focus on growing her business. He occasionally helps Blake's crew—the only man allowed on-site.

Out on the deck facing the beach, the table is set in a riot of mismatched red, white, and blue paper plates and cups that would've given Kat an eye twitch a few years ago.

"It's gorgeous!" Kat exclaims, placing a kiss on Emma's forehead. "You all did such a great job. Sunny, maybe you should be my newest hire for the home décor line."

Sunny grins.

Noah holds little Jameson curled up against his chest, the toddler's chubby hands stroking Noah's beard. Loki the dog is curled up at Noah's feet. "Tell Mommy we saved her a seat," Noah says.

When Blake sinks into her chair, Jameson climbs onto her rapidly shrinking lap. "I feel like a whale," she says, huffing.

Noah leans over and kisses her cheek. "The prettiest whale in the entire ocean," he says, laughing as Blake swats him.

"Who's ready for hamburgers?" Henry says, but Kat puts up her hand.

"Wait," Kat says, "before we eat, I have something for Blake. Well, for the baby."

She reaches behind Henry and brings out a gift box wrapped in creamy yellow paper and tied with a thick white ribbon.

Blake takes the package and opens it, Jameson helping eagerly. Inside is a baby onesie with a Camp Chickawah logo on the front and CABIN 10 FOREVER on the back.

"I love it!" Blake says, her eyes filling with tears for the second time in five minutes. "Thank you!"

Kat smiles. "Look behind it."

Blake lifts the tissue paper to find another matching onesie. When she looks up, both Kat and Henry are grinning identical, delighted smiles.

"I'm pregnant, and it's a girl," Kat says.

As Noah and Blake cheer and give their congratulations, Henry puts his arm around Kat's shoulders and squeezes; he couldn't be more thrilled about continuing his streak as a #GirlDad.

"She'll be here about five months after your daughter," Kat continues, "which means that in twelve years or so, the two of them can go to Camp Chickawah together."

Blake begins to cry in earnest, then starts laughing, wiping her eyes. Her children, her son *and* daughter, will never feel alone the way she had as a child. They'll have siblings, cousins, aunts, and uncles. An entire foundation of family to depend on.

Kat reaches across the table and takes Blake's hand. Her grief about her father has dulled to the occasional ache when she sees what a good dad Henry is to their two girls, but mostly, when she thinks of her dad she can be grateful for the gifts he gave her. The house, yes, but most important, her sister.

"Now can we eat?" Emma says, standing on her chair. "Because I am *very* hungry."

Everyone piles their plates high with food. Henry encourages Emma to try some vegetables ("at least lick them, sweetie"), and Noah slices Jameson's hot dog into bite-size pieces. Sunny keeps sneaking her phone to text someone and Henry shoots her a stern glance while Loki begs for food under the table. Blake asks Kat how she's feeling, and Kat says she's been tired lately but otherwise fine.

Later, they'll light sparklers and let the children run across the soft, sugar-white sand with the dog, then stretch out and watch fireworks bloom across the inky sky. They'll reminisce about that first Fourth of July together, how Blake and Kat teamed up to chase a different dog through the dark streets of Destin. Then they'll share stories about summer camp, how Kat convinced Blake to sneak out of their cabin in the middle of the night and paddle a canoe across the moon-streaked lake.

The little ones will fall asleep and be carried inside by their daddies, and Kat and Blake will stay outside together until long past midnight, talking and laughing or just sitting in silence, listening to the waves crash against the sand, feeling grateful for each other, for this beach house, for their father's inexplicable, unexpected, perfectly imperfect gift.

Then next year, they'll return and do it all over again.

ACKNOWLEDGMENTS

It takes a village to bring a book to life, and we are grateful for all of the people in ours—starting with our incredible agents, Joanna MacKenzie and Amy Berkower, for being so supportive and working together on this crazy idea of ours. Thank you to Cindy Hwang for seeing something in our proposal and giving us the opportunity to work with you, our dream editor at our dream imprint, to bring *The Beach Trap* to readers.

Our beta readers helped us make this book what it is. Thank you to Kathleen West, Lainey Cameron, Jill Atkins, Angela Rehm, and Katy Bachman for your insights and feedback.

We are fortunate to belong to so many supportive writing communities. Thank you to the amazing women of The Ink Tank, the Berkletes, Women's Fiction Writers Association (for bringing us together!), the Every Damn Day Writers, the 2022 Debuts, and the Eggplant Beach Writers for saying yes on a whim to a last-minute "research" beach trip!

Not only was our week in Destin fun and full of memories, it helped us bring the true Destin experience (oysters and all) to the page. Thanks to Kristin Whitcomb of Sea-Battical for the warm welcome; Dr. Randy Hammer for taking us out on his boat; Carlene Jarrett for taking us to Seaside; Webb, the bartender at The Crab Trap, for pouring strong drinks; and Lyn Liao Butler and Robin Facer for coming along for the ride.

As relative newbies in the publishing industry, we're grateful for the support and encouragement of so many writers we admire, including but not limited to Heather Webb, Liz Fenton, Kimmery Martin, Emily Henry, Christina Lauren, Lisa Barr, Renee Rosen, Orly Konig, Tiffany Yates Martin, Jennie Nash, Jamie Beck, Amy Mason Doan, Colleen Oakley, Suzanne Park, Nancy Johnson, Julie Carrick Dalton, Rea Frey, Megan Collins, Ali Hazelwood, Sarah Grunder Ruiz, and Colleen Hoover.

We'd like to thank the entire Berkley team: Claire Zion, Jeanne-Marie Hudson, Craig Burke, Angela Kim, Jennifer Lynes, Daché Rogers, Jessica Plummer, Daniela Riedlova, and of course, Sarah Oberrender and Michael Crampton for the perfect cover (we love it so much!). Thank you to Meridith Viguet and the team at Writers House, and to the team at Nelson Literary Agency. And thanks to Kathleen Carter—the best part of a date change! We're grateful to all of you for the behind-the-scenes work you do to support authors and our books.

Thanks to Dale Campbell for the support, Robin Facer for taking our author photo, and Angela Carlson for making us look better than real-life.

Alison would like to start by thanking Bradeigh. I swear I get the better end of this deal, but there's no one I'd rather share a brain with. Seriously, thank you for going on this wild ride with me. From CPs to BFFs and now cowriters, I can't wait to see where this adventure takes us. (Hopefully to Italy one day!) My family has been my biggest support system from day one. Thanks to my mom (Kathy Hammer), my dad (Dr. Randy Hammer), my sister (Elizabeth Murray), the Lewins, Hammers, Kirbys, and the

Bergers. Not only are my nephews, Dylan and Alex, two of my favorite people—but they are the only two people in the world who think I'm famous. And that's pretty cool. My friends are like my family, and I'm grateful for their support and encouragement—even when I'm writing on our vacations. Just to mention a few: all of My Girls, Meg McKeen, D.J. McEwan, Kristie Raymer, Julie Johnson, Krissie Callahan, #LibbyLove, Michelle Dash, Katie Ross, Mia Phifer, Jenna Leopold, Shana Freedman, Christina Williams, Pierrette Hazkial, Robbie Manning, the Rock Boat community, and the McGee's Sunday Funday crew. Thanks to Kristin Harmel for being my literary fairy godmother, to the 2020 Debuts, and to Stephen Kellogg, my other amazing cowriter. I'm grateful to my team at FCB Chicago for making me want to keep my day job, and to Nate and the Godfrey crew: thanks for sharing Bradeigh with me.

Bradeigh would like to thank Alison, first of all, for being my writing soul mate, world's best critique partner, and now coauthor. This journey has been a dream come true! Here's to many, many more books together, research vacations, and late nights staying up to read each other's new chapters. Hugs to the Murray Moms for the laughter, tears, and Marco Polos (Amanda Habel, Amy Rex, Erin Wiggins, Kellie Terry, Stephanie Higbee, and Suzanne James), and to all the women in my IRL book club for being my friends through thick and thin. I'm very grateful to the Women Physician Writers group and to Kristin Prentiss Ott for bringing us together (virtually). My Bookstagram community has been such a source of light and joy; there are too many accounts to name, but I want to give a special shout-out to my BLC cohosts (Angela Rehm, Meirys Martinez, Jessica Langer, Ketra Arcas, Jill Atkins, Katy Bachman, and Brandi Jarrell). I would not be a writer without my parents (Merrie and Jim Smithson), who instilled in me a love of words from a young age. Big thanks, Ellie and McLean, for being the best siblings ever. To my children (Isaac, Eliza, Everett, and Nora): thank you for cheering me on through each step of this journey. And especially, thank you to Nate. None of this would have happened if not for your unconditional, unfailing support. If I know how to write a good love story, it is because you have loved me so very well.

We would also like to thank the Bookstagrammers, Book-Tokkers, Facebook reading groups, bloggers, and everyone on social media who put our book in front of potential readers and has helped us stay connected during these pandemic days. We're grateful for this entire community, especially the Bookish Ladies Club, Andrea Katz of Great Thoughts' Great Readers, Kristy Barrett of A Novel Bee, Sue Peterson of Sue's Reading Neighborhood, Robin Kall of Reading With Robin, the Book Bonanza community, Ashley Hasty, Zibby Owens, Ashley Spivey, Mary Chase, Annissa Armstrong, and the Fab Four—Kristin Harmel, Kristy Woodson Harvey, Patti Callahan Henry, and Mary Kay Andrews of Friends & Fiction.

An extra thank-you to any reader who picked up their copy of *The Beach Trap* from an independent bookstore. Booksellers are the unsung heroes of the publishing industry, and we are grateful for all they do to bring authors and readers together. A special shout-out to Kimberly and Rebecca George of Volumes Bookcafe, Mary Mollman of Madison Street Books, Laura Taylor of Oxford Exchange, Maxwell Gregory, Pamela Klinger-Horn, and Mary Webber O'Malley.

And last but certainly not least: our readers. Thank you for picking up a copy of our book. None of this would be possible without you. We love hearing from you—so find us online at alibradybooks.net and on Instagram @AliBradyBooks.

Cabin Ten Forever!

The
BEACH
TRAP

Ali Brady

QUESTIONS FOR DISCUSSION

1. What is it about summer camp that forges such close friendships? Are you still in touch with any of your camp or school friends from when you were younger?

2. Why do you think Kat and Blake's dad left them both the beach house? Do you think he wanted to bring them back together?

3. Do you see Kat's mom as a victim of her husband's transgressions or as a conspirator? Why?

4. Why and how do you think Blake's dad was able to walk away from her for all those years?

5. How do you think Blake felt about Kat never responding to her letters?

6. Why do you think Kat held on to her anger and continued to blame Blake for so long?

7. If you had to choose between the two love interests to take you out on a date, would you choose Noah or Henry? Why?

8. What do you think of influencer culture and does it impact your life and the decisions you make?

9. If you were a social media influencer, what type of influencer would you be (e.g., lifestyle, books, food)? What would your brand motto be?

10. How did your opinion of Kat and/or Blake change throughout the book?

11. What do you think of Kat's decision to pay for Blake's grandfather's care without letting Blake know?

12. Where do you think Kat and Blake are in another twelve years? How is their relationship?

Turn the page for a sneak peek
of the next Ali Brady novel
The Comeback Summer
Coming from Berkley in Summer 2023!

LIBBY

MORNINGS ARE NOT MY FRIEND. ESPECIALLY NOT MONDAY
mornings. Especially not *this* Monday morning. It's not even ten
o'clock and I feel like everything that could possibly go wrong has.

Not only did I sleep through all three of my alarms and wake
up to find a present on the floor from Mr. Darcy, my cat, but the
driver of the 146 bus hit the brakes just as I was sipping my non-
fat sugar-free vanilla oat-milk latte, and now there's a puddle of
coffee on my shirt.

Forced to make the choice between being late and disheveled
or being *really* late and slightly less disheveled, I decided to run
into Bloomingdale's to grab a scarf to strategically cover the stain.

I tell myself conveniences like this are what make our Michigan Avenue office space worth the premium price. Although if
business doesn't get better soon, we might not be able to afford
to keep the lights on. Literally and figuratively.

As I stand in line to pay for the forty-five-dollar scarf I'll
hopefully be able to return later, I'm practically twitching with
impatience. This was supposed to be quick—we have a call with
a big client starting in fifteen minutes, and I can't be late.

In an attempt to calm myself, I reach my hand up to rub the diamond solitaire necklace I inherited from my grandmother. On days like this, I wish I'd also inherited her composure and grace. But my little sister, Hannah, is the one who got those traits— along with her slender physique.

More than anything, I wish I could call and ask GiGi what we should do to save the business she started more than fifty years ago. She'd know how to fix things. Of course, she never would've let the situation get this dire.

Not that it's entirely our fault clients have been dropping like flies. Half of the old men in charge don't trust their business in the hands of "a couple of little girls"—their words, not ours— and the other half are retiring and being replaced by slightly younger old men who don't have any sense of loyalty to the public relations firm that made their brands household names.

The one thing all our clients seem to have in common is that they're looking for a change. And some days, I honestly wish I could, too. But we can't let our grandmother down, not after she trusted her business to us. *L'dor v'dor*—her favorite Hebrew saying. From generation to generation.

With the colorful scarf wrapped around my neck, I head outside to the already bustling street. It's a perfect Chicago summer day—and I take the sun shining down on me as a sign that things are starting to look up. There's a big smile on my face as I cross the street toward our office.

The Freedman Group was my grandmother's pride and joy, next to my sister and me. As the first woman in Chicago to own a public relations firm, GiGi didn't just break the glass ceiling, she shattered it.

I grew up hearing stories about those who underestimated her—a mistake they made only once. Those naysayers (both men and women) thought Edith Freedman was just a pretty face.

They said she was in over her head. That her business wouldn't last. Of course, she proved them all wrong, becoming "one of the most in-demand public relations experts in the country," according to the *Tribune*.

My grandmother was on top of her game until the day she transitioned to the boardroom in the sky three years ago, leaving her beloved business in the hands of the granddaughters she trained to follow in her footsteps. The next generation. Me and Hannah. Who are trying our damnedest not to let her legacy die, too.

I take a deep breath and push through the revolving doors to the lobby of our office building.

The woman at the front desk smiles as I enter. She's worked here longer than I've been alive, and I have so many memories of her sneaking me a lollipop when GiGi wasn't looking. But for the life of me, I can't remember if her name is Jean or Jane or Joan.

Hannah doesn't remember either, and it's way past the polite point when we could ask. So we just mumble something that starts with a J and hope the woman's hearing isn't as sharp as it used to be.

"Good morning, Libby darling," she calls out.

"Morning, Jnnn." I lift my coffee cup to my lips, hoping it will help muffle my approximation of her name.

Jean/Joan/Jane waves as I head toward the elevator bank that will take me up to our floor—just barely in time for our ten thirty meeting. Hannah is already there, of course; she wakes up every day at six o'clock on the dot (with only one alarm) so she can run for an hour before coming into the office.

She says it helps her handle her nervous energy—which, I've heard, is a benefit of exercise. If only I was the kind of person who enjoyed breaking a sweat.

Sweets are more my thing. But unfortunately, the pint of

Jeni's ice cream I treated myself to last night didn't do anything to help curb my anxiety about our conversation with the CEO of UnderRooneys, the iconic underwear company and one of the last big clients we have left.

I've been dreading this meeting since we got the email from Mr. Rooney's assistant last week, setting up the meeting to "talk." Which is just as ominous as it sounds.

My stomach gets a wobbly feeling every time I think about it, and I hope my disaster of a morning wasn't an omen for even bigger troubles ahead. I push the button for the twenty-first floor and try to ignore the sinking feeling that GiGi would be disappointed in me.

Just before the elevator doors close, a hand slips through the crack, forcing them back open. I look at my watch and curse whoever's impatience is going to make me even later—the meeting starts in two minutes.

When I look back up, I gasp.

"It's you," I accidentally say as Hot Office Guy steps inside. I've admired him from a distance, coming in and out of the building for the last six months—but he's even more swoon-worthy up close. He's not much taller than me, but he's solid, athletic in that "I play recreational sports" kind of way. His brown hair is mussed and I wonder if he overslept this morning, too.

"It's you," he says back to me. His voice is low and textured, even sexier than I imagined in all the conversations we've had in my head. He steps close to me, so close I can smell the wintergreen toothpaste on his breath.

Hot Office Guy's blue-gray eyes drop down and I try to make myself look smaller under his gaze. His lips quirk in a half smile as he picks up the long tail of my new scarf. I silently thank the heavy foot of the bus driver as Hot Office Guy twirls the scarf around his finger.

I hold my breath as he gives it a little yank, pulling me toward him. I brace myself, hands on his broad chest, before slowly tilting my head up. There's a faint scar on his chin I've never noticed before, hiding beneath the stubble of a few days' growth.

My fingers flex against the cotton of his button-down shirt and I feel his heartbeat quicken as his lips find mine. They're full and firm, and he tastes like coffee and vanilla—the real kind, not the sugar-free stuff I drink.

His hands are on the small of my back, pulling me closer as he deepens the kiss. We fit together even better than I imagined, and I love the rough sensation of his stubble against my face. For a brief moment, I let my mind wander to how it would feel against other parts of my body . . .

The elevator dings.

"Is this your floor?" he asks, and I look up.

Hot Office Guy is leaning against the other side of the elevator, looking up from his phone with mild annoyance.

"Yeah, sorry," I say, hoping my cheeks don't look as red as they feel.

As I rush out, I scold my active imagination for getting more than a little carried away. This is what I get for staying up late last night to finish the latest CLo book. But alas, my life is not a romance novel—if it was, well, it wouldn't be my life.

I've accepted that I was born to be the chubby, clever sidekick in someone else's story. I've got a lot of good qualities—some that are great, even—but I'm just not "meet cute" material.

"LOOK WHO'S LATE," Scott, our office manager, calls out in a singsong voice. "Your baby sister had to start the call without you."

I shoot him a dirty look as I hurry down the hall to the office

Hannah and I share. Sometimes, it feels like he's the boss and we're his employees instead of the other way around. He was the last hire GiGi made before she passed away, and we haven't had the heart to fire him—even though he spends most of his time at work shopping online and watching TikTok. That's what you get for hiring a person whose greatest claim to fame is going viral in a YouTube video of himself as a six-year-old.

I'm responsible for at least a dozen of the video's seventeen million views—I can't get enough of tiny Scott standing in a department store dressing room with his arms crossed, declaring his mother's outfits either "great!" or "not great!" The video earned him the nickname "Great Scott," which we ironically use to tease him, and which he seems to unironically enjoy.

"Bee-tee-dubs—bold move with the geometric scarf. We like," he calls after me, reminding me of one of the reasons we keep him around. The man can turn on the charm when he needs to, and the few clients we still have left love him.

I take a moment to compose myself, then slide open the glass door to our office. Hannah's sitting at her desk, head bent in concentration toward the speakerphone. Her curly brown hair is up in a messy bun, a pencil stuck through it. She's rubbing her temples with her fingertips; one of her headaches must be coming on. I make a mental note to pick up some Advil for her.

My sister looks up as I walk in. Her face is pale, her eyes wide with barely concealed panic.

"Is there anything we can do to change your mind?" she asks into the speakerphone. I catch the tiniest wobble in her voice—like she's trying to be strong but falling apart on the inside—and I feel a rush of guilt for being late. Hannah hates talking on the phone and prefers to stay behind the scenes, while I handle most conversations with our clients. She's going to be an emotional wreck after this, and it's my fault. I'm the big sister; I shouldn't have left her to face this alone.

"Unfortunately, there's not," Mr. Rooney says, bringing me back to their conversation. "We've kept our business with the Freedman Group this long out of respect for your grandmother, but the time has come to move on. I wish you and your sister the best of luck."

My stomach drops the twenty-one floors to the Chicago streets where I'm afraid we might end up, out on our asses.

"Thank you," Hannah says to Mr. Rooney, her voice deceptively strong.

She ends the call and brings her eyes up to meet mine. They're glistening with tears. "It's over," she says. "I'm so sorry, I tried to change his mind, but—"

"No, it's not your fault," I say, rushing over to her side of the office, wondering if she brought up the way that we—Hannah and I, not GiGi—helped guide the Rooneys through that nasty public scandal about their factory conditions a few years back.

"I just froze," Hannah says, and I curse myself for not getting here in time to help.

"What else did he say?" I ask, although nothing good can come from playing Monday morning quarterback.

"You heard most of it." Hannah's voice trembles as she says, "They're taking the business to T&C."

I inhale a quick breath. Thomas & Company is our biggest competitor in town, and Wade Thomas was our grandmother's personal rival. He's been poaching our clients for the last two years and hasn't been secretive about wanting to acquire our company, too. But GiGi would disown us from beyond if we even considered selling out to him.

"Is this as bad as I think it is?" I ask, afraid to hear the answer.

While I bring my creativity and imagination to the table, Excel sheets give me hives. My sister is the analytical, business-minded one—she'll know the actual financial impact of losing one of our biggest clients.

"It's not good," she says, sounding defeated. "I honestly don't know how to keep us in the black without UnderRooneys."

The moment feels somber, and for once, I can't find the words to make things better.

"What are we going to do?" Hannah asks. She looks up at me with her big brown eyes, taking me back two decades, when she was seven and I was nine. The night our parents told us they were getting divorced, I promised her that the two of us would always have each other. That she didn't have to worry, because I would make everything okay.

It was true then, and it's true now. I stuff down my worries and put a smile on my face, back in big sister mode.

"We're Edith Freedman's granddaughters," I remind her. "Nothing can stop us."

Hannah nods, and exhales in relief. I sit down at my desk and turn away from her, hoping to hide the fact that panic is racing through my veins.

We'll find a way to come back from this, I tell myself. We have to.

Photo by Robin Facer

ALI BRADY is the pen name of writing BFFs Alison Hammer and Bradeigh Godfrey. *The Beach Trap* is their first book together. Alison lives in Chicago and works as a VP creative director at an advertising agency. She's the author of *You and Me and Us* and *Little Pieces of Me*. Bradeigh lives with her family in Utah, where she works as a physician. She's the author of the psychological thriller *Imposter*.

CONNECT ONLINE

🐦 AliBradyBooks
❶ AliBradyBooks
📷 AliBradyBooks